AUTHOR NOTE

Thank you for buying my book!

Taking Liberty is the follow-on to the Amazon #1 Best Selling thrillers **Killing Hope** and **Crossing Lines**.

The events in this novel are a continuation of those featured in the first two Gabe Quinn Thrillers – therefore, it is recommended to read all three in the correct sequence to ensure the best reading experience, as some key aspects of **Taking Liberty** are a carryover of situations introduced in **Killing Hope** and **Crossing Lines**.

Keith ☺

Keith Houghton

Taking Liberty
(Gabe Quinn Thriller #3)

also available
in Paperback, eBook and Audiobook

Killing Hope
(Gabe Quinn Thriller #1)

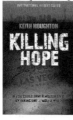 

Crossing Lines
(Gabe Quinn Thriller #2)

 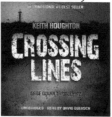

TAKING LIBERTY

GABE QUINN THRILLER #3

KEITH HOUGHTON

ISBN: 1493541447

Keith Houghton

For more information

Web
www.keithhoughton.com

Twitter
https://twitter.com/KeithHoughton

Facebook
http://www.facebook.com/KeithHoughtonAuthor

This novel is a work of fiction. Names, events, places, characters,
incidents and businesses are either products of the Author's
imagination, used in a fictional manner or with permission from the
owner. As such, all characters and characterisations are fictitious, and
any resemblance to actual persons, living or dead, is purely
coincidental.

~ For My Parents ~

June & Bill
This is all your fault

Keith Houghton

TAKING LIBERTY

"Could you give your life to save someone else?"

Keith Houghton

PROLOGUE

At this time of day, the sun-kissed sidewalk outside the world-famous Chinese theatre on Hollywood Boulevard was packed with pedestrians. Sightseers snapping iconic scenes on their cells and talent-spotting their favorite movie stars embedded in the legendary Walk of Fame. The mood was light, buoyed by the Christmassy decorations and a tangible buzz of expectancy. When it came to the absolutely must-see sights of Hollywood, this hub of old theatres, highbrow retail stores and trendy restaurants was the center of the universe on every tourist's star map. Everyone uploading images to their Facebook accounts, too busy to notice the nondescript white van as it made a left onto Orange Drive and slid against the curb.

Brake lights glowed brightly in the shade of the Roosevelt Hotel.

As far as rentals went, it was pretty unspectacular. No decals. Smoked-glass windows. Newish, but not this year's model. Clean, if you failed to notice the small streaks of ochre mud rubbed into the rims. It looked like one of the guest transports used by the hotel. Camouflaged by its ordinariness.

Perfect.

The engine died before the brake lights blinked out.

There were three men inside the van, invisible to passersby: two in the front and one in the back. The oldest of the trio, in the passenger seat, had one of those solemn faces that wouldn't look out of place on a totem pole. A military-style buzz cut forming a dark fuzz against russet-colored skin. Eyes hidden behind a pair of fashionable sunglasses – department store designer, not catwalk. He was agitated, nervous; had bitten away most of his fingernails on the ride over. Would have burned his way through a full pack of smokes had he not given up the habit back in rehab. He was the man in charge, and kept it that way with clipped commands and an unspoken threat of violence should either of his accomplices cross his path.

"You sure you know what to do?" he asked the younger of the trio, who was teetering on the edge of the backseat like a boy on a trip to see Santa.

The kid made a face. He had a softer aspect than the leader. A clod of unruly blond hair curling against an over-cooked Californian tan. One of those high-metabolism kids who can eat a horse and half a stable and still not put on an ounce of weight. He was excited, eager to press on with today's performance. Would have called CNN and NBC and handed them an exclusive had he thought of it earlier.

"Piece of cake," he beamed through pearly teeth. "I'm gonna make you guys proud and make that cop wish he'd never been born."

"No improvising."

"No problem." They'd been over this a million times. He had it down pat. Not like it was rocket science or anything. A monkey could do it. He tapped the driver on his shoulder, "Hey, don't forget our wager, man. If I make the primetime news, you owe me beers and a hot date."

The third man, the driver, kept his brooding gaze on the dashboard clock. He danced to a different tune. One of those cool, self-assured types who didn't need to argue a point to know he was right.

The passenger, the ringleader, shared none of the kid's enthusiasm. "Don't deviate from the plan," he warned. "You only get one shot at this. Make it count. Hit the target."

"Dude, relax; you'll give yourself an ulcer." The kid slid open the side door and leapt out. A cavalcade of city noise invaded the van. He went to the rear of the vehicle and pulled open the backdoor.

The cargo space was mostly empty. No rows of seats. No visitor brochures crammed into the pockets. Just a duffel bag and a pair of rectangular parcels covered in Christmassy wrapping paper. The parcels were identical, measuring three-feet-by-four, connected along one of the shorter edges by two fabric straps. The kid reached in and opened the duffel bag. Inside was a red velvety suit with a fake paunch, a matching cloth hat with a white beard attached, and a pair of big black work boots.

"Man, I'm gonna look the part in this getup."

He pulled the costume on over his tee-shirt and jeans, left his board shoes in the back of the van and laced up the boots. Then he hefted the panels against the bumper.

The ringleader joined him at the back of the van. He was bigger than the kid. Toned muscles that spoke of a tireless dedication. Maybe an obsession. "I'll be videoing from the corner. Remember what we discussed. Don't mess up."

The kid slammed the door and hoisted the parcels under his arm. "Yeah, man, I know, I got it – streaming my dazzling good looks live to YouTube for all the world to see. Make sure you get my good side and give me top billing."

"Just don't forget why we're doing this."

The kid's lips curled into a smile. "Revenge." He spoke the word with reverence – as if the sound of it would summon something supernatural.

"Restitution," the ringleader corrected.

"Hey, it's all semantics, man." The kid began to walk upslope toward Hollywood Boulevard. "Bail me if I get arrested," he laughed over his shoulder. "I mean it, dude. My life's in your hands."

"Stick with the plan," the driver called after him. "Do this right and you'll be famous."

The boulevard was teeming with visitors going starry-eyed at the movie magic. If any of them noticed him, none gave him a second glance; there were dozens of similar-looking guys coming and going hereabouts: runners, gofers, kids on breaks from the Hard Rock.

Nothing to snag the attention.

Not yet.

The kid drew a deep breath, waited for a break in the traffic, then skipped across the road. He found a free spot on the busy sidewalk near the red-liveried Madam Tussauds building, and paused to pull the hat over his head. The fluffy white beard was itchy. But he looked the part, didn't he?

Across the street, the ringleader was waiting for his performance to commence. He waved at him. He didn't wave back.

The kid turned his attention to the parcels leaning against his leg. Each was about the thickness of a portrait canvas. No string. No postage stamps. No forwarding address. Had the passersby paid him any interest whatsoever, they might have been mistaken in thinking he worked for the Post Office – when in fact he wasn't even a delivery man, not in any conventional sense.

The wrapping had snowmen on it. Nothing flashy or extraordinary.

Not yet.

He wedged fingers between the parcels and levered them apart, dipped his head between the pair of fabric straps and straightened himself up to his full height.

The sandwich board was a perfect fit.

Still no fireworks.

He started striding east along the star-spattered sidewalk, in the direction of the famous Chinese Theater, ripping the giftwrap away as he went. Visitors grouched and complained as he barged them aside, some with aggrieved expressions and some out loud. One or two didn't even see him coming and were bowled aside for their ignorance. At last, he was beginning to garner some attention. Heads turning.

But no sparks flying.

Not yet.

A dozen yards later, he was outside the legendary theatre itself – where he stopped and adopted a position facing the road. By now, most of the immediate sightseers crowding the sidewalk were looking his way. Cell phones poised in anticipation. The previously unnoticed kid in the Santa suit had something in mind. Maybe something worth recording and tweeting to their friends unlucky enough not to be in Hollywood the week before Christmas. Some of the crowd started snapping pictures. One or two jeered. More faces turned his way, both sides of the street.

But none of their eyes were lit up.

Not yet.

With the last of the wrappings discarded, the kid reached for the pull cord concealed behind the forward-facing panel, and yanked it, hard. The nylon string was attached to a trigger mechanism, which was connected to an ignition source, set to activate the stage-show pyrotechnics built into the frames of the boards.

A rolling, fizzing noise filled the air, like the sound of rushing surf.

Something popped.

Several of the nearest onlookers shied from the sudden sound, then almost fell over themselves as streams of fiery stars began to spew forth, showering the sidewalk with white-hot splinters.

Someone cheered.

Smart phones were being held aloft all over the place. Even the traffic on the street started to slow as their occupants gaped at the dazzling display. Every eye in a block radius was transfixed.

But he wasn't done.

Not yet.

As the initial flurry of activity began to subside, the kid reached for a second concealed pull cord and yanked it, hard. This nylon string was attached to another trigger mechanism, which was connected to a second ignition source, set to activate several rows of firecrackers built into the faces of the boards.

This was it. The world was about to see what revenge – or *restitution* – really meant.

Something popped.

Instinctively, the nearest onlookers drew back – but not because the firecrackers had startled them, but because the entire sandwich board had erupted in bright orange flame.

Some people started running.

Some people started filming.

Some people started screaming.

But none screamed louder or with more genuine terror than the blond kid with the sandwich board, who was suddenly engulfed in an eight-foot geyser of seething fire.

"When you're going through hell, keep going ..."

1

The Tennessee sky was the color of a Memphis Tigers jersey. Spotless, with superheated humidity blowing in from the Gulf. It was the kind of sticky summer's day that lacquers the skin in a perpetual sheen of sweat, and forms long, restless lines at water fountains.

We were in Overton Park, at the zoo; Hope, the kids and me, plus about a million other people – or so it seemed – all with the same smart idea of getting bored children out of the house and from under their momma's feet in the middle of the school vacations. No better remedy than a day trip to the Memphis Zoo, right? Doing all those patience-peeling things that happy families do on a busy weekend in the height of the season, namely: to squabble about where to eat and what to eat, to complain about long lines and waiting times, and to exist in a continual state of indecision about which exhibit to see and in what order.

Otherwise, pure bliss.

Until disaster had struck.

We were killing time at the Endangered Species Carousel. Hope and Gracie were standing by, girl-talking and giggling behind the safety barrier and a pair of melting ice cream cones. George was on the carousel, with me. Going round and round and hating it. My fault; I'd pressured him into riding the carved tiger – another great idea at the time – while I stood guard, grinning like a proud pop and feeling nauseous for it. George had pressed his mouth into a hard line and resisted my harebrained idea with a scowl. I'd had none of it.

Parenting is all about doing the stuff with ours kids that our parents never did with us.

Then, about halfway through the ride, a commotion had caught my eye. People yelling and feet falling. A youth had snatched a woman's purse and was making off with it in the direction of Primate Canyon. Instinct had kicked in and I'd given chase. No days off for this cop. Running ran in my blood. I'd caught up with the guy and wrestled him to the ground, then handed him over to the zoo security when they arrived moments later, puffing and red-faced.

When I'd returned to the carousel, feeling pretty good about myself, I'd found it stationary and with a crowd gathered. I'd pushed my way through. Hope was at the center, kneeling over George, who was unconscious, hair matted with blood, eyes rolled back in their sockets. More of the red sticky stuff on his face and on his shirt. My elation had crashed in flames. In my absence, George had fallen head-first from the ride and cracked his skull on the walkway.

All my fault.

The kind of fright in his mother's eyes that makes a father do deals with the devil.

Heart-racing, I'd rushed George to the First Aid point. A frantic Hope and a sobbing Gracie bringing up the rear. Hot blood leaking from George's scalp and lacerated cheek, dripping through my fingers and running up my arms.

No way to describe the panic burning through my gut.

Luckily, the visible damage had been superficial. Head cuts hemorrhage like burst pipes. No permanent damage on George's scan. But he had suffered a bad knock and his brain had shut down. He'd been sent home from the hospital the day after with a mouthful of candy and a war wound to charm the girls with in later life. But the invisible damage had cut much deeper than the surface scarring, lasted much longer. No salve to ease the pain of

Keith Houghton

the emotional wound that had festered away over time and never properly healed.

There was blood on my hands.

And someone was barking my name.

I materialized back into the present as if teleported, disoriented, dislocated. But it wasn't my son's blood oozing through my fingers, and I couldn't for the life of me work out who it belonged to.

Then recognition sucked the air from my lungs.

Nothing is ever what it seems.

Trenton Fillmore was a fake.

2

According to his tax records, Trenton Fillmore was a cutting-edge company accountant, but you would never figure so by looking him over. Fillmore had the mincemeat face and gangly physique of a middle-aged bare-knuckles fighter: two hundred pounds of gristly muscle, gnarly knuckles and one of those flattened noses that is about as prominent as a manhole cover on a city street. No hairline rapidly receding into a perspiring pate. No wire-rimmed eyeglasses with milk bottle lenses.

According to his sob story, Fillmore had boxed in his youth. Had gotten pretty good at it, too. Won a bunch of bouts and lost a truckload of teeth. Then something had popped in his head. A weak link. Just like that. And his fighting days were numbered. Luckily for Fillmore, he'd had a head for figures and had switched to a life of cooking books instead of throwing hooks.

Over recent weeks, I'd developed a kind of kinship for Trenton Fillmore. Not because he was a splash of color on drab concrete, but because we had something in common.

But now all that had changed.

I had his blood on my hands, dribbling from the knuckles and smeared across the front of what had been, seconds earlier, a snow-white undershirt fresh from the laundry. Worse than that, there was a bloodied shank in my fist and Fillmore was curled on the floor at my feet.

In any light, it didn't look good.

"Drop the weapon! Last chance! I won't ask again!"

There were four of us crammed into the tiny cell room of the Mental Health Unit located in the US Medical Center for Federal Prisoners in Springfield, Missouri: two inmates outfitted in khakis and whites; a dour-faced unit officer blocking the doorway; and a very worried-looking case manager with crumbs still lining his lips from his interrupted lunch.

"Drop the weapon," Frank Bridges, the perspiring case manager, repeated for maybe the third or fourth time. He was hovering halfway into the cell, a few steps in front of the duty officer, arms flung wide with palms turned upward. Classic non-aggressive body language. But the tremor in his voice was full of unspoken expletives. "What we got here is a recoverable situation. Let's all do our best to keep it that way. We don't want to hurt you, Quinn. But if we have to, we will."

It was cool in the cell, but Bridges was sweating like a whore in church.

In a small way – and I mean in a small way – I felt sorry for Bridges, and not simply because he suffered from small man syndrome. He was doing his best to tap into an old training session, conjure up suitable statements to mitigate the crisis situation. Trouble was, he'd probably spent the whole training session helping himself to the free buffet instead of paying attention.

"Back off, Bridges," I breathed, for maybe the third or fourth time. "You got this all wrong. This isn't how it looks."

My head was reeling.

How did I think it looked? I was standing over the bleeding body of my best buddy, with a *guilty as charged* neon sign flashing above my head. I wanted to drop the homemade shank, but the combination of gummy blood, shock and body heat had welded it to my hand.

"You heard Mr. Bridges." Jefferson, the unit officer, leaned in a little and made a *you know what I mean?* face.

Jefferson was a tall and chunky black guy with an eight ball afro. Normally, the kind of softly-spoken and unflappable guy who could talk mold off a wall. I'd never had any trouble from Jefferson – probably because I'd never given him any – but I suspected he could snap my neck without breaking a sweat if he had to.

"This is heading south real fast," he said. "Dugan's on his way with the Taser. And, man, that thing hurts like hell. You need to wrap this mess up peacefully, now, before things spiral out of control. Be the smart move listening to Mr. Bridges."

Hot blood trickled from the shank and splashed into the puddle forming on the floor. Fillmore wasn't moving. I could hear his breath bubbling. Only a matter of time before he exsanguinated.

Ordinarily, I'd take charge of the situation. Call the shots, the paramedics and maybe the Crime Lab techies to unplug the neon sign. But in here I was just another number. A nobody whose say-so held less water than a bucket with hole in it.

Bridges was holding out a meaty hand. Three big gold rings on the middle fingers. A single letter engraved on each, forming the word GOD when lined up together. He jangled them, like sleigh bells. "Drop the weapon, Quinn. Last chance to end this the easy way. I won't ask again."

And that's when Dugan pushed his way past Jefferson and fired fifteen-hundred volts of spiteful electricity into the soft tissue under my chin.

It was as if a heavyweight boxer had gone for the knockout punch. My head snapped back, teeth clashed and I went down for the count.

3

The worst part about the knock-down isn't hitting the canvas, it's the coming round.

Everything had a woolly feel to it. Insipid colors. I'd asked for aspirin, or even a cool sip of water to soften up my esophagus. So far, no one had obliged.

I was seated in Warden Burke's office, handcuffed. Dried blood on my hands. Gums still fizzing from the electrocution.

Over in the corner, a disheveled Christmas tree leaned against the wall, dressed like a hooker.

Burke was studying me through thatched fingers, dismissing my claims of innocence with a curl of his lips. I'd dealt with people like Burke all my life. One of those white collar bureaucrats who follow their job description as if it were scripture.

"You got this turned around," I was insisting. "Fillmore was on the floor when I got there. Do the math, Burke. While you're wasting time here trying to pin the tail on the donkey, Fillmore's real attacker is walking free."

The warden was wearing a *whatever it is you're selling, I'm not buying* face. He hadn't liked my being here from the get-go. Saw it as an imposition and a means for the federal government to eavesdrop on his operation. He rocked back in his padded leather chair and eyed me over knitted fingers. "What doesn't add up is how you came to be covered in Fillmore's blood, with the weapon in your hand."

I let him see my exasperation. I'd been over it a dozen times – how I'd found Fillmore already on the floor, how I'd thought he was screwing me, how I'd flipped him over to call him out on his prank.

"And that's when the knife popped out of his belly and conveniently landed in your hand?"

Not exactly how it had happened, but close enough to cement my guilt. Jefferson had entered the cell moments behind me, to see me kneeling over Fillmore, covered in blood. No other inmate in the immediate vicinity. How did I think it looked?

I raised myself up a little in the chair. "Look, Burke, I have no beef with you, but you're missing the big picture here. I have no reason to harm Fillmore. He's fought my corner time and again. He's the only friend I have in here. Why would I try and kill him? This is horse crap and you know it."

"I don't appreciate your tone, Quinn."

"And I don't appreciate being wrongly accused either."

"Perhaps he came by your true identity and the two of you had a falling out."

I felt the air leave my lungs.

There it was: *the motive*.

Burke's crossfire had sunk me with one torpedo.

I leaned back and fingered the salt-and-pepper Van Dyke beard I'd grown since coming to the Fed Med. It wasn't the world's best disguise – no better than Clark Kent's glasses – but when coupled with my falsified credentials, it blurred reality just enough to obscure the truth about who I was.

Burke raised his hands like a preacher about to absolve me of my alleged crime. "Besides, I'll be honest with you, Quinn. Fillmore voiced concerns about his welfare. This morning, in fact. In that very chair you're sitting in right now. He felt you and he would come to blows. He seemed genuinely fearful for his life."

"That's ridiculous! You and I both know Fillmore could knock me down with one finger. He isn't scared of me. No reason to be."

"I'm just saying it like it is, Quinn."

The phone rang on his desk.

"Don't answer it," I said through gritted teeth. "Prioritize. For once in your life, Burke, be flexible. Let's you and I go down to the infirmary and speak with Fillmore, right now. Clear this mess up."

The warden's lip curled like road-kill on a midsummer's day. I'd rubbed against his grain since day one. He didn't like my tone and he certainly wasn't comfortable taking orders from an inmate, even if I did outrank him.

He sniffed and picked up.

He nodded once, twice. I heard him mumble something into the receiver. Then he placed the handset back in its cradle and let out a tremulous breath.

"That was Doctor O'Dell. It's bad news. Unfortunately, Fillmore didn't make it. Apparently, the blade severed his abdominal aorta. He bled to death before they could operate."

I was stunned, suddenly sick to my stomach with the thought of my friend being dead and his blood still caking my hands. "That's it, Burke." My breath was fiery. "The game's over. Pick up your phone and call Mason Stone. Right now. Tell him somebody killed cock robin and I need to get out of here."

4

There is only one thing more dangerous than a paranoid fool and that's a paranoid fool with a weapon in his hand.

Trenton Fillmore was dead and I was in seclusion. Confined to a special holding cell – essentially, a cement cube with a bedroll and a narrow band of glass bricks high up – while the powers-that-be determined my guilt, or innocence, or whichever meant less paperwork.

Sometimes, redemption is as elusive as a rainbow's end: no matter how far we chase it down, it will always remain tantalizingly out of our reach.

Four long months had passed since I'd invoked a death sentence on Jacob Klaussner – aka Jack Heckscher, my friend, my confidant, my nemesis. Sixteen weeks of mental mangling and hand wrangling. But my deliberate killing of Jack Heckscher wasn't the reason I was here. Not fully, anyway. Not by a long shot.

My obsessions will be the death of me.

On the run-up to the fatal face-off with *The Maestro* in Florida, I'd shot a federal agent. Not any old federal agent and not by accident. I'd shot Mason Stone, the Special Agent in Charge of the resurrected Piano Wire Murders. Basically, my level-headedness had gone AWOL and I'd shot him in the chest – on a whim and a fear of exposure. Point blank. Not once or even twice. A full clip, with every gunshot another nail in my coffin.

How do you come back from something like that?

Luckily for both of us, Stone had been wearing a Kevlar vest at the time. He'd survived the bullet barrage and the swollen waters of Pine Island Sound with severe bruising and cracked ribs. He'd gotten away with it. I hadn't. Sometime later, I'd been arrested for my impulsive madness, processed and packaged off to the nuthouse for the criminally insane.

The deal was, to win back my freedom, I'd do two favors: one for Mason Stone and one for myself.

For my part, I'd undergone group counseling, one-to-one therapy sessions, intensive psychiatric reconditioning and enough psychological intervention to make my head spin like Regan's in *The Exorcist*. Subtly bombarded with every silent letter P in the dictionary. Worn this thick skin of mine a few microns thinner. Whether or not any of it had penetrated my thick skull was anyone's guess.

For Stone's part, I'd gone undercover and befriended Trenton Fillmore.

Distantly, I heard an exchange of hurried dialogue in the hallway outside. Heard the voices fade as their owners retreated.

I got up from the bedroll and started pacing the cell.

I'd done a lot of standing still since I'd exacted merciless retribution on those responsible for the cold-blooded murder of my wife. How did I feel about it? I didn't. I had thought I'd feel vindication, maybe even victorious. I was wrong. Vengeance had left me vacant, emotionless. Worst of all, the closure had left me directionless.

What use is a firework once it has lit up the night sky?

One emotion I did feel was anger.

Not simply because I was now holding the can for Fillmore's murder, but because my friend had been killed and I couldn't fix it. Not while I was locked up in solitary confinement. Maybe not even when I was released back into the main prison population. Not without freedom to move, to investigate, to ask awkward questions, to do what I did best: rattle cages.

Someone had gutted Fillmore like a fish and left him to bleed out. I didn't know who, or why. But I'd find out, somehow.

More than anything, I wanted to know why Fillmore – my buddy – had lied to the warden about me. I wanted to know why he'd expressed fear for his life, and at my hands. What was with that?

There was a dog-eared book on the bedroll. One of the classics. Something by Hemmingway. Left here to keep an insane inmate from going stir crazy. I could see a giant marlin and a small boat on the worn jacket. I picked it up and turned to the first page.

A former internee had scrawled the words *'You're in deep shit now, brother'* in what looked and smelled like old feces.

Out in the hallway, the voices came back.

I heard the lock mechanism rotating. I closed the book as the door squeaked open. The short, rotund outline of Case Manager Frank Bridges filled the doorway, the makings of a snarl pulling at the edges of his fleshy jowls.

"Who were you expecting," he said without preamble, "Santa Claus? Come on, get your shit together. It looks like Christmas just came early for you, Quinn."

5

Although freedom can be taken, stolen, sold, it isn't a commodity. It's a state of mind.

Physically, I was free. Not just out of solitary confinement, but the whole pig-on-a-skateboard shebang. Mentally, it would take time ripping down the razor wire.

"For the record," I told Bridges as we headed through the bleached underground tunnels leading to Building One, "I didn't kill Fillmore."

"Not for me to think one way or the other. That's between you and your maker, Quinn. Now keep your voice down; we don't want anyone getting any ideas."

It was after hours, Christmas Eve – everybody locked down early for the night and listening out for sleigh bells.

We came to a small inspection room connected to the Receiving and Discharge Unit. I'd been here previously: the first day I'd arrived at Springfield. It was a basic frisk-down area. Empty trays for personal effects stacked on a bench. Latex gloves and tubes of K-Y jelly. All the fine trimmings one would expect in such a swanky establishment.

A sour-faced attendant handed me a plastic packet containing my regular day clothes and basic effects – a wallet, a watch, house keys, that kind of thing – confiscated on my arrival back in August. He huffed and puffed as I stripped out of the prison-issue khakis. My release was keeping him here after hours, and he was making a point of showing his impatience.

"Seems you got friends in high places," Bridges commented as I climbed into a navy-blue polo shirt and stone-washed Levis. "They must have pulled some long strings to get you out during the Holidays."

I laced up my sneakers. "They're the same ones that landed me in here." I thrust out a hand. "You take care of yourself, Bridges. No hard feelings."

"None taken." A little uncertainly, he accepted the farewell handshake. His fistful of rings felt like a knuckleduster. "I'll be headed back home myself the second you're out of here. My folks live in Pasadena. I hear you're heading out that way, too. Let's do our best not to bump into one another."

The attendant cranked open the steel door leading to the processing station and ushered me through.

There was a red-haired woman in a dark gray business suit pressed up against the chest-high counter, signing a discharge sheet under the sleepy gaze of a disinterested processing officer. She was in her late-forties. Freckles peeping through light make-up. One of those hour-glass women who hadn't bought into the size zero hard-sell.

"Be right with you, Gabe," she called without turning my way.

I knew her, I realized. *Had* known her – a lifetime ago. Wasn't sure if I still wanted to.

"Rae? Libby Rae Burnett? Is that really you?"

She glanced over her shoulder as I approached, hazel eyes twinkling in the fluorescent light. She was twenty years older than the last time I'd seen her. But middle age had been kind. That, and maybe one or two carefully-placed fillers.

"Hey." She smiled one of those fulsome, lips parted smiles that pulls one from your own face and doesn't give it back.

But it was all a sham, for the benefit of the processing officer; I could see darker undertones creeping through. Worst still, I knew why.

"Rae, what are you doing here?"

She pushed the paperwork at the attendant, then flashed another perfunctory smile. "Isn't that obvious? I'm breaking out some crazy as a run-over dog celebrity cop. Now what's with the face?"

"Because I just realized you sold your soul and became a Fed."

She peeped at the FBI badge hooked over her breast pocket, as if noticing it for the first time. "Well, would y'all look at that: so I did. Then, again, so did you. And I reckon that makes us just about even." Her nose wrinkled. Freckles gathered. "Hold that thought." She balled a fist, pulled back her arm, and slugged me on the nose. The move was fast. Nothing I could do to avoid. "Now we're even," she said, shaking her hand.

6

Team Tennessee. That's how Libby Rae Burnett had once described our breakneck relationship. Bullets in the same magazine.

For almost two years, Rae and I had partnered out of the same Memphis precinct together, as green-gilled beat cops – twenty-five years ago – when life hadn't been any less of a quagmire, we'd just had more strength to wade through it.

We were in the backseat of a black sedan as it sped west, away from the federal prison, cold rainwater sluicing round the fenders. I was out and feeling the chill. Night had settled over Missouri like a wet blanket. Crystalized sleet peppering the windshield. Not many vehicles on the road; everyone home early for the Holidays.

I was massaging the bridge of my nose. "I get it, Rae. You're still angry. It's understandable. I guess I owe you an apology."

Rae's body language was all four-letter words. "What I need is for you to give me an explanation. Didn't you ever think about me?"

"More than I should." It came out before I could stop it.

Rae's stony expression softened for a moment, but only a moment. Then the drawbridge pulled itself back up.

"What's the real rub here, Rae? You didn't come all this way to give me a good old-fashioned Tennessee ass-whoopin'."

"I didn't?"

"No. I know you better than that. You've had twenty years to hunt me down and blacken my eyes. This is Stone's idea, isn't it? He knows about our past. That's why he sent you here. It's all part of his control mechanism and keeping me in check."

"Gabe, you're paranoid. Coming here was all my idea. At first, Mason refused to go along with it *because* he knew our history. I had to employ all my southern belle charm to persuade him otherwise."

I smiled darkly. Rae could always charm jumpers down from the roof.

"But I'm beginning to think it was a bad idea," she finished.

"Attacking me?"

"No, having good intentions to mend fences."

I sighed. I caught a glimpse of headlights picking out rain-soaked trees and sagging power lines. "Rae, I know my faults. Springfield introduced me to every one of them. I run away. Always have. I erect barriers and pigeonhole problems. Professionally, it's served me well. Emotionally, it's ruined relationships. I'm trying to change. Really, I am."

"And I'm happy for you, Gabe. It sounds like the Fed Med did its job. Did you a world of good and the world a favor."

Rae's gaze was paralyzing, as it always had been.

"How did Stone take the news about Fillmore?"

"Not good. He was madder than a wet hen – especially considering they'd already shipped the body out to the Greene County Medical Examiner by the time I got here."

Fast work, given it was Christmas Eve.

"Rae, you do know I didn't kill Fillmore?" There was enough graveness in my voice to give Vincent Price the chills.

For a moment she looked out through the window at the falling sleet. Then her eyes found mine and I could see her jury was still out.

It was going to take more than an apology to bridge the river of bad blood flowing between us.

7

The Gulfstream jet climbed at a steep angle into thunderous skies. Wintry Missouri dropped away, shrinking into a spider web spangle of Christmas lights.

I looked back inside the dimly-lit cabin. Rae was busy setting up a laptop on a fold-down table. Its icy glare turning her freckles blue.

"I'm not sure I'm ready to face the wrath of Stone just yet," I admitted.

"Then I guess it's a good thing we're heading out to Alaska instead." She saw my surprise and added: "We're going to Kodiak Island, Gabe, to a fishing village called Akhiok."

I hadn't heard the name in years, or thought about it in longer.

"Why Akhiok?"

"It's our assignment."

I made a face. My freedom had been short-lived. "Wait a minute, Rae. What about my agreement with Stone? With Fillmore dead, our deal's off."

"Not according to Mason. You're still under contract with the Bureau until he says otherwise. We have a job to do and so we're going to go and do it."

There it was: I was sprung from Springfield but there was no escape. Stone had every intention of keeping me on a short leash, where he could keep an eye on me, indefinitely. I couldn't blame him. I'd done some pretty stupid things on the run-up to my imprisonment. I wasn't asking for a second chance; I was already onto my fourth or fifth.

"So what's so special about Akhiok?"

"They found a body."

"Who?"

"Does it matter who exactly? I believe it was a young girl, from the village."

"The body?"

"No, the person who found the body. Are you paying attention? That is what you asked, isn't it?"

"I guess. Let me be clearer, then: *why* are we going to Akhiok?"

"I told you: they found a body. It's our assignment."

"That still doesn't answer my question, Rae."

She made a wounded face. "Gabe, it's as much as I know right now. A girl from the village found an unidentified body. No driver's license or fishing permit. Everyone accounted for in the village and no missing persons reported on the island. As far as I know, the Kodiak Police have made attempts to contact trappers and hunters in the area, but I guess it's proving difficult with the weather and all."

I was looking at her with an *I'm still waiting* expression.

"What?"

"If the local police have this covered, why is the Bureau sending agents to Akhiok on Christmas Eve? Scratch that. Why are they sending *us* and not agents from the Anchorage field office?"

"The truth?"

"It always helps."

"I don't know. I really don't. I'm following orders, just like you."

"You mean Mason Stone's orders."

She nodded. "And we're flying straight into Kodiak because that's where the body is."

I didn't hide my astonishment.

I made her explain. And it went something like this:

An unidentified body had been found in a remote Alaskan village on the southwestern tip of Kodiak Island. Signs of foul play. The local cops had flagged the suspected homicide up to the FBI field office in Anchorage as a matter of courtesy. Somehow that information had found its way south to California and, more importantly, to Mason Stone's office in Los Angeles. At his behest, the Kodiak PD had kept the body on site, breaking protocols and any number of city ordinances. The body should have been shipped out to the ME's office in Anchorage – no questions asked – while both it and any preserved evidence were still fresh and collectable. The fact that Rae and I were going to see it in situ wasn't just unorthodox, it was concerning.

It was Sanibel all over again.

And it still didn't answer any of my questions.

8

Exactly five hours later, the Gulfstream jet landed at Kodiak Airport in a squall of sleet. Snowy vortices swirling in its wake. The plane skewed on wet tarmac, jolting our teeth. I could see mounds of filthy gray snow plowed high to the sides of the runway. Everything bleak – backend of the world, bleak. A tomb lid sky, with yellowy perimeter floodlights revealing a steady veil of big snowflakes falling lazily toward an undulating landscape of white tundra.

An unearthly chill crept through the fuselage.

My wristwatch said it was a little after two in the morning, Christmas Day, Central Time. I set it back by three hours as the jet taxied toward the terminal building.

Neither Rae nor I had spoken much in the preceding five hours – a little more about our unconventional assignment and even less about Rae's twenty-year-old upset. She'd kept herself busy doing paperwork on a notebook, leaving me to sit in awe at the vast lightning storms unleashing electric mayhem over the Pacific Northwest. It seemed, for now, she'd had her fill of bone picking. But I knew it was only a matter of time before I'd have to face the inevitable and explain away my actions of yesteryear.

The jet came to a shuddering halt.

Rae broke out a pair of overnight bags stowed behind the seats and rolled one my way. "You'll be needing these; it's colder than a witch's tit out there."

I peeked inside, saw a thick parka coat and a pair of stout hiking boots, together with thermal gloves and knitted socks, plus other last-minute essentials.

"It's a woman thing," she said with a smirk. "We're great anticipators. Speaking of which, this is also for you." She placed a small cloth-covered parcel in my hand.

I unwrapped it to reveal a holstered firearm, a cell phone and an FBI badge with my photo ID attached to the wallet. Same FBI badge I'd used four months earlier, chasing down *The Maestro* in sunny California. Not the same gun.

I checked the clip in handle. It was full of shiny .40 caliber bullets. I fastened the holster to my belt. "Have Glock will travel. We expecting trouble out here, Rae?"

"I sure as heck hope not. But there's no sense taking unnecessary chances either way." She flashed me a reassuring smile. Not sure if it was for my benefit or hers.

*   *   *

A white Ford Expedition with Kodiak Police decals was waiting to collect us on the glistening apron. Snow flurries dancing in its headlights. A KPD officer with a mop of dark curly hair and a thick moustache was leaning against the hood, hands buried deep in the pockets of his padded jacket. I detected a hint of mild aggravation in his face – like we'd dragged him away from beers and a game in a bar with his buddies.

We hunched into our parkas and clattered across the wet asphalt in our brand new hiking boots.

Breath smoking, the local cop introduced himself as Officer Glenn Hillyard; pleased to make our acquaintance.

"If it's okay with you guys," he said as he loaded our bags in the trunk, "we've organized a flight out to Akhiok at first light. The forecast is for heavy snow overnight. It's too dangerous flying out there in these conditions. Meanwhile, your SAC has provisionally arranged accommodation at the Kodiak Inn."

In other words, we were grounded for the night.

We crowded inside the police vehicle and headed out of the airport at a brisk pace.

Immediately, cloying darkness closed in as the road curled northeast through the bleak landscape. It was cold, even with the heater on full. The Expedition's headlights offered up brief glimpses of dense spruce forests capped in snow, stretching away into impenetrable darkness on either side. Mile after mile of trees and black-bottomed snowdrifts. Like something out of a Stephen King novel.

Not for the first time since leaving Missouri, I pictured the image of Trenton Fillmore slain on the cell floor. Already, I had a mental list of mental suspects – just about every nut and bolt in Springfield. Plenty of motive, but not a whole lot of opportunity. For the life of me I still couldn't figure out why he'd begged the warden to keep us separated. The last time I'd spoken with Fillmore I'd been on the butt-end of a bad joke, with no hint of any fear of me or of my half-assed rebuttal.

How could I go about finding his murderer now that I was four thousand miles away?

The domineering presence of a rocky mountain loomed up in the headlights, scuffed with scree slopes.

"This isn't run-of-the-mill for us," Officer Hillyard was telling Rae over his shoulder. "Homicides are a rare occurrence out here. I think this is a first for Akhiok."

Reflective road signs warned of wildlife, camping sites and rock falls.

I could see the glow of a nearing town. Sodium streetlights pushing back at the dark to reveal wooden buildings stacked against a hillside and huddled around a harbor. All at once the forest gave way to civilization, to storefronts decked out with festive themes, to frontier businesses providing vital services to townsfolk and explorers. Variegated Christmas lights snaking around lampposts and strung across the roadway.

Through the windshield I could see an illuminated Best Western sign coming up fast. Hillyard braked at the last moment and slid the Expedition into a small parking lot adjacent to the Kodiak Hotel.

We climbed out into frosty air.

The building was a gray dry-stone affair with staggered floors stacked up against the slope. Mortuary slabs piled high. Big windows and an equally big iron anchor staked out front. Across the street, I spied rows of unmoving boats, lining long jetties, lined up like bleached skulls, disappearing into the blackness of the bay.

Impossible not to shiver.

Hillyard handed us our bags. "Sun-up's around ten-fifteen. I'll be back here to pick you up at ten-thirty, sharp. Be ready to ship out." He got back inside the Expedition and tore away up the main drag.

"Someone's in a hurry."

Rae was shaking her head. "Gabe, show some compassion. Sometimes you're about as dumb as a bag of hammers. It's Christmas Eve right now; he's probably got a wife waiting at home and toddlers tucked up tight."

There was a glass partition next to the main doors. Behind it, a preserved fully-grown brown bear was positioned in an alert pose. An over-enthusiastic hotel employee had slung a prickly Christmas wreath around its neck and hung glittery baubles from its ears.

"Do you think there's room at the Inn?" Rae asked as we pushed our way inside.

I was freezing. "Who cares so long as they have coffee?"

The lobby had been designed to resemble a hunting-lodge. Varnished pine walls rising to an open-plan gallery, complete with mounted deer heads and hung skins. There was a bushy Christmas tree in a corner, already shedding needles. Fake Christmas presents, and Mariah Carey's *All I Want for Christmas Is You* warbling in the background.

A kid in a red Santa hat smiled at us from behind the reception counter. "Welcome to the Kodiak Inn! Long journey? Can I interest you in a complimentary Christmas candy?" He motioned to a glass bowl on the counter, filled to the brim with finger-sized candy canes.

Rae helped herself. "Don't mind if I do. Gabe?"

I shook my head.

She flashed the kid her badge. "I believe we have a reservation?"

"Let me check that out for you guys." The kid tapped keys.

I gazed around the brightly-lit lobby. It felt strange, cluttered. Over the last few months I'd gotten used to seeing the same simple rooms and plain walls. Oddly, it felt claustrophobic.

"Here we go," the kid smiled. "Mr. and Mrs. Federal Bureau of Investigation. The charge for your stay has already been taken care of, I see." He slid a pair of keycards on the counter. "The honeymoon suite awaits. You can either take the elevator to the second floor, or follow the stairs."

I looked at Rae. She was looking at me. We were both thinking the same uneasy thought.

"Twin beds?" Rae speculated.

The kid shook his head. A bell tinkled at the tip of his hat. "Sorry, folks. We're fully booked for the Holidays. It's the best I can do."

"How about other hotels in town?"

The kid answered with a shrug. "You're welcome to try. But the thing is, everywhere gets kind of really booked up this time of year. The honeymoon suite is only available because of a last minute cancelation." He smiled, as if his outstanding dentistry would finalize the deal.

"Rae, it's okay," I said. "I'll put my feet up here in the lobby. There's a nice big sofa by the window. Plus, it's warm. I'll be fine."

"Alternatively," the kid said, "the room comes with a recliner."

"That's settled, then." Rae took one of the keycards and handed me the other. "The honeymoon suite it is."

9

Sadly, once they return to their old lives, many inmates return to their old ways. Even sadder, I was one of them.

My arrest in August, and my subsequent transportation straight to jail without passing *Go*, had effectively put my obsessions on hold. Living on the inside had meant I was dead to the outside. Jail time had come with basic Internet time – restricted to certain sites and under strict scrutiny. No email access whatsoever, and certainly no means to pursue my obsessions through cyberspace.

Snakeskin and *The Undertaker.*

Two murderers. Both roaming free while I'd been locked in one place. One chasing the other. Not sure if the one being chased even knew the other one was doing the chasing.

Before my arrest, *Snakeskin* aka Gary Cornslik– the disaffected ex-Fed keen to blow me to smithereens – had made a vow to hunt down and kill *The Undertaker*, who he blamed for his meltdown. And I had vowed to stop him.

Four months was a long time to be held back, knowing that those I hunted were getting farther and farther away. Warm trails cooling. A long time to be wound up like a spring, waiting to be released. All that time, going over fine details in my mind, again and again, keeping me company in the solitude of my cell. Four months of planning what I was going to do once I got out of Springfield, of how I was going to track them down, catch them, or kill them.

I hadn't bargained on Alaska.

Truth was, I had no idea where they were, or even if they had killed again. For all I knew, they might have killed one another and put an end to my obsessions.

If so, where would that leave me?

I told Rae to go up ahead of me and then snuck into the hotel's deserted business center. I charged an hour's Internet time against the room and started running Google searches. I began with the keywords *The Undertaker* and *Gary Cornsilk*, then widened the criteria to include the combinations *murder, homicide by lethal injection, ash cross, rose petals,* and separately *death, homicide by fire, incendiary bomb, burned alive.* The hits were off the scale.

I spent some time sorting through the clutter. I ignored the press references relating to the original Undertaker Case. Nothing dated beyond February. Nor was there anything in the news or any of the media feeds to show *The Undertaker* had killed again using the same MO. As for *Snakeskin* there was even less on public record. No mention that he liked playing with fire. No mention of his love for constructing booby-trap bombs. No linking him to the dead woman found in a Fort Myers hotel back in the summer. Definitely nothing connecting him to the incinerated corpse of Derrick Hives, my private investigator, found in a warehouse in Virginia a week later.

It was as if the two of them had laid down their homicidal tendencies and vanished into thin air, leaving me behind.

I should have been happy. I wasn't. I was deflated.

What had I expected – a bread crumb trail leading all the way to their woodcutter cottage in the woods?

I told myself to get a grip, and then checked my emails.

Aside from thousands of spam messages there were several from Tim Roxbury – my police detective friend from back home in Alhambra – all marked *Urgent* and none older than by a week. I went to open the first, then had a change of heart and decided to leave them for another time. Tim's wisecracking antics had gotten me in trouble and I wasn't sure I was ready to let him back into my life just yet. I continued scanning through the mass of unwanted junk instead, searching for anything sent from Eleanor Zimmerman – my dear psychiatrist friend from the Internal Affairs Group of the LAPD – but there was nothing. Not a peep.

The disappointment just kept on coming.

What was I expecting?

I hadn't exactly been the best friend in the world of late. Okay, so I'd saved Eleanor's life. Big deal. It was my fault it had been in jeopardy to begin with. Because of me, Eleanor Zimmerman had been targeted by a kill team. Because of me, she'd been kidnapped and manacled with cruel piano wires to the master bed in my home on Valencia Street. Because of me, she'd been starved for a full week and left to bleed out. Because of me, she'd been a heartbeat away from death at the hands of *The Maestro*.

I couldn't expect her to forgive. But I had expected her to let me know that she didn't.

I decided to call it a night. I retreated upstairs to the honeymoon suite and used the keycard to slip quietly inside. The lights were off. I fumbled into the bathroom, bumped an elbow on the door jamb and cursed under my breath. I closed the door and activated the low-wattage shaving light.

A ghostly apparition shifted in the bathroom mirror. In the weak orange glow, it looked like something that had just crept from a crypt. A sickly pallor. Dark rings under sunken eyes. No hint of a former Floridian suntan. Not getting any younger either. I ran the faucet, splashed tepid water over my phantom face and then used the toothbrush Rae had left out to scrub Springfield from my teeth.

Rae Burnett.

A lifetime ago, she'd gotten to know me just about as well as anyone had ever gotten to know me. Certainly, as close as any woman had ever come, aside from Hope, that is. Working long shifts together did that. Partners quickly learn their shadow's idiosyncrasies, their traits, their thought processes, what makes them tick and what doesn't. Weaknesses are exposed before strengths are identified. We anticipate and we depend. Sometimes, partners get to know each other better than they know their lovers. Sometimes the two mix and the chemical reaction is explosive.

Back in the bedroom, I could sense Rae's huddled form in the darkness, snuggled up under the linens. A crack in the drapes revealed a big recliner over in the corner, with a blanket draped over one arm. The bright red numerals on the bedside clock read 12:57 a.m. – almost four, Central Time. Christmas Day. I tiptoed to the La-Z-Boy and wrestled the boots off my feet.

"Don't mind me," Rae murmured from out of the dark, "I'm still waiting for the sandman to show his miserable face."

I put the boots under the chair. "Trouble sleeping, Rae?"

"Strange beds," she sighed. "Don't you remember?"

I felt my cheeks heat-up, was glad she couldn't see them. "From what I recall, there wasn't a whole lot of sleeping going on. We were both young and energetic. Libidos like rabbits. "

"Crazy times."

Even though Rae couldn't see it, I nodded. I knew she sensed it. For a hotheaded moment in time, Rae and I had burned brightly. Fiercely. Some folks call it chemistry. Others call it carnal. Me, I call it cowardly. For two months straight, we'd worked the streets by day and each other by night. Wrong but right. Even now, I was unsure if our union had filled a need or if there had been something deeper between us, something that couldn't be labeled as lust and seizing the moment.

"You have to admit it's undeniable," Rae said, "we were darn good together, you and me. Had things been different, we could have gone the full distance. We had everything. Sometimes I look back and wonder what might have happened if Hope had never taken you back."

The mention of my wife's name burned a hole in my chest, as it always did. Guilt does that kind of thing.

We'd been going through a rough patch, Hope and me. It happens. All kinds of excuses why. No clear recollection of the ignition source. Kids with kids ourselves, maybe. Work pressures leading to relationship stresses, definitely. One blazing row after another. Mostly trivial stuff blown out of proportion. You know where I'm coming from. No one accepting the blame and nothing ever resolved. Everything broken and nothing we could scream loud enough to fix it. Eventually, Hope had had all she could stomach of my bullheadedness. She'd left in a whirlwind. Packed up and gone home to her parents' place in the country, out near Jackson. Grace and George went with her, the whole of one summer. She'd told me it was over and she wanted a divorce. I'd flipped. Raged at the world and at my own pigheaded stupidity for pushing her away. For days, useless and foaming at the mouth. Found myself pouring out my heart to my partner in a bar one night. Found her attentive and understanding. Found myself slipping into darkness, lost in a moment that swept away the heartache and went on for seamless weeks.

But then George had broken his leg falling from a tree and the needs of my family had outweighed the needs of the two.

"Rae," I breathed. "Rae, I never meant to –"

"Love me?" she asked from out of the darkness.

And there it was: the knockout blow.

I hadn't seen it coming – not then, not now. Like the killer twist at the end of a thriller, it had sneaked up and kicked me in the gut. Is that what Rae and I had had all those years ago? Love not lust? Is that why I'd run back to

Hope the minute an opportunity had arisen, because I was scared of staying with Rae and what it would lead to? Scared that I might actually choose her over Hope?

I swallowed, dryly, glad Rae couldn't see the perplexity squirming over my face.

No arguing the fact that Hope and I had warred for months. Long enough for it to become a way of existence. Shamefully, it had impacted on our home life and had affected our children – especially my sensitive son, who loved his momma more than life itself. Instead of fighting for us, I'd withdrawn. Frustration, inexperience and the stubborn Quinn gene getting in the way. I'd never questioned my love for Hope. Not once. But I'd never asked myself about my real feelings for Rae either. Didn't realize I'd had any – not until long after the event, when the dust had settled, when it was easier to do nothing about it. Take the coward's way out.

Was it possible to be in love with two people, both at the same time?

Although Rae and I had shared many four-letter words between us, *love* had never passed either of our lips. Maybe it should have. Maybe if I'd stopped for a second to think with my heart instead of my head, I might have made different choices. As it was, the course of events had made the decision for me. On hearing about George's accident, I'd brought forward my vacation days and rushed to Jackson. Stayed there a whole month. Freed from the burdens of our jobs, Hope and I had found common ground, weeding out our issues on neutral turf. We'd patched things up. Sown the seeds of our future. A good future. Vowed to try harder, to listen, to carve out a better life for us and our children – maybe with a fresh start in another State.

I'd let Hope die thinking it was her idea to move our family out to the West Coast, when in fact all I'd been doing was running away from Rae.

I drew a deep and uneven breath. "I was going to say *hurt* you, Rae. But you're right. God forgive me, you're right. You always were."

There was a long, protracted silence in which I could hear Rae's breathing, regular and steady. Hear my heart thudding away in the chasm between fear and familiarity. I was unmoving in the dark, wondering what she was thinking, wondering what I was thinking.

Twenty years had passed between us. Two decades of hurt and hope. A lifetime of work, of children maturing into adults, of deliberately not looking back and wondering *what if?*

"I need to know," she said quietly, "do you still have feelings for me?"

I got up and padded over to the bed. I don't know why I did. It just happened. Automatic pilot, I guess. My legs and feet with plans of their own. I settled on the edge of the mattress, looked down at Libby Rae Burnett, unable to make out much more than the outline of her face in all the darkness.

I sensed her push herself up on one elbow, shimmy closer under the sheets, sensed the sudden proximity of her warmth, her breath, her fragrance. God help me.

"For the record," she said softly, "you're a bastard, and I never stopped loving you."

A hand touched mine. I should have pulled back. I really should. But I didn't. I'd been here before. In my thirties. When I should have known better, but had been too single-minded and too self-absorbed with quelling my own pain to care either way.

"I'm not sorry about the punch on the nose," she said.

"Me either."

Our hands found each other. Fingers interlocking, squeezing.

I knew what was coming. I hadn't pulled back then and I was unable to do so now.

Magnetism.

Rae tented the sheets over us. "Promise you won't flee the scene of the crime, come morning?"

"Cross my heart and hope to die."

There had always been something irresistible about Rae Burnett. Something invisible. Something that connected us through more than just time and space. I didn't know what it was. But it felt right. Always had.

"Merry Christmas," she whispered, a second before our lips touched.

10

She couldn't sleep. She had a feeling things were coming to a head. She got up and made herself a warm milk.

All told, she'd hired the services of three private detectives over the course of the past year.

The first two had proven ineffective, and she considered the drain on her finances and nerves a costly lesson in good match-making.

At first, she'd been green to the business and blind to what skills were best suited for what purposes. She'd enlisted the services from one neighborly recommendation and one from an online ad appearing on the local news website. Both private detectives had listened to her story and banked her deposits. Neither had made good on their promises or made her wishes their top priority. After a few choice words and several big checks, she'd had no choice but to let them go.

Most of the investigators she'd vetted since had specialized in proving infidelity. 'Empty hearts make for cheating minds' her mother had once said. Adultery was on the rise. The sanctity of marriage having weaker bonds these days than the glue sealing a condom wrapper. Easy money for retired cops looking to make a fast buck with as little actual legwork as possible.

Few specialized in finding people who didn't want to be found.

But things were looking up.

They were on the right track and she'd caught a glimmer of light at the end of the long tunnel.

So far, in the space of a few days, the third private detective had uncovered more significant information than she'd gathered under her own steam all year. Double the efforts of her previous hires.

She expected a location and a name anytime soon.

She finished her milk and returned to the matrimonial bed, slipping quietly under the thick comforter. She lay on her back, in the dark, next to the snoring bulk of her boring husband and stared at the ceiling.

She had a feeling things were coming to a head. It was no wonder she couldn't sleep.

11

As promised, Officer Glenn Hillyard of the Kodiak PD picked us up at ten-thirty on the dot and drove us back to the airport in his Ford Expedition. The overnight snowfall had stopped sometime before dawn, leaving the whitewashed landscape a perfect replica of the overcast sky. Christmas Day in Alaska. Cold enough to condense breath and redden noses.

"We could have called a cab," Rae told Hillyard after first wishing him season's greetings and then apologizing for our dragging him away from his family a second time.

"Ma'am, it's all part of the service," he said happily enough – although I sensed he'd be rushing straight home the second he dropped us off.

Children make Christmas, and Hillyard was visibly itching to get back to his.

We retraced our steps from the night before, following the long and winding road as it cut a channel though the snow-laden spruce forests.

I hadn't had much in the way of sleep. Then again, neither had Rae. But we weren't worse for it. Our expended energies had been replenished by a continental breakfast with a Christmassy twist and enough deep roast to make our ears ring.

"No regrets?" she'd asked, tentatively, as we'd showered and dressed.

"None," I'd replied through a mouthful of toothpaste, and meant it. I'd surprised myself with the sincerity of it. I some ways, Rae had reunited me with the human race. I was no longer a cold outsider, watching life through an unclean lens. Rae had reconnected me with something deep and unspoken. Something beyond the physical. Something healthy. Something Hope would have wanted me to have, after her, of that I'm sure. Not much in the way of the kind of conversation Rae had hoped for, but sometimes actions do speak louder than words.

Let he who is without sin cast the first stone.

I watched Rae Burnett as she chitchatted with Hillyard about everyday stuff, supporting the conversation in the way that only women can do. There was a noticeable change in her demeanor this morning. It was visible. Her whole body language was more of a whisper than a shout. A glow in her face. Eyes bright. Cheeks flushed. Everything softer and brighter. Smiling for no apparent reason. She looked like she'd found rekindled love and been up all night getting reacquainted. I wondered if I looked the same.

"Does this constitute a conflict of interest?" I'd asked her, around eggs-over-easy.

"Shoot, Gabe, I won't tell if you don't."

The thing about age is, the older we get the more we make a point of getting to the point. We learn that time is too precious a commodity to waste on formalities. Rae and I both knew where we stood. Both older and hopefully wiser. We'd cut to the chase and made up for half a lifetime of being apart.

And something had changed inside of me.

For the first time in recent memory I had a weird sense of happiness. It was frightening and yet exciting. Like holding your newborn baby for the first time, unsure if your shaking hands were up to the task. I didn't want it to end, but at the same time I was scared by the responsibility.

The universe has a way of lulling us into believing, right before it rips reality open and lets us fall right through.

I watched Rae lift Hillyard's spirit with her affable nature, dazzled by it.

Keith Houghton

I was acutely aware I'd opened a box. Not exactly Pandora's, but no less packed with potential calamity either. I'd set the contents free. Unleashed possible mayhem. I wasn't sure if I could put them back or even if I wanted to.

Our connecting flight consisted of a six-seat Cessna seaplane with amphibious floats painted a luminous yellow. It took off from a dock on the edge of the Kodiak Air Station and clawed its way into an overcast sky brightening in the east. It was a little too cramped and rickety for my liking. Everything rattling. I spooned myself into a plastic seat at the very back and clung on as the small plane hugged the rugged coastline, headed southwest.

"The runway at Akhiok is down for maintenance," the pilot shouted above the drone of the propeller. "There's a seaplane base at Moser Bay. That's as far as I go. A boat will pick you up there and take you the rest of the way."

I gaped through grubby windows as the lunar landscape opened up in the burgeoning light. A lumpy sky the color and texture of old muslin. Visibility: fair. Wind chill factor: freezing. On one side, I could see an uneven white landscape of deep snow and black rocky outcrops, fractured by ice-covered streams and mountains shrouded in layers of curling mist. On the other side, a beaten panel of flat pewter water stretching out into the misty Pacific as far as the eye could see.

"You doing okay back there?" Rae called over her shoulder.

"I haven't thrown up yet, if that's anything to go by."

Everyone who knows me knows I'm a bad flyer. Despite the cold, I had sweat streaming down my sides.

"Akhiok is a Native fishing village located on the island's southernmost tip," the pilot was shouting in his tour guide voice. "It's the remotest community on Kodiak Island. Fewer than eighty inhabitants and just a handful of buildings. Most are private dwellings. There's a school and a small medical clinic. It's also home to the historic Russian Orthodox church, built at the turn of the twentieth century."

I phased him out, stared through the window at the flawless ocean and thought about the flawed passage that had brought me here.

The ghosts of demons past.

We all have them.

I'd swept up more than most over the years. An entourage of hell hounds, soul-suckers and psychological leaches. Together, they formed an invisible force field of denial. The downside was their steady power drain on my psyche.

But I was on the mend – or at least I had been.

Prison had taken my liberty but not my time. Plenty of empty hours to think about the final condemning moment that had certified my place in the asylum: that cheerless day in August, caught in the middle of a hurricane, caught with my guard down, caught red-handed. Up to that point, I'd dedicated eighteen months of my life to the relentless pursuit of the man who had wrecked it. I'd shunned everything else: people, friendships, work. I'd become insular, paranoid and, in the end, dangerous. I'd seen spooks in every shadow and even tried to kill an innocent man just because he'd flipped my switches.

But I'd learned my lesson, right?

*   *   *

Like a skimmed stone, the seaplane skipped as it hit the water, then plowed a furrow into it, using the sudden friction to absorb its momentum. I lurched in my seat. The pilot cut the power and we coasted toward a big, roofed jetty jutting out onto the icy bay. I could see several stubby boathouses on the snowy shoreline. No signs of life. He nudged the Cessna against a large square platform at the end of the pier and we jumped out onto the weathered gray timbers.

It felt colder down here. Icicles fringing eaves.

There was a small aluminum skiff moored on the other side of the platform, with a solemn-faced Alaskan Native in a blue-and-black lumberjack coat seated by the outboard motor. He looked like he'd been sitting there all night. Looked about ninety years old and probably was. A roundish face as chiseled as an island outcrop.

"We're looking at a sundown at approximately four-twenty," the pilot called after us. "There's more snowfall on the way – which makes it unsafe flying after dark – so make a point of being back here with at least an hour to spare. I'll wait as long as I can, then I'm out of here. You have my number. Call me if you're unable to make it back in time. Happy Holidays!"

The granite-faced boat captain helped Rae into the flat-bottomed skiff.

"You picking up strays today?" she asked cheerfully as we climbed aboard.

"Highlight of my week," he replied without a kink in his stony expression. "Beats dead beavers."

There was a small pool of water in the bottom of the boat, with a pair of tatty life preservers forming an island in the middle. They looked as old and as weathered as their owner.

Rae nudged one with the toe of her boot. "Are we expected to wear these?"

"Only if you intend on going in the water," he replied.

I said my hellos and settled up near the bow. The boat captain revved the outboard. Gasoline fumes stung at my nose. Slowly, the skiff angled itself away from the jetty, then picked up speed, bow tilted slightly skyward.

The seaplane bobbed in our wake.

Next stop: Akhiok – the scene of the crime.

I didn't know what to expect. I have attended countless crime scenes and have as yet to come across any that are identical. I still wanted to know why Stone seen fit to send two of his agents all the way out here. No question he knew more than he was telling. But what?

We headed south at a leisurely rate of knots, keeping close to the coast. We passed through the narrower neck of the bay, then followed the ice-locked shoreline out west. The black water was mirror-flat, reflecting an inky facsimile of the monochrome sky. Looked cold enough to freeze anything with less than a two-inch layer of blubber.

I huddled inside the parka, the cold air forcing tears in my eyes.

Rae was busy engaging conversationally with the deadpan boat captain and showing a genuine interest in the smallest details. Men are clumsy in comparison: *You see the game last night? What did you think? They were robbed of a win, weren't they?* I listened to her voice, to her undulating southern inflection. I warmed to it like a child with his ear pressed against his mother's chest.

I didn't know what was going to happen between Rae and me, later, but I was already selfishly looking forward to it.

Prison has a lot to answer for.

Finally, our destination came into view: a scattering of structures, jutting out of the frozen tundra like snow-capped tombstones; one or two columns of lazy smoke climbing from metal chimney stacks out back; a few other fishing boats of varying sizes moored up against the curve of frozen beach, including a big fancy private motor cruiser that wouldn't have looked out of place at the Shoreline Marina in Long Beach. Otherwise, no signs of inhabitation.

The boat captain steered the skiff toward a small boat launch slanting into the still water. There was a man waiting for us on the concrete slope, just back from the water's edge: another Alaskan Native in a padded black coat and one of those Russian-style fur hats with the ear-warmers. His rounded face was as sullen as the sky. Behind him, a necklace of footprints stretched back up through the snow and into the village.

The skiff moaned as the aluminum hull grounded against the concrete slipway.

The guy in the furry ushanka offered his assistance to Rae as we climbed out. I could see a shield-shaped patch sewn to his sleeve: a brown bear with the words *Kodiak Police* stenciled above it. Same badge I'd seen on Hillyard's winter coat.

"Quinn," I said, extending a gloved hand. "And this is Special Agent Burnett."

"Officer Locklear," he acknowledged with a nod. "Welcome to Akhiok. I'm sorry your visit isn't under better circumstances."

We left our boat captain behind and followed Locklear into the village. Brittle ice cracking and fracturing under our boots. Breath smoking from our lips. Frigid air fingering through every seam.

The place looked abandoned. Snowed-under. Compacted gravel roads eroded into wide ruts and rimmed with hardened black snow. Buildings silvered by the elements. Rolling hillsides of virgin white snow veined with jet black rock in the background. Top of the world.

"We're a small, tight-knit community," Locklear explained as we navigated frozen puddles. "Nothing like this has ever happened here before. Everyone's shocked. Especially Julie."

"Julie's the one who found the body?"

He nodded at Rae, "Yeah. Julie Tsosie. She's eleven. She's still pretty shaken up."

Finding a dead body could do that, I knew.

"I realize it's Christmas Day," Rae said, "but we'd like to speak with her, if possible."

"Not a problem. I'll make the necessary arrangements."

"This body," I asked, "where did Julie find it?"

"On the beach, down by the water. It was around midnight."

"We'd like to see that, too."

"Sure. I'll take you there after we've seen the doc."

Sanibel came to mind, four months earlier. Another body had been found on another beach. I'd been called in to inspect that discovery, too, and ended up being drawn into a life-and-death battle with my ghost of Christmas past. This was becoming a pattern.

"Where's the body now?"

"Medical clinic."

We arrived at the main street: basically, a wider thoroughfare formed by individual buildings shouldering both sides of a gravel roadway. Everything looked old, worn, held together by the ice and snow and countless rusting nails. Rudimentary Christmas decorations were hung from window frames. Locklear pointed the way and we headed toward a long wooden structure with sky-blue sashes. Even before we got there, I could see Santa Claus had beat us to it.

*　　*　　*

He was a big old guy, in his seventies, wearing a bright red Santa outfit and leaning against a hand rail at the top of a short flight of wooden steps. He was thick-set. Loose muscles draped over a big frame, like damp laundry slung over a drying rack. He had one of those wind-blasted seafarer's faces: rugged red, salt-stripped, with a thick white garland of beard hanging between the ears. The beard was real.

"Merry Christmas, Gabe Quinn!" he hollered as we approached. "Didn't figure we'd meet again under these kind of circumstances. But hey ho, ho, ho."

I could feel Rae's inquisitive gaze burning into the back of my neck. I ignored it. I climbed the steps, removed a glove and shook his outstretched hand. "Paul. You're looking well. It's been a while."

"Going on eighteen years, as a matter of fact. I see you've become something of a celebrity in the meantime." He saw my flinch and added: "Anytime that showbiz lifestyle of yours gets too much for you to bear, you should consider moving to Alaska. You'd fit right in; we're all running away from something up here. When it comes to freedom and no questions asked, nothing quite beats the forty-ninth. Plus, we get cable." He spotted Rae and tipped his head. "Ma'am."

"Hey."

"Rae, this is Paul Engel. Paul's the resident doctor hereabouts."

Rae accepted his handshake. "Special Agent Rae Burnett. Pleased to meet you, Paul."

"Same goes, I'm sure."

"Paul came up here on a fishing expedition about twenty years ago and never went home. Isn't that right?"

He grinned, "Guilty as charged. Used to run my own surgery down in Vegas, but I swapped the big city lights for small-town America. And can you blame a guy? Take a look at this place. I might be ancient, but I'm not too old to recognize a good thing when I see it."

Rae was nodding. "I take it y'all know one another, and how?"

"It's a long story," I said. "I'll tell you later."

Engel held the door open and we crowded into a narrow hallway smelling of burnt toast. It grew stronger as we followed the doc deeper into the dimly-lit building. I glimpsed storage rooms filled with what looked like packing crates on either side. Snow-white drifts of packing peanuts.

We came to a small, darkened room at the back of the building. It was an extension of the main structure, an annex – cold as a meat locker. There was a letterbox window facing north, opening out across a Christmas card scene of snowy terrain and barren mountains.

Engel pulled a cord by the door and a fluorescent bulb sputtered into life. The room appeared to be a basic *patch-'em-up* first-aid stop on the frontier of nowhere. Glass-fronted cabinets lined the walls, stocked with bandages and potion bottles. Trays of surgical implements stacked on a long worktop. A stainless steel sink in one corner and an 80's boombox wedged onto a shelf in another. By the looks of things, nothing purchased this century.

There was a collapsible trestle table pushed up beneath the window. A green tarp formed a pyramidal mound on its surface, about three foot tall. Engel wheeled the examination table out into the middle of the room, positioned it beneath the sober glow coming from the overhead strip light. I was already having flashbacks to Sanibel. Same kind of setup, only this was sixty degrees cooler.

Engel hooked fingers under the edge of the tarp. "Hope you both have strong constitutions."

"Cast iron," Rae answered.

Like a magician revealing a neat trick, Engel peeled back the waterproofed covering.

I heard someone gasp. Not sure if it was Rae or Officer Locklear, or me.

*   *   *

The tarp had been hiding a body.

It was positioned on the examination table in a seated posture with the legs crossed – the classic lotus position – leaning slightly forward with the hands curled into fists behind the crease of the knees. Chin nestled against a concave chest in the same way as someone practicing a yoga pose. Everything perfectly balanced.

But that wasn't the worst part.

Now I knew the origin of the burnt toast smell: the body had been set alight and baked to a crisp.

"You can breathe," Engel said.

I didn't want to, but I did, through clenched teeth. "You found it like this?"

He nodded, "As a matter of fact, in this exact position. It was still ablaze when we got there. Had to douse the darned thing with snow to put it out."

Morbid fascination tugged me closer.

Every square inch that I could see was blackened and flaky – like a potato left too long in barbeque coals. The intense heat had melted away most of the soft tissue, including the lips and the eyelids. The face and skull were almost skeletal. Boiled egg eyeballs, solidified into milky glass orbs. Remnants of ears shriveled against the blackened skull. Jaw slack and unhinged. No sign of any hair or clothing. Everything overcooked, charcoaled. The entire torso was marbled with red cracks where the seared skin had tightened and split, probably under sudden cooling. Even so, the fierce temperature had hardened muscle onto bone, locking the corpse in its present death pose. It resembled a storefront mannequin exposed to blast furnace heat, cracked and blistered. Some of the scorched skin had flaked and fallen to form black soot on the metal examination table.

Engel rolled a portable lamp out of a corner and powered it up. He angled the cone of light so that it lit up the cremated corpse and cast a gruesome shadow of it across the floor.

"Judging by the size of the ribcage and the pelvis region, I'd say it's a fully-grown male."

Rae moved closer. "Have you determined a cause of death?"

"Isn't that self-explanatory?" Locklear answered before Engel could. "The poor guy burned to death."

"No," I countered. "Agent Burnett is right. There's no way anyone alive could burn to death and remain in a seated position. This person was already dead when the killer set him on fire."

"Unless he was drugged," Engel offered. "I checked inside the mouth and there is evidence of smoke inhalation."

"It's possible he used a paralytic," Rae breathed.

Locklear made a face. "Why would anyone do something like that?"

"Because he wanted this guy to know he was burning alive," I answered. "That's why."

Either way, it wasn't a nice way to go: surrounded by snow and water, yet unable to raise even a finger to extinguish the all-consuming flames.

"Y'all smell that?" Rae said. "It's like a gas station in here."

I sniffed, smelling beyond the burnt toast, caught a whiff of something sharp and chemically.

"It's Bombe Alaska."

We glanced at Engel.

"As in the after dinner dessert," he said. "You splash dark rum over Baked Alaska and then ignite it."

"The killer used an accelerant?"

He nodded. "And flambéed his victim. We found a thermos flask near the body. It contained traces of gasoline."

"You kept this thermos?"

Engel pointed to a silver flask standing on the worktop.

With gloved fingers, I picked it up and unscrewed the lid. Felt fumes scratch at my sinuses. "So, the killer drugged the victim, seated him in the lotus position and then drenched him in gasoline, right before turning him into a human candle."

Each subsequent layer of skin and flesh igniting as it had boiled off moisture and broiled muscle. Fat liquefying into hot wax, accelerating the blaze.

I shuddered at the thought. "We'll need this sending over to the Anchorage Crime Lab, together with the body." I turned to Officer Locklear. He was looking like a kid called to the principal's office. "And there are definitely no villagers reported missing?"

"I triple checked personally. There's no one missing. I grew up here. Everyone knows everybody else. It doesn't take long to notice if someone's unaccounted for."

"What about visitors?"

"None currently lodging in the village itself."

"And outside of Akhiok?"

He nodded, "There are a couple of hunter camps inland by Olga Creek and one or two out by Dog Salmon Flats. Not many this time of year. Mostly fishermen looking for trout and halibut. Come the summer months, when the salmon are flying, we're overrun."

"Fewer suspects, then. That's good. Has anyone questioned them?"

"The coast guard deployed a chopper yesterday afternoon. They were unable to get a complete inventory."

"How so?"

He shrugged, "We're a small force out here. We don't keep track of all the comings and goings. We're a few hours from the mainland by boat. Anyone with a decent setup can come here undetected and leave just as easily. The truth is, some trappers don't want to be found. This is the last great wilderness. People are free to come and go as they please."

"And to commit murder," Rae commented.

Locklear's mouth formed a slanted line.

"What about closer to home," I said. "Anyone in the village likely to do anything like this?"

Locklear seemed appalled by the insinuation, like I'd just called his mother ugly.

"No, not here. We're not like that."

"But someone killed this guy," I said. "Aside from the girl who found the body, didn't anyone see anything?"

He shook his head inside the fur hat. "I canvassed the whole village. No one saw a thing."

"This girl," Rae said, "Julie Tsosie. What was she doing out on the beach at midnight?"

"The Tsosie residence is close to the beachfront. Julie's bedroom has a direct line of sight. She says the fire woke her. She was curious. She went to investigate."

"So she went down there in the dead of night without informing her parents?"

Again, Locklear looked offended, but held it in. "Like I say, Akhiok's a small community. It's a safe place."

I nodded at the burned body. "Try convincing this guy. Did you process the crime scene?"

"As best we could, given the conditions. We brushed back the snow and the ice, but we didn't find anything suspicious. We took pictures, before and after."

"We'd like copies," Rae said.

"How many sets of footprints, in the snow directly around the body?"

Locklear's eyes rolled to the ceiling and back. "It's impossible to say, for sure. It snowed overnight. There were multiple overlapping tracks. Some completely snowed over."

"The thing is, it was chaos down there," Engel explained. "Julie fetched her parents first. Then some of the local boys heard the commotion and came over. At first everyone was more focused on putting the fire out. Nobody was worrying about standing on the crime scene. We didn't even realize it was a crime scene until the flames were out and we saw it was human."

Rae's brow was wrinkled. "After which you contacted the Kodiak Police straight away?"

Engel nodded.

"And exactly when did you arrive, Officer Locklear?"

"As soon as it was light."

I huffed. "Ten hours later."

I could see the first signs of unease creeping across his face. He was thinking our questions had a touch of hostility to them and his defenses were rising accordingly.

"Overnight visibility was poor," he said through tight lips. "There was a weather advisory in place. Even under the best conditions, flying by night is dangerous here. We came just as soon as we could. The body had been removed when we arrived."

I turned back to Engel.

"Well, sure, it was my decision," he admitted. "Figured we couldn't leave it down there on the beach. The weather was closing in fast. I knew it was important preserving it."

While everybody else had merrily trampled the crime scene.

"We're going to need shoe tread impressions from everyone on that beach," Rae told Locklear.

He nodded, stiffly. Looked a little hot under the collar after our grilling.

"Fortunately," Engel said, drawing my focus back to the body. "The teeth appear intact. Maybe good enough to cross-check against dental records?"

"Maybe." I brought the lamp in closer and examined the burned fingertips. They were completely melted. Zero chance of an ID that way.

Something caught my eye.

I repositioned the lamp again and peered closer. "Paul, you got a pair of tweezers at hand?"

I heard him rummage through a tray of implements. He came up with the goods and placed a pair of metal grips in my hand. I leaned in, close to the burnt flesh, trying not to breathe too deeply.

Rae came alongside. "Found something?"

"Not sure." I used the tweezers to lever open the fingers of the left hand – just enough to shed light on the small sliver of something foreign that had caught my eye. "Got any alcohol, Paul?"

"A few bottles of finest single malt in the other room. Or are we talking its less flamboyant cousin, rubbing alcohol?" He handed me a plastic pump bottle.

I slid the spout in the gap between the fingers and squirted isopropyl onto the crisped flesh. Heard it crackle and fizz as it soaked in. I pulled gently with the tweezers until the object sprang free.

Rae was on my shoulder, "What is it?"

I held it up to the spotlight, turned it over. "Looks like the remnants of a credit card."

It was a melted wafer of plastic, roughly oblong in shape, completely wrinkled along one edge. I went over to the steel sink and rinsed it under the faucet, then used a paper towel to wipe away tar.

Locklear and Engel were both on their tiptoes, like I'd found a winning lottery ticket and they wanted in.

Under the light, I reexamined the object. The plastic had bubbled and buckled. Browned. One side no more than a discolored blur with a stripe of black magnetic tape, relatively unscathed. On the other side was a scuffed image of what appeared to be a fishing boat and the traces of some colored text.

"Rae, take a look at this."

She leaned closer, eyes narrowing. "It's a photograph, printed into the plastic. Could be an advertisement. Some kind of fishing excursion?"

"Companies pay high dollar for in-pocket realty," I said. "Which makes this a room key."

"You mean from a hotel?"

"Not just any old hotel, Rae. I'm thinking it's where the victim was staying. Or, better still, where the killer was holed up, and maybe still is."

12

We had a keycard, but it didn't automatically come with a room. Neither had we any way of knowing which hotel it belonged to; the reverse side was too blurred-out to distinguish any hotel logos. Alaska was a big place – the biggest State in the Union – with hundreds of lodges, motels and guest houses spread unevenly throughout its six-hundred-and-sixty-three-thousand square miles. In every sense, the clichéd needle in the haystack. No saying that the keycard was even tied to a hotel in Alaska. Visitors came here from all over the world. It could prove impossible making a connection.

When faced with the prospects of a monumental search, it's wise to narrow the criteria before committing valuable man hours.

I got Officer Locklear to contact his colleagues back at base and had them set about compiling a list of accommodations located within a few hours' traveling distance of Akhiok. We knew the victim had traveled to the Kodiak Archipelago. Maybe he'd hired a local boat captain or even a floatplane taxi to get him here. Chances were, he hadn't been a day-tripper from Anchorage – which meant some kind of lodging in the area. No privately-owned bed and breakfasts. No fishing lodges with a handful of rooms. Only those lodgings big enough to use electronic keycards.

The fact that the victim had had the keycard clutched in his fist meant something. I had to find out what.

With his colleagues making the checks, Officer Locklear led us back through the sleepy village toward the smoked-glass bay. The whole place was deathly silent. No kids out building snowmen or sledging in the deep snowfall. No locals spreading Christmas cheer. No boats coming and going. In fact, no movement at all. Somebody had been murdered and everyone was indoors for the Holidays.

"You didn't mention you'd been here before." Rae pointed out as we crunched over compacted snow.

"Rae, I've been to lots of places before. Besides, it was a long time ago. It didn't seem relevant."

We worked our way down to the frozen shoreline, coming out onto the snow-covered beach about two hundred yards farther around the thin crescent, west of the boat launch. Across the black water I could see our skiff still jammed up tight, but no signs of the boat captain. We slipped and slid over snowy shingle until we arrived at a place where Officer Locklear assured us was the crime scene location. After another night of unbroken snowfall there was no evidence that anything had happened here, least of all a murder.

He pointed out the slightest of depressions, "The body was right here."

"Which way was it facing?"

"That way. Out across the bay."

I looked around at the deserted curve of beach. It was a brilliant white contrast to the dark water. I looked at the lumpy islands huddled across the bay, at the larger land mass of the Aliulik Peninsula jutting across the horizon like a humpbacked whale. The sky had brightened some more. Searchlights of weak yellow sunshine were probing through clouds weighted with snow. I could see freezing fog clinging to the rocky islands out in the bay, and what looked like a bald eagle far out against the patchy sky. Behind us, the snowy tundra inclined to form hills and mountains, with a scattering of structures braced against the chill in the foreground.

"Which one is the Tsosie residence?"

"Right next door to my family home." Locklear pointed to the nearest building, about twenty yards back from the beach. Yellow window frames against gray wood.

"You live here, too?"

"Not exactly. Not these days. My family still do."

"Don't forget we'd like to speak with Julie," Rae reminded him.

Locklear nodded. "It's Christmas Day; she should be home."

Along with everybody else, I thought. Everyone keeping their distance, both from the murder scene and from those investigating it.

Small town mentality.

We were about to return to the medical clinic when Locklear's cell phone chimed. He dug it out and answered, nodded, once, twice, then:

"It's the Kodiak Inn," he said as he hung up. "The keycard's an exact match."

13

Sixty minutes later, out seaplane splashed down at Kodiak Air Station and we piled out.

I'd told Locklear to stay with the body until arrangements were made to ship it out to Anchorage. I had thought he'd be inconvenienced with the prospects of hanging around the fishing village another day or two. I was wrong. He'd smiled through his gloomy countenance for the first time. Locklear had family in town; spending Christmas in Akhiok was a gift.

Officer Hillyard picked us up in his KPD taxi and Rae apologized profusely for our dragging him away from his family again. *No imposition*, he said. All the same, he broke the speed limit getting us to town, roof lights flashing and sirens wailing. Not a whole lot of other traffic to contend with.

We arrived at the Kodiak Inn to find the same happy-go-lucky receptionist working the front desk as the night before.

"Long shift?" Rae commented.

"Great overtime pay," he answered back. "What can I do for you guys? You need a turndown?"

"What we need is to see your guest list."

I held up the melted keycard. "Or better still, tell us which room this belongs to."

The cheery clerk placed a card reader onto the counter. "It's against protocols – and I could seriously get my knuckles rapped for doing this – but since it's Christmas and you're the Feds, go ahead and slide her in."

I worked the warped plastic into the slot, so that the surviving bit of magnetic tape went in first. It was a tight fit. Not quite straight. The kid tapped at a keyboard, said to give the card a wiggle, then tapped some more. I saw him scan the information flashing up on his computer screen.

"Room two-oh-nine."

"What's the name on the booking?"

"Mr. Nathan Westbrook."

"When did he check in?"

The kid peered at his screen. "Let me see . . . He checked in at the weekend, for a total of a one week's stay."

I leaned on the counter. "Was a credit card used to make the reservation?"

Another glance at the screen. "No, not in advance. According to our records, Mr. Westbrook is a call-in customer who paid for his entire stay in cash. It looks like his MasterCard was swiped into the system for the security deposit."

"We'll need a copy of that." I saw his brow wrinkle, and added: "We're the Feds, remember?"

He pressed keys and a printer whirred into life. He handed us a printout.

I looked it over: Westbrook's MasterCard information with an expiration date deep into next year.

The kid slid a new keycard from a pack. With his fingertips, he pulled out the melted one, handed it back, then slid the new card into the machine. He tapped a key, then handed it over. "Take a right at the landing and it's just down the hall."

We went up the stairs to the gallery, turned down the first hallway and counted doors until we came to Room 209. There was a paper swingy dangling from the door handle: a cartoonish drawing of a yawning bear with the words *Beware! Sleeping Grizzly!* scrolled above it.

"What are we thinking here?" Rae whispered. "Is Westbrook the victim or the killer?"

I got out my Glock. "Let's take no chances either way."

I waited for Rae to ready her own firearm, then inserted the new keycard into the door lock. There was a whir, a click, and a little green light lit up. I leaned on the handle and shouldered open the door, following the Glock into the guest room.

Rae was tight on my heels. She peeled off, into the bathroom. I headed into the bedroom area, sweeping the iron sights across a King-sized bed facing a multifunction cabinet. There was a writing desk in the corner, with a swivel chair tucked under. A blood-red sofa over by a brightly-lit window. The last hotel room I'd snuck into had presented me with a surprise dead body on the bed. Not this time. There wasn't even any indication that the bed had ever been slept in. Everything was smoothed down and pillows plumped. No signs of a suitcase. No loose change piled on the nightstand. No used clothes discarded on the floor. No Nathan Westbrook.

I heard Rae shout: "Clear!"

I holstered the Glock. "Same here, Rae."

Then I pulled open drawers: all empty. I examined the multifunction cabinet: a flat screen TV, a microwave oven, a small refrigerator. I opened the cooler. The miniature liquor bottles, soda cans and candy nibbles all looked present and correct. I went over to the writing desk. There was a lamp, a telephone and a hotel welcome pack on the leatherette inlay. The complimentary notepad hadn't been written on, but the big mirror hanging above the desk had.

"Rae, you better come take a look at this."

She joined me in the bedroom, eyes narrowing as she read the words written across the mirror. "Oh my gosh, Gabe. What's with that?"

"I think it's Westbrook's last dying thought."

Five uppercase words had been scrawled on the glass, at chest level, each letter gone over several times to make it stand out. It looked like they were written in blood, but was probably red permanent marker:

THIS IS ALL YOUR FAULT

The letters were slightly leftward-leaning, with a curling arrow sprouting out at each end, pointing upward at the reflection of my dumbstruck face.

"Rae, I think the local cops might have jumped the gun. We only went along with the homicide scenario because Locklear and his cohorts had reported it that way. They assumed it was a murder because it's unthinkable somebody could commit suicide by torching themselves to death. But now I'm thinking they got it backwards. I'm thinking this isn't a homicide, Rae. It's a suicide. Which means we came all this way for nothing."

*   *   *

Fact: if I had a dollar for every dead end I'd ever gone down I'd make the Forbes Rich List, easy.

As it was, Rae wasn't buying it. She had her arms folded defensively across her stomach, with a doubting twist hooking up her lips.

"If that's the case," she began, "where are Westbrook's personal possessions right now? Take a look at this place, Gabe. It's spotless. Who goes anywhere these days without credit cards and a cell phone? According to your doctor friend, there wasn't even a watch on that corpse. No wallet. No money clip. I don't believe for one second Westbrook traveled here with just the clothes on his back."

Rae had a point. Women have an inimitable ability to sense reality askew. But I also knew that some suicides cleaned up and put their house in order before taking the plunge.

"Locklear and his chums didn't process the crime scene properly," I said. "It's possible Westbrook's personal effects could still be on that beach. Buried under all that snow. Or even out in the water. You heard what Paul said: there were people all over that crime scene. It was dark. People kicking up shingle. Throwing handfuls of snow on the flames. It was organized chaos."

"So how do you explain the lack of toiletries in the bathroom?"

"Maybe he didn't bring any."

"Not even a toothbrush?"

"Maybe he wasn't into personal hygiene."

"You men." The kink in her lips drew into a pucker; she still wasn't investing in my theory.

The more I thought about it, the less I was too. "I guess some things can't be rationally explained, Rae. Suicide victims don't necessarily think logically. If Westbrook did come here with every intention of taking his own life, I don't think he was too concerned about having minty fresh breath while he was planning a funeral pyre."

Rae's frown deepened.

"Okay, I know. I'm being insensitive."

"At least you recognize the fact. And that's a huge step forward. All the same, this message just about qualifies as the strangest suicide note I've ever seen."

Rae was right. Most suicide notes were confessions rather than accusations. But I'd seen enough suicides over the years to know not every person contemplating taking their own life quoted chapter and verse beforehand, or left a lengthy Dear John conveniently wrapping up their life. Pushed to the point of suicide, few people thought with pure logic. Many were accidental deaths: cries for help that went too far and ended badly. Some by attention-seekers. Some by those who simply turned out the lights without any fuss and faded away.

I wasn't sure which category Westbrook fell into. Judging by his note, he blamed himself for something unforgivable. Something so terrible that it had driven him to flee this world.

I aimed my cell phone at the mirror and snapped a picture.

"It's classic self-condemnation," I said. "You can see it now: Westbrook standing right here, despising his own reflection to the point of making this very public statement. Look at the number of times he marked each letter, Rae. He was desperate to get it out, to stress his self-loathing, to make sure those that came after him knew it."

"I'm not so sure, Gabe. I'm having a hard time believing it's a suicide. Why would he use a paralytic?"

I shrugged. "Until the Tox report comes back, we don't know for certain that he did."

But Rae's jury was still out. "What if we rewind a little here? What if this is the killer's room, and Westbrook's the killer?"

"And somehow the victim got his hands on Westbrook's keycard?"

She nodded, "You have to agree, it better explains why this place looks so spick-and-span. Westbrook removed any trace of himself before leaving."

"Aside, that is, from the nutty note on the mirror."

Rae smiled. "Touché. Come on, let's check the guest list. See if any names pop up."

"Such as?"

"Such as someone who hasn't been back to their room in two days. Otherwise known as a victim."

14

What were the chances of a killer and his victim renting out rooms in the same hotel? Then again, what were the chances of our having a reservation there, too?

We headed back downstairs. Rae placed a call to the Kodiak Police Department, requesting backup. I got the chirpy clerk on the front desk to print out a list of all guests booked in and out during the preceding two weeks. Told him that the room upstairs was now officially a crime scene and that no one must enter, especially Housekeeping.

I tapped fingers on the counter. "While you're at it, check who hasn't accessed their room in the last twenty-four hours."

The kid tapped keys. "You guys are determined to make me earn this overtime, aren't you? Let me take a look at the messenger system."

The guest list was lengthy. A full house. Mainly single males and couples, in town for business or for visiting family over the Holiday period. I managed to get a third of the way through before hot adrenaline erupted in my chest.

"What's wrong?" Rae asked as she came off her cell. "You look like a serial killer just climbed in through your bedroom window."

"One just did," I breathed, jabbing a finger at a name on the list. "This prize-winning psycho, right here."

*   *   *

The word *coincidence* is a convenient contrivance to discredit the incongruous. It's a mouthful, but true.

Rae took the printout from my hand and read the indicated name out loud – in the same moment the clerk on the counter came up with the same result:

"Gary Cornsilk."

It meant nothing to Rae, and even less to the kid in the Santa hat. But to me it meant everything.

"You know this person, Gabe?"

I knew him, all right. But mostly by another name. A name I had given him on a whim, in accordance with his scaly face and his reptile skin boots:

Snakeskin.

Adrenaline was burning a hole through my sternum.

Since my arrest in the summer, a day hadn't passed by without *Snakeskin* invading my thoughts. Early on, I'd made it my mission to hunt him down once I was freed from Springfield. Make him pay for the callous murder of Hives, a private investigator I'd hired to do my dirty work. But mostly I'd thought about how I would stop him from finding and killing another serial killer, the killer who had become my prime obsession, the killer I knew as *The Undertaker.*

I held Rae by the elbow and moved us out of earshot of the desk clerk. "Cornsilk is ex-FBI. He was based at the Memphis Field Office. That was until he had a mental breakdown earlier this year and the Bureau put him out to pasture."

"It still doesn't explain how you know him."

The kid behind the counter was leaning over and trying his best to eavesdrop. I turned our backs to him. "There was this farmhouse, in Jackson. It came to light during our investigation into The Undertaker Case. We suspected it was the killer's family home. An FBI SWAT team was sent in under cover of night, to investigate. What we didn't know at the time was The Undertaker had rigged the farmhouse with incendiary explosives. When Cornsilk opened the front door, all hell broke loose. Two agents were killed and four were seriously injured."

Rae was nodding. "Now that you mention it, I remember the incident. I was in and out of the Memphis field office for a while. I knew most of the old school there, including Nielson who was Watch Commander that night. From what I recall, he took a nail through his windpipe and the last I heard he was talking through a machine."

"Did you ever cross paths with Cornsilk?"

She thought about it, shrugged. "It's a possibility, I guess. I didn't know everyone by name. Maybe if I see a photo?"

"Well, it'll have to be one taken before that night. The liquid explosive melted most of his face and all of his humanity. The Bureau sent him to rehab, but he failed every psych evaluation they put him through. They were left with no choice but to show him the door."

Rae was looking at me suspiciously. "You sure know an awful lot about some guy we pink-slipped. Either you have a good memory for names and incidentals or there's something crucial you're not sharing with me."

Inescapable female intuition. Caught me every time.

Truth was, I didn't want to tell Rae everything I knew about *Snakeskin*. Not because I couldn't, but because *Snakeskin* was my secret. My pet hate. Mine to hunt down, my way. I didn't want anyone else coming along for the ride, joining in, and interfering with my obsessions. Even Rae.

Rae's diamond-bit eyes were drilling through my hard outer shell, set to strike a vein of truth at any moment. No way was she letting this one slide.

"Gabe, talk to me," she said, quietly but firmly, "right now. I mean it. It's no coincidence he's here and so are we. Tell me everything you know."

I heard myself say: "The concise version is, Cornsilk is a vindictive son of a bitch. He blames me for his life going down the toilet. He came after me, Rae, down in Florida. He tried to kill me, twice. Tried incinerating me with thermite."

Therapy had left me with loose lips. I hated it.

Rae's eyes were wide, appalled by the thought of Cornsilk trying to do me harm. But there was something else behind the horror. Something like skepticism. I could never pull the wool over Rae's eyes.

"But you weren't responsible for his meltdown."

I almost smiled at her choice of phrasing. "True, but he blames me for his downfall nevertheless. It was my case, Rae. I okayed the operation in Jackson. To him, I'm as guilty as the person who planted those fire bombs. And he's coming after everyone involved."

I couldn't keep it in. I'd already told her too much.

She was quiet for a moment, thinking it through. Frown unmoving, possibly hardening. I could sense my vague explanation being rolled out and examined under a microscope. Picked at. Undone. I hadn't mentioned that *Snakeskin* had also made his intention to kill *The Undertaker* quite clear, but I could see she was about to reach that conclusion without my prompting.

Luckily for me, Officer Hillyard and a fellow female officer bustled in through the main doors just as Rae was about to voice it.

"Dispatch says you need urgent assistance?"

Rae made a pained face. "We do. And we're so sorry for dragging y'all out here again so soon."

"It's no problem, agents." Hillyard had crumbs in his bushy moustache. Looked like pumpkin pie. "What's the emergency here?"

I handed him a keycard. "Room two-oh-nine. Treat it as a crime scene. No one goes in or out until Forensics get here."

Hillyard nodded to his partner and they both disappeared up the stairs, armed with a roll of black-and-yellow police tape.

I turned back to Rae. "Okay. My hands are up. You were right. I was wrong about the suicide angle."

She smiled. "What's this – another apology? Oh my. That makes two in a row. Remind me to send your counselors a *Thank You* card. So, we're in agreement Cornsilk killed Westbrook?"

"I'm leaning toward it."

"You're leaning? I thought you didn't believe in coincidences?"

"I don't. I'm just having a hard time coming to grips with the discovery, that's all."

My brain was wading through the data, bogged down with details.

It was too unlikely that Cornsilk – someone with an unhealthy obsession with fire-starting – would be guesting by chance at the same hotel where another guest had been burned to death. It was reasonable to assume therefore that Cornsilk was involved – that he had followed Westbrook to Kodiak, intercepted him at some point, possibly administered a paralytic and then torched him to death on the beach in Akhiok. The question was: why?

What frustrated me the most was the fact we'd been here all night, barely feet away from a crime scene and breathing the same air as Gary Cornsilk.

So close.

"You know," Rae said, "there's a chance Cornsilk is still here, right now, in the hotel."

Was it too much to hope for?

Cornsilk's was a first floor room located at street level along a short hallway. The clerk activated yet another keycard and we slipped down the hall with weapons drawn.

There was an identical paper swingy hanging from the door handle.

Repeat performance.

I slid the keycard in and out, waited for the green light, then leaned on the handle and shouldered open the door. We rushed in. Same as before. Rae peeling off into the bathroom, while I headed into the bedroom area.

I heard Rae shout *clear!* and I echoed it back.

The room was an exact copy of its overhead neighbor. Unlike Westbrook's, this one definitely looked lived in. There were garments on an unmade bed, hooked over the back of the swivel chair and even scattered on the floor. Mainly short-sleeved shirts and boxer shorts, plus one or two pairs of blue jeans.

Snakeskin had an untidy nest.

I went over to the blood-red sofa as Rae came in. There was an open carry-on suitcase propped against the cushions. I peeked inside: more clothes and incidentals, travel tickets, boarding card stubs, survivalist magazines. Unsurprisingly, no sunblock.

Rae pulled open the fridge. "Half a pepperoni pizza in here."

"Looks like Cornsilk's still in town," I said.

Through the window I could see the grille of Hillyard's police SUV parked nose-in against the metal safety barrier. I picked up the room phone and dialed internally to the room directly above us.

"We're downstairs in one-oh-six," I told Hillyard as he answered. "In what we believe is the killer's room – which means he could return any minute. We need you to move your vehicle and make your presence as low-key as possible."

"I'm on it," he said and hung up.

There was a handful of paper receipts on the writing desk. Looked like local eateries and a downtown convenience store. A couple of leaflets advertising things-to-do-and-see in Kodiak – one of which had a sheet of paper folded inside the flap. I held it by the edges and turned it over. There was a picture of a marina on the cover: white boats floating on reflective blue water, with the words *Minky's Charters* splashed across a navy sky.

I unfolded the printout. It was an invoice, for a boat rental, dated a few days ago. A pleasure craft called *Free Spirit*.

"Looks like Cornsilk hired a boat," I said.

"Explains how he traveled to and from Akhiok undetected."

I noticed Hillyard through the window. I leaned over the AC unit and rapped knuckles against the glass. He paused with his fingers hooked under the door handle of his Expedition. I pressed the brochure against the pane, so that the picture of the marina was clearly visible.

"St. Paul Harbor," he shouted, then pointed across the street. "I'll pick you up out front."

*   *   *

I left Rae holding the fort and headed out. I jumped into the waiting police vehicle. Hillyard hit the gas and the Expedition accelerated up the main street. It was early afternoon, midweek, but everywhere was closed for the Holidays. Everyone at home, roosting with their eggnogs. Children more absorbed with packaging than presents. We made a right at the first intersection, tires crunching on the gritted blacktop.

"What are we looking for?" Hillyard asked.

"A vessel called Free Spirit. And a guy with a melted face, if we're lucky."

He glanced my way, waiting for an explanation.

"The killer looks like Freddy Krueger's half-brother. You can't miss him if you try. He rented the boat a few days back. Possibly to ship Westbrook, the victim, out to Akhiok."

The roadway descending into an area of wooden port buildings and various retail stores, all closed. A hundred boats moored in the marina to our right. Mostly fishing craft of all shapes and sizes. Some covered in blue tarpaulins, bedded in for the winter.

"One more thing," I warned as we bailed out, "he's dangerous. If the boat's here and you sense he's on board, retreat and wait on backup."

The marina consisted of four long piers with slips either side, jutting out of the main jetty like bristly antennae. Not many empty berths. One or two weathered fishermen giving us the eye as we scuttled down the main ramp leading onto the waterfront. I could smell brine and diesel. Hear gulls cawing in the distance. Hillyard went to the first pier. I ran onto the second and started scanning boat names.

Sea Otter, Throwback, The Aurora, Bad Mistress …

Something froze me in my tracks. It was a beaten-up fishing boat with battered hull rimmed with old car tires. It had a flying bridge and a pair of whip aerials. Everything weathered and faded. Rusting bolts leaking orange stains over flaky white paintwork. The name on the stern read *The Undertaker.*

A shrill whistle blasted across the harbor. I turned to see Hillyard signaling from down near the end of the first pier. I saw him point to a small vessel berthed in the very last dock.

Free Spirit – had to be.

Heat blossomed in my chest.

I signaled acknowledgement, then hurried back down the jetty. My cell phone rang as I reached the connecting pier.

Rae Burnett.

The heat intensified. Had Cornsilk returned to the hotel and Rae was calling for the cavalry?

Her tone sounded urgent, but not panicked: "Gabe, I've come across a drum of fishing wire in the closet, together with cutters and a reel of duct tape. Didn't you say Cornsilk made bombs?"

I didn't answer – mainly because the heat had choked my throat. I could see Hillyard at the far end the wooden walkway, his police-issue firearm extended as he inched toward the back of the charter craft. I stuffed the phone away and picked up the pace – running full steam in his direction, boots clattering against the ice-slicked wood. I saw him step completely onto the boat. I went to holler a warning – in the exact same moment an intense ball of brilliant orange fire ballooned at the end of the pier, completely enveloping Hillyard.

Keith Houghton

15

Fact: light travels faster than sound. Fact: thought processes don't.

I ran straight at the expanding sphere of gas and debris without slowing. Reaction-time on a go-slow.

For the first few heart-stopping moments, the fireball blossomed in silence, pushing an invisible wave of heat and concussion pressure out across the marina. I saw what looked like a broken marionette being yanked backward on invisible strings, flying up and away from the blooming inferno. My pace hadn't slowed any. Neither had the adrenaline squirting through my system. The marionette struck the mast of a boat on the other side of the pier and fold in half as it fell in an arc toward open water, trailing gray smoke. Then the blast front caught up with the visuals and the din of the explosion boomed across the quayside. The compression wave hit like a sledgehammer, bowling me off my feet. I went slithering across the decking as the nearest boats lurched in their berths, recoiling from the detonation. They smashed into one another. Wood splintering. Metal creaking. A swell of water swamping over the pier and rushed my way. I rolled to my feet as the energetic fireball plumed skyward, carried aloft on a donut of black smoke. Fiery debris rained down. Smoky projectiles peppering the nearest boats and hissing as they hit the water. I splashed into a sprint and reached the burning, fractured end of the pier at full speed. Without giving it a second thought, I shucked off my coat and dived into the frigid black water.

*   *   *

It was like being sucked out of an airlock into the freezing vacuum of space. Merciless. Deadly. As the liquid ice encased, every bit of my body reacted, badly. Muscles cramping. Blood retreating. Steel talons scratching over exposed skin. I wanted to scream with shock, but my mouth was clamped shut, preventing precious hot air from bubbling out of my pancaked lungs.

In TV documentaries I'd seen goose-greased people bathing in icy Scandinavian lakes. Wondered how their bodies had tolerated the near-death temperatures. Now I knew. They didn't. Cold stress caused the nervous system to withdraw, so that it could concentrate on keeping the internal organs heated. Instant numbness was the consequence, starting at the extremities and working inward. The longer the skin shed heat faster than it could be replaced, the more the body was prepared to sacrifice. Death was an inevitability.

I estimated a couple of minutes, tops, before my body would start shutting things down.

I didn't stop to worry about it.

I kicked and pulled through the biting water, just beneath the surface. Ignoring the waves of pain slamming into my super-chilled brain. I dragged hand over hand, forcing forward, flesh numbing, nerves screaming, lungs aching.

Twenty yards, I figured. Maybe less, I hoped.

Endurance swimming had never appealed to me. Sure, I could do the basics: crawl a few lengths and tread water for a few minutes. Maybe swim thirty seconds underwater. But this wasn't a heated swimming pool. This was an open-air harbor in Alaska, filled with arctic water, in late December. No comparison. No way I could hold my breath and swim twenty yards without the punishing pain pulling me down to my doom.

I broke the surface and sucked in air.

There were bits of boat ablaze all over the place, bobbing on the rippling water. Some of it still raining down, fizzling. I could hear the main fire raging away like a netted dragon, ten yards behind. I could hear plastic popping, timbers crashing. Secondary eruptions spewing flames and lesser shockwaves out across the immediate marina.

Already, my clothes were as heavy as a suit of armor. I trod water, desperately scanning the uneven surface, trying to fight gravity. I spotted something that didn't look like a piece of floating wreckage and pushed toward it. It looked like a blackened face, staring skyward, unblinking.

I clamped chattering teeth together and plowed on with muscles filling with slurry. Slush Puppy blood. Chainmail clothing. Somehow, miraculously, I reached Officer Hillyard and scooped his scorched face clear of the water. No idea if he were alive, unconscious or even breathing. His head rolled into my hands and stared up at me with bomb-blasted eyes. It was only then that I realized the explosion had not only killed Hillyard, it had beheaded him in the process.

16

Here's another fact: people die around me – acquaintances, partners, friends, loved ones. Seemingly anyone who comes too close to my curse.

I was perched on the steel back plate of a Kodiak City Fire Department truck, swaddled like a takeout burrito in a fleecy blanket and a foil wrap. Mildly hypothermic. Mood as black as the harbor water. I was thawing out, slowly. Feeling was returning, slowly. Most of it was bad.

There was a jumble of emergency vehicles crowding the wooden wharf: shiny red fire trucks and black-and-white police cruisers with their light bars blinking. The crackle of radio chatter. Emergency personnel on scene. All of it a blur. I had brain fog. Not from the concussion of the blast, but from immersion hypothermia.

Compared to Hillyard I was the epitome of good health.

Rae pushed a foam cup into my hand. "Right now you need to drink this. You look like you couldn't tell your ass from a hole in the ground."

I put the cup to my mouth and sipped over tingling lips. Coffee, black, sugar-loaded.

"Thanks."

I'd already been interrogated by the surly Chief of Police, then asked the same bunch of circular questions by one of his morose detectives. Then once again, partly to double-check my story, but mostly because it diverted their attention away from the recovery underway in the harbor below us. I'd blabbed through the brain fog, told them about our discovery at the Kodiak Inn, about the fire-bomber who was ex-FBI, about him being our prime person of interest linked to the body found on Akhiok's seafront, about him booby-trapping the boat he'd rented from *Minky's Charters*, and about Officer Hillyard taking the full brunt of the blast, head-on.

For what it was worth, I'd given the chief a description of *Snakeskin*. He'd summoned all hands on deck, issued a BOLO – a *be on the look-out* – to his officers and to the port authorities in charge of Kodiak's harbors and airport, then left in a whirlwind. I'd gotten one of his men killed on Christmas Day and somebody had to tell his family. Not me; I'd done enough.

I decided I hated Gary Cornsilk with every cell of my body.

Other than going inland and sitting it out, he'd have nowhere to run. Not with his poster-boy looks on show and his only private means of leaving the island now resting at the bottom of the marina. Eventually, he'd have nowhere to hide. Sooner or later he'd surface. Sooner or later there'd be a confrontation.

Every cop on the island had a glimmer of determination in their eyes.

Snakeskin had just killed Christmas.

"Shoot," Rae said. "The press are here."

On the roadside running parallel with the marina, I could see crowds gathered. Onlookers taking pictures. Some pointing. One or two with shoulder-mounted video cameras. Looked like the whole of Kodiak had made the effort and turned out for the Christmas Day fireworks.

"Just in time to film the gory bits," she added.

The firefighters had extinguished the flames at the end of the pier, but not before the inferno had blackened the nearest boats and burned a large section of the jetty away. Scorched paintwork and smoldering timbers all around. Debris scattered over tarps. Ballerinas of smoke pirouetting out across the bay. As for the source of the explosion – the charter boat *Free Spirit* – she had blazed and then sank, leaving an oily swirl on the flotsam-strewn water. Arrangements were being made to get a crane onsite to winch the wreck out, but it was Christmas and no one was picking up.

Down on the jetty, paramedics were unfolding a black body bag on a gurney. The Coast Guard had already deployed frogmen to recover Hillyard's remains. It was looking like a difficult task in the fading daylight.

A sour tang burned on my tongue.

Cornsilk had killed twice in Alaska.

First Nathan Westbrook and now Officer Glenn Hillyard.

I didn't think Christmas Day could get any worse.

I was about to be proven deadly wrong.

17

His blunt thumb tracked across the embossed name on the credit card, as if reading braille.

Gary Cornsilk.

He knew by using the First Tennessee Visa anywhere in the western world the authorities would immediately locate him. Pinpoint his exact whereabouts and trace his movements. Maybe even send in the marines – providing they weren't otherwise engaged in liberating some oil-rich region that most eleventh-graders couldn't find on a map of the world if their lives depended on it.

Alternatively, he could lie low. Wait for the smoke to clear before rolling out the next stage in his play and turning up the heat elsewhere.

People were looking for him.

Satellites eyeballing from a hundred miles high.

He slid the card back inside his billfold and swapped the wallet for a Zippo lighter he'd picked up at some unmemorable airport gift stall. He liked it. It had a special meaning. There was a flattened American Indian tribal chief head embellished on the metal. Turquoise feathers in the headdress. A face like rolling thunder.

He flicked the lid and marveled at the flickering flame.

He'd always thought there was something magical about the exothermic process of combustion.

Something addictive.

Something godlike.

He ran his palm over the flame, delighting in its hot caress.

People were going to pay with their lives.

And he'd just got started.

18

On the remote chance Cornsilk was the only person in town to miss all the police activity, officers had taken siege of the Kodiak Inn and laid down the law. All available police personnel had been commanded to convene – including those pulled in on their day off. No one was complaining; an officer had been killed in the line of duty. This was top priority and the cops were cracking down.

I couldn't blame them. I didn't have the heart to tell them that *Snakeskin* was unpredictable, crazy, but not nearly crazy enough to come back for his gear. The explosion had been heard right across the city. It was unlikely *Snakeskin* didn't know the score.

The hotel was in lockdown.

No one was coming in or out without having their ID's scrutinized under a magnifying glass. More cops combing the entire complex, methodically, making sure Cornsilk wasn't holed up somewhere inside. Officers checking out the surrounding buildings, parking lots and even the Dumpsters. Anyone kicking up a fuss was being frisked and cautioned. I couldn't blame the KPD for being heavy-handed. One of their own had died. Blown-up in broad daylight. Word was that Hillyard had been popular. A dedicated family man. Understandably, his colleagues were angry, with a growing appetite for justice served cold. If Cornsilk was still on the island, the only way he was leaving was in a casket.

"I've spoken with the Anchorage field office," Rae was telling me as I shook out the change of clothes courteously supplied by the hotel management. "Just as soon as they can rustle up the manpower, they're sending over a forensics team and people from the bomb squad. All being well they should be here before dusk."

Less than an hour. I didn't fancy their chances.

We were shoehorned into the small office behind the reception counter. It smelled of donuts and printer cartridges. Rae had her back turned while I peeled off sodden clothes and dropped them in the trash. Strange behavior given our nighttime antics. The jeans were a little low-cut but otherwise a decent fit. The white tee-shirt had *I Heart Kodiak* emblazoned across the chest, with the image of a fierce brown bear on the reverse. Very touristy. I covered most of it up with a red-and-black hooded flannel shirt. Luckily, my discarded parka, cell phone, badge and gun had escaped the watery surge unscathed. Not so the hiking boots. I was back to wearing my shabby sneakers. In a way, I felt like me again.

I ran fingers through hair thickened with sea salt. "I guess it's as good as it gets."

Rae nodded her approval and we returned to Cornsilk's room. We asked the cops to clear out while we looked the place over. The first few hours following a homicide are vital, with the likelihood of an apprehension rapidly diminishing thereafter. The freezing water had woken me up to the fact I had a job to do.

I wanted to find something to point to where Cornsilk might be, right now. I wanted to catch him and make him pay for murdering Hillyard in cold blood. I wanted to grab him before he killed again.

I started with the items Rae had told me about on the phone.

There were several plastic soda bottles in the closet, all empty. A drum of wire and a reel of silver duct tape on a shelf, together with a pair of cutters and various plastic clips. The tools of Snakeskin's trade. Mindful of booby-traps, I lifted the lid on a plastic box, to find it full of micro-switches and other electronic stuff, including high-charge batteries like the kind used to power camcorders.

Down on the carpet I spotted a dusting of a white sugar-like substance. It was too grainy to be cocaine. I got on my haunches and gathered a sample into a small heap, picked up a pinch between thumb and index finger and rubbed the tiny crystals together to cause friction. Something caustic stung at my nose.

"Traces of ammonium in here," I called to Rae, who was out in the bedroom, taking Cornsilk's room apart.

"I thought you said he preferred thermite?"

"He does. Or did. Today's blast blew that boat to smithereens. I guess he's evolved his MO to include fertilizer bombs."

Save the incendiaries for close-quarters. Upscale to higher energy explosives for bigger targets.

Officer Hillyard had stood no chance.

I shuddered at the thought of finding the boat first, or even Rae getting to it before any of us.

As with all bombers, Cornsilk's methods of murder and madness were indiscriminate.

"According to the brochure, Minky's Charters is based in Whittier," Rae called.

"Whittier? Where's that at?"

"A short drive south from Anchorage, by the looks of things."

Anchorage: the most accessible Alaskan airport from anywhere inside the continental US. If *Snakeskin* had flown into Anchorage, he'd picked up the ingredients for the fertilizer bomb in Whittier. Any old hardware store would do. No way would he risk carrying bomb-making ingredients on a commercial flight. He'd bought the stuff locally, loaded it on the rented boat and brought it out to Kodiak – with a view to a kill.

"Any signs of a return flight ticket, Rae?"

"Not that I can see. I've checked everywhere I can think of. My guess is, if he has one, he has it with him."

The BOLO would stop *Snakeskin* using it.

Keith Houghton

I rinsed my hands in the bathroom sink and dried them on a fluffy white towel. I leaned against the worktop and thought about the close shave I'd had in Sanibel, caught in *Snakeskin's* deadly spider's web. Cornsilk had taken me by surprise back then. Hit me with a Taser. I'd woken to find myself strapped to a chair in the middle of a complex network of wires spanning the living room in Jack's place. An incendiary device barely feet from my face. Crisscrossing cables connected to micro switches. A timer counting down. No way out. I'd faced certain incineration. That was until Jack Heckscher – aka Jacob Klaussner – had come to the rescue at the last minute, foiling *Snakeskin's* plan.

Rae appeared in the bathroom doorway. "Any progress?"

"Aside from bomb-making equipment, nothing. You?"

"I turned out all his pockets. Practically ruined his suitcase pulling the lining out. I did find this." She held up a booklet.

"A road map?"

"Not just any ordinary road map."

Back in the bedroom, Rae unfolded the concertinaed booklet and spread it out across the bed. It was big. At least three feet by four. A driver's map of the US of A. Each individual State color-coded, with key attractions highlighted. The kind of treasure map that foreigners pick up in airports to keep their minds boggled at the enormity of the nation. I smoothed it down and looked it over.

Snakeskin had used a red marker pen to highlight certain road routes, to circle specific towns and to place cross markers on key locations. Probably the same marker pen used to write the message on Westbrook's mirror. The highlighted routes formed a branched system of red veins across the heart of the country, in all directions. Crosses and circles seemingly randomly scattered. There were words, too. Mostly dates. Some names that looked like they could be hotels. Some that definitely belonged to people. The name *Hives* was underlined twice in Virginia. And a sad face drawn over Jackson, Tennessee. My eyes traveled southeast to Florida, where they found a circle around Sanibel Island, with the words *'Goodbye Gabe Quinn'* splashed across the Gulf of Mexico.

Rae came in close. "It looks like he's been hunting Westbrook for some while. See, the oldest date goes back to February, with the latest being here in Kodiak, last week."

Not just hunting down Westbrook, I knew. This map documented Snakeskin's pursuit of me and everyone he wrongly believed had played their part in ruining his life. I had no idea how many innocents were on his mental hit list. No idea how many nameless victims he'd already burned to death across the country. What I did know was that Westbrook had led him here. What I didn't know was a damned thing about the guy whose crisped body was stinking up Paul Engel's examination room.

"What do we know about Westbrook?" I mused out loud.

"Aside from him being in the wrong place at the wrong time? A whole bag of nothing." Rae got out her phone and started tapping manicured fingernails against the screen. "The Bureau has an app," she said as her fingertips danced on the glass. "It allows field agents to log into the system remotely."

I made a face. "The FBI has an app?"

"Actually, we have several. They're preloaded into your phone. They're all voice-activated. Just about the handiest is Find-A-Fed. Sounds corny, doesn't it? But it's quite useful. It's an electronic phonebook listing every agent's contact numbers. A real lifesaver when you're in a tight spot." Her brow crinkled as she scanned information. "What?"

Keith Houghton

"You wouldn't believe how many people there are called Nathan Westbrook. I mean, really. There are dozens."

"So narrow it down. Cornsilk is only interested in people directly involved in ruining his life. It's a safe bet they're either in law enforcement or connected to it."

Rae swept fingertips over the screen. "Okay, let's see . . . ah, this is better. We have a Detective Nathan Westbrook."

"A police detective?"

"Seems so. Was he part of your investigation into The Undertaker?"

"Not that I recall. Where is he based?"

"Looks like he's time served with the NYPD – in fact, most of his career is with them – plus a shorter stint with the Reno PD."

"Reno?" I chewed cheek. "I was in Vegas when Cornsilk got injured in Jackson, but the Reno PD weren't involved in the case."

I scanned the map, focusing on Nevada. There was a skull-and-crossbones drawn in red over Las Vegas, but no markings anywhere near Reno. There was something that looked like a phone number written along the blue ribbon of the Hudson River in New York, however, but no names.

"What else does your app say about Westbrook?"

"He's unmarried. No children. Decorated twice for bravery. Worked both Vice and Homicide. And . . . there's currently a missing persons notice filed against him. According to the FBI database, Detective Nathan Westbrook went missing last year."

"So what was he doing in Kodiak?"

19

Rae pulled up everything the Bureau had on Westbrook and handed me the phone. I read it with a strange sense of déjà vu prickling at the nape of my neck.

Nathan Westbrook, a decorated police detective, had disappeared under the radar fourteen months ago. No suspicious circumstances. He simply hadn't shown up to work one day. He hadn't called in sick either. And he hadn't booked any vacation days. His lieutenant had sent a unit to Westbrook's home that afternoon – following several unanswered attempts to contact Westbrook through his landline and cell numbers – only to find him not there. The next day, a subsequent search of the property had shown no evidence of foul play, but signs that Westbrook had emptied his closet and drawers, seemingly packing for a trip. Neither his police ID nor any other personal effects (such as his driver's license and his passport) were found in his home. No mention to his next of kin (namely his widowed mother living in a home in Upstate New York) that he was anywhere other than where he ought to be. His on-the-job partner had spent the next week running checks to see if Westbrook's credit cards popped up on the system. They hadn't.

Detective Nathan Westbrook had vanished without a trace.

Until now.

"Where was he this last year?" I wondered out loud.

"By all accounts, off the grid."

"I know that, Rae, but why? Why did he just vanish without warning like that?"

Keith Houghton

"Maybe he got himself involved too deeply in something he couldn't control and he went into hiding. According to his jacket he worked Vice for a while. It's possible an old enemy caught up with him. People disappear for any number of reasons, Gabe. Not all of them are logical or even obvious."

I made a dissatisfied pout. "So how did he come to play a part in Cornsilk's disfigurement? Officially, Westbrook disappeared *before* The Undertaker Case. Months before Cornsilk was blown up in Jackson. We know Cornsilk's intentions are to wreak revenge on those he believes wronged him. So where does Westbrook fit into all that?"

"And you're asking me? You know more about The Undertaker and Cornsilk than anyone, Gabe. What if Cornsilk knew Westbrook previously and was settling an old score?"

"I guess." But it didn't feel right. My *Uh-Oh Radar* was picking up ghosts and sounding a silent alarm.

I was about to air more doubts when the room phone rang.

Rae looked at me. I looked at her. The usual.

The last time I'd been in a hotel room with the phone ringing unexpectedly it had turned out to be a serial killer on the other end of the line, enticing me into a deadly game of cat and mouse.

I pressed the receiver to my ear.

"Hello? Agents? You guys there?"

"Who is this?"

"It's Danny, on the front desk. Listen, there's something you guys should know. Mr. Westbrook rented out a safe deposit box. I have a key, if you're interested."

"We'll be right there." I nodded to Rae and we rushed back downstairs.

I'd noticed the safe deposit boxes in the back office – basically, a row of six gray metal compartment lockboxes, like the kind used to take mail deposits in apartment blocks – but hadn't thought anything of it.

"It's the one at the far end," the kid from the front desk told us.

I took the master key from his hand. "We'll take it from here." I shooed him outside, waited for him and his disappointment to disappear before opening the small metal door. "No saying there's anything in here, Rae."

But there was.

Not Westbrook's wallet. Not his passport or his even cell phone.

It looked like a clear plastic envelope with something like a postcard inside.

I reached in, held it by a corner, and pulled it out.

The white rectangle of card had handwritten words on it. Faded black ink. Even fainter, the printed word Kodak running in repeat rows diagonally.

"What is it?" Rae asked over my shoulder.

"Looks like an old photograph."

Curious, I turned it over.

And that's when the day went from disaster to devastation.

*   *   *

The conscious mind is slave to the body. We think we are in control of our physicality, that our thoughts influence the nervous system, that we pull the strings. We are wrong. Dead wrong. Consciousness is a non-paying passenger. It is the unconscious mind that commands the body. For most of the time, it is content to let the consciousness believe it has the wheel. But when survival comes into play, when that fight or flight instinct overrides all logic, the conscious mind is told to buckle up and shut up.

My body reacted automatically. Muscles expanding like the pistons in a steam engine. Lungs inflating. Heart squirting richly oxygenated blood into my system.

Keith Houghton

Nothing I could do about it.

My unconscious mind was in overdrive. I clung on as my legs backpedaled, turned and rushed me out of the office. Distantly, I was aware of Rae tagging along behind, trying to grab me by the arm, trying to slow me down. I heard her voice asking: *what was wrong?; where was I going?; what was happening?; why wouldn't I stop and speak to her?*

Impossible to say anything.

Not because I was tongue-tied – which I was, without doubt – but because speaking it out loud would be worse than saying Candyman five times in front of a mirror.

Vocalizing it out loud it would make it real. And making it real would be . . . *final*. Suddenly, I needed air; I was suffocating!

My cement-filled legs carried me down the side of the hotel and into the small parking lot. I was impervious to the cold, shielded by superheated blood, and oblivious to the other cops staring at me like I was buck naked and foaming at the gills. From my faraway perch I saw my hands brace themselves against the hood of a pickup and I clung on as my body folded at the waist, winced as a geyser of sour black coffee gushed up my throat and splashed over the snowy asphalt. There was barely enough time to grab a scalding breath before another rush of acidic bile drilled through my nostrils.

In over thirty years of adult life, I could only remember ever feeling this way once before: on discovering Hope, my beloved wife, bound with piano wire to the master bed in our Alhambra home and bleeding to death at the hands of a cold-blooded killer. Back then, the cavalcade of conflicting emotions had hit me like a cannonball and had killed my hope in more ways than one. This was on a par. Emotionally unfathomable.

It was one of those life-altering moments where the universe sucks itself into a finite dot and crushes you out of existence.

I spat out acid and came clattering back into my body with a bang. My vision was pulsating. Discordant drums pounding out a death dirge in my ears. With a shaking hand, I wiped goo from my lips and forced freezing air into boil-in-the-bag lungs.

Reality was shaking at its foundations. An emotional earthquake, vibrating from the core outward, like the Death Star moments before it exploded.

I looked up to see Rae, standing a few feet away, a desperate look of heartfelt concern pushing back her perplexity.

"I need to go back to Akhiok," I gasped.

She went to protest, but I raised a hand, doubled over again and gagged up a mouthful of yellow goop. Abdominal muscles squeezing the life out of me. Everything straining.

"Gabe . . ."

I straightened. The world spun, then clamped down.

"I don't know what's happening here, but I'm coming with you."

"No."

She grabbed me by the arms. "Then at least level with me. You're scaring the living crap out of me. One moment you're fine, the next it's like you've got the plague."

I shook her loose. "Rae, I have to do this, alone. Don't try and stop me." I pushed past her, past a pair of gawking cops.

She rushed in front, blocking my way. She had demons in her eyes. "Dammit, Gabe. We're supposed to be a partnership here. Team Tennessee, remember? You can't just go hightailing it on a whim. Not without first telling me what's got you shaking like a hound dog trying to shit a peach pit."

I sidestepped her and continued toward the street.

Keith Houghton

"We're not done talking this through just yet!" she called.

I hit the sidewalk and carried on walking. I didn't look back. All I could think about was Akhiok.

"Gabe!"

I was numb. Rae's pleas rebounding off my icy shell like bullets against Superman's chest.

"At least take your coat!" she shouted. "You'll freeze to death out there!"

Better than being burned to death.

I flagged down a passing police cruiser and fell inside.

20

Absently, his blunt fingers sought out the scar on the side of his face. He studied his mutilation in the grubby restroom mirror, recollecting how he'd come by it and whose fault it was. The thickened skin acted as a permanent visible record of his interaction with his archenemy. You could say, revulsion etched into his face.

Once or twice he'd considered cosmetic surgery. Several esteemed surgeons had recommended this or that. A skin graft from here to cover this bit there. Stem cells to regenerate degenerated flesh. Smoke and mirrors.

He'd opted for none.

The scar was an indelible tattoo. A reminder of a debt unpaid. Soon to be collected.

He caressed it with his blunt fingertips.

There was no sensation of feeling on the surface, but he could feel it deep down inside.

And it felt like hate.

21

The floatplane bumped and rocked on switchback thermals. Another death-defying flight. I was too dazed to worry about it falling out of the sky. If it did, it would be a blessing.

Through pulsing eyes, I watched mist-shrouded mountains slip by. Shadows lengthening as daylight faded rapidly in our wake.

The days were short here in wintry Alaska. Blink and they were gone. The pilot had agreed to fly me to Akhiok on the proviso he'd turn around and fly home the moment he dropped me off. Nightfall was swiftly approaching. No choice but to spend the rest of the day in Akhiok and hold out until tomorrow.

My cell had rung continually for the past fifteen minutes. I'd switched it to silent mode.

Leaving Rae in the dark was cruel. Leaving her to oversee the cleanup at the Kodiak Inn was irresponsible. Leaving her at all was insensitive. But right now none of it made one iota of a difference. I wasn't in control. I had no choice.

Sure, Rae didn't deserve my abandoning her. I knew that. She certainly didn't deserve my sealed lips and mulish attitude. Nothing I could do. My hindbrain was calling the shots. This non-paying passenger had hitched a ride on a runaway train and there was no stopping it even if I wanted to.

And, so help me God, I didn't want to.

*   *   *

The seaplane vibrated like a baby's rattle as it scuffed dark water. It cast off speed, then coasted to the canopied pier at Moser Bay.

"I called ahead," the pilot shouted over the drone of the propeller. "Pete's on his way. Should be here in about thirty minutes." He checked his watch. "Okay, that's it. Daylight's burning fast; I've got to head back now. You have my number. Call me in the morning, first light, and I'll come pick you up, whenever you're ready."

I fell out onto the weathered jetty and slammed the hatch. The pilot fed juice to the engine and the floatplane angled away from the pier. I watched it rip across the bay, leaving twin gouges in the dark surface before lifting into the sky, wobbling back the way we'd come.

I had the hooded shirt buttoned up to my chin, but the insidious chill was petrifying skin.

I waited for the noisy Cessna to be swallowed up by the lingering mist. Waited for the silence to come rushing in before drawing a lungful of frigid air and howling like a wolf.

*   *   *

The tortured cries ricocheted around the bay, echoing off the frozen shoreline, overlapping like a remixed dance tune. I howled some more, adding to the audible mayhem. Kept at it, full volume, until my lungs threatened to burst and my throat had become linguini.

There was no one to hear. Not out here at the backend of the world. I might as well have been on the dark side of the Moon. No one to tell me to stop being so damned noisy and so inconsiderate toward the local wildlife. Not that I would have complied. Some things are worth screaming about.

Finally, all yelled out, I fell to my knees on the decking, suddenly swamped by slamming waves of emotion. I let them crash. I went with the flow, rolled onto my back and stared through spotting vision at the bruised sky. I lay there for long minutes, cursing everything I knew and anything I didn't. I dug nails into the splintered boards and contorted like a man gripped with delirium, and maybe I was.

The bruised sky deepened from purple to black. Shadows visibly stretching out to meet. Daylight dwindling into western waters. Stars rising. Temperatures plummeting.

I pounded my fists against the planking until my bones hurt. I yelled and thrashed some more like a landed fish.

Then, through ringing ears, I heard the distant hum of an outboard motor, and dragged myself to unsteady feet.

22

Twilight had morphed the bleak Alaskan coastline into an alien world.

The boat captain had sensed my darkling mood from afar and had kept his deadpan comments to himself. Maybe he'd heard my howls and knew better than to pry. *Weird guy from the outside – been here a day and already gone stir crazy.* His expression had remained impassive as I'd climbed aboard. Hard to say one way or the other if ferrying federal agents to and from Akhiok broke the monotony for him or made it all the more conspicuous.

And so I rode the squared-off skiff in silence, hood up over my ears, face blank, eyes blanker. All of my energy was directed inward. I was like a Cray supercomputer: nothing special to look at, but a trillion calculations going on in the inside. Committed, and grappling to get a handhold on the ungraspable.

*   *   *

Night fell without a sound.

We made a landing at Akhiok, the skiff moaning as it grounded against the cement launch. I think I murmured a *thanks* to the boat captain before following my hurrying feet inland, over crisping snow. Breath fogging from my lips.

The fishing village looked about as lively as a cemetery in the dead of night. No lights visible anywhere. No living soul to humanize the place.

I stuffed frozen fingers in the hoodie's pockets and skittered along the gravel road leading away from the beach.

The cold was almost unbearable, seeping through the plaid shirt. I gritted my teeth to stop them chattering insanities.

I didn't know what I would do once I got to my destination. I just had to get there. I was being pulled along by an invisible chain, compelled by something primeval, something genetically encoded, something I couldn't quantify or hope to explain.

My brain was in mush mode. Spark plugs misfiring.

A deathly quiet hung in the air, deadening sound.

No one on the main stretch. Still no lights visible anywhere. The place looked abandoned, dead. A zombie uprising just around the corner.

No signs of life in the medical clinic either.

I leapt up the steps and tried the door: locked. I banged a fist against the flaky wood, waited. No sounds of anyone opening up. No signs of Paul Engel or even Officer Locklear for that matter – so much for him keeping guard. I banged harder, longer, with both fists until my hands ached. Then I waited some more. Still, no answer. Something like frantic fear spread through my chest. I snatched a glance both ways down the main street. Still no lights visible. No curious villagers coming out to see what all the noise was about. Hard to see anything in the cloying dark.

It was as if I were the only human left on Earth.

My penance, perhaps. My own private hell. The worst kind imaginable: just me in it.

I dropped from the steps onto the frozen dirt and went down the side of the building. Even darker here. I fumbled my way round back, slipping and cursing over splintered lengths of timber. The backyard was buried under three foot of compacted snow. I dug my toes in and climbed up, leaning on the rear wall for support. I walked my hands across the rough wood until I came to the letterbox window set in the annex.

The window formed a rectangular maw trimmed with icicle teeth.

I stooped and stuck my nose against the cold glass.

Darkness had transformed the backroom of the medical clinic into a black cave of indistinct shapes and uncertain depth. Monsters crouched in corners. The only thing remotely discernible was a metal oblong in the middle – the examination table, right where we'd left it. Only now there was no sign of the tarp-covered body.

Demon claws scratched at my stomach.

I raised an elbow and struck the glass. Just like that. I did it before realizing exactly what I it was I was doing, which was breaking and entering. Illegal, in any State – especially in my state – even with an FBI badge stuffed in my pocket. I didn't care. Jagged shards hit the floor inside the building and shattered noisily, slewing across the tiled floor. Too late now. I pulled the shirt sleeve over my fist and smashed away lethal daggers until the gap was big enough to climb through. Then I slung a leg over the rough rim, pivoted my forearms on the frame and rolled into the backroom of the medical clinic.

The air still stank of barbecued flesh. I felt bile scald my throat. I fumbled for the pull cord, scanned the room as the fluorescent bulb lit up. The monsters huddling in the corners instantly vanished, revealing nothing but my own wet boot prints and a lawn of broken glass. I'd made a big mess. Too bad.

What had Engel done with the body?

I pulled open the door and entered the main building. Aside from the light spilling out of the backroom, it was dark. I followed my shadow down the hall. Four doors in total, two on either side, directly facing each other. I came to the first pair and opened the right-hand door, felt for the light pull and ignited another sleepy strip bulb.

It looked like a doctor's waiting room: several faux leather chairs positioned around a wooden coffee table. Fishing magazines fanned out on the surface. A water dispenser in one corner. A plastic cheese plant in another. There was a long alcove set in the opposite wall, with a receptionist's desk minding its own business. Room enough for a small metal filing cabinet and a waste paper basket. No signs of anything untoward.

I turned and opened the opposite door, yanked on the light.

This was Engel's consultation room. There was an old desk and two padded chairs. The usual stationery and office requirements cluttering up the worktop. Shelves stacked with dog-eared medical books, subscription materials, reference manuals, journals. Framed certificates certifying Engel's clinical achievements, including the University Of Nevada School Of Medicine. Nothing fancy. A locked cabinet for storing controlled drugs. And a small safe hunkered in the corner.

There were photos pinned to the walls – mostly depicting Engel standing on a weather deck at the aft of a fishing boat, happily holding prize-winning catches up to the camera. It looked like the same swish cruiser I'd seen anchored up in the bay when Rae and I had first arrived in Akhiok earlier. A handful of pictures with smiling Alaskan Natives – including Locklear and the boat captain – taken against green tundra grasses and summer skies.

I moved on to the next pair of doors. The demon had begun to sharpen its claws on my stomach wall. Sparks were flying. Both rooms were identical storage areas. An assortment of packing crates, some stacked, some with their lids off, several large enough to hide a body. Mounds of packing peanuts on the floor.

Why was I even thinking that Engel had hid the body?

I had no reason to think Engel had done anything improper – aside from the fact the body was missing. Maybe my present state of mind was overreacting. Maybe there was a perfectly reasonable explanation. I wasn't hopeful.

I inspected the bigger boxes, whisked hands through packing peanuts, chopped through bubble wrap lasagna, and came up with nothing.

The body wasn't here.

The demon claws were ripping through.

What was Engel's game?

I tried the main door, this time from the inside: still locked, with no signs of a key. Fired-up, I retreated back through the building, hoisted myself up and through the letterbox window and clambered out into the snow.

A dog howled somewhere.

Vaguely, I remembered Locklear saying his family had the house next door to the Tsosie residence. Maybe he could shed some light, or in the very least explain why he'd abandoned the body. I pulled up the hood and set off at a sprint, pounding impatient boots against the frozen gravel. The Locklear place was a hundred yards distant, tops. I hadn't run this far in over four months, and it showed.

I came to the Locklear homestead and drummed palms against the front door. I could hear faint music bleeding through the wood. It sounded like Christmas songs tinkling from a stereo, maybe country. I banged some more. The door rattled against its surround. I heard footfalls approaching. Heels clacking. The door cracked open with a whine, just enough to reveal a sliver of illumination and the silhouette of a small elderly woman. Mountain mist hair floating above a sandstone face. The cheery discourse of folks enjoying Christmas together washing around her.

"Ma'am, I know it's Christmas and I'm sorry to disturb you. I'm looking for your son, or maybe your grandson. Police Officer Locklear?"

She gawped at me as though I were speaking mandarin. I repeated the question, this time less forcibly.

Suddenly her rheumy eyes grew big as saucers and she reached out a skeletal hand. "Have you come for me?"

I baulked.

There was movement behind her. I looked up to see Locklear striding down the hallway, a hot beverage in his hand. He was out of uniform, wearing a dress shirt and jeans. He murmured something to the old woman. She shrugged and shuffled back down the hall. Her disappointment was tangible.

"This is a surprise," he said with a nod. "Is everything okay, Agent? You scared my grandmother; you look like the grim reaper in that getup."

I threw back the hood. "You're supposed to be guarding the body, Locklear."

"Is that what this is about?" His chest rose and fell. Clearly, I was disturbing the family festivities over something Locklear regarded as an unimportant breach of protocol. He sucked a sip of his beverage and smacked his lips. "Okay, so I took the liberty of staying home with my family for the evening. It's Christmas. It's not like anything was going to come of it. We're a hundred miles west of civilization. No one's going in there. I left the doc to lock the place up." His mouth curled at one side. I recognized the expression: *get lost*. "Look, we're just about to sit down and eat. There's enough to go round. It's freezing out there. You're welcome to come in and join us." He stepped aside. It was a feint, done to move the spotlight off his sloppiness.

I shook my head. "You don't get it, Locklear. I gave you one task and you couldn't even do that. You're supposed to be guarding the body. And now it's gone."

His face folded into a frown. All at once, all trace of Christmas cheer melted away like the springtime thaw. I didn't wait for the floodgates to open.

"Where's Engel?"

"The doc? Home, I guess. Are you sure the body's gone? It's dark. The eyes can play tricks. I don't mean any disrespect, but did you take a good look?"

I stepped back. "Just point me in the right direction."

He went to put his drink down on a hall table. "Tell you what: let me get my coat and I'll come with you."

"No. I don't need a babysitter, Locklear. Just tell me where he's at and I'll find my own way."

"Good luck with that. The doc doesn't live here in the village. He has a place out past High Rock."

I knew the landmark from a distant memory. It was out across the bay somewhere, east of Moser, on another offshoot of Kodiak's crenelated coastline. I also knew the only way to access it was by sea.

"You got his number? Call him."

A little reluctantly, Locklear dug out his cell. "I'm sure it's just a misunderstanding," he muttered as he dialed a number.

I didn't know what part of a missing body Locklear thought was a misunderstanding. What did he think Engel had done – taken it home for Christmas dinner?

"It's ringing," he said, then stuck out his lower lip. "And going straight to voicemail."

"Any other number?"

"Only the clinic. And you say he's not there, right?"

I turned on my heels and started back the way I'd come. I had no intention of wasting time trying to find the boat captain; I could pilot the skiff, find my way there, somehow. Point and go, right?

I heard Locklear call from behind:

"Do you even have any idea where you're going, Agent Quinn? Those waters are treacherous after dark. Full of submerged rocks and rip currents. You're crazy if you think you can make it on your own."

I didn't tell him I already had a certificate proving as much.

I cut down an alleyway between buildings, disturbed a bunch of rats trying to break into a garbage can.

I should have stopped, taken heed of Locklear's warning. I didn't. Couldn't. Desperation is a logic suppressant. It makes us stupid. And stupidity makes us act impulsively.

My legs rolled into a sprint. I was focused solely on my objective. Twenty yards later, I came to the three-foot drop-off where the sea had cut away the land to form the narrow band of beach. I dropped down onto frozen shingle and sprinted along the line of black water, heading for the cement slipway.

I was almost there when a long, flickering shadow began dancing around on the snow ahead of me. My shadow. I glanced over my shoulder. Locklear had suited up and was tracing my steps with the beam of a bright flashlight.

"Wait up!" he shouted.

*   *   *

We all choose which path to walk. No one forces free will. Coercion, manipulation and obligation are sweeteners, sugarcoating our bad choices. But in the end, it's all down to us.

I didn't think twice about dragging Locklear away from his family at Christmastime. His choice. Maybe I should have.

"It doesn't make any sense," he was complaining as he gunned the outboard motor. We were in the skiff, heading out into darkness. "Why would the doc move the body?"

"I have no idea, Locklear. It wasn't where it was supposed to be and that's all I know." I didn't add *and neither were you* – because I could see the realization was already screwing up his face.

"You're thinking he's moved it to his house?"

Locklear caught on quick.

"For what reason?"

I had no answer. Not yet. But it was my intention to find out.

According to Locklear, Engel's place was located on the shore of Deadman Bay: a popular fishing stretch located a mile or so northeast of Akhiok. Ordinarily, in daylight, getting there by boat was a straightforward affair of navigating around a pair of smaller islands, then crossing the mouth of Moser Bay. At night, with only a salting of stars to guide the way, it was suicidal – unless you had a local tour guide at the helm, that is.

"Sure you know where you're going?" I asked.

It all looked the same to the untrained eye.

We'd been heading out to sea, out into pitch blackness, for some time.

"Relax; I've got this."

Away from the shelter of the shoreline, the skiff was rising and falling on long swells, slapping the surface and spaying icy saltwater against my skin. Seasickness had never worried me. But the prospect of getting lost out here on increasingly choppier water was tightening up my gut.

"I know the way." Locklear's response was cool bordering on bored. "Close to the islands there are many more dangers. You'd be advised to sit down, agent, before you fall overboard."

I was agitated. More reasons than one. No way could I sit down.

Truth was, we were a couple of hundred yards out and already I couldn't see Akhiok. The fishing village had completely vanished in the dark. So, too, had the humpback islands. Night had swallowed us whole. Just about the only features I could make out were the inland mountains covered in dark gray snow, and even they were nothing more than indistinct blemishes against the smattering of stars.

"Try Engel's number again."

Locklear made a disgruntled noise and offered up his phone, "Be my guest. I'm busy navigating by starlight and memory."

I selected the last number dialed and jammed the phone to my ear. The number rang out. I heard the call make a connection, heard Engel's voice, went to speak, then realized it was just his answering machine message kicking in.

I handed it back to Locklear. "What happens if there's a medical emergency and you can't get hold of Engel?"

"We bring in the air ambulance from Kodiak. Anything less serious usually waits until morning."

Like everything else around here, I thought. Come nightfall, the entire place dropped off the edge of the world and fell into a coma.

"See over there on the left, those lights? That's the doc's place."

I squinted in the general direction. Barely visible: a swarm of dim lights nestling together in the dark like fireflies. No idea where the sea stopped and the land started. No sense of scale or distance. Mistakenly, I had thought we were still heading out into open waters.

"It's easy to lose your bearings out here." Locklear had read my mind. "Good thing I came with you, agent. Left to your own devices you'd be a dead man come daylight. "

The skiff moved on an intercept course, settling onto smoother water as it approached the land. The jumble of Christmas lights grew bigger, resolving into the individual squares and rectangles of windows. Within their glow I could see the shape of a tall building and several smaller sheds off to one side.

"Engel's place looks big."

"It is. Bigger than most of the fishing lodges hereabouts. The doc had it specially constructed. It's the only private residence on the island with three floors."

"Why'd he need all that space?"

"In a word, freedom. That's what you get out here, agent. Freedom by the bucket load. No one poking their noses in your business or snooping round your backyard. Mostly, mainlanders come here to escape the rat race."

Locklear's answer didn't explain why Engel had built himself a small hotel in the middle of nowhere.

Now I could hear music, rolling out across the water to greet us. At first I thought it was the rumble of distant surf crashing on a pebbly beach. But as Engel's place grew bigger, it became recognizable as something more artificial. Something synthesized. Not my kind of music. Not Engel's kind of music, I would have thought. It sounded like a hundred robotic woodpeckers hammering holes in a steel pylon. Electronic beats, ebbing and flowing on the stiff breeze.

Locklear saw my scowl. "It's called Trance. Sounds better on ecstasy – or so I'm told."

"Is that Engel's poison?"

"It isn't mine."

The stilted shape of a long jetty emerged out of the darkness. With it came a 40-foot motor yacht moored alongside. Lights out. All aerodynamic lines, with a distinctive black paint sash running the full length of its white hull. It was the same swanky cruiser I'd seen in the photos in Engel's consultation room and in Akhiok earlier.

Not bad for a retired physician from Nevada.

A metal ladder descended from the pier into the black water. Locklear brought the skiff against it and cut the outboard.

"Stay here," I told him as I hauled myself out.

"Sure?"

"Positive."

He handed me the flashlight. "Okay. Just don't be too long. The meter's running."

Stiffly, I sprinted down the slippery boards.

My legs were shaking, but not from the trip over.

The demon in my belly had clawed its way out.

It wanted answers. So did I.

23

A gravel track led up to the house.

This close, Engel's place was more like a modest motel. A big rectangular box, covered in seamless metal paneling and painted sky-blue. Modern Georgian, if that makes sense. Judging by the amount of windows, more than two dozen rooms spread over three floors, easy. Every window ablaze with light – mostly glowing yellow or stark white. One or two electric blue. An outpouring of light that brought a false dawn to the immediate area and threw long shadows out across the snowy tundra.

No signs of a front lawn sleeping underneath the blanket of snow.

It sounded like a rave party was underway inside.

Three long concrete steps gave rise to a large main door. A polished steel fascia. It had a small porthole of thick red glass set in the center, shining like the Eye of Sauron. I banged a fist against the thick metal. If it made a sound, I didn't hear it; booming dance music was pummeling my eardrums. I banged with both fists, but my efforts were lost within the din.

"Engel!"

I kicked the door. Shouted out his name again. No reply. No surprise. An atom bomb could have gone off and you wouldn't have heard it.

I stepped back and inspected the first-floor windows. A half dozen either side of the door. None open and none lower than head height. All with stout metal bars crisscrossing the glass, inside and out. Panes that looked thicker than normal, maybe even bulletproofed. What was Engel up to here? The place looked like a small fortress.

Everything braced and reinforced. Hard to imagine just how loud the music was on the inside.

I looked higher. More metal bars on the next level of windows above. Same above that.

What was with all that?

I made my way down the side of the building, around a large snow drift mounded up against the house – ten foot tall and compacted halfway up the side windows. I passed through contrasting bands of light and shadow and came round back. There was a cluster of outbuildings with heavily-padlocked doors and dark, barred windows. Tool sheds with snowy roofs, set back against the tundra. More sloping snow drifts. A mountain of propane gas cylinders of various colors and sizes, thirty, easy, stacked on their sides. A larger barn in the middle with a caged lean-to running its entire length, possibly a canine compound. There was a big cube-shaped tank on stilts to one side of it, with pipes running into the barn – probably feeding juice to a power generator. A tangle of thick cables reached out of the barn's roof, suspended on tall poles, some branching off to other outbuildings, but the main bunch entering the house about two thirds of the way to the roof. Ten foot below that, a sturdy canopy ran the entire back of the house length, extending six foot out over the backyard. Beneath this sloping roof was another stout metal door and more barred windows blazing with light. Electronic dance music just as deafening. But there was something different here: a long dark opening in the aluminum siding, protected by the canopy. It looked like a built-in garage, with the corrugated steel roller shutter pulled halfway up from the ground.

A way in.

I stooped inside and shouted out Engel's name. It was pointless. My voice was instantly drowned in the waves of music crashing through the walls. I lit up the flashlight and scanned the garage. Its beam picked out work benches, a circular saw, a lathe, tools pegged to the walls. It looked like a carpenter's workshop, only it was the cleanest workshop I'd ever seen. No sawdust or wood shavings on the poured concrete floor. Just a few darker stains that looked like old oil patches. Either Engel was a clean freak or he hadn't turned any wood in here in a very long time.

The beam fell on a door at the back, at the top of three concrete steps.

I went for it, pushed it inward. A cavalcade of earsplitting trance music stampeded over me. Beyond was a short passageway. Again, I hollered Engel's name. No answer. I flicked off the flashlight and ventured deeper inside. The passageway ended at a T-junction. A wider corridor running left and right, cutting the first floor in half. No pictures on plain cream walls. Several arched openings leading off into big rooms, two to the right and three to the left. No internal doors. No way to tell where the dance music originated. It reminded me of a certain night in a certain nightclub on Santa Monica Boulevard. The synthesized sound seemed to be seeping from every surface.

"Engel!"

Nothing – except for a hoarse throat.

I made an educated choice and headed left. More archways this way, and what looked like the foot of a staircase.

The first opening on my right led to a wide hallway running down the middle of the house, front to back. More door-less openings located on both sides, and what looked like the back of the front door down at the far end, heavily braced. More locks and bolts than a Manhattan loft.

"Engel!"

Still no response.

I continued on, attracted to flickering light coming out of the next archway along. I paused to peer inside. It was a sizeable living room. Blood-red walls with big white hunter trophies: elk heads sporting impressive antlers, huge fish in glass cases. Three big sofas were arranged in an arc around a large bear skin rug, facing one of the biggest flat screen TVs I'd ever seen. Sixty inches, easy.

The TV was the only source of light in the room.

But it wasn't showing primetime TV – at least none I'd ever seen. This was hardcore porn. Sixty high-definition inches of it. Looked like sadomasochism. Two males in black masks, doing dastardly deeds to several chained women. Naked bodies cavorting, writhing, doing things that porn actors do to earn a living. Unnervingly, everything moving in time with the insane beat pounding through the house.

This was Engel's private space and I was intruding. And now I knew something about him I wished I didn't.

Collateral damage.

I needed to know where Engel had moved the body, and why. Sometimes turning over stones means finding creepy crawlies.

I turned my back on the TV, ready to explore some more. The music sounded like it could be coming from upstairs. Maybe that's where I'd find Engel – holding a one man acid rave.

I stopped dead in my tracks.

There was a man standing beneath the archway leading to the hallway. He had on a brown leather apron and work boots, and not a stitch of anything else.

Even in the flickering light I could see it was a pissed-looking Paul Engel.

And there was something in his hands, pointing my way.

At first I thought it was a broom handle, then I realized with a start that it was something far more deadly.

Alaskan's call them bear insurance.

We call them 12-gauge shotguns.

And I was intruding.

*   *   *

Cops are trained to react. Our reflexes aren't any quicker, but our life-or-death decision-making is generally better informed.

I had a fraction of a second to assess the situation before Engel blasted my insides all over the plasma TV.

From Engel's' point of view, he'd stumbled in on somebody invading his private lair. Out here, in the back end of nowhere, it would have come as a huge surprise – and one he wouldn't take lightly. Who would? The fortifying of his home attested to the fact he'd protect his personal domain tooth and nail. I was silhouetted in the bluish light flickering from the big TV behind me. No way could Engel see who I was properly. No way could he see my face. I was just a human-shaped shadow blotting out his beloved S & M.

And I was intruding.

The god-awful trance music was too loud to verbally confirm my identity. That left me with only one choice: I raised the flashlight, intending to switch it on and illuminate my embarrassment.

And that was my mistake.

No amount of police training can account for stupidity.

Engel must have thought it was a handgun.

I couldn't blame him; so would I, in the same circumstances.

Still in that split second I saw his fist tighten around the shotgun's trigger and knew that if I stayed put, I'd die. I threw myself sideways – in the exact same moment blinding light erupted from the business end of the 12-gauge. The big plasma TV exploded, spewing out sparks and glass and plunging the room into total darkness. Both booms lost amid the thunderous drum rhythm raining down from above. I rolled across the bear rug and hit the end of a couch, came into a crouch, heart pumping, the flashlight suddenly igniting in my hands and giving me the willies. I snatched a suicidal peep over the arm of the sofa.

Engel was nowhere to be seen.

I ran the flashlight beam across the room.

Still nothing.

Looked like Engel had unloaded the 12-gauge and then taken flight.

Insanely, I flew after him.

*　　*　　*

Everyone who knows me know how I feel about foot chases. I'm leery, to say the least. Dark alleyways are bad. The insides of abandoned buildings are worse. In comparison, running after someone through a brightly-lit house should be a jog in the park, right? Wrong. They are all dangerous. There's no way to predict where those being chased might suddenly decide to stand their ground and fight it out. No way to tell what traps might lie in wait. Every corner has the potential to be fatal. Every turn bringing you one step closer to a deadly confrontation or a lethal obstacle.

Cops are trained to expect the unexpected. We are programmed to protect, to err on the side of caution. I hadn't been a cop in ages.

I flew straight out into the corridor and caught sight of Engel's work boots disappearing up the staircase at the far end. I launched myself after them, reached the foot of the stairs in time to see Engel's naked posterior disappearing down the second floor landing.

I dug in and leapt up the stairs three at a time.

I had no idea what I was going to do if Engel turned around and came at me with the shotgun. Maybe I was hoping he'd see my face this time and come to his senses. Maybe, at his age, Engel's eyes weren't what they used to be. Could I take the chance?

I hit the landing on a roll. Incredibly, the mind-numbing music was even louder up here. Walls vibrating. Jackhammer drumbeats drilling into my chest cavity, turning my ribcage into a glockenspiel. I couldn't even hear myself think. It was as if I had my head pressed against an amplifier at a rock concert, loosening teeth.

I was in a long hallway of plain plaster walls. One closed door after another, either side – each locked with a 12-inch surface bolt. Another staircase leading up on an angle at the far end. A glimpse of Engel's legs disappearing up those very stairs. I had long since given up trying to answer why those being chased invariably head to loftier heights. Maybe it's the illusion of freedom the higher we are away from the earth. Maybe it's sheer stupidity.

I fell into a sprint, reached the stairs and bounded up to the third floor landing. Fewer rooms up here. Same plain walls. Same bolted doors. About three-quarters of the way down the hall: a pull-down aluminum attic ladder ascending into a hole in the ceiling. I went for it. I know Engel had. I gazed up into the dark hole, then clamped teeth around the flashlight and pulled myself up. If the metal creaked, I didn't hear it. I paused before the top rung and poked my head into the darkened attic space, felt cold air push at my face. I switched on the flashlight and scanned the beam across stacks of flattened packing cartons. One or two leftover packing peanuts on the boards. No signs of Engel. But there was an open skylight, up near the apex.

Engel had gone out onto the roof!

I climbed inside the attic and made my way between the piles of cardboard, came to the hatch and peeped through. Freezing air poked tears from my eyes. There was a slope of thick snow on the roof, its top surface hardened with ice. Beyond, a nighttime view across Deadman Bay and down to the jetty where Locklear waited. I wondered if he'd seen Engel come out onto the roof and was wondering what the heck was going on.

I know I was.

As for Engel, he'd inched away from the skylight, out along the snowy peak. He was stooped forward, his back to me, using the shotgun for balance like a tightrope walker. Work boots fighting for grip.

Where did he think he was going?

I clambered halfway out of the skylight and clung to the window frame. Snow and bits of ice skittered down the rooftop and rained to the ground. I shouted his name, but my throat was still raw from all the howling I'd done.

Besides, Engel wasn't for stopping. There was ice underfoot and we were thirty foot up. No way was I going out after him. Believe it or not, there is a limit to my madness. I trained the flashlight on the back of his head and, one last time, yelled out his name.

Unbelievably, Engel stopped, balancing on the apex of the roof like something out of the Cirque de Soleil. Ice particles whirling around him.

I didn't know if he'd heard me above the din of the music or if he'd gone as far as he could go. Either way, he began to shuffle around on the icy angle, boots slipping and slithering as he stabilized his balance with the shotgun.

He was going for a standoff, I realized with a start. And I was a sitting duck, stuck halfway through the window.

I saw the shotgun come round to point my way. I saw his ruddy Santa Claus face light up in the beam of the flashlight. I moved it out of his eyes, but the damage had already been done. Light-blinded, he hunkered forward and brought the muzzle up to bear. No way could I jump aside this time. The muzzle came up. I wished myself small. But the sudden movement had affected his balance. He was trying to correct it. The muzzle kept going up. One of his boots slipped off the apex. His knee buckled and his shoulders sagged. The shotgun pointed skyward. Lightning flashed from the end of the barrel. Then Engel was sliding backward down the slant of roof, gouging out twin furrows in the snow as he went. His arms wheeled, trying to right his balance. Boots scrabbling for purchase as he slid, uncontrollably, toward the abrupt edge and the thirty-foot drop to broken bones or even death.

Nothing I could do.

I watched, numbed by cold and shock, as Engel tilted backward over the edge and seemed to hang in the air for a moment – like Wile E Coyote in the Roadrunner cartoon – before plummeting from sight, a swirl of snow following after him.

*   *   *

At first I didn't move. Disbelief had me glued to the spot. Then reality kicked me up the rump and I dropped clumsily back through the skylight. I rushed down through the house, wading through the sea of earsplitting music. My mind was spinning, harassed by the hellish noise and the thought that Engel had met with an untimely end.

My fault.

I'd wanted answers, and now my bullheadedness had probably gotten a man killed.

No way could Engel have survived, not intact.

But I had to see it for myself. Call it morbid confirmation.

I didn't slow until I was in the carpenter's workshop at the back of the house. Then I eased off as I approached the opened shutter, eyes frantically searching the snowy backyard for signs of Engel's broken body. Nothing immediately visible. I ducked outside. Still no signs of a fatal fall. I panned the flashlight across mounds of shoveled snow, over icy ruts, up across the sheds and the power cables. Still nothing. I came out from beneath the canopy, and that's when the sky fell in on top of me.

*   *   *

According to science, everything falls to earth at the same rate. Engel wasn't the exception to the rule. It should have taken him less than two seconds to hit the ground and crack like an egg. He should have been lying out here in the snow, staring skyward with dilated eyes. That was almost a minute ago. No way he could have defied the laws of gravity and waited to drop his two hundred pounds on my head, all at the right moment.

It was only as his boots connected with my shoulders and his weight flung me face-first into the ground that I realized what had probably happened:

Engel had hit the power lines on his way down. The tangle of cables had partially broken his fall. But the real lifesaver had been the metal canopy running along the back of the house. He'd dropped onto the smaller roof and come to a full stop. Probably shaken and bruised but no worse than that. Then he'd waited for me to venture blindly out before resuming his fall.

And I'd walked straight into it – or under it.

Engel was determined to dispatch his intruder, one way or another.

His full weight slammed me into the snowy dirt, flat on my stomach. Air whooshing from squashed lungs. Freezing slush squelched up my nose and into my eyes. Instinctively, I tried to raise my head and breathe, but Engel had other plans. I felt the hard, ridged sole of his work boot press firmly into the back of my neck and pin me down like a bug on a board.

I was facedown, eating snow. Engel couldn't see who I was. In the red-and-black hooded shirt I must have looked like a trespassing hunter. One of those very people Engel had secured his home against. I felt something firm dig into my back between the shoulder blades and realized it was the muzzle of the 12-gauge.

Engel was going to blast buckshot right through me!

In the eyes of the law, he had every right. I was on his property, uninvited. It was dark. I'd given chase. No court in Alaska would condemn him for taking out a home invader.

But I wasn't finished yet.

I slammed my hands against the deck and pushed with all my might. But Engel had most of his weight on the one foot pinning me down, and the other was suddenly stamping on my lower back. Pain exploded through my spine, sending electric fire coursing down my legs. My body flinched and bucked automatically. But Engel's weight against my neck kept me from moving an inch.

This was it.

Yet another backyard brawl.

Yet another unglamorous moment where my life could end in a heartbeat, facedown in the dirt on a cold and starry night.

And I was powerless to prevent it.

I felt the muzzle dig even deeper. Nothing I could do. I felt my lungs scream for air.

No way out.

I felt a judder as the trigger went *click*.

* * *

It is said, that in the moment before we die, our life flashes before our eyes. Mine didn't. I was too busy cursing myself for being so damn stupid.

Miraculously, Engel's weight lifted.

I twisted my face sideways out of the mud and sucked in precious air. I coughed and spluttered and blinked to see Engel taking off again. The world was on its side, cracked. Through streaming eyes I saw him sprint across the vertical backyard and disappear down the side of the horizontal house.

Only two shells in the shotgun, I realized.

Had Engel loaded three, I'd be dead right now.

I scrambled to my feet, wiped cold slush from my face, and gave chase.

Sucker for punishment.

*   *   *

Who really knows why people react the way they do?

I clattered down the side of the house, almost losing my footing in my haste, almost going down again face-first. I had no idea why Engel was making a bolt for it. He could have simply retreated into his workshop, rolled down the shutter and battened down the hatches. He had the place shored up like Fort Knox. There was little chance of a heavily-armed SWAT team breaking their way in, let alone an unarmed me.

I came round the front of the house. Engel was already out on the jetty. He wasn't alone; Locklear was blocking Engel's escape route. They were deep in a heated exchange. It looked like Locklear was pleading with Engel to desist and see sense. I ran on bendy legs toward the beach. I saw Engel heft the 12-gauge and slam the butt into Locklear's stomach. The Kodiak cop folded like a bad hand of poker and crashed to the deck. His furry ushanka rolled across the timbers like roadkill.

I hammered down the gravel track and leapt onto the jetty, sliding onto the boards in the same instant Engel leapt onto the back of his motor yacht. Locklear was writhing round on the full width of the planking, struggling to breathe. The twin engines on the cruiser spun into life. The boat started to creep away from the dock, kicking up frothy white plumes behind it. I went to hurdle Locklear and take my chances making a jump for it, but Locklear was reaching up with a desperate hand, his panicked face sucked in like a popped balloon. Engel's strike had kicked the air out of him. The distraction was enough to allow the gap between the yacht and the jetty to widen beyond the point of a successful leap, and I came to a slippery halt.

The motor yacht picked up speed and took off.

I rolled Locklear into a crouched position and held on to him until his stunned diaphragm rebooted. I watched as the cruiser roared away into the night, disappearing within seconds. It sounded like it was heading east at an increasing rate of knots. I tried to follow it with my eyes, but it was impossible. I did spy something else, though. Something far out across the bay. Something higher, and in the air. It was an intense white dot, glowing brighter and bigger by the second. Smaller green and red lights becoming visible with it.

"That'll be the US Coast Guard helicopter, out of Kodiak," Locklear wheezed.

I pulled him into a seated position and patted his back. "You okay there, Locklear?"

He shook himself. "Only thing wounded is my pride."

"I can't believe that crazy old son of a gun slugged you. What did he say?"

"Nothing, except for me to get the hell out of his way." Locklear pushed himself to his feet. He trudged over to his hat and scooped it up.

"What the hell was he thinking?"

"I don't know. I've never seen him behave that way before. Looked like the devil was after him. What happened back there?"

"Aside from a mess? Engel must have thought I was an intruder and tried to fill me with buckshot. When that didn't work out, he hightailed it. What I find harder to understand is why he didn't stop the second he realized you were with me."

Locklear made a *to hell if I know* face.

I mirrored it with one of my own.

The recognizable roar of rotor blades began to rip across the bay, cutting through the dance music and rumbling off the nearby cliffs. The intense white dot had grown into a powerful searchlight, lancing through the dark. Within seconds, a red Dolphin helicopter came into view, fifty feet up, coming right at us across swirling water, the din of its turbine completely drowning out Engel's rave party. The searchlight swept suddenly along the jetty, then dazzled our eyes. A second later, the whole pier shook as the chopper thundered by overhead. Snow and ice rose in its wake. The Dolphin pivoted on a dime, then settled onto the beach, sending more snow aloft.

I braced myself against the fierce downdraft and worked my way off the jetty. Locklear was tight on my heels, holding onto his hat.

A hatch popped open. A woman in a parka jumped out. She stooped her way across the shingle toward us. Mahogany hair blustering like windswept flames. She looked about ready to punch someone. Probably me.

"Glad to see y'all having a regular beach party out here while I run my sweet ass off doing all the legwork!" she shouted.

"Rae, I can explain."

"Save it, Gabe. There's been a development. We've had a hit on Cornsilk's credit card. He used it to book a seat on a flight to LAX. We have less than five hours before it lands in LA. This is our best chance to grab him before he disappears on the mainland. We need to go! Now!"

I didn't need telling twice.

24

The Coast Guard helicopter leapt vertically into the night sky, taking us with it. My stomach followed a second later.

Rae and I were seated opposite each other, knees touching in the cramped space. Everything shaking noisily. Everything rattling, including me. Rae was doing everything to snare my gaze while I was doing everything to avoid it. The flight technician checked our safety harnesses and gave a thumbs-up. The chopper swung dangerously low over Engel's brightly-lit house, gusting snow off the roof, then began hurtling inland.

"How'd you know where to find me, Rae?" I shouted above the roar of the engine.

"I tracked your cell phone's GPS signal," she shouted back. "You know, Gabe, it's really impolite not to pick up when a girl calls. I've been trying your number constantly since you scooted."

"I'm sorry, Rae. I had it on silent. It's just that . . ."

"What? Don't go giving me any more bullshit, Gabe. I've had it with you. I mean it. No more running round like a chicken with its head cut off. You owe me an explanation for disappearing back there like that." She leaned forward and nudged my knee. "I'm serious. Right now you're scaring the bejesus out of me. Whatever this is, we're in it together. We're partners, don't forget. I have your back. I need to know you have mine."

"I do."

"So level with me."

I had a hornet in my mouth. A whole nest of them in my stomach. Rae could see it. She could see the turmoil churning behind my taut expression. She knew there was something terribly wrong. Something that had caused me to take flight. And I knew she wouldn't let up until I let her in.

Strangely, I wanted to.

I reached into my pocket and drew out the photograph burning a hole in it, passed it over.

Rae's eyes narrowed. "The photograph from Westbrook's lockbox?"

It was still inside its plastic envelope. She took it from my hand and examined the picture. I saw her brow crease and her freckles try to flee her face.

"What is this?"

I said nothing.

She turned it over and read the words scrawled on the back, glanced up, "This makes about as much sense as a trapdoor in a canoe. Is this for real?"

I nodded, tightly.

"But I don't understand, Gabe. Why would Westbrook have this photo, of all things?"

Still, I said nothing. The truth had me gagged.

Freezing mist was streaming past the hatch window, illuminated in the navigation lights. I could feel it thumping at the fuselage, knew that it would take just a second or two to pop my buckle, open the hatch and let the fog swallow me up.

Then what?

A death fall to the craggy peaks below.

I fixed my gloomy gaze back on Rae and saw the penny drop behind her eyes. I saw the color drain from her face. Rae had seen enough of life to know that not everything came with a money-back guarantee.

"This is bullshit," she breathed.

"No," I said.

"I don't believe you, Gabe. I don't believe *this.*" She waved the photograph at me. Tears were beginning to pool in her eyes, magnifying her pupils.

"I can't change what it is, Rae." My voice was hoarse, split with upset. "It's the real deal. No matter which way you cut it."

The five-by-seven color print was the picture of a woman and a young boy. The woman looked around thirtyish. The boy looked about five or maybe six. They were hugging, smiling, looking deliriously happy. *Were* deliriously happy. Not a care in the world. A snapshot of pure mother-and-son love, frozen in time.

It had been taken on a day trip to the zoo on a bright, tee-shirts-and-shorts summer's day. One of those vibrant Technicolor days that sticks in the memory, like a fly in amber.

I knew all about it because I'd had one just like it. A long time ago. The same one, in fact.

The same perfect, glorious moment in time, right before the universe had changed.

A tear trickled down Rae's cheek. "Gabe, you need to explain this to me right now. Why does Westbrook have a photo of your wife and son in his possession?"

The truth will always come out.

I drew a shaky breath, sensed the demons poised to pull open the hatch and suck me out. "Because Westbrook isn't his real name, Rae. It's an alias. A dead cop's stolen identity. Nathan Westbrook is a cover for The Undertaker. And The Undertaker is my boy. Westbrook is George. He's my son."

25

I'd taken George to Alaska for his thirteenth birthday. Just the two of us. Father and son, pitted against the elements and play-acting old-world pioneers. A coming-of-age for both of us, out in the wilds.

It seemed like a lifetime ago. Someone else's.

We'd spent a short but memorable week on Kodiak Island, scouring the narrow rocky beaches around Alitak Bay. Exploring the many inlets and rivers, searching out brown bear, then running a mile when we'd spotted one.

Amid our adventures, George had spent long hours sitting by the water, by himself, watching the reflections of clouds scudding across the bay. He'd spent an equal amount of time inspecting the configurations of rocks and pebbles making up the shoreline. Come to think of it, I'd never seen him more content, before or after. The remoteness somehow complimented his own.

For me, our Alaska trip had been a chance to spend a week of quality time with my son, to make up for years of my job taking priority. For him, it had been a means to prove his worthiness – not to me – to himself and especially to the untamed world.

We'd both returned home irreversibly changed. Me, with a little more fearful insight into my son's introversion. George, with both feet planted firmly in men's boots.

He'd always wanted to come back, but I'd never found the time. Twenty-some years later, he had.

Tears were tumbling down Rae's cheeks. "George is The Undertaker?"

It seemed unthinkable, *was* unthinkable – that the little boy she'd once known had grown into a killer.

137

But every killer starts out as a child. And no parent knows for sure if theirs will be the one.

I waited for the flight tech to look the other way. He had a headset on, but I didn't want him eavesdropping. I'd known all along I'd have to come clean with Rae about George and our terrible family secret. Never like this, though. Not so soon. Not under these circumstances.

"Rae. I told you: Cornsilk is obsessed with payback. His main goal is to kill me and The Undertaker. Westbrook is The Undertaker. And The Undertaker is an alias for George. Somehow Cornsilk found out he was using Westbrook's identity and followed him out here. I'm guessing he overpowered him and left him burning like a beacon on that isolated beach. Why else would Westbrook have a picture of Hope and my son, with the words *Momma & Me* written on the reverse, unless he and Westbrook were one and the same?" I didn't hold back. I'd never spoken those words to anyone out loud before. Not even to myself. It should have felt awkward. It didn't.

Rae was staring at me like someone who had just been told something bad had shown up on a scan and it needed taking out, immediately. I felt implications impinge on her world, felt bad for her.

"Who else knows?"

There were only two people that I was aware of in the whole wide world who knew with absolute certainty the true identity of *The Undertaker*. I was one and Cornsilk wasn't the other. Even though Cornsilk had killed *The Undertaker*, in his eyes he'd killed Westbrook. Not George.

"Mason Stone. That's about it."

It took her all of two seconds to put together everything she knew about *The Undertaker*, about me, about my son and about how I'd ended up in the asylum. It didn't make for light reading. Surprisingly, it didn't repulse her either. Instead, she popped the buckle on her safety harness and threw her arms around me. The flight technician went to intervene, but she shook him off. She pressed her damp cheek against mine and clung on. I felt hot breath against my ear, felt her body quake as she squeezed me hard.

"Gabe, I am so sorry," she breathed. "It must have been awful for you. A living nightmare. You should have told me."

"I couldn't." It was the squeak of a mouse, of a coward. Another lie. I squeezed her back, but I felt like a fraud.

Truth was, I had plenty of people in my life who cared about me – Eleanor, Sonny, Grace, Celeste, plus a dozen others – people I could open up to if I really wanted it that way, to confide in. They would have listened, empathized with my situation, offered advice, and probably encouraged me to turn my serial killer son in to the authorities. Let them handle it. But not one of them would have understood my reason for keeping George's secret, my secret. Not sure if I did.

Rae was sobbing. Not for George, but for me. But I didn't deserve her sympathy. My deadly intentions had gotten my son killed. There was no way back from that.

I held on to her, letting her cry the tears I could no longer shed myself.

No matter how many times we go through the process of losing loved ones, it never gets any easier.

There is no manual for dealing with death. No crash course for the cursed. No way to shore up the mind, the heart or the soul against the emotional tsunami. Each time the surge touches us, it is as cold and as cruel as its first contact.

Snakeskin had murdered my murderous boy.

And I hated him for it.

Most of all I hated myself.

Not for failing to prevent it, but for feeling relieved.

26

Less than thirty minutes later, we were back on board another private charter, bound for Los Angeles.

Rae hadn't let go of me the whole time – not until the Dolphin helicopter had deposited us on the apron at Kodiak Air Station and we'd stooped our way to the waiting jet. Learning my secret should have revolted her, made her see me for what I was. It should have killed any feelings she had for me. It hadn't. To her, I was a damaged bird with a broken wing and she was prepared to do everything in her power to patch it up and make it fly again. To me, I was a lost cause.

I didn't have the heart to tell her that some things are irreparable.

The jet broke through a thick layer of cloud and leveled out beneath a canopy of stars. Rae was making coffee in the small galley. I was watching ice crystals growing on the plastic pane.

Out of respect, Rae hadn't pried any deeper. All the questions concerning the hows and the whys behind George becoming a serial killer were courteously postponed. For now, she was being understanding, soothing, consolatory. In time, when the upset subsided, she'd peel away my layers of deceit until the complete and unadulterated truth was exposed.

Maybe when she saw my rotten core she'd loathe me the way I loathed myself. Maybe for my own good.

"Thanks," I murmured as she handed me a steaming mug. "You didn't go into detail about how you discovered Cornsilk's flight."

She dropped into the facing seat. There were tears in her eyes, magnifying the hurt. "We found it on a hunch.

I had the airlines check bookings made prior to the BOLO being issued. I figured there was a chance Cornsilk had seen us at the hotel before the boat went *ka-boom* and decided to scoot while the going was good. At precisely twelve-fifteen this afternoon, he used his First Tennessee Visa card online to make a reservation on the three-twenty-five flight to Anchorage."

Literally minutes before the BOLO went out.

"Gabe, I don't know this guy from Adam, but I swear he could fall into a barrel of shit and come out smelling of roses."

Rae always had a way with words.

I sipped the coffee. "What time is he expected at LAX?"

"Eleven-thirty tonight. His connecting flight was out of Ted Stevens at five-fifteen."

I checked my watch, added an hour on for the time zone difference between Alaska and California. Four hours. That's all we had before Cornsilk landed in LA. Even with the jet on full throttle, I wasn't sure we'd make it.

"You went back to Akhiok to be with George," Rae said suddenly. "I understand that now. Once you saw that picture you realized the burned body was his, and you had to be there, with him. So why were you were someplace else? Where was that?"

"Paul Engel's house. George's body wasn't in the clinic when I got there. Engel had moved him. Don't ask. That's why I was out there. I was looking for answers."

"Did you find them?"

"No. I just ended up with more questions. Engel had this weird setup going on. Plus, he tried to kill me, twice."

Rae's eyebrows met in the middle.

I ran through the course of events that had taken me to Deadman Bay in the thick of night and to the frosty confrontation with Engel. I told her about Engel's sadomasochistic porn movie and about how I'd chased him to the roof.

"But you didn't find George's body?"

There was a thistle in my throat. "No. I've put Locklear on the case. Let's see what he comes up with."

I'd left the Kodiak cop to investigate in my stead. I'd given him explicit instructions to search Engel's property with a fine-toothed comb, told him to call me with news the second he found the missing corpse – *my son's body* – and to warn me the moment Engel showed up.

Best of a bad situation.

Right now I was more focused on catching Cornsilk: the killer of my boy.

I stared into the coffee, at the swirling blackness, knowing it mirrored my own. *Snakeskin* had killed my son and something ugly was stirring deep within my hypothalamus. I'd never subscribed to the biblical justice of an eye for an eye, but the more I pictured *Snakeskin's* milky orb, the more that ugliness within me wanted to pluck it out and crush it under the heel of my boot.

27

Her heart was beating so fast it made her feel lightheaded.

The private detective had phoned with good news.

She knew he would; she'd read it in her horoscope.

Her husband was worried she was wasting her time, their time. The family-run business had taken a hit these last twelve months. Their income had halved. They were at risk of defaulting on their mortgage payments, bank loans. The minivan had been repossessed. Her husband was worried she was investing too much of herself into lost causes. Chasing ghosts while the rest of her life, their life, fell into chaos and ruins. He was worried it was making her ill. She needed to let go, move on. He didn't understand, could never understand the force driving her forward.

It was in her chemistry. As unalterable as her DNA.

Nothing else mattered except this.

The investigator hadn't told her all the details – she didn't need to know everything, even though she'd asked, pushed – just the necessary facts to give her stamp of approval on his next paycheck, plus expenses.

He'd got a lead. He'd tapped into a friend who worked for the FBI. He'd come up with a name. He was running checks, making calls and asking questions. Essentially, earning his extortionate fee.

She was getting nearer.

She had a name and soon she'd have a location.

It was good news. The best.

Her heart was beating so fast it made her feel lightheaded.

28

By the skin of our teeth, we landed at Los Angeles International Airport with minutes to spare. Even with all the plugs pulled, our pilot had made no guarantees we'd arrive at LAX before the passenger plane carrying Gary Cornsilk touched down. As it happened, a strong tail wind had given us an unexpected push and we'd left hot rubber on the tarmac at precisely 11:22 p.m. – exactly eight minutes before the Boeing 737 carrying Cornsilk had berthed at Terminal 3.

We hit the ground running and didn't stop until we'd arrived at Cornsilk's gate.

Rae had left me to stew in my silence, pretty much for the past four hours. No good will ever come of prodding a sleeping bear with a stick. I am a firm believer there is a time and a place for talking. This wasn't one of them.

Besides, my obsession was all-consuming.

We were met at the mouth of the airbridge by a half dozen heavily-armed Airport Police and their unsmiling sergeant. Rae had phoned ahead and advised security about our interest in the Alaska Airlines inbound flight from Anchorage – in particular, of its murderous passenger with the melted face – and controllers had apprised the captain of the situation. The crew were asked to expedite passenger disembarkation, without giving the game away – which can be asking a lot from people who know there's a killer onboard.

Rae issued orders and we shoehorned ourselves into the angle of the airbridge where it joined the plane, a few feet from the curved fuselage. All of us waiting impatiently as the technicians completed their checks and then opened the hatch.

No way was Cornsilk going anywhere except straight into custody, or to hell if I had my way.

Rae had one hand on the heel of her gun, the other balled into a fist. I was clenching my teeth so hard my jaw hurt.

"Y'all remember: we need to take this sumbitch alive right now," Rae called to all present. "No excuses, mind. Let's keep this simple and clean."

Of course, it didn't apply to me. As the father of a murdered child I was exempt. Now I knew how it felt from the other side of the interview table. All those times I'd spoken with hurting parents. All those times I'd offered reassurance. All those times I'd been understanding, while trying to glean information out of their grief, anything to help find the killer of their child. All those times I really had no idea about the pain they were going through. Empathy can be as objective as it liked. Pain is subjective. It changes us. No more so than with the death of a child. It had hollowed me out and filled me up with demons. *Snakeskin* could rot in hell for all I cared. I had a bullet in the chamber of my cleaned-up Glock and a steely glint of vengeance in both eyes. If he so much as sneezed out of line, I was prepared to cut the head off the snake.

A loud clunk sounded as the hatch swung out and then sideways. Everybody tensed.

Inside the plane, a pair of flight attendants gave us solemn nods of acknowledgement as the first passengers began to filter out.

"Merry Christmas," Rae said to each passenger as they passed by. "Nothing happening here. Move swiftly along. Thank you. Keep moving. Y'all have a wonderful Christmas now."

We were all fervently scanning faces, looking to match the description I'd provided of Gary Cornsilk: a medium-build guy of American Indian descent, early-thirties, military-style tattoos, with one side of his face melted away and one unblinking eye as white as a bird's egg. No way would anybody overlook a face like that. Anyone who had ever dreamed of monsters under the bed knew their own *Snakeskin*.

"How many, all told?" I called to one of the flight attendants as passengers streamed by, flashing us wary looks before moving on and up the tunnel.

"Thirty-seven."

Quite a tally for Christmas Day.

I'd already counted twenty, without spotting anyone who looked remotely like Freddy Krueger. Mostly business people and regular folks returning home for the Holidays.

I sensed the uniforms stir restlessly around us.

The last stragglers came out: an old guy with a fuzzy gray beard and crooked teeth; a chubby guy in a business suit several sizes too small; a giggling couple of youths with backpacks and cheesy grins, and then . . .

"That's everyone," the attendant stated with a shrug.

Rae and I exchanged confused glances.

"Step aside," I said.

Our police party poured inside, eyes scanning the cabin down the length of their guns. On the surface, it looked empty – aside from the usual mess that normally tidy people leave exclusively on planes: discarded blankets, newspapers, garbage. No signs of *Snakeskin* trying to slither inside an overhead compartment.

"How many toilets?"

The attendant pointed, "One here. Two at the rear of the plane."

"Go ahead," Rae said. "I've got this one."

I nodded and worked my way down the aisle – a pair of Airport Police in tow – checking between seats as we went. Still no signs of *Snakeskin* curled under a tray table. Nothing to indicate anything suspicious.

I came to the lavatory cubicles in back. The concertina doors were folded open. No signs of anyone hiding inside. I swept back the curtain on the galley and scanned rows of metal lockers, a transparent garbage bag filled with paper cups and food wrappers. No hint of any invertebrates.

Snakeskin was nowhere to be seen.

Damn.

"What now?" the sergeant asked.

"Get your people to double-check everyone leaving the airport," I said. "Tell them to detain anyone even vaguely fitting Cornsilk's description."

He nodded, curtly, and waved his men out.

I regrouped with Rae at the plane's exit. She was already on her cell, head tilted to one side, curls spilling. I heard her asking questions and making incredulous sounds, figured she was speaking with Departures at Ted Stevens and it wasn't sounding good.

"Don't tell me," I said as she came off the phone, "he failed to board."

She nodded. "None of the airline staff recall seeing anyone matching his description."

Double damn.

"But he was definitely on the first flight out of Kodiak?"

Again, she nodded. "No one is confirming a visual ID, but Ticketing claim his boarding card was scanned."

I was in no doubt that Cornsilk had known we were onto him. As Rae had suggested: probably spied us at the Kodiak Inn, looking into the room registered in Westbrook's name. He'd known he'd stand a better chance of escaping if he got off the island, known that travelling by land would offer a greater opportunity to avoid detection, known we'd go chasing down the connecting flight even if he skipped the plane in Anchorage.

Snakeskin had spied his chance and had given us the slip.

It was a clever move, leaving us red-faced and empty-handed.

Worst still, we were over two thousand miles distant to do anything about it.

29

He waited in the shadows, hardly breathing, watching his prey.

The man with the comb-over had no idea he was being followed, or who was doing the following.

Comb-Over had gone about his business all day, oblivious. A gazelle chewing grass while the cheetah slinked.

Christmas Day had been mostly quiet for Comb-Over, but busy. He'd run an errand for his miserable old mom, then called round at a friend's house for a glass of Christmas cheer. The errand had reminded him that being an only child with aging parents sucked, while the visit had reminded him how lonely he'd be without kids of his own once age sucked the life out of him.

Later, he'd spent some time indoors, at his parents' place, watching TV with his feet up, while his decrepit dad grouched about ungrateful kids and reruns.

It was a picture of Christmas bliss, copied across America.

Now Comb-Over was picking up a few last-minute items from a convenience store. It looked like a carton of milk and a pack of beer. The milk helped sate his dad's ulcer while the beer helped sedate his mom.

From the shadows he watched Comb-Over cough up a twenty dollar bill and tell the owner to keep the change. Then he sauntered across the empty lot to his dad's Town & Country.

He had no idea that this would be his last day on earth.

He watched him get in the car, place his purchases in the passenger foot space, mouth a silent prayer.

He had no idea anyone was sitting in the shadowy backseat.

Comb-Over let out a sigh as the needle stabbed his carotid artery.

30

Whichever way you looked at it, it was a mess.

Rae got on her phone again and broke the news to our counterparts at the Anchorage field office. There was a very slim chance Cornsilk was still in Alaska. They'd send field agents to the airport and notify the port authorities to be on the lookout for our fugitive. The same went for the border agents operating the crossings leading into Yukon and British Columbia. I wasn't hopeful. Cornsilk had at least a six hour head start. The likelihood of him still being within reach was remote. More likely he'd hitched a ride on a vehicle heading south and already crossed the border into Canada. If so, he was as good as gone.

Snakeskin was in the wind.

And it was an ill one, for us.

31

"We need to go back to Alaska, right now," Rae said as we marched through the airbridge tunnel.

I put the brakes on and caught her by the arm. "Rae, wait. Not yet. There's something I need to take care of here, first."

She looked puzzled. "Cornsilk killed George. What's more important than going after him?"

"You're right: nothing. Trust me, Rae, catching up with Cornsilk is my number one priority. He killed my son. Believe me, I am focused. I know you're pissed he gave us the slip and so am I, but we need to go about this the right way."

"And if we stop now his trail will go cold overnight." She was uncomfortable with the thought of losing momentum and it came through in her tone.

I let out a ragged breath. "And that's why we've scrambled every available field agent and border control officer in Alaska – for all the good it will do."

Her eyes narrowed. "You think it's already too late, don't you?"

I nodded. "If I were him I'd be as far away from Alaska as humanly possible. He's had a good head start on us, Rae. He'll be long gone by now. I don't want to waste our time rushing back there if we need to be concentrating our efforts elsewhere. For all we know he could be on his way down here."

"To Los Angeles? Why?"

"Because he made that reservation for a reason. He had dozens of options to choose from. He could have sent us anywhere in the country, or even oversees. If he had no intention of making the flight, why book it to LAX?

Sometimes, Rae, we make choices unconsciously. Maybe he had every intention of coming to Los Angeles and the reservation was automatic."

Rae didn't look too convinced. "Okay. So what are you saying exactly, that we wait and see if he makes an appearance?"

"I'm saying the last place we need to be right now is back in Alaska. Plus, take a look at us both: we're running on fumes. It's late. We haven't slept since I don't know when. Let's get some sleep, recharge, then catch up again first thing in the morning. In the meantime, I'll speak with Locklear, see if he's found anything at Engel's place. Anchorage has our numbers; they'll call if they get anything on Cornsilk."

"Gabe, you shouldn't be alone tonight."

"I'll be fine."

"No you won't. You just found out your son is dead. I'm worried for you." She reached out a hand.

I stood my ground. "Rae, I said I'll be fine."

"And excuse me if I don't believe you. Okay, so I understand you're out to get Cornsilk for what he's done. So am I. But you're bottling everything up. I'm worried that pressure will keep on building and sooner or later you'll blow. I don't want you doing something crazy when that happens."

"Crazy is what I do, remember?"

"All the more reason why you shouldn't be alone right now. Come home, with me. Please."

I was tempted – sorely – by the offer. Being with Rae – *being physically intimate with Rae* – not only sent me to a better place, it also felt right. And nothing had felt right in a very long time. I was in no doubt Rae Burnett was good for my soul. Truth was, I wasn't sure if it worked both ways.

32

It was after midnight. No stars visible through the murky yellow overcast of reflected city lights.

I was in the back of a taxi, heading northwest on Lincoln Boulevard, away from LAX. The driver had the windows down. Warmish air was blowing in. But the clement Californian climate was unable to chase away my chill. It seemed the freezing Alaskan temperature had embedded itself in my skin – *under my skin* – leaving me with the shakes. Cold thoughts snowballing in my head.

Rae had called me a *selfish sumbitch* as we'd gone our separate ways. No argument there from me. This wasn't her show and I didn't want her mopping up my tears.

I paid the fare and got out on the roadside along Admiralty Way in Long Beach. The smell of salt was heavy in the air. I could hear distant music thumping from a big yacht down in the marina: rich kids snorting coke and comparing Hollywood smiles. I crossed empty lanes toward the hotel situated directly on the Marina Del Rey harbor front. It was an upmarket property, supplying lavish accommodations to people visiting the seaside community. Not the kind of place my own travel expenditure had ever stretched to.

The hotel lobby was quiet. Most guests either in bed or watching on-demand movies. I could see a wafer-thin male receptionist with short blonde hair, busy ogling a computer screen in the back office. I pushed through the door leading to the stairwell and made my way to the eleventh floor. The elevators were keycard-operated. A security setup designed to stop non-paying guests from accessing the upper floors. Possibly for Health and Safety reasons, the stairs hadn't been factored into the equation.

My destination resided halfway along a hallway dotted with maritime prints. I came to the desired door, hesitated, then rapped knuckles against the wood. I was acting on an assumption. The last time I'd been here I'd made a grave error. Not this time. I heard movement coming from within. I stared at the spyhole, knowing that there was an eye checking me out on the other side.

The door opened to reveal the spitting image of Sean Bean, the movie actor, dressed in a Pink Floyd tour tee and stripy lounge pants. But this wasn't Sean Bean. He wasn't even a movie actor. His name was Mason Stone: a Brit with dual-nationality – formerly a top inspector with the London Met, now working for the US federal government out of Pennsylvania Avenue. But he could have passed as Sean Bean in any light. He had the same gray-grizzled chin. The same soulful stare through baggy eyes.

"Bloody hell, Quinn. You never fail to amaze. If you're here delivering Christmas presents, you're late. Haven't you seen what time it is?"

I didn't answer.

There was a snarl scraping away at the back of my teeth.

I'd anticipated this moment since discovering the photograph in Westbrook's lockbox.

Some of the snarl leaked out as I propelled myself at Mason Stone, hands outstretched.

*   *   *

It was the last thing he expected.

I grabbed him by the neck of his souvenir T-shirt and used the momentum to force him backward and off-balance. Caught off-guard, Stone backpedaled, eyes widening. I had the advantage, the element of surprise. It should have been a breeze knocking him off his bare feet. It wasn't. Stone's loose muscles were a camouflage for his core strength. He didn't crash to the plush carpeting as expected, with me on top, probably about to throttle him. Instead, he rotated at the waist as we toppled into his suite. He threw both arms upward and under my own, effectively breaking my grip, then used my momentum against me, spinning me aside. The power balance shifted. Suddenly I didn't have my footing or any kind of an advantage. I landed heavily on the thick carpeting, face first. Ribs popping. Stone stepped out of reach and looked down at me with thick ridges furrowing his brow.

"For God's sake, Quinn. Remind me to get you fixed up with judo lessons. That was amateurish beyond embarrassment."

I kicked him on the back of his knee. His leg buckled. His shoulder dipped. I rolled to my feet and rushed him, head down for the tackle. I wrapped arms around his waist, buried my shoulder in his stomach and pushed him back against an ornate side table. Wood grated against plaster. Stone's shoulders slammed into a painting, knocking it askew. A vase of fake flowers toppled to the carpet.

"Watch the bloody furniture, Quinn."

I punched him in the side. Not hard enough to do any real damage – just enough to knock the wind out of him. He responded by sliding a python-like arm around my neck and squeezing, hard. In the same heartbeat, he spun round on the spot – so that we were now facing the same way, but with me stooped in his stranglehold – and proceeded to apply the pressure. Stone was going for a blood choke. I went to elbow him in the groin, but suddenly my vision was spotting, the world spinning, ears ringing, and then . . . blackness.

33

That night – spent fidgeting and worrying as George had undergone scans in St. Jude Children's Hospital – had been the scariest of my life to that point. Chasing down bad guys through shadowy alleyways hadn't come close.

Nothing compares to a parent's fear when their child's life hangs in the balance.

The scan results had taken a lifetime coming through.

Hope had sat there stewing, slightly tearful, while I'd paced the hospital corridor, quietly raging at myself for letting it happen, for letting George fall from that carousel. Hope hadn't verbally condemned me for leaving George while I'd run after the purse-snatcher. She hadn't needed to. The terror in her eyes had been enough to slip the hangman's noose around my neck.

And the torturous wait had pulled it tight.

Parenting is just about the most rewarding job in the world, and just about the hardest.

But when it goes wrong the blame rests solely on our shoulders.

George had cracked his skull on his fall from the carousel. He'd remained unconscious the whole ride in the EMS vehicle, and even during his tests in the hospital.

"Following this kind of trauma," a young doctor, seemingly fresh out of med school, had told us, "it's not uncommon for the brain to shut itself down. It gives it time to repair."

"In other words, our son is in a coma."

A confirmative nod. "Right now, it's likely his brain is undergoing damage assessment and fixing what it can."

Although George had bled profusely from his head wound, the MRI scan had shown no signs of any internal bleeding. Thank God. No brain swelling to speak of. Some unusual misfiring, possibly caused by the blow, or his *condition*. No signs that he wouldn't make a full recovery, or at least return to the healthy boy we knew and loved.

It hadn't stopped us from fretting like traitors before a firing squad.

"Can't you at least bring him out of it with drugs?"

"In our experience, we've found it's better to let the patient's brain decide on the right time. Your son took a big knock. His whole nervous system went into shock. The coma is temporary. It's his brain's way of recharging. We expect he'll wake sooner rather than later, and with no adverse side effects."

We hadn't been convinced.

Worrying parents are programmed to think the worst. It's our paternal instinct protecting us, preparing us for any eventuality.

Twenty-four hours later, George had surfaced from his catatonic sleep.

But something had changed in him.

I'd seen it in his eyes.

Something a little wilder, a little more *basic*. Visible only when he'd looked my way.

34

I was sucked out of the blackout with a slurp, feeling woozy.

"What the hell do you think you're playing at, Quinn?"

I was seated in a big comfy chair in a nicely-appointed lounge area, propped up on plumped pillows. Around me, a series of opulently-decorated rooms were visible through open doors, each with panoramic views out over the nighttime marina and on to the dark Pacific Ocean. The place looked like something straight out of a French Renaissance château. Heavy brocade drapes and gilded portraits. There was even a baby grand piano with its lid raised and sheet music ready to be played.

The world brightened into focus, like sunshine after a storm. There was a man in a Pink Floyd tour tee seated opposite. A gun on the lap of his stripy lounge pants. My gun.

"So here we are once more," Mason Stone spoke as I heaved myself a little straighter in the chair. "I've poured you a cup of tea with plenty of sugar; it'll take the edge off things."

There was a fine bone china cup sitting on a matching saucer, placed on a small ornate side table next to my chair. A tan-colored liquid almost to the brim.

"Milk," he added. "The way tea's meant to be drunk. None of that wishy-washy see-through stuff that tastes like ditchwater."

My lips peeled into a snarl. "I'm not here for a tea party, Stone. Give me back my gun."

"What, and put myself in harm's way?" He tut-tutted. "I don't think so, Quinn. Clearly, not with the mood you're in. Remember what happened the last time I left you alone with a loaded weapon? Been there, done that. Got the tee shirt with the bullet holes still in it."

"We both know I made a mistake. I've learned my lesson."

"So I can see. You turned over a new leaf, but felled the tree to do it. Is that how you meet and greet people these days, charging in and trying to wrestle them to the ground?"

"Only those who mess around in my life." I kept my snarl visible. "You set me up, you pompous son of a bitch."

Crossed lines emerged on his brow. "Don't be so bloody melodramatic."

"You knew it was George, up there on that beach. You knew he'd been murdered."

"And that's where you're wrong, Quinn. Yet again. I wasn't sure. Not for definite. That's why I sent you there, to prove one way or the other. My money was on your son being the killer, not the victim."

"So you sent me there to confirm it?" I blew superheated breath through my teeth.

"I was shocked to hear the truth. Seriously, Quinn, I'm sorry for your loss."

"Just tell me everything, Stone. From the beginning. Start with how you came to know George was The Undertaker. We never got the chance to discuss it on Sanibel Causeway."

"Only because you lost the plot and shot me umpteen times." He spread his hands. "Anyway, it was easier than you think. I'm surprised you missed it, considering your obsession to find him."

"Just get to the point, Stone."

"So, I was reviewing The Undertaker Case files –"

"Looking to catch me out."

"– looking to fit together pieces of the puzzle." He let out a long sigh. "You know, Quinn, it's not you versus everybody else. The world isn't out to prove the mighty Quinn wrong. We're not all out to get you and reinforce that paranoia of yours."

"So why were you snooping into my case?"

"By that time it wasn't your case. You were off doing Disney World and topping up your Floridian suntan while everybody else was picking up the pieces of your fallout. I had no interest in The Undertaker Case. I'd heard about it. But it was closed. It was only when one of our SACs sent me the files to look at –"

"Which SAC?"

"Does it matter?"

I made a face.

"Our Special Agent in Charge at the Las Vegas Field Office."

"Hugh Winters sent you my case files?"

"Together with a note saying he believed you'd made a right pig's ear of it, too. He felt the case needed reviewing. I agreed to take a look. I didn't expect to find anything – certainly not a different suspect. As far as Director Fuller was concerned, the Bureau had caught his niece's killer."

"Harland Candlewood – who later died because of the beating he got from Winters' henchmen."

"Albeit after incriminating evidence was found in his hotel suite and he subsequently resisted arrest."

"That's a bunch of horse crap and you know it."

"Not according to the official report. At that point in time, Candlewood was the prime suspect. Not only was there a booby-trap bomb inside his suite, he was also the CEO of the company whose employees were being picked off by The Undertaker. Right then and there, he was good for it all."

"It doesn't excuse their murdering an innocent man." I got to my feet and started pacing, burning off nervous energy. "Besides, this is inside out. Winters believed Candlewood was guilty. Why did he push for the case to be reopened?"

"Simple. He cited his prime reason as yours and Inspector Maxwell's failed apprehension of a suspect in the Stratosphere Tower *after* Candlewood had already been hospitalized."

Sonny Maxwell's police report had somehow found its way onto Winters' desk and alarm bells had rung. Winters would have subpoenaed the CCTV recordings for the cameras in and around the Stratosphere's observation deck. He would have found that they'd been deactivated minutes before our fatal face-off which had seen *The Undertaker* seemingly falling to his death. No doubt he'd questioned Sonny about it, learned that she hadn't glimpsed the suspect's face.

"Winters has a personal agenda."

"I'm aware of that. You and his wife had something going on, and Winters took umbrage. It didn't cloud my judgment."

"The trouble with Winters is he can't move on. It was a long time ago, before I was married." I stated it for the record, to be clear. "And long before Angela married him. So what happened?"

"Remember the hotel surveillance tape you got from the Ramada Inn on Vermont?"

We'd seen our first glimpse of *The Undertaker* in fuzzy black-and-white. A hotel security camera had filmed him skittering across the Hollywood Hotel parking lot, frame by frame, taking another of his victims, a down-and-out called Helena Margolis, to her doom. The recording had been made on old VHS tape. Scratchy and low-res.

I nodded, "We sent it over to the Crime Lab for processing."

"Which they did. But for one reason or another it got filed away with the rest of the evidence. Perhaps after the case was closed and you quit. The image they managed to pull out was still grainy, but it was good enough to run through face recognition software and give us a hit."

"George was in your system?"

"He was arrested on a class B misdemeanor when he was twenty-five, for patronizing a prostitute."

I hadn't known. Not something he'd ever tell me.

"There was a ninety-seven percent chance the face on the Ramada surveillance tape belonged to George Quinn, your son. It was too coincidental to dismiss. I went through the rest of the case files with fresh eyes. There were things the killer did, moves he made, details he left behind that only someone who knew you personally could have done. I was left with only one conclusion."

George Quinn was *The Undertaker.*

"You must have had an inkling."

I shook my head. "Sometimes we're too close to something to step back and see the bigger picture."

Truthfully, I'd had no suspicion George was the killer at the time. Who would entertain the notion of their own flesh and blood being a psychotic murderer? Sure, he'd given us moments of concern over the years – doesn't every son? George had been born with a condition, but not one which stopped him functioning normally in society. In our eyes, he'd overcome earlier drawbacks. He'd struggled through academia, but had blossomed out in the workplace. No reason to ever suspect he was a killer. Even when our investigation had traced *The Undertaker* back to our home State of Tennessee, even when he'd used a set of my old handcuffs at a crime scene, even when he'd left one of my prized cufflinks on a body buried under a silo in Jackson, even when one of his former psychiatrists had turned up as an old homicide in Philly, I'd failed to connect the dots. Either that, or my unconscious mind had protected me from the truth, pulling close the cloak of denial.

"How did you link George to Westbrook?"

"He used his flagged alias."

I nodded. "Westbrook was a cop, who went missing. He was on the Bureau's database."

"Three months after Westbrook went into the system, his details showed up on a flight from Newark Liberty to McCarran. It was flagged for the Bureau to look into – which we did. Apparently, Westbrook had paperwork permitting him to escort and transfer a mentally-ill prisoner through Liberty."

"Jamie."

Stone nodded gravely.

I hadn't spoken her name in a while and my throat crackled like an old vinyl LP record.

Jamie Garcia, my police partner during our hunt for *The Undertaker*, had traveled under her own steam to Staten Island, to investigate a strong lead. She'd tracked down a possible survivor – the one that got away, as we knew her – intending to speak to her in person. As far as I'd known, Jamie had arrived in New York in one piece. Then, shortly thereafter, she'd slipped under the radar and we'd lost all contact. The next I'd seen of her was as a hostage of *The Undertaker* in our fatal showdown at the Stratosphere Tower, over one thousand feet above the glittery Las Vegas Strip. An encounter that had cost Jamie her life and me my sanity.

"So, he flew with Jamie from New York to Las Vegas."

"Using Westbrook's identity to facilitate his passage, yes. We put a request to the Las Vegas field office to intercept him on his arrival at McCarran. But your manhunt for The Undertaker was in full swing at the time and the request got pushed down to the bottom of the priority list. That's where Westbrook's trail went cold."

"Until he booked a hotel room in Alaska almost a year later."

"Bingo."

There was ice in my belly. Stone had known about George and his serial killing habits long before he and I had first met on that hazy dawn on Sanibel Beach. While I had been looking under the wrong rocks for my obsessions, Stone had found *The Undertaker's* true identity. Undoubtedly, Stone had looked into me, too, and discovered I'd quit the LAPD for sunnier skies. Then he'd played a waiting game. The only certain fact in his arsenal for tracking *The Undertaker* being the killer's use of Westbrook's ID. He'd known if he waited long enough, the ID would be used again. And when it was, Stone would be there to catch the Westbrook impersonator: *The Undertaker* – George Quinn, the killer, my son.

Like all great investigators, Mason Stone had the cunning of a fox and the patience of an ambush predator.

For all his claims of being able to see into the future, George hadn't anticipated that.

I stopped pacing; it was becoming tiring. "What I don't get is why you kept the truth about Westbrook from Rae. You just sent us to Alaska, blind, on the basis of investigating a homicide. You should have come clean, Stone. Saved a little heartache on both parts. I don't understand all the secrecy."

"I told you: I wasn't sure."

"Bull crap."

I turned and opened the glass French doors leading out onto Stone's balcony. Suddenly, I was feeling dizzy, nauseous. I needed fresh air.

A salted breeze blew at my goose-bumped skin. All at once the fight had gone out of me, replaced by overwhelming sadness and possibly the first inklings of defeat. Foolishly, I had thought I'd get away with my dark secret – at least until I'd brought George into custody. I was wrong. Stone had known about George all along, chasing my son while I'd been lazing around in the Sanibel sun.

My intransigence had been my undoing.

And my son's.

I felt sick.

George's death, Jamie's death, Harry's death – it was all my fault.

I gripped the metal balustrade and stared out across the nighttime marina. I could see partygoers on the open deck of a big motor yacht, drinking, socializing, a million miles away from the cold thoughts growing icicles in my head.

Stone had hung back. Then Lady Luck had given him a golden handshake: back in LA, *The Maestro* had resumed the Piano Wire Murders. Stone had spied his chance to bring me onboard, keep me close so that he could keep an eye on me, knowing that I, too, must be looking for my serial killer son, and that there was a chance I could lead him to a capture. Stone had used me, I realized. I couldn't blame him.

I sensed the Brit come alongside. Big hands wrapping around the balustrade. "You and me, Quinn, we're not that different. We're both peacekeepers. We try and right the wrongdoings of others. Redress the balance between good and evil. But we're human. We make mistakes. Often bad ones. Our intentions are just, but not always justified. I'm not the enemy. I gave you what you wanted. I sent you to Alaska to finish the job."

"Only Cornsilk beat me to it."

Stone's soulful gaze roved the myriad of moored boats. "Gary Cornsilk. Our very own disaffected agent gone serial. Agent Burnett told me all about him: how he went after you in Florida, how he killed that private dick of yours. Cornsilk was an unknown variable. We had no way of knowing he'd go after your son. Looking back, I should have arranged your release from Springfield the moment we got the Westbrook hit."

Rage squeezed my gut. "Why hold back?"

"Because my job is about striking balance. At that moment in time, the information you were sent to acquire from Trenton Fillmore trumped everything else."

"Even Cornsilk burning my boy to death?" It came out a croak, through a constricted windpipe. "Thanks for prioritizing, Stone."

"Don't shoot the messenger, Quinn. You kept Cornsilk to yourself. You had ample opportunity to tell me about him after Sanibel. That's on your head."

For long moments we lingered there in silence: Stone, the epitome of laidback; me, quietly seething; both knowing that my obsessions had been the death of others.

"I'll make arrangements to have your son's body brought back to LA," Stone said at last.

But I shook my head. "No. That's my job." I didn't want Stone knowing about Engel and the fact he'd taken George's body. Not right now. I wasn't sure why. Maybe because I wanted to find out first. "Cornsilk's out there. I need your help finding him."

"And you'll have it. Cornsilk is just as much our problem as he is yours. We've circulated his photo to law enforcement agencies nationwide. If he so much as double parks we'll find him." He leveled his soulful stare on mine. "The Bureau is right behind you on this one, Quinn. But there's something we need to clear up first. What went wrong with Trenton Fillmore?"

*   *   *

News up: Stone hadn't sprung me from Springfield because he'd learned about the homicide in Akhiok and assumed George was involved. His first reaction had been one of reticence. He'd held back, observing things as they unfolded in Kodiak. He'd broken me out of the asylum because Fillmore had died – taking with him the precious information I'd been sent there to extract – not because he'd been concerned about protecting my feelings.

Shamefully, I hadn't thought much at all about my dead friend from the Fed Med since shooting off to Alaska. His hot blood dripping from my hands seemed like a distant event. In another life. Not thirty-six hours earlier. The mystery of the burned body had swept me up and then *Snakeskin* had blown me away.

"There's nothing to tell, other than somebody shanked him to death. End of story."

"Any idea who?"

"Take your pick. That place is full of loose screws. Any one of those crazies could have slipped in and taken him out. Can we do this debriefing some other time?"

"No, Quinn, we can't. You brought this on yourself by storming in here. Look, I know you and Fillmore were close. I'm not insensitive; I know this is difficult for you after all that's happened. But we need answers. We need to know who had a motive, or better yet, the opportunity."

I stared out beyond the marina to the dark Pacific. I pictured Fillmore curled up on the cell floor in a pool of sticky blood. "Not counting me, just about everyone had access. Especially the unit officers. There's an open house policy at Springfield. It allows inmates free movement between buildings. As for a motive, like the rest of us, Fillmore did his best to stay out of trouble, but he wound people up the wrong way. He liked playing pranks. He got under the skin. Made enemies. Besides, Springfield is a federal prison for the mentally sick. People like that don't need motives. You only need to comb your hair the wrong way and they take exception."

"No one said there wouldn't be an element of danger."

Fillmore had saved me from a lot of it. His big brawling physique had kept the bullies at bay. Saved my skin. In many ways, I owed Trenton Fillmore my life. But I hadn't been able to save his.

"If it's any consolation," I said, holding my thumb and forefinger less than a half inch apart, "I was this close. I had Fillmore on the brink of telling me everything. The whole nine yards."

"But he went and spilled his guts for someone else."

I let Stone see my disapproval.

A wave of chatter drew my eyes back to the partygoers crammed on the luxury cruiser. Giggling girls dressed as sexy Santas. Rich boys in tuxedos trying to impress. All of them having what they thought was fun. Kids untouched by homicide and vileness. Their faith in the world as yet untarnished.

Trust is thicker than blood.

I'd spent three months building up Fillmore's trust. Three months convincing him he could confide in me, that I was on his side. Three months constructing confidence while I lied through my bare teeth about my own history, about my real identity. Nothing I could do about it. I was on an assignment for the FBI, undercover. Only key prison staff privy to my mission. As luck would have it, I'd become Fillmore's only friend at Springfield – the only other sane person wearing prison-issue khakis he could depend on. I'd kept the guards off his case while he kept the other inmates out of my face. We'd had each other's back. Brothers in chains. But when it had come to the crunch, I'd let him down. Big time.

"Frank Bridges had me peeing in a beaker," I said, "while somebody was shanking Fillmore."

"Is that standard procedure, patients undergoing drug screens in the middle of the afternoon?"

I thought about it. "I guess it wasn't uncommon. They like to keep things random in the hope of catching lunatics deliberately avoiding their meds."

"Or from taking each other's."

"The point is, we had this thing, Fillmore and me. We'd meet up for a game of pool, same time every day. It was one of the devices I used to gain his confidence."

"You mean you let him beat you."

"Sometimes. Bridges knew about the arrangement. He'd never interrupted us before. When I got to the recreation room, Fillmore wasn't there. I waited five minutes before going in search."

"And that's when you found him bleeding out? Doesn't it strike you as a little odd he should be killed right before he's about to come clean?"

It had crossed my mind, more than once. The timing was impeccable. For three whole months, Fillmore had remained a locked safe. All his secrets secure inside. I'd spent weeks working on his combination, without any of the tumblers falling. Then, the day before Christmas Eve, something had changed. He'd spoken about his accountancy work for the first time at length. Nothing of any real value. But it was an opening. I'd glimpsed inside the safe, had a hint of the information I'd been assigned to obtain. I'd retired to my cot that night, knowing when the next day came Fillmore would tell me everything.

"They killed him to keep him quiet." I realized. "They got to someone on the inside and they silenced him."

"Exactly my worry. It points to someone tipping them off."

I smirked, "It explains why you've been one step behind Fillmore's employers the whole time. Somebody in the know has been feeding them information. That's why the operation's been beset with setbacks, Stone. Congratulations. It looks like you got yourself a mole."

Suddenly, the Brit looked even more cheerless than usual.

I knew what he was thinking: if Fillmore's death was a deliberate act of sabotage, then its implication was sweeping. At best, it meant an immediate and in-depth scrutiny into the backgrounds of everyone with inside knowledge of the operation. No stone left unturned, so to speak. Checks into the private lives of prison officers and special agents alike. Who owed what to whom, and why. Who had a lifestyle open to exploitation. Who had the balls to pull it off. At best, it indicated a major leak which could deflate Stone's showboat and sink it faster than he could bail it out. At worst, it had cost Fillmore his life and maybe the lives of all those we were trying to protect with our undercover operation.

"So what happens now, Stone? You going to ship me back to the workshop for more panel beating?"

The comment actually pulled a wry smile from his lips.

"Don't think for one minute I haven't toyed with the idea. Burnett told me what happened in Alaska. She's worried about your coping mechanisms. I'm worried you'll kill somebody innocent. For your own good and for the welfare of everyone around you, I ought to send you straight back to Springfield, Quinn. I'm not convinced you're fixed. I'm not entirely sure if it's even possible. You're an unexploded bomb. You can put on a brave face all you like. Fool everyone into believing you're okay. But I know how shock works. When you least expect it, it sneaks up and bites you on the arse. And that's when you're at your most dangerous – because that's when you're liable to self-destruct and end up eating your gun."

"The last bad picture I saw painted like that, they called it a masterpiece."

Stone sniggered. "Yeah, you're one of those all right. But for all the wrong reasons. Quinn, I know what makes you tick, remember? I know what motivates you. You won't rest until you bring down this Gary Cornsilk character, with or without my consent. But I have this niggling doubt, this little voice of caution whispering in my ear, warning me to keep you reined in and as far away from trouble as possible. And therein lies my dilemma." He studied me though eyes so narrowed they could have been closed. "What to do about Quinn? Compassionate leave may be the right course of action, but I'm not certain it's the best thing for you."

I let my dark wishes show. For all his pomp and ceremony, Stone understood me. He knew I couldn't let sleeping dogs lie. He knew I'd do everything in my power to hunt down the killer of my child. Wouldn't anyone? He also knew my obsessive nature could work for both of us: he'd get an embarrassing ex-Fed off the streets and I'd get closure, maybe even start the long mend.

"What's the compromise?"

One thing I had learned about the Brit's style of command: there was always a middle ground with Mason Stone.

"You pull in your slack. Get your act together and make Fillmore's murder count for something."

"I'm already onboard with Operation Freebird."

"Make it fully. I need you focused and present. And I know that's asking a lot, given the circumstances. But let's finish what we started. Help me stamp out the nest of vipers that cost Fillmore his life."

"And what do I get in return?"

"Cornsilk's all yours."

35

Empty streets rolled by like scene changes in a stage play. Everything two-dimensional. Shuttered stores and dark alleyways, differing only by their location. I spread myself across the backseat of the taxi and dialed the cell number given to me before leaving Alaska.

On the surface, I had plenty to be happy about. Conditionally, I was a free man. My certificate of lunacy had been filed away. Behave myself and it would remain that way. I had a good job with the government. A nice home on a quiet street far away from trouble. A doting daughter on the other side of the country. An old relationship with the promise of a new start and a hopeful future. And my wife's murderer doing life in solitary, with no hope of parole. Plenty to be cheerful about, right?

I should have been in a celebratory mood. I wasn't.

My son was dead and it was all my fault.

Realization kept coming up and punching me in the teeth. Razor wire wrapped around my heart. There was a hole inside of me where something had been ripped out. Maybe my soul. It had filled up with hurt and pain and the terrible sensation of utter loss – a strangeness I was all too familiar with, but wished I wasn't.

No child should die before their parents. It goes against the natural order of things. Like the sun setting and never rising again. It felt like I didn't have any right being alive. Just breathing made me feel guilty. Losing Hope had crippled me emotionally for long hard months. It had stripped me bare, left me raw, like an exposed nerve. I'd barely recovered, barely found my feet again. Each day an ordeal. Forcing myself to exist in a vacuum in which I couldn't breathe. I wasn't sure I had the strength to go through it all again.

The number rang for a while, then a tired voice answered a muzzy *hello?*

"Locklear, it's me: Quinn."

I heard the Kodiak cop pull himself together on the other end of the connection. "Agent Quinn? It's late. What time is it? Where are you?"

"Forget that. Did you find the body?"

"The body?" I heard his metal cogs grating. "You mean the body from the clinic? Huh, no, I didn't. Listen, I'm in the middle of something. Can I call you back in the morning?"

"Are you kidding me, Locklear?" I didn't hide the aggravation in my tone. Locklear's attitude was borderline blasé. "What did you find at Engel's place?"

"Nothing."

"Nothing?" Now there was disbelief in the mix.

"I can't make it up, agent. I went through the whole place room by room. I even checked under the beds. Everything was in order. The doc's a respected member of our community. He's a stand-up character. What were you expecting?"

An upright guy with a penchant for S&M. I chewed lip. What had I hoped Locklear would find, aside from my son's cremated corpse and enough loud speakers to kit out a rock concert?

"If he has nothing to hide, why did he run?"

"Simple. You spooked him and he panicked."

"Which doesn't explain why he knocked the wind out of you, Locklear."

I heard him snicker, "That was my fault. I tried grabbing his shotgun. He just overreacted. I'm expecting he'll turn up when he's calmed down, say he's sorry and buy me a beer."

I wasn't convinced. "What about those outbuildings?"

"Far as I can tell, mostly storage. One housed a generator. Another is being used as a dog kennel. Everything checked out." I heard Locklear yawn loudly. "Look, do we really have to do this right now? It's late. I looked everywhere. There was nothing suspicious."

I held the phone in front of my face and stared at the word *Locklear* on the glowing screen. "Listen to me, Officer. I need you to go back over that place with a magnifying glass. Take sniffer dogs if you have to. Check every nook and cranny, twice. Look for concealed spaces. Engel stashed that body somewhere. While you're at it, go through that clinic of his. This is a Bureau priority. Mess up and the only job you'll have on the force is cleaning the station house toilets."

"Okay, okay. Give me a break, agent. I'll get to it. First thing in the morning."

"I'm serious, Locklear. This comes all the way from the top. Call me the second Engel shows up. Get it?"

"I got it, agent. Loud and clear. Message received and understood. Merry Christmas," he yawned and hung up.

Stone would have called Locklear's attitude *bloody useless*. I hovered on the side of deliberately difficult.

I spat out the wasp buzzing round in my mouth and jammed the phone back in my pocket.

*   *   *

I had a bunch of reasons to go home, but none of them seemed to matter all that much right now.

Difficult times ahead.

At some point in the very near future I had to call Grace. I needed to tell her the terrible news about her brother. And not just Grace. George had a wife – Kate, my beautiful daughter-in-law – who also had a right to know. He'd disappeared from both their lives, a year ago. I wasn't on my own. The devastation was far-reaching. I'd be expected to remain strong, shoulder their upset, but right at this minute I felt weak, old. How was I going to begin to explain why George had been burned to death in Alaska?

Delay. It was a coward's tactic, but it was Christmas and I couldn't bring myself to ruin it for them, forever. Losing someone close leaves a black stain on the calendar. Besides, I didn't have a body and no conventional funeral can be arranged without one.

Maybe I could hold off telling them until I'd brought George back and *Snakeskin* to bear.

Out of habit, I went somewhere other than home first. The taxi dropped me on Main Street in Alhambra, swiftly made a U-turn in the road and then screeched away, back toward LA.

It was almost 2 a.m., Thursday, and my body clock was keeping the wrong time. Like my father used to say *'Even a broken clock is right twice a day.'*

Stone had given me back my gun, with instructions to show my face at a case meeting twelve hours from now. With Fillmore gone (and with him his precious information) our group needed to talk new tactics. The nest of vipers Stone had referred to was an ongoing Bureau investigation known as *Operation Freebird*. It was an all-inclusive FBI undertaking, overseen by Washington, DC, and run from Stone's office on Wilshire Boulevard. As part of the deal keeping me out of the courts for the attempted murder of a federal agent, I'd been working on *Operation Freebird* since my involuntary reassignment to Springfield. My part had involved going undercover and drawing information from Trenton Fillmore, to help Stone prosecute his case against a human trafficking ring. The ring was bringing Russian girls into the country to be used as private sexual slaves. They were using Fillmore's accountancy skills to launder money through several shell companies. My part – essentially getting names and locations from Fillmore - had failed. Not sure where that left me. All the same, Stone wanted me onboard, still –

probably to keep an eye on me. The upside of it was, when it came to hunting down *Snakeskin*, I'd have the full resources of the FBI at my disposal, plus a federal seal of approval to deal with him in any which way I liked.

And I liked the thought of doing something really bad.

I came to the 24-hour convenience store with the bar in back, pushed against the glass door without even noticing the place was drenched in darkness. When the door resisted, I stepped back and scanned the dark frontage.

Winston's has been around forever. Okay, maybe not quite prehistoric, but enough time for it to weld itself to the bedrock hereabouts and become something of an institution. The worse-for-wear watering hole isn't everyone's idea of a good time, but it serves a purpose – primarily, to give insomniacs someplace to hang out in the wee small hours.

Frowning, I checked my watch.

No lights on inside. No neon-blue fly zapper bringing down bugs in the window. Even the faded *Winston's* name sign, which was normally backlit, was out.

A card hung on the inside of the door. I'd never noticed it before. It was a rectangle of beige cardboard rimmed with silver tinsel. Faded red letters saying *Go Home – We Are*.

I frowned again, then remembered it was Christmas Day night. So much had happened in the last thirty-six hours, it was no surprise I was distanced from the Holiday festivities.

Even Winston Young deserved one day off each year.

I crossed the quiet street and headed home.

It was a calm winter's night in Alhambra. Cool by Southern California standards, but not in Alaska's neighborhood. I had the hooded shirt undone, working up the heat as I marched along Valencia. Even in the dark, the old street looked unchanged since the last time I'd been here. Maybe less fuller foliage on the trees and fewer flowers in the window boxes. But it had the same smell, the same familiar feel I always associated with home.

The house on Valencia.

The scene of two cold-blooded crimes against two women in my life, both at the hands of *The Maestro*. Could I still think of it as home after all that had happened?

Home is where the heart lies, right? But when the heart lies where is home?

Truth was, since Hope's death, I'd contemplated selling the house on Valencia, more than once. Not exactly prime real estate, but a nice enough neighborhood, especially for younger families with kids. Easy commuting into LA and the greater Metro Area. I'd be happy to get back what I'd paid for it. Move on. Start anew. Lay demons to rest. With a lick of paint and some TLC it would make a fine family home again someday. Suffer a bunch of happy kids running round it. A loving husband and wife making plans and putting down roots. Banking on a place to invest memories. But there was low demand on crime scenes these days. Aside from weirdos or groupies, who wanted to live in the house from *Psycho*?

I moved through cones of yellow street lighting, following the undulation of the worn sidewalk. Christmas lights sparkled in garden trees. Illuminated snowmen and snow-women huddling in glowing groups, smiling at me as I passed. Flashing reindeer on rooftops, being chased by portly Santas. All was normal in the suburbs.

But murder was on my mind.

I wondered what Rae was doing right now, and realized I was already missing her. In the space of twenty-four hours she'd had a huge impact on me. Team Tennessee all over again. She'd reawakened old feelings, old stirrings I'd thought fossilized, buried. Given me something to live for and perhaps to die for.

George.

Suddenly, hot bile burned at my throat. I came to a juddering stop and leaned against a light pole, grabbed a lungful of air.

Grief hits in waves. It crashes against our emotional shores, dragging us dangerously out of our depth. Sometimes the surge brings fresh insights into what lies beneath, but most of the time it just erodes.

I swallowed down the bile and moved on.

I had twelve disposable hours before the case update meeting in which to get my head around losing my son for the second time and to find out which stone *Snakeskin* had slithered under. For now, I was on the Bureau's payroll. Like it or lump it. Stone had the power to send me back to the Fed Med anytime he saw fit. I didn't like it. I didn't have much choice. No one was interested in my sob story. If I wanted to be free to chase Cornsilk my way, I had to show willing, help them crack the Russian sex ring.

Besides, I felt obligated to nail the son of a bitch responsible for Fillmore's murder, whoever that might be.

Stay busy. Stay focused. Stay in control. Most of all, stay out of trouble.

I could hear a dog barking in a faraway backyard. A warring couple having a heated row in an upstairs bedroom, something about overcooked ham and a dominating mother-in-law.

Welcome home.

My house on Valencia was right where I'd left it. Nothing special. A two-floor dwelling set back from the roadside behind an uneven patch of grass and a weeping cherry tree. I lingered where the crazy-paved front walk greeted the sidewalk, and looked the old place over.

For the most part, I have good neighbors; they know what I do for a living and they stay respectfully out of my business, which doesn't bode well for the upkeep of my property. Mine isn't the only overgrown plot on the street, but it's no excuse. I'd let things get a little out of

Keith Houghton

hand since Hope's death. Let the grass grow tall and the need for major repairs grow short. More important matters to attend to, I guess. I used to keep on top of things, take pride in pulling up weeds and painting the boards. Didn't seem much point anymore.

After a long summer of unchecked growth, the property should have looked like an abandoned parcel of land. One of those backwoods ramshackle affairs you see in scary B-movies. It didn't. Someone had cleaned the place up: the front lawn was trimmed to within an inch of its life; the paintwork was proudly sporting a new winter coat; the cracks in the driveway were smoothed over with a fresh skim of cement. In fact, the whole place looked plumped up – as if it were an inflatable that had been losing air for a long time and somebody had plugged the leak, then breathed new life into it.

Crazily, I glanced up and down the street, wondering if I'd inadvertently stopped at the wrong house. My old jalopy wasn't on the drive – then I remembered Agent Melody Seeger had wrecked it when she'd run over Gus Reynolds in the summer.

Curious, I jangled keys out of my pocket and cautiously approached the front door.

No unread junk mail jamming up the mailbox. No muddy work boots growing roots by the stoop. No signs that the mice were at play while this cat was away.

The key fit the lock perfectly. Again, I scanned up and down the street before opening the door, foolishly feeling like an intruder in my own home.

Last time I'd been here the place had smelled of disinfectant and various astringents used by the crime scene cleanup crew – better than a whiff of evil, but only marginally. I'd found my good friend and therapist Eleanor Zimmerman at death's door in the master bedroom. *The Maestro* had shackled her to the bed with piano wire and left her there to bleed out – in the same way Hope had been left there to die eighteen months earlier. A repeat performance commanding no applause. Now there was a definite trace of baked cookies in the air and maybe even a hint of vanilla from one of those scented candles they sell at department stores.

Had Martha Stewart taken up residence in my absence?

I waited for my eyes to adjust to the gloom. Everything looked neat and tidy. Windows washed. Wood polished. Carpets vacuumed. The Pearson's across the street had spare keys. Maybe the housework was nothing more out of the ordinary than a good neighbor doing a good deed.

I dropped keys in the dish on the hall table and shucked off the hooded shirt. I thought about making a coffee, then decided against it. I was pumped all right, but I hadn't slept properly since Springfield. I had a long day ahead. Two assignments to divide my time and keep me on the streets. Instinctively, I wanted to be proactive, call every phone number on Cornsilk's tourist map, to get out there and sniff out *Snakeskin's* slimy trail while it was still warm. But despite my mental gears whirring away, physically I was beat. Soporific Sanibel had put my insomnia to rest. It had reset my circadian system. I no longer survived on caffeine and catnaps. Bed was the smart move whichever way I looked at it.

I was about to retire when I noticed a pencil-line glow drawn around the basement door.

I halted with my foot hovering over the first stair tread.

The light was on in the basement, I realized.
Somebody was in my house!

*   *   *

I wasn't expecting Goldilocks. I didn't check who'd been sleeping in my bed or eating me out of house and home. Omitting Cinderella, fairytale characters rarely do the

181

dishes. I slid out the Glock and eased open the basement door. The light was definitely on down there, casting long oblong shadows up the wall from the wooden steps. Either my new housemaid had left it that way by accident, or there was somebody in my den.

If an Englishman's home is his castle, then an American man's den is his home. Put simply: any kind of invasion will be met with absolute force.

I squinted against the light as I tiptoed gingerly down the first wooden steps. Without descending more than halfway I couldn't see beyond the squared-off outcrop where the first floor formed the basement's ceiling.

I hollered: "Police!" Then remembered I was FBI. I didn't correct myself verbally. Either way, there was no response. No interlopers scurrying to escape.

I followed the Glock down more steps, got low enough to grab a peek underneath the outcrop.

Not only had somebody invaded my sanctuary, they'd kindly rearranged the furniture, too. The big projection TV was moved over to the far wall, covering most of my *Undertaker* notes still pinned there. Facing it, with its back to the stairs, was my big leather La-Z-Boy. The computer desk was pushed over to one side, with cardboard packing boxes stacked on and around it, no signs of the desktop. Handwritten words on the boxes such as *party gear, personals, paperwork.* The collapsible cot bed from the storage room upstairs was installed against the opposite wall, with linens neatly folded open. The beer cooler was chilling out next to the recliner, with an opened bottle of two-year-old *Samuel Adams Octoberfest* standing to attention on its surface.

My basement. My cooler. My Sammy Adams.

Heat bloomed in my gut.

I descended another two steps.

The TV was turned on. What looked like a chick flick was playing in silence on the screen. I could see a tearful Julia Roberts giving lip service to a grinning

Cameron Diaz. A curly cable stretched across the gap between the TV and the La-Z-Boy, where it joined up with a pair of big padded headphones sitting either side of a man's head, back to me.

My home invader was watching the TV!

I jumped the remainder of the steps and came round between the cot and the La-Z-Boy. Glock aimed. Heart thudding.

The intruder was sprawled across the recliner, unclothed, apart from a pair of shocking-white Calvin Klein boxer shorts. Fortunately for me, there was a bucket of *Redenbacker's* popcorn on his lap. A big stupid grin was splitting his big stupid face. He was lapping up the chick flick with a fervor, so engrossed in it that he hadn't seen me sneaking up and aiming the gun at his too-close-together eyes. I lifted a foot and jabbed his knee with the toe of my hiking boot.

The popcorn promptly launched itself into the air. He tore off the headphones and gawped like an adolescent found trying on his mom's underwear.

"What gives, Tim?" I asked as it started raining popcorn. "Why are you in my house and who the hell gave you permission to drink my beer?"

36

I have known Tim Roxbury longer than is good for my health.

We first met in January, during my investigation into The Undertaker Case. I was power-napping in a parking lot at the time. Pendulous drool and a bib full of broken potato chips. He was an Alhambra PD motorcycle cop back then, checking out a suspicious-looking sleeper in an old jalopy. We'd hit it off like The Odd Couple confined to a phone booth. A few days later, Tim went on to save my self-respect after I was drugged in a nightclub on Santa Monica Boulevard. Six months after that, during my investigation into the Piano Wire Murders, he'd effectively trashed that same self-respect after a botched chase culminating in the death of an innocent citizen, Gus Reynolds.

Detective Tim Roxbury of the Alhambra PD wasn't exactly the Robin to my Batman. More like that pesky Donkey in the Shrek movies.

I kept the Glock centered on the small indentation between his eyes. "Give me one good reason why I shouldn't arrest you for breaking and entering."

His hands were in the air, flapping. Popcorn popping from his mouth. "Jeez Louise, Gabe – how about, because I'm your friend?"

I kept the Glock aimed.

"And because this isn't what it looks like," he added, fishing for tips.

I made a disgruntled grunt and stowed the gun. "I'll tell you exactly what this looks like, Tim. You spied your chance to take over while I was away. You moved in. Made yourself right at home. Okay, so you've done the place up.

Caught up on all the jobs I'd been meaning to do these past two years. You've given the old place a new lease of life. Probably brought smiles to the faces of all my despairing neighbors. You took siege of my basement. Got merry over Christmas on my beer. You entertained yourself with my dead wife's DVD collection, I see. And you didn't bargain on me coming home for the Holidays. Doesn't make it okay. How am I doing so far?"

He lowered his hands. "You got me dead to rights, Gabe. Go ahead, throw the cuffs on and march me off to jail." He nodded at the logo on my shirt. "What's with the Kodiak tourist tee?"

"It's a long story. And not really any of your business."

"You're angry."

"You broke into my home, Tim. I have every right to be angry."

"Well, that's not exactly true. One of your neighbors aided and abetted. She gave me a key."

"Under false pretenses, no doubt."

"No, not at all. Mrs. Pearson knows me from my patrol days. She had no problem handing it over."

"Did she know you were staying?"

"Sure. She even baked me a pie. We've been throwing Tupperware parties ever since." He stuck out his tongue. There was an indentation in it, made by a previous piercing. "I guess we have a lot to talk about. Didn't you miss me even a little bit?"

"Like an abscess in a root canal."

Tim got to his feet and opened up his muscly arms. A six foot something side of tanned beef in white boxers. He waggled fingers. "Come here, come on. It's Christmas! Give your old pal a big hug."

I made weary a face. "Don't make me regret not shooting you, Tim. I'm making coffee. Then you're going to explain yourself in full." I retreated to the stairs. "And put some damn clothes on."

"Why, does my sexuality make you nervous?"
"No, because it's my house and that's the rule."

37

On the whole, people have genuine reasons for behaving the way they do. It's always different when you're in the box than out of it. Often, we act on impulse – *seemed like a good idea at the time* – or make decisions based on a set of personal rules and parameters built up over time and through experience, rather than the hard facts. We all are different, which means, given the same set of circumstances, we are likely to think something totally different and act accordingly.

Tim's story had a tent pitched in both camps and went something like this:

As of the end of September, the fortysomething rookie detective had lived with his mom in rented accommodation on Kendall Drive – less than a mile as the crow flies from my house on Valencia. His mom had battled with emphysema for a number of years and had finally lost the war. Since Tim's name hadn't been on the tenancy agreement, the landlord had decided to sell rather than lease, and Tim had found himself homeless. Instead of doing what anyone in his position would have done – namely renting someplace else or staying at a motel until the right bachelor pad came along – he'd moved into my home and used what money he should have been paying out in rent to do the house up. According to Tim, he'd been keeping a voluntary eye on my place since I'd fled to Florida in February. With my vanishing into thin air, Tim's moving in had killed two birds with one stone. He'd sweet-talked Mrs. Pearson into giving him my spare key, then he'd kicked off his pink cowboy boots and settled in.

I wasn't happy about his home invasion. Who would be? It wasn't like Tim was family, or an old and needy friend or anything. But I was mindful of the fact he'd made good in my absence. The new improved me had brought out the old amenable me, and somehow I understood. My life wasn't a Dickensian drama; I wouldn't see anyone out on the streets at Christmastime, even if they got paid for it.

"To cut a long story short," Tim breathed as we drank coffee at the breakfast nook in my tidy kitchen, "it was never meant to be a permanent solution. The area had a spate of burglaries while you were away. They broke into a house a few doors down. I spent the night. Then, before I knew it, one thing led to another and the Holiday season was here. Look, Gabe, my sister has a place over in Pomona. I'll give her a call. See if she can squeeze me in. Don't worry; I'll be out of your hair come morning."

"Tim . . ."

"No, seriously, Gabe. I don't want to be an incongruence."

"Encumbrance."

"It's a small one-bed apartment and she has three kids and another on the way. Then there's the two dogs. German Shepherds both. But I'm sure there's room on the couch."

I sighed, "Tim."

He looked at me over his coffee.

"There's no need to rush. I'm not heartless. I understand you're in a tight spot. I know it's not easy finding a new place this time of year. Truth is, I'm through fighting over lost causes. Charity begins at home, right?"

Tim gawped at me like I'd just confessed undying love. It was the last thing he'd expected. "You mean it?"

I nodded. Sometimes living with an itch is better than scratching the skin away and opening things up to infection. "Let's face it, I'm hardly ever here as it is. And I am grateful for all the hard work you've put into the old place. You've done a fine job of making it habitable again.

The least I can do is let you stay on until you get fixed up with a place of your own."

His face lit up like one of those illuminated snowmen. "No catches?"

"Just don't get under my feet or start mothering me."

"What about bringing guys home?"

"Don't push it, Tim."

He tapped his cup against mine. "Okay. You got yourself a deal."

We drank coffee.

Tim's company wasn't as uncomfortable as it had been a year ago. Like fungi on a tree trunk he'd grown on me. Or I'd mellowed. Not yet close friends, but I had a feeling it was Tim's goal.

"Say, now that we're on speaking terms again," he began, "what did you make of my emails?"

"The truth?"

He nodded.

"I didn't read them."

"You're joking?"

"No, Tim, I'm not. I've been busy working undercover. I haven't had time to read emails or get my nails done."

Tim made a huffing noise, got up from the breakfast bar and disappeared into the living room. A few moments later, he returned with an iPad and slid it across the granite counter.

"You have got to see this. You won't believe your eyes. For all of sixty minutes it was hot property on YouTube. And I mean blazing. In total, there were at least twenty other videos just like it. I succeeded in downloading five – including this one – before YouTube pulled the plug on them all."

Frowning, I tilted the iPad to get a better view. There was a jerky video playing, on full-screen. A crackly soundtrack of scratchy traffic noise punctuated with horrified screams. I put my readers on and peered closer.

The homemade movie had been filmed outside on a busy street from a camera phone held at arm's length. It looked like a few famous Hollywood landmarks in the background. I could see crowds gathered in the periphery of the shot – many of them holding up smart phones, all of them looking shocked or spellbound, all of their attentions focused on a gushing column of orange fire in the middle of the screen. At first I thought it was a protest march and somebody had torched a full-sized human effigy. Then I realized with horror that there was movement within the fire. Arms and hands thrashing futilely at the flames. The semblance of a face melting away.

"What the hell is this, Tim?"

"It happened last week. On the sidewalk outside Grauman's Chinese Theatre."

"Somebody went up in flames on Hollywood Boulevard?"

He nodded. "Seems unbelievable, doesn't it? The place was jam-packed with visitors, too."

I could see. Dozens of pausing passersby, all there to enjoy the Christmas nostalgia, but all witness to this horror show instead. I watched with morbid fascination as the burning figure fell to its knees and collapsed face-first to the glittery sidewalk. Arms and legs still twitching.

"By the time anyone thought to grab an extinguisher, the poor shmuck was burned beyond recognition. What a way to go, huh?"

I froze the blazing video. I'd seen enough. This was too close to home right now and I was getting itchy feet.

Tim took the iPad from my hands and flicked at icons on its screen. "Hollywood Boulevard was closed down for two hours while the emergency services cleaned up. I hear they had to scrape him off the sidewalk."

The coffee in my belly was turning to tar.

"Why are you showing me this, Tim?"

He spun the iPad back my way and touched the *play* icon on another downloaded video. "Watch and all will become clear."

Against my better judgment, I looked on.

This second home movie had been shot from a different angle. By the looks of it, filmed from across the street. Same crowds gathered. Same sunny day in LA. Same guy in the middle of the shot – only at this point in the recording he wasn't engulfed in flame.

Curious, I spread my finger and thumb across the screen. The image zoomed in to show the guy was dressed in a Santa costume, complete with fluffy white beard and black buckled boots. Nothing extraordinary for Hollywood at Christmastime. He was standing on the curbside, facing the road, with the famous Chinese theater in backdrop. A sandwich board hung over his shoulders. Fountains of bright sparks were spurting out into the air on either side. Fiery plumage drawing attention. I could hear people wondering out loud what the guy was doing. I could see onlookers pointing. The guy in the Santa suit looked like he was part of a promotional campaign. One of those gimmicks to lure punters off the street and into one of the nearby restaurants. Then I noticed the writing on the sandwich board, and zoomed in until it completely filled the screen.

No lunchtime discounts here. No exclusive show tickets for the Cirque du Soleil at the Highland Center.

Just five uppercase words written in bold red paint:

THIS IS ALL YOUR FAULT

I watched, mouth drying, as fire swept suddenly across the lettering and turned the sandwich board into a raging inferno.

*   *   *

"Breathe, Gabe, or you'll force me to give you mouth-to-mouth."

I gave Tim a *back off and rethink* scowl. I poured scalding coffee over my tinder-dry throat. Didn't feel it go down.

I'd seen those exact same words scrawled on the mirror in Westbrook's hotel room in Kodiak – *in George's room* – written by Cornsilk's homicidal hand. Seeing them again here could only mean one thing: *Snakeskin* had killed in Hollywood before coming to Alaska. No other way to explain it. He'd burned somebody to death on a crowded street at the height of the business day. Everything caught on camera.

I knew the connection. But how had Tim made it?

He saw the question bubbling its way through my scorched larynx and reached for a stack of mail at the end of the counter. "I wouldn't have given the videos a second thought, if I hadn't seen this first." He picked up a postcard from the top and handed it over.

"You read my mail?"

"It's a postcard," he countered. "It's not marked top secret."

I looked at the glossy picture on the front. It was a panoramic cityscape taken at night from an aerial viewpoint. A necklace of illuminated hotels encrusted with jewels, with a taller structure in the foreground. A sweeping concrete column with big glass observation windows reflecting the night-time neon. There was a splash of text across the image: *Stratosphere, Las Vegas*.

The tar in my belly turned to pitch.

Showdown with *The Undertaker*.

A cold Nevada night at the wrong end of January. The tallest tower west of the Mississippi. A thousand foot above the glittery Las Vegas Strip. After a week chasing a psychic serial killer, I'd come face to face with my son, and my whole world had fallen from a great height. George had abducted my new police partner, Jamie Garcia, and my old

FBI friend, Bill Teague, taken them hostage. In a crazy twist to make me feel his pain, George had blasted away one of the big windows with Jamie's gun and then thrown her out into the gaping maw. He'd attempted to do the same with Bill. But Sonny Maxwell of the Metro PD had shot him twice from behind. George had fallen through the deadly hole, taking Bill down with him. Miraculously, I'd managed to grab hold of Bill, pulling him to safety as George had fallen away, seemingly to his death. I'd made a split second decision. Saving Bill had meant killing my boy. I'd learned later that George had survived. He'd BASE jumped to safety, gotten his wounds patched up, and promised me my pain had only just begun.

Feeling sickly, I turned the postcard over and saw my name and address written on the reverse, in red marker, together with the words:

THIS IS ALL YOUR FAULT

"When did this arrive?"

"Early last week – a few days before the videos went viral."

"And you just happened to be surfing YouTube at the time they were all uploaded?"

Tim made a hurt expression. "I don't think I like your tone, Gabriel."

"And I don't like the fact you broke into my home, Timothy. Get over it; I did. Now level with me."

He chewed some cheek, then said: "This won't work if you resent my being here. I really do appreciate your charity. I'm more than happy to pay my way. But you've got to stop with the guilt trip."

"It's been a long couple of days."

"Besides, there's no big mystery here. A friend of mine works the afternoon shift at the Hard Rock. He was running an errand when the human torch decided to go nuclear. That second video, he shot it on his cell. Called me up afterwards. As soon as I saw those words, I remembered I'd already seen them on this postcard, and emailed you right away. Only you didn't read my emails."

"Let me see the rest of the videos."

Tim queued them up on the media player, then set about making a fresh jug of hot black.

Except for the video shot by Tim's friend, the other four were all filmed from the same side of the street, but from slightly different perspectives. Three started with the guy already ablaze and pretty much told the same story as the first two.

The fourth was different.

It didn't even begin with its attention on the guy in the Santa suit. It was a longer clip. A typical tourist capture – sweeping up and down the street and randomly zooming in and out as it filmed the various sights of Hollywood Boulevard. More than a minute passed by before I spotted the guy in the Santa suit appear in the crowd, walking directly toward the camera. He was already drawing attention as he cut a swathe through the crowds, elbowing people aside and eliciting terse retorts. I watched him take up his position on the sidewalk, then reach down and pull a cord attached to the edge of the sandwich board. Sparks began to fly. The crowds all turned to face the display, forming a six-deep semi-circle around him. They pointed their smart phones, going starry-eyed as the sparks showered the sidewalk. I saw him pull another cord and that's when everything went up in smoke. The video jerked as the crowds withdrew instinctively. The *ooh's* and *ah's* turned to screams and holy exclamations. Within a heartbeat, the guy in the Santa suit was completely enveloped in seething flames.

I stopped the playback and skipped right back to the point where the recording had switched to a westward view down Hollywood Boulevard. I centered the image to where I'd pictured the guy first appearing in the crowd, then pinched the screen until it was zoomed in to the max.

"Seen something?" Tim asked as he placed a coffee cup on the counter next to me.

"I'm not sure. Maybe."

I was interested in seeing where the guy in the Santa suit had come from. He hadn't just materialized on Hollywood Boulevard with a heavy sandwich board. And no one could have walked very far in those cumbersome Santa boots. It suddenly occurred to me that maybe *Snakeskin* had given him a ride – in which case, maybe there was a vehicle and a plate number, and possibly a lead.

Big blurry heads moved across the screen.

The zoom exaggerated the camera shake, making it difficult to watch. Through a gap, I spied the guy in the Santa suit and hit the *pause* icon.

He was barely a fleck of red and white, with only his upper half visible above a fuzzy landscape of blurred heads. He appeared to be standing on the street corner outside Madame Tussauds, facing the opposite corner. No sign of the sandwich board. I rewound the recording by just a few seconds and ran it again. Indistinct shapes shifted across the screen. Then I was presented with the same glimpse of him standing on the street corner. The person shooting the footage hadn't caught him in the frame prior to this point. I let the recording resume. The image jiggled about, affected by the shooter's movements. I saw the guy in the Santa suit raise a hand – maybe in a wave – right before the camera angle shifted and the crowds blotted him out completely. I waited, watching, hardly breathing. Several long seconds later, the shapes parted to reveal big red words coming toward the camera:

THIS IS ALL YOUR FAULT

I pinched the screen and zoomed out a little, just enough to reveal the guy in the Santa suit in full. Paused it.

His face was masked by the fluffy white beard and low-quality camera-work. No way to make a positive ID.

He looked about six foot and of average build. No identifying features other than the fake portly belly and maybe a wisp of blond hair sticking out from beneath the Santa hat. On the outside, the sandwich board looked ordinary enough. But it had been packed with pyrotechnics, designed to maximize attention. Hollywood Boulevard was a busy place at that time of day, I knew. Hundreds of people milling about, all spellbound as the real fireworks had kicked in and engulfed the guy in flames.

Snakeskin had burned him alive and in public, without actually striking the match himself. I wanted to know why.

"He had an accomplice," Tim said. "Didn't he?"

I nodded. "Reckon so. What did the police say about this?"

"Nothing special. I knew it was significant, so I asked around. As far as I could determine, the LAPD put it down to an accident and chalked it up as a stunt gone wrong."

"And what do you think, Tim?"

His too-close-together eyes widened. "The great Celebrity Cop's asking my opinion?"

"Don't blow it."

"All right. I'll take it under advertisement."

"Advisement."

"That's what I said. Okay, let's look at the facts. You received a postcard with the same phrase on it that later showed up on some guy torching himself to death in public. Want to know what I think?"

"That's what I'm waiting to hear."

"It isn't the work of chance. He wanted you to make the connection. He wanted you to sit up and take notice."

"Who?"

"The guy who set up this poor sap. The accomplice. Gary Cornsilk. See, Gabe, I'm not as stupid as I look."

*   *   *

I wasn't sure about his last statement, but I was sure Tim had seen more than he was admitting to.

He saw my reaction and made a *brakes-on* gesture. "Jeez Louise. Relax. I haven't been stalking you, if that's what you think."

"That's not what I'm thinking, Tim. I'm thinking you've watched more than Hope's copy of My Best Friend's Wedding. You've seen the video of Hives being burned alive, haven't you?"

He made a blameless face. "What do you want me to say? You didn't exactly leave me with much in the way of choice. It was in the DVD player when I moved in. Imagine my surprise when I accidentally came across this Hives guy going up in flames."

I pushed back from the breakfast bar. "Exactly how did you connect Cornsilk to his snuff movie?"

"I'm a detective, remember? I'm good at my job. Like when I connected Gus Reynolds to the Piano Wire Murders."

"Tim, Gus Reynolds was an innocent bystander, who died because we chased after him and because I was crazy enough to buy into your off-the-wall conspiracy theories."

If Tim was offended by my challenge, he didn't show it. "You mean because Melody Seeger deliberately ran over him. That's what really happened that night, Gabe. You were set up. We were set up. Seeger had her sights on you from the second you set foot in LA. She was working with The Maestro, silencing anyone they thought could give their game away. You've got to stop blaming yourself for things outside your scope of effluence."

"Influence," I corrected.

"Yeah, well, it's all a piece of crap whichever way you look at it." He rested his big forearms on the counter. "As for Cornsilk, I asked Wayne Stuber."

"Who's Wayne Stuber?"

"Your friend from Winston's. The guy with the dreadlocks and the miserable mug."

"You mean Dreads?" I realized in ten years of knowing him I'd never learned his real name. Dreads had always preferred it that way. After all, I was a cop and he was antiestablishment.

"I've known Wayne for years," Tim continued. "I dated his older brother for a while. Cute kid with great glutes. He had this way of dislocating his hips so that he could –" He saw my disapproving frown and caught himself. "Anyway, his family still live in the neighborhood, out by the elementary school? I knew about the agreement between you and Wayne, and so I worked it to my favor. I convinced him we were working together."

"And he coughed up the whole enchilada, just like that?"

"Only about Cornsilk. He didn't betray you, if that's what you're worried about. At first he didn't want to play ball. Then I explained he wasn't covered by data protection or client confidentiality, and that the three of us were all on the same side."

In August, Dreads had unearthed Cornsilk's FBI discharge papers, after Cornsilk had tried blowing up Jack's Sanibel home with me inside. Months later, Tim had told Dreads about the guy with the melted face he'd seen on the DVD in my player. He'd given Tim the information, thinking he was helping me out.

"So I know all about Gary Cornsilk. Dumb shmuck. It doesn't take a genius to figure out he's the one behind the human torch."

"He came after me in Florida," I said.

Tim's face was a picture. I proceeded to tell him about the car bomb and the booby-trap setup in Jack's place. I didn't mention my exploits in Alaska – no need, not yet.

A glance at the wall clock told me it was four hours past my bedtime. Institutionalized. "I need sleep," I yawned.

"Any objections to my finishing the romcom?"

"Knock yourself out."

Tim headed down to the basement. I made my way to the living room and fell into the couch. I pulled one of Hope's crocheted throws over my tired frame. It smelled of Jasmine and kindled memories of happier times.

I rolled onto my back and stared at the ceiling.

I had a head full of hornets. Their collective buzz sounding like flames searing into flesh, cracking and crackling.

I was home.

But it didn't feel like home anymore.

In the past two years, my life had been turned upside down and crushed flat by the weight of loss. My wife had died and now my son was dead. Half my family gone and what was left of it in ruins. This place used to be alive with the shouts of teenagers, the thunder of music, the weary complaints of parents. Now it was silent. Dead. All those happy memories vacuumed up and dumped in the trash.

I sniffed at the throw, wishing Hope was here.

Tim had done a great job sprucing the place up, but to me it felt like a tomb. I could feel the ceiling pressing down. The master bedroom lay directly above. The scene of two terrible crimes against two women in my life. One had died and one had left me for dead. I hadn't been upstairs properly since finding Eleanor Zimmerman wired to the bed at the hands of *The Maestro*. Not sure I ever wanted to again.

Sooner or later I'd have to put the place on the market.

There was no way Tim could crash here indefinitely.

I wasn't even sure I could.

I lay perfectly still for some time, going over the falling domino events since leaving Springfield. I got to the part where I'd realized George was the victim on the beach and felt the upset surge. I tried my best to hold it at bay, but it forced tears into the corners of my eyes and left me with a vile taste in my mouth.

I knew delaying to deal wouldn't postpone my pain. I knew there was worse to come, more floods of tears, more angry fists clenched at the heavens. Right now I was still deep in shock mode and it was allowing me to function, to hold things together, to appear intact and collected. But I knew it was only a matter of time before the pressure built up to the point where I'd self-destruct.

I tried sleeping, but my dampened eyes and the demons laughing from the shadows prevented it. Eventually, I took out my phone and dialed Rae's number. I didn't know why, other than to sate a seed of an obsession. She answered after a dozen rings. The lilt of her voice helped deaden the buzzing in my brain.

"Gabe?" She sounded sleepy and rightly so. "Is everything okay?"

"Just missing you," I confessed.

"Already? That's so sweet. Damn you, Gabriel Quinn. I'm missing you, too." I heard her giggle, softly, sleepily. "Listen to us. We're regular sad examples of middle-aged teenagers."

"I spoke with Stone."

"I thought you might."

"We came to an understanding."

"That's promising. Really, a good thing, Gabe. I know y'all have your differences and all. But he has your best interests at heart. I know he does. I'm glad y'all worked something out. He speaks favorably of you. He holds you in high regard."

"You'd never guess so."

"Forgive him, Gabe; he's a proud Englishman. Stiff upper lip and all that, I guess. Bless his soul, he really does care. I told him about Alaska."

"He said as much. He also knows about George."

"Gabe . . ."

I listened to her breathing, used it to regulate my own. My heart was skipping beats for all the wrong reasons.

"I don't know what to say."

"Rae, you don't need to say anything," I said. "It's okay. I'm okay."

"Where are you?"

"Home."

"Me, too."

"Where?"

"A nice little house overlooking the ocean, just off Sunset. An inheritance and a fixer-upper," she added before I could ask how she'd afforded Pacific Palisades. 'Do you want to come over?"

"At a push, I can be there in thirty minutes."

I was tired, exhausted, but I would run on hormones, all the way to Rae's bedside, without a second thought. I'd spent four months in a cell, but the house felt even more claustrophobic.

"Gabe, I'd like that. Be careful. But please do rush."

38

Ironically, the Glenn Frey song *The Heat Is On* was warbling from the car stereo as he drove the nondescript van through the sleepy neighborhood, at a crawl.

He'd moved the beat-up Town & Country into the deep shadow behind of the convenience store before transferring Comb-Over's dead-weight into the rented vehicle. Wedged him in tight in the cargo space, in among the jerry cans brimming with gasoline. Then he'd driven southwest on Route 66 to the Pacific Ocean, soft rock hardening his ears.

Comb-Over had been a naughty boy.

He had to be taught a lasting lesson.

One of the few things his daddy had taught him was: play with fire and you risk burning fingers.

The fast-acting paralytic was keeping up its end of the bargain. Comb-Over was tranquilized, unable to move anything but his diaphragm, and maybe his eyelids – at a push.

Comb-Over didn't have to die right now. Not just yet. He could watch and learn. Gather together a few more sparks of life to flash before his eyes when his end came.

Brake lights shone briefly as he reached his destination.

He killed the engine. The music died.

Silence and darkness – two of his favorite things.

He reached for the Zippo lighter on the dash, flicked it open with his blunt thumb and watched the flame leap high.

The heat was on and bridges had to be burned.

39

Contrasts. My life, in a nutshell. The eternal struggle between good and evil.

Was it possible to be deliriously happy and dangerously bitter, both at the same time?

I borrowed Tim's motorcycle and set out for the address Rae had given me over the phone. I hadn't ridden a motorbike in a very long time – not since Hope and I had been young and childless – and I wasn't sure I could pull it off. But the Indian Chieftain fit like a glove and did most of the work without complaint.

"You sure you don't mind?" I'd asked Tim as he'd wheeled his prized possession out of my garage and given me a quick guided tour of the controls.

"Sure, but I owe you. Just do me a favor and bring her back in one piece. This baby is my dream machine."

And so I drove through the night, propelled by burgeoning love and yet pulled back by it, too. A dichotomy of emotions tearing me in half. Right now, I didn't want to be anywhere else other than in Rae's arms. Right now, I didn't want to be anywhere else other than chasing down the murderer of my son.

Opposing forces. Two halves pulling in opposite directions. Ultimately, something would snap.

Maybe me.

I gunned the engine and leaned into the ramp as it curved through the Harbor Freeway interchange. Then I floored it as the pavement leveled out. Not much traffic on I-10 westbound. I pressed the speedometer into the triple figures. Made long, sinuous ins-and-outs around the occasional slower vehicle. Wind in my hair. Vibrations purring. The sense of sheer speed and freedom, intoxicating.

I thought about my insane son and about how far he'd fallen from grace. I couldn't deny I'd played my part in his downfall. I saw that now. Therapy had rinsed the silt from my eyes. I hadn't just ignored his condition, I'd run away from it – like I had done all my life. Running genes ran in the Quinn family. According to George, I'd always put my work ahead of him, and he was right. Sometimes we have no choice. Sometimes we do. Deliberately, I'd buried myself in my work, aiming for one promotion after another. Out of the house more than in it. I'd let Hope deal – perhaps because she'd been better at it than me – never once stopping to think that I'd given her no choice. I'd always believed that when it came to ailing children, mothers coped better than fathers. Lame excuse. My absence had alienated my son and hammered a wedge between his mother and me. While I had turned a blind eye to their emotional needs, George had cleaved to his momma. I'd grown apart from them both and I hadn't seen it coming. The devil had spied his chance and taken siege of the space between us. It was my fault they were both dead. The hurt in my barbed wire heart was a small price to pay for what I'd done.

I noticed flashing lights in the bike's side mirror, and automatically eased off the gas, dropped back to the speed limit.

I thought about Rae and about where we were headed. I was still in a daze with it all. Shocked on two counts. I kept pinching myself and expecting to wake up. Unquestionably, being with Rae felt good. I couldn't deny it felt right. Look what I was doing! Rae's coming back into my life seemed too good to be true. I was hoping it wasn't. The last thing I wanted was for our rekindled relationship to burn itself out before the kindling had caught. I knew I was running from my pain, but I wanted to be with her in every sense of the word. Better still, I knew she felt the same way. We were like hormonal kids: we just wanted to spend every waking moment in each other's company, and to hell with everything else.

But everything else was the reason we were together.

A police cruiser shot past, doing eighty, easy, chased by red-and-blue specters sweeping along the retainer walls.

In short, the last two years of my life had been nothing less than a catastrophe. I didn't believe in beating a woe-is-me drum. But with Rae entering the picture I'd had a glimpse of something better, something brighter. When you're flat on the floor the only way is up, right?

I spied more emergency lights flashing in the mirror. I heard the high-pitched wail of multiple sirens. A second later, another police cruiser screamed by, followed by two more, both sides of the Chieftain.

They tore away into the night and darkness enveloped.

My thoughts turned to *Snakeskin* and to the YouTube videos showing his gruesome handiwork for all the world to see. I shuddered at the thought of meeting with such a grisly end. I was in no doubt Cornsilk was behind the killing; it had his name written all over it. But why? And who was the guy in the Santa suit? There were far easier ways to get my attention, if that had been his aim – unless it was all about the show. Was that it? Had *Snakeskin* wanted a public spectacle, an exhibition of his madness just to make me sit up and take notice? In his warped mind I knew I was his number one enemy. What I didn't know was if Cornsilk had learned of my incarceration at Springfield and gone solely after my son instead. If so, why kill someone in broad daylight on Hollywood Boulevard? What was I missing?

More than a dozen hours had passed since *Snakeskin* had dropped off the radar in Anchorage. He could be anywhere in the Pacific Northwest by now, thumbing rides or using public transportation. Farther afield if he'd travelled by air. No chance of tracking him until he started a paper trail. But he would turn up – of that I knew. *Snakeskin* was on a mission to avenge those he blamed for spoiling his good looks. If I didn't catch up with him first, I knew sooner or later he'd come looking for me.

I spotted the end of the freeway coming up, fast, and eased off the gas. The Chieftain thundered through the McClure Tunnel, then powered up again as it emerged onto the Pacific Coast Highway.

A salty breeze blew through my hair.

Rae's address resolved to a quiet lane that coiled around a cliff top in Pacific Palisades. Last house on the left, she'd said. It was an upmarket neighborhood of multi-million-dollar homes overlooking the Santa Monica Bay. About six zeroes above my pay grade. She'd insisted it was a fixer-upper, an inheritance, but I couldn't help wondering how Rae could afford its upkeep on her paltry Bureau salary.

I caught the right turn at West Channel and accelerated up the incline, with the dark Pacific unfolding behind me. The Chieftain chewed up the road. I leaned into the left curve, realizing I actually liked motorcycling, and then braked and made the next left onto Corona. Almost there. Butterflies performing aerobatics in my belly. I screwed a little more juice out of the throttle and leaned into the long right curve. Top of the cliff now. Impressive views of the night-washed ocean opening up. A tree-lined lane with big houses owning exclusive views.

Up ahead I could see a police cruiser parked lengthways across the road, barring passage, its roof lights splashing Christmas colors across the roadway.

I slowed, shifting down gears. The Chieftain's hot engine popped and clacked.

Beyond the black-and-white I could see more flashing lights belonging to several police cars parked helter-skelter on the street. Farther still, a pair of blood-red fire trucks from the Santa Monica FD with their neon blue turret lights illuminating nearby houses. I slowed the bike to a crawl. There were people out on their front walks, dressed in robes and slippers. Some gathered on the sidewalk, holding concerned conversations. Cops keeping them back. Firefighters unreeling long hoses and hooking them up to curbside hydrants. Through the shadowy trees I could see intense flames licking at the sky. Bright as molten gold. A house ablaze, with a churning column of black smoke reaching for the stars.

The cop manning the makeshift roadblock flapped a hand and I brought the Chieftain to a stop against the curb, pulled off the goggles.

"What's going on here, officer?"

"House fire," he said, matter-of-factly. "Looks like it's got a good hold. Road's going to be closed for quite a while. You'll want to back up and go down Altata."

I could smell the burn, feel the heat of it on the sea breeze, even from this distance. Be in no doubt – house fires are deathtraps. Especially those with a timber construction. Once the flames take hold, anyone unlucky enough to be inside is likely to remain that way.

I glanced up and down the street, trying to make out the big houses hidden behind the sidewalk trees.

"You live here?" the cop asked conversationally.

I knew what he was thinking: middle of the night, some bearded middle-aged guy in a lumberjack shirt and an *I Heart Kodiak* tee, sizing up the lay of the land.

"Just visiting," I answered. "As a matter of fact my partner lives here."

There. I said it. It was official.

"You got some ID I can see, sir?"

I sighed and brought out my FBI badge.

He squinted at it. "Oh, okay, Special Agent Quinn. Give me one second and I'll see about expediting your passage through here. Which is your partner's house again?"

"Last one on the left."

The cop's face paled. "Last house? You sure about that?"

"Positive."

"Then you've got yourself a serious problem, agent, because that's where the fire is and no one has come out of there alive."

*　　*　　*

If fear is the spark that ignites the touch-paper of the nervous system, then adrenaline is the body's combustible gunpowder.

And I went off like a rocket.

I'd hurdled the hood of the cruiser and hurtled into a sprint before the cop had spoken the last word. If he went to holler a warning I didn't hear it; the rush of blood to my head was booming. All at once my legs were pounding like pistons, accelerating my feet into a blur across the asphalt. Arms working the air. Teeth barred as muscles fizzed. All I could think about was getting to the last house on the left, and to . . .

Rae!

Hers was the house ablaze. I could see luminous orange serpents writhing against its timber walls. I could hear wood splintering. Plastic popping. Paint sizzling. I could see flaming Medusa heads poking out of broken window panes, hear their tortured screams as they raged at the night air. I heard hot glass shatter. Support beams creaking like the last dying moans of a shipwrecked galleon. I could see burning tumbleweeds of fire cartwheeling along the roof tiles. Thick acrid smoke belching skywards.

I shot between a pair of patrol cars. Several startled cops were slow to react. No one was expecting some nut, fresh from the nuthouse, making a direct dash to the fire.

All I could thinking about was . . .

Rae!

We'd spoken, barely thirty minutes ago. I knew she was home. If she weren't being comforted out on the street by a friendly neighbor or a Fire Department paramedic, then she was still inside the house. Still inside that raging inferno. And that meant . . .

I was so focused on the wall of flame that I failed to see the two firefighters intercept my mad bolt. But they saw me coming. They reached out big arms and grappled me against the shiny paneling of one of the fire trucks. Gloved hands holding tight. Terrified words spewing from my mouth: *I had to get into the house! Rae was in there! I had to get her out! They had to let me go!*

The fire burned brightly, cackling in a mocking tone.

A couple of burly cops took charge and manhandled me facedown on the hood of a police cruiser. I kicked and I thrashed like an apprehended drug dealer with pockets stuffed with crack cocaine. But they clung on, yanked my arms behind my back and threw on cuffs. More terrified words spewed forth: *they had to let me go! Rae was in the house! I had to get in there and get her out!*

But I wasn't going anywhere.

Flames soared high, pulled by spark-filled smoke.

The whole of Rae's house was afire. Every bit of wood blanketed in red-hot flame. No way was anyone going in without getting burned alive. No way was anyone coming out unless they already were.

With my cheek pressed firmly against the metalwork, I was unable to do anything except observe, helpless, as firefighters aimed hoses at the rampant blaze. The infernal beast fought back. Hissing and reeling.

Rearing up as the flaming serpents hissed and slithered for cover.

Vomit clawed at my throat.

I couldn't believe what I was seeing. No sign of Rae out on the street or sitting on the back plate of an EMS vehicle. I couldn't believe her house was on fire and she was inside.

"Cut him some slack," I heard someone shout. "He's a Fed."

Heavy-duty hands rummaged in my back pocket, then flipped me over. A no-nonsense beat cop compared my sickly pallor against my photo ID.

"She's a Fed, too," I blurted, voice racked with panic. "In there! This is her house! She's my partner, dammit! You've got to get her out of there!"

*   *   *

There are times in our lives when we feel utterly useless: listening to George's doctor tell us about his tangled brain chemistry for the first time; Hope lying in a coma at Cedars-Sinai, her prognosis grim; Jamie Garcia falling to her death from the Stratosphere Tower at the hands of her killer. This was one of them. Irrationally, I wanted to rush through the flames, do the superhero thing, find Rae and carry her out to safety. Realistically, I already knew it was too late.

Blood thumped behind my eyes.

Nothing I could do. Nothing anyone could do. The cops removed the handcuffs, but kept me restrained – they assured me for my own safety – while the firefighters did their job.

Despite the punishing heat, there was Alaska pack ice floating round in my belly.

No way could anyone have survived in that hellfire. *No way.*

40

Hardly any traffic on the road this time of night.

He drove the rented van west along the coast highway, out toward Malibu, listening to Jim Morrison trying to set his night on fire.

His blunt fingers strummed against the wheel. He was feeling exhilarated, mildly optimistic. One step closer to sealing the deal. To the final play. The showdown at the end zone.

Everything going according to plan.

In the cargo space behind him, his silent passenger rolled around on the floor, conscious but unable to lift a finger of protest.

Not dead.

Not yet.

41

It consumed the best part of an hour to completely put out the blaze in Pacific Palisades. One of the longest hours of my life, for sure. All the while, itching to rush in there, to rescue Rae, to do something. No way anyone was going in until it was absolutely safe to do so, and then only the Fire Department assessors in the first instance.

Throughout, I watched, nauseous and disbelieving, numbed, as the fire dwindled under the relentless deluge. Rage throttling my throat. The beast did its best to take refuge in the farthest reaches, but eventually the hoses exhumed the blackened remains of the house. A shattered shell of smoldering timbers emerged through the smoke. Wet burn in the air – horribly reminiscent of the boat bomb in Kodiak. Spectral lights revealing brief glimpses of skeletal wood and smoking limbs.

A soot-faced platoon commander splashed his way toward me through the black water coursing down the street. "Someone said you're the next of kin."

"I'm her partner," I breathed.

"I'm sorry for your loss." He confirmed it with a difficult nod. "We found the body in the bedroom. If it's any consolation, she was probably asleep and didn't know anything about it."

There it was: the irrefutable proof.

Rae was gone.

My old flame had died. But she hadn't been asleep. She'd been waiting for me. And now she was dead. Burned to death in her own home.

I steadied shaking legs against the patrol car and gasped for air.

All of a sudden the world was spinning crazily out of control.

Rae was dead!

The platoon commander shouted: "Get this man some water. And somebody get the detectives down here; this is now a crime scene."

Through acidic tears I stared at the blackened hulk of Rae's home. Every emotion imaginable fisting me in the gut.

Rae was gone.

No doubt about it now. Burned alive in her own bed. And I'd been too late to save her.

Someone handed me a glass of water as ashy flakes began to fall from the sky.

It was Christmas in California and it was snowing the remains of Rae's house all over the street.

*　　*　　*

I know procedure.

As raw recruits, it is drummed into us until we know it by rote. Every public service has its protocols. I haven't always followed them. In this case, I had no choice. It was the Fire Department's call. Not much I could do anyway. Even the yawning police detectives, who had shown up last minute, had to acquiesce to the FD's investigators sifting through the burnt debris.

Someone had died in the house fire on Corona, and a cause had to be established.

I sipped at the water. It tasted like vinegar.

Mute minutes dragged themselves painstakingly by.

All but one of the fire trucks cleared out, leaving overlapping tire tracks in the ashy snow. The police cordon stayed put. Most of the residents returned to their homes, to a restless rest of the night. Hard to sleep with red-and-blues lighting up the neighborhood. A van from the Scientific Investigation Division arrived. A pair of forensics techies got out and suited up, then carried heavy kit bags into the ruins of Rae's home.

I paced; the wait was torturous, draining.

Eventually, an inspector in firefighter gear came out of the wreckage, removed his helmet and spoke with the platoon commander. The big chief pointed in my direction, then waved the yawning detectives to come join him in a heated confab. The inspector came over, pulled off his heat-retardant gloves and stowed them in his helmet.

He offered a hand, "Morrissey. I'm an investigator with the Fire Department."

"Quinn."

"Commander says you're FBI."

I nodded. Steel neck sinews unyielding.

"The victim was your partner?"

I didn't say *in more ways than one.*

"A professional heads-up," he said. "We've confirmed what the chief suspected. We're formally treating this as arson. We found evidence of an accelerant used extensively throughout the property, and several five-gallon jerry cans out in the yard. Looks like the fire was started in several key locations, which then spread rapidly throughout the residence. Judging from the amount of accelerant, we calculate it took it less than two minutes to completely overwhelm the house."

Plus anyone unlucky enough to be caught up in it.

I rocked back on my heels under the weight of his words.

The fire had been started deliberately. Fiery demons had raged around the house, consuming everything within minutes. Rae hadn't stood a chance.

Rae had been murdered!

"Forensics also thought you'd like to see this." He held up a clear plastic evidence bag. "It was in the victim's left hand."

I was numb from the neck down and dumb from the neck up. Everything zooming in and out. With uncooperative fingers, I took the bag from Morrissey's hand and examined it in the beam of a headlight. Inside was a small rectangular wafer of blistered plastic.

"Looks like a credit card," Morrissey pointed out.

But I knew otherwise. It was a hotel keycard. Melted and blackened. Same thing I'd seen on my son's burned body in Akhiok.

All at once I knew what had happened to Rae and her fixer-upper. I didn't want to believe it. I couldn't process the terrible truth.

I was still gawping at the evidence bag when a black Suburban screeched to a stop and Mason Stone jumped out. Aptly, he looked ashen.

"Bloody hell, Quinn. What happened?"

"It's Cornsilk," I breathed over a cotton candy tongue. "He's burned down Rae's home with Rae in it. He's killed her, Stone. He's killed Rae."

*   *   *

"From here on in, I'm in the cremation business," *Snakeskin* had told me by way of a DVD recording sent to my home, back in August. "Anyone who crosses my path will go the same way as your private dick. I'm coming to get you, Quinn. You and everyone close to you. I'm going to make you pay for what you did to me. You and The Undertaker. Make you feel my pain. Then I'm going to kill him first and then you second. So break out those marshmallows, detective; your life is about to become a living hell."

Snakeskin kept his promises.

It was as if someone had gotten hold of all my dried-up emotions, chopped them into little pieces and thrown them in the air.

"Cornsilk?" The ridges on Stone's forehead were forming a question mark. "But Cornsilk wasn't on that plane."

"No," I agreed, tightly, "and we neglected to put eyes on the following arrivals. As far as we were concerned, he was on the run. It didn't seem reasonable to think he'd follow us to LA on the next plane out, even using an alias."

Inconceivable to think he'd come after Rae. But he had. *Snakeskin* had gone to the last place we'd look, then done the unexpected.

"He killed her, Stone. He poured gasoline all over her house and torched her in her own bed."

Stone looked like he'd just been told he had terminal cancer. He slammed big hands against the hood of the Suburban and cursed against the night.

I was lightheaded and heavy-hearted – otherwise empty, as if I were a hollow carbon copy of myself. An empty vessel, ready to play home to a whole host of demons.

A breeze picked up and scattered my shredded emotions to the wind, mixing them with the ashes of the house.

Morrissey gave us the grim thumbs-up and we were allowed into the crime scene as a professional courtesy. Officially, it wasn't our case – not yet, anyway. But come morning, the West Bureau police detectives would accede to the FBI's request to turn it over to Wilshire. They'd have no choice in the matter – not when one of our own had been killed, and by a serial killer we were already chasing.

Robotically, I followed Morrissey across the soaked front lawn, leaving smudged footprints in the fake snow.

"You sure the two of you are game for this?" Morrissey asked as we slipped plastic shoes over our own.

The hard line of my mouth was answer enough.

Truth was, I didn't want to see Rae's burned remains, but I didn't have the strength not to.

Rae was dead!

Stone was equally silent. Jaw muscles twitching. The suggestion of a low growl rolling around in his throat. The closest to him losing it I'd ever seen.

"All right, then stay with me. I don't need to tell you to be careful." Morrissey handed us patrolman's flashlights and we followed him into the razed ruins. The homicide detectives stayed outside, sucking lemons. I didn't care.

The house stank of damp wood smoke and the toxic tang of melted plastic. Everything blackened. Everything sodden. Loose plaster raining from waterlogged ceilings. Timbers weeping. Charred debris all over the place. Whole sections of the upper floor and roof had burned away or caved in, exposing devastated rooms and the hazy night sky above. One or two inner walls had collapsed into splintered piles of wood. Furniture had blazed or melted into unrecognizable slag heaps. Broken glass underfoot. It looked like hell and smelled like it, too.

Our flashlights picked out pools of inky water, islands of soggy plaster.

We came to a flight of metal stairs, shone our flashlights over the wrought iron framework. It was only half supported by the scorched brickwork behind what had been an impressive central fireplace, more ornamental than functional. Grated treads piled with wet soot. I swept the beam over a broken ceiling. I could see night sky framed by charred rafters. Ashy snowflakes falling lazily.

"Keep to the wall as we go up and tread exactly where I do."

Metal groaned as we climbed.

More loosened plaster crumbled and fell.

My heart was in my stomach and my stomach was in my mouth.

We entered a dark tunnel that had once been a hallway. Dagger shards in broken mirror frames reflecting frightened faces. Our flashlights illuminated black stripes running up the walls and over the ceiling. Fiery tattoos forming a ribbed throat.

Welcome to the mouth of Hell.

We came to the master bed. It was a sizeable area facing the Pacific Ocean. Probably a lovely place in which to wake and savor the splendid views through the big picture window, or slumber in the perfect sunsets. No more. Part of the roof was missing and most of a walk-in closet had folded in on itself. Bits of ash swirled in the air and glass teeth snarled at us from the remnants of the window.

I halted, halfway into the room, legs leaden, bile bulldozing up my esophagus.

The crime scene investigators had rigged up a pair of portable lamps on the floor space. Their brilliant focus was on a black mound in the middle of the room. It resembled a burnt-out bonfire, but it was actually the remains of a King-sized bed, together with its burned linens and pillows.

Morrissey and Stone ventured a little deeper. But I was rooted to the spot. Nailed to the blackened floorboards by fear and disbelief.

There was a ghastly apparition within the exposed mesh of the mattress. A crisped corpse, seated cross-legged in the classic lotus position. Curled fists clenched in the crease of the knees. Head tilted slightly forward. The intense heat had burned off the clothing, most of the skin and all of the hair.

Bile pressed against my barred teeth, stinging at the back of my nose.

"Don't contaminate my crime scene," Morrissey barked as he saw me go green.

No hope.

I turned and puked in the doorway.

*   *   *

When tragedy strikes, we have two options: give in or hit out. My world had imploded – a collapsing star, moments before going supernova – and all I wanted to do was explode.

But I had no intention of going under. Shock had me focused and there was little room for falling apart. I had every intention of killing Gary Cornsilk.

The realization should have startled me. It didn't.

Snakeskin had killed my son and then my lover. Killing their killer was the only train hurtling down my one-track mind.

Everything else was on the backburner.

Once, I was a religious man.

Once, I was a police man.

Once, I was a family man.

Once I was on my own with Gary Cornsilk, I'd be none of the above.

42

Exactly two hours later, I was co-chairing an impromptu meeting at the Bureau's field office on Wilshire Boulevard.

I didn't want to be there. I didn't want to be anywhere. Not even in my own brain. But I knew the best way to pick up Cornsilk's trail was with the full scope of the FBI behind me.

Didn't mean I'd need their help once I caught him.

". . . as of now this is our number one priority," Mason Stone was saying to our gathered audience. "All vacation days are cancelled and all other non-emergency case work will be put on hold or farmed out. That includes our work on Operation Freebird. Until Gary Cornsilk is captured, this office will live, eat and breathe this case."

A murmur of resolve passed through our midst.

All told, there were more than fifty of us filling up the airy room with the big glass windows overlooking the corrugated Santa Monica foothills. Emergent dawn light shortening shadows. The alarm had gone out and every available field agent had shown up for the emergency debrief. Men and women pulled away from their families the day after Christmas. Some seated, most standing. Early morning coffee warming cupped hands. Serious expressions fixing faces.

A special agent had been murdered and the Holidays were over.

Behind me, a trio of eight-by-ten photographs were taped to the wall, together with printouts of Cornsilk's records – including the failed mission in Jackson, his psych evaluations and his discharge papers. It didn't make for interesting reading. One of the photographs showed a thirtyish male of American Indian descent – a copy of

Cornsilk's original Bureau ID. He had a clean-looking face with coal-black eyes and no signs of disfigurement. The second eight-by-ten was the same picture only this time digitally-doctored to represent how Cornsilk looked today, based on my description. It showed in detail his scaly skin and his milky unseeing eye. Not quite Freddy Krueger, but close enough to give sensitive souls nightmares.

Over the preceding fifteen minutes, I'd brought our gathering up to speed on everything we knew about Gary Cornsilk. Voice monotonic. Jaw dystonic. In broad brushstrokes I'd painted out the bleak backdrop behind his disfigurement – the incendiary booby-trap bomb planted by *The Undertaker* in Jackson – as well as Cornsilk's attempts to do the same to me in Florida. Everyone was in agreement that Cornsilk was a prized nut job. I went over the more recent events in Kodiak that had seen a police officer killed and Cornsilk giving us the slip. *Snakeskin* was a slippery son of a bitch and I impressed it on my listeners. We'd already requested flight manifests on all passenger aircraft arriving in the Los Angeles area between midnight and three in the morning. In that small window, Cornsilk had landed in LA and then proceeded to orchestrate an elaborate crime scene. It begged some believing – so much so that I was leaning toward the theory that *Snakeskin* had planned it long before coming to California. Of course, there was one other explanation we hadn't discussed yet: he had help.

"I've spoken with the Chief of Police," Stone told our group. "The LAPD have our backs on this one. All patrol officers are being briefed on a rollout basis."

"What about the surrounding areas?" someone asked.

"Again, the same applies. All the Sheriff's Departments and police forces within a hundred mile radius are now on the lookout. We've reaffirmed the nationwide APB and alerted all our field offices."

Gary Cornsilk had made the FBI's Most Wanted – which was ironic, considering when he was FBI he'd been their least wanted.

We were all agreed that Cornsilk couldn't have gone very far in the time between starting the fire and our discovery that he was behind it. State Police were now on high alert, looking for anyone remotely fitting Cornsilk's description using the state highways or Interstates. While Stone and I had been shaking off shock, Rae's neighbors had been questioned about suspicious vehicles on the street after midnight. So far, no one had reported seeing any. But Cornsilk had gotten there by some means other than walking. Already, we'd sent out summons to all the rental agencies at the airports and surrounding districts, requesting copies of their customer lists.

The kill map we'd found in Cornsilk's Kodiak hotel room was being scrutinized by Bureau specialists. Phone numbers were being traced and dialed, and addresses were being checked out across the country.

Two hours into the hunt and the Bureau's media wizards had already worked their magic on the Internet. Bulletin boards and news portals everywhere were showing Cornsilk's pictures – and would continue to do so until further notice – with instructions to call their local FBI office or police department should anyone make a positive identification. A press release had been drafted and dispatched to the various media outlets, including local and national networks. This was a major assault. A federal agent had been murdered, burned to death in her own bed, and it was hot news.

I am a firm believer that many hands make light work. Our hope was that an informed and vigilant public would act as our eyes and ears on the streets. Millions of unofficially deputized public agents, all looking for the killer with the snakeskin face. As yet, the Bureau wasn't offering a reward in exchange for information. But the more time passed without a result, the more a financial stimulus was an inevitability.

Rae was dead.

It still hadn't sunk in properly through my thick skull.

I kept thinking I was stuck in a nightmare. I kept pinching myself. I didn't wake up.

Rae was dead and part of me was dead, too.

Sure, the temptation was to go to pieces. Rant at the injustice of the world. Scratch my eyes out with acid tears. But I'd already used up every curse and expletive known to man, and some not, following the discovery of my son's death yesterday. I had to keep a lid on it – for Rae's sake, for my sake – otherwise I'd explode and be no use to anyone. And that would fit in with *Snakeskin's* plan perfectly.

No way was I giving him the satisfaction.

All the same, I was desperately conscious of every wasted second passing us by. I was itching to get out on the streets, run down leads and shake rotten apples from trees. The last place I wanted to be was in an air-conditioned office discussing strategies over breakfast muffins.

"What do we know about the keycard?" someone asked.

"We believe it ties up to a hotel room," I answered. "As yet we do not know which one. Forensics are examining it as we speak. A small part of the magnetic stripe survived the heat. If they can access the information contained on that strip, it should give us a unique identifier."

Stone cleared his throat. "Remember, Gary Cornsilk is ex-FBI. That's his advantage. He knows how we operate. He knows where we'll be at any given point in our investigation. It's also his disadvantage. He won't expect us to be unconventional. So let's concentrate our efforts on doing the unexpected. Let's think outside the box. Surprise him.

"Once we're done here, I want all of you who haven't been assigned specific tasks to liaise with the local law enforcement. Go out on the streets. Squeeze every criminal informant and rattle every cage. Call in any favors you have. Be unpredictable. If Cornsilk isn't on the road he'll need a safe place to hide. Somebody will know something, have seen something, heard something. Make some noises, people. Let everyone know we mean business and that we won't rest until Cornsilk is caught."

"This bastard killed one of our own," somebody spoke up. "Are we going for a capture or a kill?"

A ripple of agreement passed over our gathering.

"Fair point," someone said. "Burnett was a good kid. If I get into a tight spot with this guy, I'm not about to play nice."

Stone glanced at me as the ripple of unrest grew into a wave. He knew what I was thinking, because it was advertised all over my face.

"Let me make this perfectly clear," he said as he scanned the room, "I'm just as angry as you are. I'd love nothing more than to rip Cornsilk to pieces. We lost one of us today. Not by some accident or act of God, but by the hands of a cold-blooded coward. Agent Burnett was a great asset to this department and to the Bureau. More than that, she was a dear friend to me and to many of you gathered here.

"Believe me when I say no one is more determined than I am to make Cornsilk answer for his crimes. But this office will not tolerate mortal retribution, from anyone." Another granite glance in my direction. "This department does not operate a shoot to kill policy. Not today or any other day. If you want to do Agent Burnett a service, you will do this by the book. We capture Cornsilk, alive. We make him answerable. We are the law, ladies and gentlemen. We must uphold it even if it kills us doing so."

The wave of discontent turned into murmurs of unification.

Crowd mentality. Stone had the gift.

And I had to face it: *Snakeskin* was no longer my personal pet hate. By targeting a federal agent other than me, he'd elevated his status from simple lowlife to the FBI's Most Wanted lowlife.

Privately, I had planned on chasing after Cornsilk my way, then metering out punishment, again my way. But now the whole of the FBI was on his case, nationally, and my own personal crusade was overrun. Ironically, the extra manpower left me feeling powerless.

I looked at the third photograph taped to the wall. It was a blow-up of Rae's Bureau ID. Soft fiery hair falling in thick swags. A spattering of freckles under a bewitching gaze. Full lips pulling smiles from everyone who laid their eyes on them.

My heart ached.

Beneath the photograph were the words *Special Agent Liberty Rae Burnett*, but to me they read *this is all your fault*.

43

Even with a federal warrant rushing them along, people still drag their heels.

The airlines gave up their complete flight manifests an hour after our requesting them. They weren't worth the wait. Turned out the only evening flight out of Anchorage and bound for LA had been the one we'd already checked. To say I was disappointed was an understatement. I was at a loss to explain how Cornsilk had pulled it off.

One flight. Thirty-seven passengers. Zero Snakeskins.

I was still crunching the numbers, on my own, when Supervisory Special Agent Lee Bishop appeared in the conference room doorway. Bishop was in his mid-forties and confined to a wheelchair. He had a blond thatch and wore wire-rimmed eyeglasses. One of those faces that has mocking down pat. I hadn't had much dealings with Bishop since coming into the office this morning – just enough to know he had authority issues and that he and I wouldn't get along if we were both stranded on a desert island together.

"I heard you got the flight manifests," he said. "So, how's it going? I've got an eye for names. Do you need any help going through them?"

Bishop had come into Stone's team during my stint in Springfield. Bishop had broken his back on the job in New York City, falling from a fire escape in pursuit of a felon. After rehab, the Persons with Disabilities Program had chained him to a desk. The limiter had filled him with resentment. Rae had warned me about Bishop during our return flight – that basically he was an asshole with a chip on his shoulder. Worst kind, in my book. Of course, his disability had nothing to do with it; he was an asshole even before the fall.

"Don't get excited," I said. "This was a complete waste of time. Cornsilk isn't on the list. There was just one incoming flight – the one we checked – and he wasn't on it."

Bishop wheeled himself into the room. "Christmas, when all said and done. Stands to reason, I suppose. Have you thought to check with the private charters? My reasoning is, if he didn't fly with the commercials, there's always the independents. It doesn't stretch the imagination to think he could have hired a private plane. I know I would, given his desire to remain undetected."

I made a face. "Cornsilk was discharged straight onto disability. Unless he won the lottery or robbed a bank I can't imagine him squandering upward of fifteen thousand dollars on a one-way ticket to LAX." I pushed a printout across the table. "All the same, I like to dot my i's and cross my t's. You'll find every private charter company operating up and down the West Coast on there. Only two late night flights arriving from the Pacific Northwest. And not one mention of any passengers named Cornsilk or even fitting his description."

Bishop had a snicker hanging on his lips. "So how on earth do you propose he got here, Quinn? He waved a magic wand and hey presto."

I didn't like Bishop's attitude. I wasn't on my own.

"I'm working on it. Tell you what, Bishop, instead of worrying about my part of the play, what about your end of the deal? Any luck with the traffic cameras?"

Bishop had been put in charge of liaising with Caltrans – the California Department of Transportation – specifically to review all the footage gathered by their live traffic cameras in and around Santa Monica within the hour immediately preceding the first nine-one-one call, and also within the hour immediately thereafter. Routine recordings from roadside surveillance cameras, gas stations and tourist webcams also fell under his remit. It was our hope that one of them would pick up Cornsilk's melted face behind a steering wheel. Then we'd have a make, a model and maybe even a plate number. In Florida, *Snakeskin* had escaped in a red Jeep Wrangler, with tags issued in Tennessee. I'd already put its memorized license plate into the system, only to learn that the vehicle had been totaled by its insurance company shortly after being found burnt out in Tampa, the same day he'd tried frying me alive in Jack's place.

Bishop was giving me the eye – one of those *I'm going to knife you between the shoulders the moment your back's turned* kind of looks.

"Actually, we're on top of it," he said. "My boys and girls are sifting through the data. As you'd expect, there's a lot to wade through. We're triple-checking. We wouldn't want to overlook a vital clue because we weren't being thorough." He pushed the printout back across the conference table. "As in the words of Earl Monroe: just be patient, let the game come to you, don't rush, be quick, but don't hurry."

I broadcast my discontent. While the rest of us were pulling out all the stops in the hunt for Rae's killer, Bishop was happily quoting basketball players of yesteryear.

A phone jangled on the conference table, saving me from saying something I wouldn't have regretted. I reached over and picked up. It was Deputy Medical Examiner Sarah Kuesel, patched through from the switchboard, and calling from the LA County Coroner's Department. I listened to her request to have me call over there ASAP. I queried it, but she refused to go into detail over the phone.

"That was the ME's office," I told Bishop as I hung up. "You'll have to excuse me; I need to go."

"Then I'm coming with you," he said as he wheeled ahead of me toward the door. "I'll drive."

I tried to protest, but Bishop was having none of it.

44

Antisocial. That's what I'd become since losing Hope. Like a turtle, I'd reeled in my head at the first sniff of danger and ignored the world as it fell apart around me. Don't get me wrong – I had plenty of friends, acquaintances and work colleagues to help fill up my time. Difference was, I chose not to.

Many of those friends, acquaintances and work colleagues had known Hope. We'd socialized together as couples. Without Hope by my side I'd stuck out like a unicycle in a tandem race. Self-preservation had pulled me back, pulled me in. At first as a survival mechanism, then later as the norm.

I'd learned something about me: I didn't have a problem with my own company, so long as I didn't talk too much.

Following Hope's death, I'd retrained myself to depend solely on Gabriel Quinn, to look after number one and to come and go on my own timetable. So when somebody I didn't particularly want to share my time with insisted on gatecrashing my party, I tended to take offense.

"How'd you end up in the chair?" I asked Bishop as he drove the specially-modified Suburban east on Wilshire. I already knew, but somebody had to make conversation. "I heard your rehabilitation was a complete success. No physical reason preventing you from walking."

Some people shy away from being direct about disabilities. Sure, Bishop was in a wheelchair, but he was still a grown man, still an asshole according to Rae. Nothing wrong with his brain or his voice box. I had no intention of treating him with kid gloves.

"Have you been checking up on me, Quinn?" he smiled falsely.

I pouted. "Just trying to ameliorate the awkward silence, that's all. Don't read into it more than that."

"Actually, talking about it is therapeutic. The doctors say my ongoing condition is psychological. I just need a little more work, a little more time. According to the physiotherapists . . ."

I tuned him out. I watched the busy streets roll by instead, only half listening as he spun his leisurely tale about chasing some bad dude up a fire escape and ultimately falling into the alleyway below, hitting every switchback on the way down.

It was a sunny December day in LA. A cornflower sky with fibers of white gauze out over the Pacific. Christmas decorations brightening up storefronts and power poles. Folks returning unwanted or faulty gifts, or hoping to bag a sale item. The epitome of normalcy on the day after Christmas.

But the urban landscape looked strange, somehow.

Not strange as in the strange way it had looked the last time I'd returned to California – after spending six months on a barrier island with nothing but pick-headed pelicans to keep me company. That time, everything had looked rundown, crowded and unpleasant to the eye. This time, everything looked big, busy and brand new. But the only thing to change was me, I knew. Prison life had dulled this blade. Spending endless hours staring at the same four walls had pulled in my perspectives and shortened my horizons. Everything here seemed spaced out, oversized and much greener than Los Angeles had any right to be, this time of year or any other.

Bishop jammed on the brakes, jolting me forward against the seatbelt. We were at an intersection. Signals on red.

"Welcome back," he smirked. "For a while there I thought you'd slipped into a coma."

I loosened up the belt. "Get over yourself, Bishop. We're conducting a manhunt on the back of an agent's murder; I have good cause to be distracted."

"Speaking of which," he began, "how well did you know Agent Burnett?"

I scowled at his prying.

"It's a straightforward question," he added as the lights turned green and we moved through the intersection. "No hidden meanings. Liberty Rae Burnett. How well did you know her?"

Bishop was beginning to chaff my hide. "It's none of your damn business, Bishop. Just keep your eyes on the road and stop trying to take a peek under my hood."

He snickered, "It looks like she's pulled the wool over your eyes the same way she has with everybody else."

I gave him the full weight of my scowl. I wasn't in the right frame of mind for this line of questioning. "What do you mean by that?"

"I mean she was your partner. The first thing partners do is have a conversation about each other's backgrounds. Personal and professional. So I'll ask again: how well did you know her?"

I sighed superheated air, "Bishop, you're really beginning to grind my gears. I've gone through fifty years of life and never had reason to pop anyone in a wheelchair. But there's a first time for everything. Now get to your damn point."

Bishop had a big stupid smirk ballooning up his face. "You don't know, do you?"

"I know you're wearing my patience dangerously thin."

"You really have no idea why she dropped her going-places job in DC and signed up with Stone. Basically, moving five rungs back down the career ladder."

Rae had told me she'd requested the temporary transfer to LA in order to assist Stone with *Operation Freebird*. Essentially, she was on loan from Washington. No mention of a demotion. No mention of staying permanently in LA either. As far as I was aware, she had every intention of leaving once the nest of vipers was stamped out.

"The thing is, Quinn, she hasn't been completely honest with you. Burnett didn't come here solely to lend a hand with Operation Freebird. She rushed to Stone's side because he was missing her. That's right. You've been played like a bad hand of poker. Stone and Burnett were lovers."

*   *   *

My first reaction was to pop Bishop on the mouth for speaking ill of the dead. My second reaction was to doubt everything that had happened between Rae and me, and then to pop Bishop on the mouth.

Instead, I grabbed at the steering wheel. "Pull over!"

It was reflexive and stupid. Street full of traffic. The Suburban lurched in its lane. Someone honked in a passing sedan.

Bishop smacked my hands away, "Are you crazy? You're going to get us both killed!"

I grabbed at it again. "I said *pull over!*"

The Suburban lurched again, tires screeching on the pavement.

Bishop had no choice other than to swing the SUV against the curb and hit the brakes. Alloys grated concrete. "No wonder Stone had you committed," he snarled. "You're completely out of control."

I flung open the door and dropped onto the sidewalk. "Go back and do your job, Bishop. Find me an image on those surveillance tapes. And stay the hell out of my business."

I slammed the door in his face and walked away.

Bishop crept the Suburban along the curbside and rolled down the passenger window. "There's one other thing you need to know, Quinn," he called. "You might want to look into Burnett's background a little deeper. Don't be a fool and get by on blind trust alone. If she didn't come clean about her and Stone, what else was she hiding? Ask yourself where she got the money to pay for that place in Pacific Palisades."

He was still jabbering away as I backed up, slipped behind the SUV and crossed the street.

*   *   *

Rage is a dangerous thing. It leads normally placid people into committing the vilest of crimes.

Springfield had had a lasting impression on me.

I performed deep-breathing exercises as I marched along Mission Road, visualizing fields of flowers and hopping bunnies – all through a clearing red mist.

Breathe. Control. Release.

I watched Bishop's modified Suburban make a right at the next signals and disappear down the road.

Other than pure mischief, I had no idea why Bishop would stir the pot and try to blacken Rae's image. Admittedly, I only knew what Rae had told me about the intervening years between us.

What didn't I know?

Bishop's accusations had hammered nails of doubt in my head, I realized. Two blows in quick succession, leaving me dazed and seething.

I crossed the entranceway to an abandoned building, only distantly aware of my surroundings.

This was a well-worn area of town. Yellowy weeds pushing through cracks in the sidewalk. Vacant plots, overgrown and decayed. Sagging chain-links and boarding blighted by graffiti. I stormed past one auto glass repair shop after another. I was all fired up, ready to punch someone or something.

My cell phone jangled.

I dug it out and barked a *what do you want?* into the microphone.

"There's dried soot all over my bike," came a man's voice. "Thanks a bunch, buddy. She's a real mess. All the intakes are clogged up and probably the valves, too."

"Tim?"

"Jeez Louise, Gabe. You promised you'd look after her. I'm megally disappointed."

"Tim, I'm sorry. I'll make amends. I'll get it professionally cleaned. I promise. And there's no such word as megally."

"That's not the point, Gabe, either way, and you know it."

"You're right. I said, I'm sorry." Up ahead, I spotted a pair of youths cross to my side of the street. Baggy jeans and baseball caps. Body language shouting out *we's gonna roll you over real good, grandpa*. "This isn't a good time, Tim. What do you want?"

"I just saw the breakfast news and nearly choked on my Cheerios. Your partner's been killed. Jeez Louise. Why didn't you wake me?"

"More pressing matters."

The two youths were conspiring between themselves, eyeing me up and down and flexing fingers as they came my way. I knew what they were thinking: some middle-aged guy in a sports jacket, jeans and sneakers, a mile outside his comfort zone. Easy pickings.

"Aside from freaking out over my bike, I just wanted to pass on my condolences," Tim was saying. "Plus, I've been thinking more about our human torch."

"Tim . . ."

"Gabe, hear me out. Least you can do."

I had my gaze locked on the approaching double act. The shorter of the two had slid his right hand inside the front of his jacket. The other had slipped what looked like a steel knuckleduster over his fist. Both were wearing menacing faces.

"So, I called this guy I know who works security at Madame Tussauds. He used to work the door at the nightclub on Santa Monica Boulevard, way back in the early days. You remember the discothèque, don't you, Gabe? The one where you very nearly got your ass –"

"Tim, just get to the point."

The youths were checking out the street, confirming there was no one to witness what was coming up.

"Okay, okay. We know the guy in the Santa suit acknowledged someone across the street. Probably this Gary Cornsilk character. So I figured something might show up on the Madame Tussauds security cameras. Maybe even a vehicle they were using. For a limited time only, the tapes are available for us to view. Tell me where you are and I'll come pick you up."

My pair of impending assailants were almost upon me. Ten yards, tops. I could see their chests rising and falling as adrenalized blood was pumped into muscles. Jaws clenched. Eyes unblinking.

"I'll call you back," I said, and hung up.

The shorter of the two started to pull his hand from beneath his jacket. I was quicker, practiced. I had the Glock out and aimed before he could do the same with his 9 mm.

"Take it easy, boys," I said. "Mine's bigger, with a hair trigger. So keep walking; I haven't got time for any of your shit right now."

I kept the gun on the shorter guy as they inched past me on the sidewalk. Backs to a chain-link. I could see they weren't happy about having their master plan crushed. No easy money today, fellas. Foolishly, the kid with the 9 mm still looked like he fancied his chances.

"Try it and your momma will be visiting you in Evergreen Memorial, every other Sunday," I said, just to make sure he understood my exact frame of mind.

I didn't put the Glock away until they were out of sight.

45

I hadn't visited the Coroner's Department in Boyle Heights since The Undertaker Case. I showed my badge and made my way to Benedict's office. It hadn't changed one bit. It still had its distinct haunted house smell and body parts in bell jars on shelves, magnifying the macabre. All the freakiness of the fairground without any of the fun.

There was a woman seated behind his desk. She was in her mid-thirties, with long chestnut hair and one of those faces that wouldn't have looked out of place at a soccer moms convention.

"Where's Benedict?"

"Visiting family in Honolulu." She got to her feet and held out a hand. "Agent Quinn? Deputy Medical Examiner Sarah Kuesel."

"Pleased to meet you, Sarah. What gives?"

"First off, your house fire victim didn't die in the house fire."

I felt my forehead ripple.

"There's no trace of smoke inhalation. No thermal damage in the upper respiratory system. In fact, no signs that the victim succumbed to hypoxia." She saw the quizzical expression drawing down my face and added: "I think you better come take a look for yourself."

I followed Kuesel down the hall in the direction of the autopsy rooms. I wasn't in any particular rush to inspect Rae's burnt remains; 1 was trying desperately hard not to let it be the last image I ever had of her. I wasn't being given a choice. It felt like I'd swallowed a lump of lead and it was weighing me down.

Kuesel shouldered open a steel-paneled door and flicked on lights.

The child within me gasped.

Transplant an operating theater into a shower room and you're somewhere close to the autopsy room in the bowels of the ME's facility. Function over form. None of the pearly glows and trendy backlighting seen in the movies. Racks of stainless steel surgical instruments and rinse-down everything. The scalpel-sharp smell of disinfectants.

Standing proud on a central leg in the middle of the tiled floor was a gunmetal plinth. A multi-bulb halogen lamp was poised over it, like a multi-eyed alien, illuminating a charred human body.

But something was wrong.

Now that the corpse was removed from the wreckage of Rae's bed, I could see it was the wrong shape entirely. Even allowing for the fact that the ME had laid the body out flat, it was impossible to ignore the distended midriff. It was a bulging, bloated waistline and XL in anyone's wardrobe. Its limbs were short, chunky.

"This is why I asked you to come down here and see for yourself," Kuesel said as the confusion screwed up my face. "I've met Agent Burnett. I know she has balls, but this unlucky soul lying here has testicles. Your house fire victim is male, which means this isn't Agent Burnett."

*   *   *

If a hole had opened up beneath me then and there I would have fallen through it gladly. When it didn't, I was left to gape like an idiot, unable to compute Kuesel's disclosure.

"Rae's alive?"

It sounded unthinkable. A contradiction. Hard to speak it, let alone believe it.

"Agent, I can't guarantee that. But I can confirm she didn't die in that house fire."

Impossible hope blossomed in my chest.

Rae was alive?

Breath shortening, I moved closer to the plinth and ran my disbelieving gaze over the charcoaled corpse. In the sobering light I could see it wasn't Rae. No way. The whole arrangement was wrong. Too small, too fat and very much the wrong gender.

The blackened ruins of Rae's bedroom, coupled with the fact I'd expected her to be burned alive in her bed, had fooled my eyes into seeing what my brain had anticipated.

"So who the hell is this?"

"Good question. I'm still waiting on a dental match. What I can say is this is definitely a fully-grown male. Five foot and slightly on the overweight side."

I was catching flies, heart pounding. All morning I'd been buried alive under six feet of grief, suffocating under the weight of Rae's loss. Now the deputy ME was digging me out and suddenly I was blinded by the light.

"Furthermore, he died from an artificially-induced cardiac event. I found an injection mark in the soft tissue behind the left ear. I ran checks and found lethal quantities of potassium chloride in his system."

All at once I was breathless, but in a good way. "Sarah, you're good."

"I know; I've had the best teacher." She smiled, then nodded toward the body. "Allowing for the unusual heating and cooling, the liver temperature points to a time of death around two this morning."

While I was banging on *Winston's* door and getting nowhere, Cornsilk was killing this John Doe and leaving him in Rae's house. But why?

"I didn't find any identifying marks such a tattoos or implants, but I did find these three gold rings, all on the right hand."

She handed me a plastic dish. There were a few flakes of crisped skin in the bottom, together with three man-sized gold bands.

"Each has a separate letter engraved in the gold," she said, pointing. "Line them up and they spell the word DOG. Maybe your victim's a gangbanger?"

I blinked twice, disbelieving my own eyes for the second time. I had a pain in my throat; something squeezing combustible hormones from my thyroid gland and trying to strike a match.

"Sarah, I know who this is. And this homicide just got a whole lot weirder, real fast."

46

On the back of a phone call, Mason Stone showed up fifteen minutes later, looking like he'd run it all the way across town. I'd broken the incredible news about Rae and he'd broken every speed limit getting here.

I hadn't tackled him about Bishop's claim – not yet. With the sudden turn in events it didn't seem vitally important right now.

"Tell me this is some kind of sick joke," he said as he blustered into the autopsy room.

"Take a look for yourself, Stone," I said. "And then tell me I'm joking. This isn't Rae's body. It's a guy called Bridges. He was my case manager at the Fed Med."

Stone was staring at me like I was speaking backwards. "The body we found in Rae's house, it's Frank Bridges?"

"I know it sounds farfetched. And I'm still having a hard time believing it myself, but I'd recognize these rings anywhere." I showed him the three gold bands in the plastic dish, rearranged to spell the word GOD. "Bridges wore them with pride. Jangled them in everybody's face every opportunity he had. He was a believer and wanted everyone to know it."

Stone was shaking his head. "Frank Bridges? Bloody hellfire."

The information was slow going in. Even slower digesting all the ramifications. None more so than the giddying fact that Rae hadn't died in her house overlooking the Pacific.

Rae was alive!

I nodded at the crisped corpse. "Take a look for yourself, Stone. This body is the right size and shape. The rings are definitely his. I know the dental records will come back and say the same thing. This is Frank Bridges."

Stone examined the body on the plinth like it was an alien autopsy. "How the bloody hell did he end up here?"

"I asked myself the same thing, at first. Then I remembered something. Before I left Springfield, Bridges mentioned he was coming home for the Holidays. Said his folks had a place in Pasadena. It wouldn't be impossible for Cornsilk to intercept him and –"

"Hold that thought," Stone interjected, raising a hand. "Why on earth would Cornsilk kill Bridges? There's no connection. What's his motive? How did he even know about him?"

Trust Stone to throw a wrench in my works.

I drew a speculative breath. "Right now, I have no idea. But this is unquestionably Cornsilk's work. Positioning the body in the lotus position, leaving a hotel keycard in the left hand, setting the victim alight – that seems to be his signature lately.

"It's an exact copy of the Akhiok homicide. We know Cornsilk is targeting me and we know he's threatened to kill anyone who stands in his way. I'm the link to Bridges. It's possible Cornsilk found out I was hidden away in the Fed Med. Maybe he kept an eye on me. I don't know. Maybe he made a note of who I interacted with, then added them to his hit list."

Stone's brow was scrunched up. "Tenuous doesn't even come close, Quinn. Cornsilk has no reason to go after Bridges, or anyone else not directly involved in his payback scheme. You're clutching at straws."

"I didn't say it was perfect, Stone. I'm thinking on my feet here."

"Then think harder. Killers kill for a reason. Not just to piss you off."

I sighed, "Look, Cornsilk is a prize nut job. Just because his choice of victim makes no immediate sense to us, doesn't mean it isn't important to him, or where he leaves it."

"Added to the fact your timeline's all out of kilter. Just take a step back and look at this, Quinn. Everything's too tight. It doesn't feel right. I don't buy for one second Cornsilk had time to get down here from Alaska, kill Bridges and then set Burnett's house on fire in the tiny window of opportunity you're giving him."

"You're right. And I've already been thinking about that. From the get-go, Rae and I assumed Cornsilk had fled Kodiak after we'd discovered his room at the Kodiak Inn. He used his credit card to purchase the two-leg flight from Kodiak to LA. But he wasn't on either. According to the airlines, the eleven-thirty arrival at LAX was the only flight out of Anchorage heading this way last night. Cornsilk used it as a decoy. Now I'm thinking he eyeballed us the night before, on Christmas Eve, when Rae and I first booked into the hotel. He left Kodiak then, not the next day. He's been here all along."

Stone was wearing his trademark look of weary skepticism. I was throwing theories in the air like clay pigeons and he was happy to shoot them down all day long.

"I'm sorry, Quinn. It still doesn't add up. If Cornsilk arrived in LA yesterday morning, why throw you a bone by booking the fake flight? It doesn't make sense. The decoy led you straight back here. Why not leave you thinking he was trapped on Kodiak?"

Truth was, I hadn't thought it through that far. Stone's argument made more sense than mine. But my *Uh-Oh Radar* felt like it was onto something. I couldn't ignore it.

"Sure, he knew we'd come rushing back to LA. Bridges was here. For some reason we don't know as yet, Cornsilk wanted him dead, on his timescale, and he wanted me to find the body." I looked at Mason Stone, sudden fear welling in my chest. "Maybe it's all about putting me in the crosshairs, so that he can finish what he started down in Florida. He wants me to burn alive, remember? And on his terms. And that's why he didn't kill Rae. He abducted her instead."

"To what end?"

"To get me to where he wants me. He's going to use Rae as bait."

47

In any abduction scenario, time is of the essence. I didn't need to convince Stone I was right. Rae wasn't dead – at least, not that we knew of. She wasn't answering her cell and there was no reports of anyone fitting her description being admitted to any of the local hospitals. The only conclusion left was that *Snakeskin* had abducted her.

Stone got on the phone and instructed his underlings back at base to expand the scope of our manhunt to include kidnapping. The nationwide APB was updated to include Rae's description, with copies of her Bureau photo ID circulated to every agency. The spotlight of our task force would now concentrate on the safe recovery of an abducted agent, with everyone working double shifts until she was safely returned to the fold.

The manhunt had shifted up a gear, increasing its impetus. Only a miracle would keep *Snakeskin* out of sight and undetected. And I didn't believe in miracles.

Rae was alive!

My brain was banging around in my skull like a boxer's speed ball struck by a world champ.

Now that I knew the victim's true identity, I had to believe Rae still lived. The more I thought about it, the more I could feel the positivity in every fiber of my being. Our invisible tether. Unbroken. If *Snakeskin* had wanted her dead he'd have done the deed in her own home, wouldn't he?

At a pace, Stone drove us away from Boyle Heights in his shiny black Ford Mustang, grille lights blinking, forcing slower vehicles aside.

By now, I was convinced *Snakeskin* had taken Rae for one reason and one reason only: to lure me to my own fiery fate. Exactly how that would all pan out, I had no clue. Not yet. At this point, it was impossible to fully predict *Snakeskin's* end game – other than my own cremation – but Rae would definitely play a part.

Somehow, I had to turn the tables and beat *Snakeskin* at his own game.

But I was fearful over Rae's welfare.

In the back of my mind all I could picture was the guy in the Santa suit, sent on a suicide mission for all the world to see. What if *Snakeskin* had something equally horrifying in mind for Rae?

We were racing northbound on the Santa Ana Freeway when Stone's cell chimed. While Stone took his call, I dug out my own phone and dialed Rae's number. I heard her phone ring, and started to feel giddy. Then a *not in service* message kicked in, and deflation pressed the air out of my lungs. The Fire Department investigators hadn't found her cell in the debris of the bedroom, nor anywhere else it was likely to be. They had found her burned purse on the kitchen counter, with her fire-damaged FBI ID still inside. No cell and no firearm. I had thought Cornsilk had taken them as trophies, but now I was thinking maybe there was a small chance Rae had hidden them on her person. Maybe *Snakeskin* had bitten off more than he could chew.

"That was the SID," Stone said as he hung up. "Forensics managed to pull information from the keycard. It resolves to the Imperial Motor Lodge in Springfield."

"That's right across the street from the Fed Med. Why there?"

"That's what I need you to find out."

I shot him a glare. "You mean you want me to go back to Springfield? Forget it, Stone. There's no way that's going to happen. Right now, saving Rae is my number one priority. You've got to appreciate that. Rae needs me here, looking for her. She's my partner. You made it that way. Delegate and send somebody else."

I could no sooner deny Rae my whole undying attention than a flower could turn its back on the sun.

"You misunderstand, Quinn. This isn't a request, it's an order. You're going to Springfield, and that's the end of it. Whether you like it or not, Bridges is your responsibility by way of association. You might not agree with that, but that's the way it is. I need you to go and find out why Cornsilk is pointing us back to Springfield. Don't worry about things at this end; I'm more than capable of holding down the fort while you're gone."

He swung the Mustang across two lanes of traffic and took the next exit. The sports car thundered through the Bill Keene Memorial Interchange and out onto Harbor Freeway, southbound.

"Don't do this, Stone. And don't make me beg."

He put his foot down. The engine responded with ease.

"Here's my concern: if I let you stay here you'll play straight into Cornsilk's hands. And that could end badly for Burnett. I know you, Quinn. You're the definition of a bull in a china shop. If you're right and Cornsilk intends using her as bait, he'll have no choice but to keep her alive until you're where he wants you, which is here, in LA."

In other words, if I stayed out of town it would buy Stone and our task force more valuable time to track down Cornsilk. Keeping me at a distance was the best choice right now. Not for me. For Rae. Didn't mean I had to like it.

"I'll release an updated press statement," he continued. "Say we're investigating a lead in another part of the country and that you're personally overseeing it. That way he'll know you're not here."

Stone wanted me out of the way. Maybe so he could rescue Rae and catch Cornsilk for himself. Add another glittering accolade to his trophy cabinet. Or maybe because there was something deeper.

I looked sideways at the Brit, wondering about Bishop's words as we passed a sign for the airport.

Was there any truth to his claim?

48

An untidy patron had spilled sugar on the tabletop, and a slapdash waitress had overlooked it. He tapped the Zippo against the wood, watching the grains dance and take flight.

In his line of work, he knew a thing or two about abduction situations.

From the outside, the van windows appeared blacked-out. But the vehicle wasn't soundproofed. He couldn't risk his prisoner kicking up a fuss and rousing attention. He knew he had to keep her quiet and compliant, and that meant keeping her system topped up with strong sedatives.

Luckily, he'd had the foresight to bring plenty with him.

He rubbed the lucky Indian head motif with his blunt thumb.

They had a long journey ahead of them. Other passengers to pick up along the way.

She had to remain submissive, zombielike.

He kept his eye on the white van parked by itself out in the diner's parking lot as the sloppy waitress took his order.

49

Tires squealed as the Gulfstream jet slapped wet tarmac and skipped down the runway at Springfield-Branson. It was a dull day in Missouri. A sky as leaden as a pan full of buckshot, already darkening in the east. Thirty-six hours of bombarding sleet had reduced the landscape into a muddy battlefield.

I checked my watch: almost two in the afternoon. I moved the hands on by two hours, to make up for the time zone difference. Sundown in forty-five minutes.

Stone had phoned ahead and an agent from the Kansas City Division had been sent to meet and greet.

I still wasn't happy about being here. No choice.

I waited impatiently on the damp concourse, resisting the urge to shiver as a black Buick Enclave came to a stop and a young blonde woman stepped out. She was slim, gray-suited, and looked no older than twenty-one.

"Special Agent Kelli Woods," she announced, offering her hand. Her grip was firm but fair.

"You guys get younger all the time," I smiled. "Makes me feel prehistoric."

My comment triggered a smile of her own. It was pleasant enough and full to bursting with brilliant white teeth. "I'll take that as a compliment – I think. If you must know, I turned thirty this year."

"You did? Oh my. What's your secret?"

"Plenty of bottled water and sunblock, even in winter." She continued to smile brightly as we climbed into the SUV. "Gum?" she asked as I buckled up.

I obliged, conscious of my plane breath. "Thanks."

"Pleasure."

Woods drove us out of the airport, eastbound on West Division Street, steered us down the road with confidence, seventies soft rock whispering from the stereo. Something about a new kid in town. There was a pair of designer sunglasses in the center console, right behind a bottled water. A yellow post-it on the dash saying *Pick up Tucker – Don't Forget!!!*

"Smells like Christmas in here."

Woods motioned to a Little Tree air freshener hanging from the rearview mirror. "Cinnamon apple; my absolute favorite. Hope you aren't allergic. It helps mask the smell of dog."

I glanced around the interior. "They let you pick up your pet in a motor pool van?"

"Not officially. Stop looking; he isn't here! When it looks like I'll be working longer than expected, I pick him up and leave him with my sister. I'm really sorry about the hairs; I Scotch-taped as many as I could. He's one boisterous Border Collie."

"Don't tell me – you need all the exercise he can get."

"Exactly!" She tittered. "You're smart; I like that."

"It's a wonder the dinosaurs went extinct."

The Enclave rumbled across the overpass spanning I-44. Below us, double lanes of semi-trailer trucks crossed the State. Sagging power lines holding up the overcast.

"How was your flight?" Woods asked conversationally.

"Bumpy."

I'd spent most of it chewing my cheek and worrying about Rae. Feeding nerves through a shredder. I'd called Stone a dozen times, for updates, and each time he'd assured me he'd call me the second the manhunt caught a break. We were a further five hours into the search for *Snakeskin* and so far we were still treading water. Nothing on the traffic surveillance footage, and no word on the streets. It was as if he'd slithered underground and taken Rae with him.

Oddly enough, I'd drifted in and out of a fervent sleep during the flight. Middle of the day sleep – the kind that leaves you with a hangover without the happy memories. There had been a time when I'd gotten by on power-napping and caffeine alone. Not any more. Internment had reset my body clock. The sleep had been fitful and filled with nightmarish images of Rae standing on the beach at Akhiok, against a thermonuclear sunset, her fiery red hair aloft and her freckled skin aflame.

"Please don't take this the wrong way," Woods said softly, "but you look like you could do with freshening up. There's wipes in the glove compartment."

I reached in and retrieved a pack of make-up cleansers. "It's been a long couple of days. Must have flown over of eight-thousand miles between here, Alaska and California."

"Helping out Santa?"

"If only." I pulled down the visor. A set of keys landed in my lap.

"Spares," Woods said. "Heads up: I'm ditzy, okay? I'd forget my own head if it wasn't screwed on."

I blinked at my puffy eyes in the mirror. I looked like something out of a Roald Dahl tale. Halfheartedly, I rubbed a wipe in a circle over my gray-grizzled chin and forehead. Then replaced the keys behind the visor. "Nothing a strong coffee couldn't fix."

"Okay, so let's do something about that. I'll stop at the next gas station. Or there's a waffle house on the way, if you can handle the cholesterol."

"Clogged arteries might be the only way to keep me warm right now. Either sounds great." My belly had been rumbling for hours. I realized with a start that I hadn't eaten anything substantial since I'd breakfasted with Rae in Alaska, yesterday.

Woods cranked up the heater. "Better?"

"Yeah, thanks. Thin Californian clothes. So, Special Agent Woods, what do we know about the Imperial Motor Lodge?"

"The illustrious Imperial." Her tone was sarcastic. "One time, it used to be the main place to stay in these parts. Congressmen have boarded there. Now it's a nondescript motel with a low-key aspect, known for the occasional prostitution arrest. It's also a hangout for biker gangs when they're passing through town. Nothing extraordinary for this neck of the woods, not these days. I spoke with the manager by phone. He says the room in question was rented out the day before Christmas Eve."

"Do we know by whom?"

"He says it was a black guy. He paid cash for the week. That's all he remembers."

We crossed a busy intersection. Woods pulled into a red-liveried Kum&Go gas station on the corner and tucked the Enclave in front of the convenience store.

"Back in a jiffy," she said and left me with Boston's *More Than a Feeling*.

I watched the comings and goings. People going about their business. Refueling their vehicles after the mad pre-Christmas rush. No one knowing or even caring that I was sitting here, with the pressing weight of the world on my shoulders.

All I could think about was Rae.

She was alive!

My cell rang.

"What does a guy need to do to get a little attention around here?" came Tim's voice on the other end of the connection. "I'm still waiting for your return call."

"Extenuating circumstances," I apologized.

"I guess I'm used to it. Listen, I'm thinking about cooking Chinese tonight. Peking duck and egg fried rice. My way of making up for imposing on your hospitality. Give me a rough idea when I can expect you home."

"Tim, honestly, you don't need to include me in your plans. Besides, I'm in Missouri. We got a break in the case and I'm chasing it down. No clue when I'll be back."

"Missouri? Great. Then I guess I'll have to take a look at those tapes by myself." He sounded genuinely disappointed.

"Tim, I'm sorry. If you find anything, send me photos."

I hung up as Special Agent Kelli Woods came out of the store, carrying a coffee and a paper bag. I leaned over the driver's seat and opened the door.

"Double-shot and donuts," she said as she handed over her purchases. "Otherwise known as the coronary diet."

"I won't tell if you don't." I opened the bag and instantly got a buzz from the sticky sweetness. "You abstaining?"

"After yesterday's binge, you bet."

We double-backed through the intersection and headed south. Twilight rushing in from the east. Specks of icy rain on the windshield ahead of it. Headlights coming on as the murk descended. Like most highways, US Route 160 was nothing special to look at. Cloned fast-food outlets and auto-repair shops. I made light conversation around mouthfuls of donut: partly to learn how and why Kelli Woods had decided to join the Bureau, but mostly to keep my dogged thoughts from worrying about Rae.

Woods was happy to talk and easy to talk to. She seemed a good, hard-working kid with the right kind of attitude. Focused more on doing her job to the best of her abilities rather than which options offered the easiest route to promotion. These days, it came as a breath of fresh air. She was single (not by choice; she simply hadn't met Mr. Right yet), lived in a quiet neighborhood near Swope Park (where she jogged with her dog every morning before breakfast), and came from a long line of lawyers (stretching right back to the early days of the Pendergast era). Otherwise, she seemed grounded.

"'Course, my dad wanted me to follow in his footsteps, but I wanted to get my hands dirty." She laughed breezily. "And so here I am."

The intersection with Sunshine Street was coming up, clogged with late afternoon traffic. It was strange to be back here again in such a short space of time. The Fed Med was a mile or so east of here. Hard not to think about Trenton Fillmore and his hot blood dripping through my fingers.

I drained half the coffee and put the cup in a holder, brushed donut crumbs out of my wiry Van Dyke.

Before the signals, Woods steered the Enclave into an offshoot leading to an area of small businesses huddled around the crossroads. A dilapidated neon sign for the Imperial Motor Lodge was lit against the darkening sky. *Vacancies* glowing pink. The motel was hidden behind a gas station, and was a single-floored building with grayed net curtains at the windows and one or two suspicious-looking vehicles parked out front. One of those rundown roadside motels you see on the outskirts of every town, and continue to drive by.

We pulled into a parking bay next to a white police patrol car with Springfield Missouri PD decals. Woods reached over to the backseat and handed me a bulletproof vest with big FBI letters on it.

"You never know," she said. "Better safe than sorry."

We climbed out. It was cold. Specks of icy rain falling from a sky blackened with the stuff. Woods flashed her badge to the patrol officer seated in his vehicle.

He dropped the driver's window and handed her a keycard. "Room eleven, straight ahead. No one's been in or out or near while I've been here."

Not surprising, I thought, there being a squad car parked up out front with its lights on.

We donned our vests, then made our way to the specified door. It looked just like all the others in the row: in desperate need of paint. I glanced at the window: heavy drapes drawn behind a dusty net curtain.

By the book, we got out our handguns.

Woods banged a fist against the wood. "FBI! Open up!"

We waited. No sounds of movement coming from inside. She banged again. Still no answer.

"What are you expecting to find here?" she asked as she slid the keycard into the lock.

"A reason," I said. "But I'm not holding my breath."

As usual, I'd spoken too soon. The air inside room eleven of the Imperial Motor Lodge in Springfield smelled bad, bad enough to wrinkle the nose and close up the airway.

*   *   *

My Glock went in first and I went in ahead of Woods.

"FBI!" we both warned.

It was dark inside.

Woods threw on the lights and we scanned the lackluster room. It was a standard motel setup: tired twin beds with brown throws and faded linens, both made; cheap prints in even cheaper plastic frames, blending in against jazzy wallpaper last sold in the 70s; a wooden dresser with an old portable TV on the top, dusty; beaten carpet tiles trying unsuccessfully to hide a lifetime of abuse.

Woods' face was pulled in on itself. "What the heck is that smell? It's like a sewer in here."

I could see why.

The bathroom door was partly open. No lights on inside, but a slice of illumination from the bedroom revealing a bathtub and what looked like a dangling arm and half a torso. Skin grayed by death and fingers piped full of purple blood.

"Dead body," I said, holstering the Glock. "In the bathroom."

I walked over, pushed the door open fully, then winced at the overpowering odor as it slapped me in the face.

"Oh my gosh," Woods breathed over my shoulder. "That is seriously screwed up."

Sadly, I had to agree.

Someone had taken their own life in the bathroom.

The arm and torso belonged to a middle-aged man. He was completely naked and suspended in a semi-standing position by a nylon cord garroted around his neck and anchored to the shower head. Arms dangling loosely at his sides, knees bent, legs crossed. The cord was pulled as taut as a guitar string, slicing into the flesh and cutting off the blood supply to his brain. Face dark purple and bloated. Bloodshot, bulging eyes, staring lifelessly into the tub.

I switched on the bathroom light and the gruesome scene came alive in all its terrible detail.

"OMG," Woods gasped.

Sometimes death knows no dignity. In the last few moments of life, the decedent's bowels had emptied. Flushed by fear. Stress had liquefied the feces, spraying them down the backs of his legs and all over the insides of the bathtub. I could see scuff marks where his feet had grappled for grip, slipping and sliding with no hope of a purchase.

Woods was gagging on the putrid stench. "I'll go see if I can find a wallet, some ID."

"No rush," I said. "I know who this is."

*   *   *

Two hotel rooms and two apparent suicides, both in two days. The first had turned out to be a homicide. No surprise if this turned out to be one, too.

Woods and I regrouped outside the motel room and sucked on fresher air for a while. Dusk had descended and icy rain was falling. A vertical veil of wannabe sleet, tapping on the wooden roof covering the wraparound walkway and making nearby power lines hum.

Woods cleared her throat, "So who is it?"

"His name is Gentry O'Dell. He's the general doctor over at the Fed Med."

"Honestly? I'm pretty sure that's the last thing you expected."

"Doctor O'Dell?"

"Finding a suicide."

I nodded. "That's just it, Woods. I'm not convinced it is. I'm here on the back of another homicide in LA. That victim – a guy called Frank Bridges – had a keycard for this room in his hand, which means either he was here or the killer was."

"Or both."

"Or both." I thought about that: Cornsilk being here, at this motel, tracking down Bridges and taking the keycard with him. Seemed like a tall order. "Here's the rub, though: Bridges also worked at the Fed Med, together with Doctor O'Dell. It's no coincidence they're both connected to this room."

"So you're thinking the same killer killed both victims?"

"No."

"But . . . ?"

"Bridges was killed and then burned. That's the killer's MO. This is someone else's work."

"Assuming you're right about it not being a suicide."

"Woods, you're a hard nut to crack."

"Thank you." She flashed a smile.

"But there's no way this is a suicide. I don't know if you noticed, but there are soap suds still in the bottom of that tub, mixed in with the diarrhea."

"Nicely spotted."

"Thank you back." I flashed my own smile.

"So he showered before pulling the plug."

I let her see my smile fade.

"Sorry, Quinn. Humor is a kneejerk reaction with me."

"Whatever gets you through it, Woods. Soaping the tub makes traction impossible against the glaze. Even if this was a suicide and he changed his mind halfway through, he wouldn't have been able to do a damn about it."

"Which means he was deadly serious about killing himself."

"Or he was murdered and the killer wanted to make it look like a suicide. Besides, how many suicides have you seen who hanged themselves buck naked?"

"None. But then again this is my first hanging."

I made a pout. "Trust me, Woods, I've seen enough to know that most premeditated and determined suicides like to check out looking their Sunday best. The last time I saw anything remotely like this it turned out to be a homicide, and right now this has all the same hallmarks."

"Okay. I'm happy to go along with your assessment. Let me get my stuff and we'll go over the room ourselves, before I call Forensics in." Woods disappeared behind the Enclave.

I signaled to the uniform still seated in his squad car. He put down his coffee, got out and came over.

"We have a four-nineteen in here. You need to call this in. Get your homicide detectives down here ASAP. This is now a crime scene. Until we get more agents on site, make sure nobody comes near."

"Yes, sir." He nodded and returned to his vehicle.

Woods reappeared with Latex gloves and Maglites. We ventured back inside. The stench wasn't as bad the second time around, diluted by the influx of damp air. Woods went for the dresser. I headed for the closet. Inside I found O'Dell's clothes, all neatly hung, with socks stowed in shiny shoes. I heard Woods opening and closing drawers behind me. I slipped gloved hands into pants' pockets: all empty. I checked the jacket: same thing. I pulled out the socks and tipped up the shoes: nothing.

"We have a suicide note over here," Woods announced. "And a wallet."

She was standing by the nightstand between the twin beds. I padded over. There was a sheet of paper slipped under a black leather billfold. I picked up the note. Sure enough, it was a typed letter, addressed to no one in particular. It consisted of a single paragraph containing unimaginative phrases such as *I can't take it anymore* and *God forgive me*, finished at the bottom with the doctor's signature, handwritten.

"See," Woods winked.

"Ye of little faith." I swapped the note for the wallet and peeked inside. I saw several credit cards issued by Louisiana banks, all with the doctor's name embossed on them. About a hundred dollars in assorted denominations, a few business cards for local companies, a driver's license behind a plastic window, and a solitary coin wedged in, next to O'Dell's photo.

I shook it out into my palm, played the Maglite over it.

Woods leaned in close. "What is it?"

"A nickel." I turned it over, curious. "Any more loose change anywhere else?"

"None that I've found."

"So why did he have a single five-cent coin in his wallet?"

"Perhaps it's a keepsake. It looks like one of the newer commemorative designs. You can't be thinking it's significant."

"Woods, when you get to my age you learn the devil is always in the details. Never overlook anything at a crime scene."

I looked more closely at the nickel, turning it round in the beam of the Maglite, wishing I'd brought my readers with me to Missouri.

"Use your phone," Woods said, seeing me squint. "You can zoom in with the camera function."

I nodded. "I knew that."

She smiled. No fooling her.

I did as suggested, studying the enlarged image on the phone's smart screen.

The coin had been issued in 2006. It had an image of Thomas Jefferson's Monticello residence on the reverse and a forward-facing image of the third president himself on the obverse. The universal US motto *In God We Trust* curved along the upper edge and another stylized word appeared below – one which ignited hot fire in my belly.

"What is it?" Woods asked, seeing my reaction.

"If I'm right about this, I think I know who killed O'Dell."

*   *   *

We left the uniform guarding the crime scene and set off in Woods' Enclave, headlight beams illuminating drizzle, wipers clearing slush off the windshield.

"Where are we going?"

I was squinting at my cell phone, using the FBI app to find an address. I brought up a map and showed it to Woods. The phone's glow lit up her frown. She pulled out into rush hour traffic, and we headed east on Sunshine. A steady stream of red-and-white lights, made fuzzy by the incessant rain.

"Are you always this impulsive?" she asked.

"You wouldn't believe it."

"Next question: who's your suspect?"

"It's complicated," I answered. "A couple of days ago I was an inmate at the Fed Med." I saw her mystified glance and tried to explain. "It's not what you think. I was there undercover, and had been since the summer."

"You were inside for four months?"

It sounded unbelievable. No one would willingly do time in a federal penitentiary for the criminally insane without being a little bit crazy themselves.

"I was there to extract information from an inmate. The Los Angeles Field Office is currently investigating a human trafficking ring bringing sex slaves into the country. This other inmate was locked up for tax evasion, plus mental issues which were probably the reason he forgot to pay his taxes in the first place. I guess it took a little longer than planned."

"Was it ultimately successful?"

"Unfortunately, no. Someone shanked him to death on Christmas Eve."

"Ouch. I bet you were gutted, but not as gutted as him."

I looked at her, flatly.

"Funereal humor," she smiled. "Keeps me sane. Say hi to your old home."

I glanced through the passenger window. The Medical Center for Federal Prisoners was on our right, separated from the road by about three hundred yards of grassland and trees. Hardly any lights anywhere. Hard to make it out in the deepening twilight. I didn't feel a pang of nostalgia.

"His name was Trenton Fillmore. He was an oddball. He didn't open up easily, and when he did he spoke in riddles."

"I have a two-year-old niece just like that."

Keith Houghton

"I'd spent months winning his trust and cultivating his confidence. Come Christmas Eve, I had him on the brink of telling me everything I needed to know."

"Can I be nosy and ask what that was?"

"First off, Fillmore was an accountant."

"Who didn't pay his own taxes?"

"Apparently." Just like home decorators who never get around to doing their own. "Our investigation had linked him to the human trafficking ring. As far as the Bureau could establish, he acted as their accountant and a means to launder money. Don't ask me how the connection was made, because that happened before I came onboard. What I do know is the Bureau had no idea who was running the show."

"And this Fillmore character was your only link to the top dogs. So how did the investigation get its legs?"

"A dozen dead bodies in various stages of decomposition showed up near a hiking trail in the Santa Ana Mountains in California. Mostly teenage girls, maybe one or two in their early twenties. They all had sustained sexual trauma in common and all had signs of repeat beatings. What's more, they each had the same Cyrillic tattoo on the inside of the right elbow."

"Russian prostitutes."

I nodded. "At least, that's how it looked at first. Access roads into that part of the Saddlebacks were put under twenty-four-hour surveillance and photos of the victims were shown around known red light areas. Over a three week period, no one returned to the dump site, and the word on the street was that no one had ever seen those girls before."

We came to the intersection with Glenstone Ave. Woods chose the right feeder lane onto Route 65. It was fully dark now. Unrelenting sleet. Wipers working overtime. Woods saw my face and cranked up the heater.

I wiped condensation from the passenger window. "The high levels of sexual abuse pointed to sexual slaves rather than forced prostitution. According to the State Department, there's upward of fifty thousand females trafficked into the country each year. The private sex slave trade accounts for a small percentage of that. It's almost impossible to police. There are no pimps or places of employment. The girls are sold to the highest bidder and are never heard from again."

"Until they show up dead."

"We don't know what the setup is with the dead girls yet. It looks like the dump site has been used for at least a year." Some of the bodies had taken root, while others had been ravaged by wild animals. "We're thinking they're the disposables."

"Thrown out with the trash?"

"I guess. We live in a throwaway world, Woods. Humans are no exception. If you have enough money and the right connections you can just about buy anything."

We came to the busy intersection with Battlefield Road and waited on one of the left-turn lanes for long minutes while everyone had their turn.

Absently, I checked my watch. I thought about Rae, felt panicked and utterly useless. I had no idea how close Stone and the rest of the task force were to securing her location. Probably not at all – otherwise I would have heard something by now. The radio silence also meant that Cornsilk hadn't been in touch with any demands.

What was he doing with Rae?

I drew an unsteady breath as the signals changed.

Not far along Battlefield, Woods made a right turn and then a left. It was a quiet neighborhood of individual homes set back from the street behind trimmed lawns and leafless trees. No sidewalks. Ordinary Pleasantville. More neon reindeer and chubby snowmen casting cheerful glows within the cheerless sleet.

Woods pulled up outside one of the residences. "Here we are; this is the place. I take it this is your suspect's home?"

"We'll see." I looked the house over.

The first floor was taken up by a double garage and a brick entranceway. The second floor had a wood fascia and slits for windows. It looked like a regular family home in a regular neighborhood. But unlike the other properties hereabouts, there were no Christmas ornaments in the yard. No lights visible in the house. But there was a silver-colored Nissan Sentra in the driveway. Both the trunk and the driver's door were open. Through the rain I could see someone leaning into the car. It looked like a big guy.

We got out and walked up the driveway, peppered by rain. I had the Maglite in hand, scanned it in the open trunk as I neared. The beam played over a bulging suitcase and a lumpy duffel bag, together with packets of various foodstuffs and bottles of soda.

"Going someplace?" I shouted.

The big guy twisted out of the car like he'd been stung on the rump. He straightened to his full height. He was a tall African American with an eight-ball afro. He squinted in the beam of the Maglite, one hand lifting to shield his eyes. "Quinn?"

"Hello, Jefferson," I said. "Looks like you're all packed up and ready to take a long trip. I hope it's someplace a little warmer than here."

The unit officer from the Fed Med blinked and shook his head, as if by doing so he'd clear me from his vision. When I didn't disappear, he said: "Get the hell off my property. You have no business being here."

"Bridges is dead." Sometimes being direct has more impact.

Jefferson's mouth opened and closed in time with his blinking.

"Your co-conspirator was murdered, back in LA. That's why I'm here. Someone gave him a lethal dose of potassium chloride and then set him on fire. That why you're running?"

Jefferson slammed the trunk lid. "Bridges knew how to make enemies and keep them. Sooner or later some unhappy parolee was bound to seek him out and grind their ax in his face. Now if you'll excuse me, I'm just about to leave. Best if you get your girl here to back up that car of yours." He went round to the driver's door.

I blew sleet off the tip of my nose. "Don't you want to stop a moment and catch up? We just came back from the motel room. The one at the Imperial Motor Lodge."

Jefferson came to a sudden stop, like he'd walked into wet cement. He turned to face us and blinked against the Maglite. I could see something like volcanic fear pluming in his face. Steam about to issue from his ears.

"We saw what you did back there: Doctor O'Dell's faked suicide. Mind telling me what was with that?"

Jefferson didn't hesitate. He launched himself at me like a surface-to-air missile. I should have expected him to make a move. I hadn't – not against two armed federal agents. But cornered rats rarely lie down and die. They fight their corner, to the death.

Jefferson came at me too quick for someone his size. I had no time to react before his big hands had struck me in the chest and bowled me backward off my feet. I hit the wet pavement, shoulders-first, grimaced as pain slammed through my back. The Maglite went skittering across the lawn. Also taken by surprise, Woods was in the process of pulling out her sidearm. Jefferson had seen it and wasn't for slowing. He knocked her hand away from the gun, grabbed her arm and twisted it up her back. I heard her squeal as I scrabbled to my feet and got out the Glock. Jefferson put Woods between us and clamped a big paw around her throat. He released her arm and grabbed her gun, stuck the muzzle in the gap between her vest and her pelvis.

"Don't!" I barked.

"I told you to keep your nose out, Quinn. See where it's got you? Look where we are, dammit. This is all your fault."

I leveled the Glock at his face. "You don't want to do this, Jefferson. It's only going to end one way and that's badly."

"I told you to keep your nose out," he repeated. "You were supposed to believe O'Dell took his own life. Now you've gone and messed it all up."

I could hear the desperation in his voice, see his hand tighten around Woods' throat. Jefferson had the strength in that one hand to snap Woods' neck, I knew. Maybe pull off her head. She was staring at me, eyes wide, every muscle tensed, probably thinking the same thing.

"Let her go and we'll talk this through. I know you, Jefferson. You're not a natural born killer. You wouldn't kill unless you were absolutely pushed to it." I took a gamble and raised my hands. "See. No one's about to push you to kill again. You know me. We can talk. Work something out. Maybe strike a deal."

Jefferson started backpedaling toward the driver's door of the Sentra, taking Woods with him. He hadn't moved either hand from their threatening positions.

"Her name's Kelli," I said. "She's an innocent party in all this. She didn't even know your name before coming out here. Can you feel her pulse thudding away behind your hand? Kelli's a good kid. Going places. She has a dog that depends on her coming home. She's not the enemy. We're here to help."

Suddenly, he aimed the gun at me and fired. No warning. Totally unexpected. The street lit up momentarily. Automatically, I sucked myself into the thinnest profile possible. But the bullet had passed by wide before I'd moved and bounced off the road with a *crack*.

A dog started barking in a neighbor's backyard.

"What the hell, Jefferson!"

"I was aiming for the damn tire," he shouted.

Jefferson wanted to run. He didn't want us following.

Contrary to popular belief, hostage negotiation isn't about building relationships. It's about surrender, on both sides. What are you willing to give up to make them give up?

I turned toward the Enclave and shot out the front tire myself. Air whooshed and the vehicle tilted into the curb.

I swiveled back. "Satisfied?"

Both Jefferson and Woods were staring at me like I'd bitch-slapped an old lady walking by with her lap dog.

"Throw your gun across the street," Jefferson commanded.

"Only if you promise me you're not going to harm Kelli. Otherwise I'm going to need it to do the same to your head as I did to that tire."

Jefferson had backed up all the way to the open car door. "Best just to do as I say, Quinn. Longer you stand there with that gun in your hand, the more I'm inclined to make rash decisions."

"What if your neighbors have kids? We wouldn't want one of them coming across a loaded weapon on their front lawn. You wouldn't want that on your conscience too, Jefferson."

"Empty the damn clip." The desperation was giving way to mild annoyance. Already, he wasn't thinking straight. He could have settled with simply separating the clip from the gun, but he was going all the way.

Keeping my hands visible, I dropped the magazine from the grip and let Jefferson see me empty the remaining fourteen bullets into my cupped palm. I stuffed them in my jacket pocket and slid the magazine back into the Glock.

"Now toss it across the street."

"Okay. But remember: we have a gentleman's agreement here. You're not going to harm Kelli. You're going to keep her safe. She's relying on you to keep her safe, Jefferson. You hear me?"

"I hear you, Quinn. Now toss the gun."

I twisted and pitched the Glock onto a lawn directly across the street.

My heart was thudding, but I couldn't feel it.

"Now do the same with your car keys."

I made a face. "Oh, come on, Jefferson. Give a little, will you? I'm doing all the bending backwards here."

He jabbed Woods' handgun into her pelvis. She stiffened. The hand on her throat stifled a yelp.

I raised my hands and showed open palms. "Okay, okay. Only I don't have them, see."

"Get them," Jefferson growled in Woods' ear. "And no tricks."

Woods slid a shaking hand into her jacket pocket. The movement was difficult; made awkward by her tension. The hand came out with the car keys dangling from her fingers.

"These the car keys, Quinn?"

I nodded. "Sure looks like it."

He nudged Woods with the gun. "Throw them inside the car."

She did. Again, awkwardly. I heard the keys hit the Nissan's dashboard and land in the floor space.

"Now back the hell away, Quinn. Get in your car and lock the doors."

"If I do, will you promise to release Kelli?"

"Not yet. She's coming with me." He was thinking on his feet. Brains in his size twelves. "I'll leave her down the road. That's what I'll do. You let me go. I let her go. We all come out of this happy."

I wasn't sure about Jefferson's definition of happiness. There was no way he was getting away with his role in O'Dell's death.

I started moving back down the driveway. "It'll be all right, Kelli. Jefferson's a man of his word. Aren't you,

Jefferson? He just made a mistake, that's all. He's learned from that now. He's smarter than to make that same mistake again."

Woods was staring through wide and fearful pupils. Wet blonde hair plastered to her head and neck. Didn't look like she was believing a single word I was saying.

Probably the worst situation she'd been in, period.

I reached the Enclave, opened the driver's door and climbed inside, locked it after me. Immediately, the windows started steaming up. I wiped away condensation and watched through the rain-pebbled glass as Jefferson forced Woods into the Nissan. She went in backwards, had to shimmy across the center console to get to the passenger seat. He went in after her and slammed the door. I saw the vehicle's lights come on. Bright beams lighting up the twin garage doors and dimming as he turned the ignition. I toweled sleet off my face with the cuff of my jacket. The Nissan reversed off the driveway and out onto the street, so that it faced the Enclave: headlights blinding. I made an *okay* sign with my index finger and thumb, and the Nissan rolled by, taking Special Agent Kelli Woods with it.

50

Did I trust Jefferson to do the honorable thing? In not so many words he'd admitted to playing a part in O'Dell's murder, maybe even pulling the whole thing off by himself.

Did I trust Jefferson to release Woods unharmed? I wasn't about to test it by giving him the chance. No way was I willing to risk Woods' life, all to prove a point.

Jefferson had made his choice. Free will. Now I was making mine.

As soon as the Nissan passed by, I leapt out of the Enclave and retrieved the Maglite from the lawn. Then I rushed across the street and used it to recover the Glock from the neighbor's yard.

I saw the Nissan make a left at the head of the lane. Jefferson was taking it easy. No breakneck getaway driving here. I clambered back inside the SUV and dropped the passenger visor, caught the spare keys and started the transmission. I put the blower on the windshield and the wipers on max.

By the time I'd performed a U-turn and reached the junction at the head of the lane, the Nissan was about a hundred yards away. I left the headlights off and gave chase.

The punctured tire slapped against the pavement, in rhythm with my pulse.

There wasn't a whole lot of traffic on these residential back roads. A good thing. One or two oncoming vehicles flashing their lights when they spotted the Enclave with a flat tire emerging toward them in the dark. Some crazy guy driving with his lights out in these inclement conditions. Damn asking for trouble. Damn right.

I didn't have a plan. I was improvising as I went along, wrestling with the steering wheel just to keep the SUV from ditching off-road. I knew if I ruffled Jefferson's feathers too much he'd likely get twitchy and shoot Woods by accident. I couldn't take that risk. That meant no cops. No squad cars with their sirens screaming and their roof lights intimidating.

I rummaged out my phone. "Find a fed," I said at it.

The screen lit up and a synthesized voice replied: "Thank you for using Find-A-Fed. Please speak the name of the agent you wish to contact."

I glanced at the glowing screen. "Kelli Woods." Technology is yet to flip my switches.

"Thank you," the voice acknowledged. "Dialing Special Agent Kelli Woods."

I heard her number ring.

I had the Nissan's tail lights in my sights. Jefferson was still taking it easy on the sleet-slicked asphalt; doing twenty-five. I had no idea where he was headed, other than in the opposite direction to the airport. He'd planned a drive. Possibly a lengthy one judging by the travel rations stashed in the trunk. All I had to do was hang back and out of sight and wait for him to pull over, drop Woods on the roadside, then I could call in the cavalry and take Jefferson into custody. Straight forward, right?

Brake lights brightened as the Nissan approached the junction at the end of the road.

The phone stopped ringing.

"Quinn?" It was Woods' voice. She sounded deadpan.

"Can you put me on speakerphone?"

"You are."

I saw the Nissan make a left.

"Jefferson?"

"What do you want, Quinn?"

"Reminding you of our deal and that you're a man of your word. You leave Kelli by the road, alive and unharmed, and you're free to drive away. She's an innocent party, remember?"

I reached the junction. Crisscrossing traffic, regularly spaced. Red-and-white lights cutting through the rain. I didn't want to lose sight of the Sentra. I turned left across the street, gunning the Buick and cutting it close to an oncoming vehicle. I accelerated into my lane as the car behind me rushed up and honked its horn, long and hard. I was a nuisance with my lights out, endangering other road users. I flicked on the headlights and put my foot down. The popped tire sounded like a gofer wrapped round the wheel.

"What the fuck?" I heard Jefferson say from the speaker. "You're behind us!"

He'd heard the sounded horn, then its time-lagged echo down the phone. I was busted.

The Nissan lurched and begin to speed away. I stepped on the gas. No way was I going to lose them.

Then something unthinkable happened.

The Nissan zigzagged in the lane, abruptly, dangerously. Screeching tires slipping on the icy surface. Woods must have snatched at the wheel, trying to foil Jefferson's escape plans. I saw the Nissan's interior briefly light up as if lightning had struck. Then I heard the gunshot burst out of the phone's speaker and felt fear erupt in my gut. The Nissan's rear end fishtailed. I braked, hard, as its front wheels left the blacktop and ploughed into the broad run of city grass separating a wooded area from the roadway. The Nissan bounced across the uneven ground, tore through a single-strand barbwire fence and went nose first into a dip.

I reacted automatically. I yanked the wheel and held on as the Enclave went off-road, too, after the Nissan. The car behind me sounded its horn again as it zipped by. The Enclave bounced, tearing the wheel from my grasp.

The flat tire flapped off and banged on the underside of the fender. The exposed wheel hub went to earth, burying itself in the softer surface and digging deep. Momentum dragged the back end of the Enclave around in a half-circle and the SUV came to a shuddering standstill, facing the road.

Headlights rushing past through the downpour.

I leapt out.

The Nissan was butted up against a tree, half its right fender concertinaed. Hood steaming in the cold damp air. Lights still on and engine still running. Twin gouges in the lawn behind it. Snapped barbwire and an uprooted fencepost lying on the trunk. I slithered down the grassy slope. The driver's door was open. The light was on inside. I slid to a stop and pulled out the Glock, remembered stupidly that I hadn't reloaded it.

But Jefferson didn't know that.

I crouched and looked inside, down the barrel of my gun.

Woods was still seated in the passenger side. She looked shaken, pale, but she was alive.

"That was one helluva ride," she gasped. She saw the concern mangling up my face and added: "I'm okay. My vest absorbed the impact. Knocked the wind out of me. I don't think he meant it to go off." She winced. "Oh, mama. I think I've broken a rib."

"Stay here," I said. She still had her phone in her hand. "Call for backup."

She nodded. "He went into the woods. Be careful. He has my gun."

*   *   *

The headlight beams from the Sentra lit up the first few rows of trees, but after that it was pitch black in the woods. Tangled undergrowth and treacherous tree roots. I was about ten yards in when I realized I could have brought the Maglite and made my life a whole lot easier.

Too late to go back now.

I paused to listen. The canopy was soaking up a good deal of the ceaseless sleet. Even so, I could hear dripping water all over the place. The muffled sounds of tinder soaking up moisture. Distant waves of traffic up on the roadway.

I dropped the magazine out of the Glock and refilled it with bullets from my pocket. Counted thirteen – unlucky for some. One missing. I felt around in the jacket. Number fourteen had slipped into the lining and was out of reach. Thirteen was thirteen more than I hoped I'd need. I slapped the magazine back and strained eyes to penetrate the gloom. Nothing but the dark hulk of trees disappearing into the murk.

I had no clue which way Jefferson had gone. Maybe if I heard him thrashing across the forest floor . . .

Movement a ways off to my left, deeper in the woods.

Jefferson.

I was sure of it. I went after it. Slipping and tripping. Scrabbling under low branches. Grabbing onto mossy trunks to stop me going face first into the mushy undergrowth.

A hundred strenuous yards later I emerged onto a foot trail. I was saturated, scratched and breathing hard. Steaming in the cold night air. I scanned both ways with the Glock. Everything shadows and blackness. The rain had turned the trail into a muddy stream. It ran at an angle across a slope, then curved downhill through more trees.

My crashing through the undergrowth in the dark had sapped precious energy. It was a fair bet Jefferson was feeling the pain, too, and had opted for the easier downslope escape route. I wiped sleet out of my eyes and splashed along the trail. Sneakers sodden and heavy with rainwater, squelching. I reached the curve where the trail sloped downhill and paused to listen.

And that's when a tree toppled on top of me.

I was there, but it didn't make a sound.

It was Jefferson.

He'd lain in wait, in the dense scrub. Probably exhausted. Done. Thought it better to knock me out and effect his escape without me hounding his heels.

He impacted me from the side and we hit the forest floor like two sacks of wet sand. Cold rainwater gushed around us. Mud spattered my face. His big hands went straight for my throat. I kicked and hit out, managed to get a fist into his ribs. He was puffing hard. So was I. Entwined, we rolled as one. Suddenly he was on top of me, straddling me at the waist. A big bear, squeezing the air from my lungs. Sleet pelting my face.

His big paws clasped themselves around my throat.

Jefferson wasn't going for the knockout, he was going for the kill!

I sputtered out dirty rainwater.

No way was I going to die in a muddy rut.

Sometimes I learn my lesson.

I swung my hand with the Glock in it and struck the butt hard against his temple. I could have shot him. I could have unloaded the full clip into his side. But I wanted Jefferson alive; I wanted answers.

Jefferson's spine straightened as he sucked in air. The strike had sent an electric landslide cascading through his brain. He blinked and threw back his head. I didn't give him the chance to shake himself out of it. I pushed him in the chest and heaved him off. He crumpled to the ground, breaking twigs, and started mewling like a baby.

I rolled to my knees on the waterlogged trail, shook out my handcuffs and locked one loop over his right wrist. I went to do the same to his left, then had a change of mind. I locked it over mine instead. It was a difficult trek back to the road. Dark. Plenty of opportunity for Jefferson to give me the slip, even cuffed.

He moaned and shook his head.

I staggered to my feet and kept the Glock pointed his way. "Get up, Jefferson. You're under arrest for the murder of Gentry O'Dell and the abduction of a federal agent." I nudged him with the toe of a soggy sneaker. "I said get up!"

"You broke my damn eye socket," he groaned. He pushed himself to his knees. He was soaked to the bone. Blood leaking from his eye. Shakily, he got to his feet and touched fingers against his temple.

We faced each other in the woods. Blinking away sleet. Jefferson's back was to the trail as it sloped downhill and out of sight. I was aware he was bigger and heavier than me. Take a second to turn the tables.

All at once Jefferson made a gurgling noise.

I saw his eyes roll back and the whites come up.

He must have gotten up too fast. Blood rushing into his size twelves and saying adios to his head.

I dug in my heels; knowing what was coming.

Still gurgling, he toppled backward.

The handcuff chain snapped me forward and I went after him.

I hit the mud again, belly-first, as Jefferson crashed onto his back. The Glock sprang from my grasp. Then we were sliding down the shallow gulley. Rolling and bumping. Swept along by the muddy water. Jefferson's dead weight dragging us down.

*   *   *

You've seen it in the movies: the hero coming unstuck and whooshing down a mudslide. It looks like fun. It isn't.

Every rock and tree root whacked me on the way down. The Kevlar vest cushioned a little, but only a little. I bumped and bounced, towed by my connection to

Jefferson. The slippery slope had to end somewhere. The surrounding forest was a blur as we tumbled faster and faster. Then, without warning, we were sliding out of the trees, out onto an open expanse of mud and rock. Jefferson feet first. Me on my belly, head first, riding a wave of liquefied mud.

I could see what looked like a drop coming up. Someone had excavated a large area out of the woods, leaving behind what looked like a large meteor crater. A couple of hundred yards in diameter, easy. A torrent of muddy water was flowing over the edge and out into space. No idea how far it went down.

And we were heading straight for it.

I tried locking a desperate hand on a rocky outcrop as I passed it by, but my fingers scraped it without getting a fix.

Too much momentum.

Jefferson skewed on his side. He was still out of it. I tried digging my free elbow into the landslide, using it like a rudder to steer us away from the onrushing drop. Submerged stones cracked my bones. But it was no good; Jefferson's mass was calling the shots. No way I could slow our descent or change the inevitable.

I flapped my loose hand, frantic to grab a handhold and stop him from pulling me over.

A second later we reached the drop-away and Jefferson's limp body skipped over the edge.

*   *   *

Miraculously, my flailing arm hooked around an exposed tree root jutting over the rim of the crater. Instinctively, I clamped fingers around the spongy wood and clung on for dear life. The anchor point brought me to a juddering stop, side-on to the drop-away, one leg dangling over, and the other taking up the tension. But it didn't stop Jefferson's full weight from snapping down hard against my arm and shoulder. *Crack!* Muscles straining. Sinews stretched to snapping point. I clenched teeth and let loose a throaty growl as pain rocketed up my arm. Then I screwed my eyes shut and howled, gasping for air. Then howled some more as continuous pain lanced through my wrist and up my arm. Bones grinding. A steady stream of icy water washing over me, trying to sweep me over the edge.

But we'd stopped, and right now that's all that mattered.

I clung on, flat on my stomach, looking down at Jefferson who was swinging on our handcuff link like a bear-sized pendulum. Water tumbled over him and continued to fall through thirty feet. A sheer drop. Survivable if the floor of the crater was soil and grass. No such luck. I could make out mounds of rubble. Slabs of whitish rock almost luminescent in the dark and the drizzle. Big puddles with rocky islands. This wasn't a meteor crater, I realized. It was a quarry. And the leftover rocks directly beneath Jefferson made it a deadly drop.

I tried squirming in the mud, trying to downgrade my predicament from perilous to precarious. Jefferson's bulk kept me where I was – two hundred and fifty pounds of dead weight, pinning me down. My grip on the root was doubtful, worsened by the wetness and my withering strength. There was only so long I could keep hold before either my strength gave out of Jefferson's weight ripped off my hand.

I'd been here before, more than once: prone, suspending someone else's life from my fingertips. Most with grim outcomes. No reason to think this dire situation was going to end any way but in a bad way. For me, included.

Gravity is a killer.

Jefferson moaned.

I blinked mud from my eyes.

He was coming to; rudely awakened by the torrent of muddy water gushing over him. He shook himself like a wet dog and renewed pain coursed up my arm.

"Quit wriggling!" I yelped.

It felt like Jefferson was going to rip my arm from its socket. Tendons burning fire. Muscles screaming. The bracelet was biting into the skin of my wrist, adding blood to the watery mix.

He gaped around him, dazed, then down at the drop hanging beneath his feet. Realization made him squirm.

"Keep still, dammit!"

His neck twisted and his gaze met mine. I saw his big brown eyes take in the situation, and the severity of it.

"We got ourselves in a real state," he shouted, spluttering and blinking away the water flowing over his face.

"Just quit moving around, will you? And I'll haul you up."

A flash of teeth. "You and I both know that is never going to happen."

I tried pulling. Pain seared. My wrist couldn't take much more.

"How'd you find out, Quinn? How'd you know about me and O'Dell?"

"He left a clue behind," I said through gritted teeth. "A nickel with Thomas Jefferson on it. That's your full name, isn't it? Thomas Jefferson."

"And you made the connection."

"That's what I do; it's my job."

"I guess O'Dell was one smart cookie. He didn't deserve to die. Least, not like that."

"So why did you do it, Jefferson? Why kill O'Dell?"

He didn't answer. He reached into the small of his back. His hand came away with a lump of black metal: Woods' gun. He'd had it tucked in his waistband the whole time. He turned the muzzle in my direction.

"Forget it, Jefferson. Shoot me and there's no way back. We can do this. I can get you out of here. Just hold on. Help is on its way."

He coughed out water, blinked. "None of this was my choosing, Quinn. We both know there's no way back from this for me. Sometimes other forces act against us and give us no choice. He made me do it. I have a son. He lives with his mom. He's in college. He's a good kid. Makes his father real proud." He raised the gun. "He said he'd kill my son if I didn't go along with it. Best thing for all concerned if it ends here."

He put the muzzle against the chain holding us together.

"Wait!" I yelled. "Who made you do it?"

"Trenton Fillmore."

The revelation made no sense to me, but his face was deadly serious.

"Trenton Fillmore made me do it. God knows I didn't want to. Never come close to doing anything like that before. But he gave me no choice. You understand me, Quinn? I had to protect my son. Do what had to be done to save him, at any cost."

He pressed the muzzle hard against the chain. I stared down at him, water gushing along my pulsating arm.

"Do me a favor?" he said. "Tell my son I'm sorry for not being there when he needed me."

Lightning cracked and thunder boomed around the quarry.

Separated from the chain, Jefferson dropped away and fell to his death on the jagged rocks below.

51

I have danced with death a dozen times and yet the timing still takes me by surprise.

Stunned, I lay there for long painful moments as icy water snaked through my clothes, staring at Jefferson's unmoving and broken body on the rocks below.

My mind was spinning, whirling, thoughts crashing together like debris in a tornado. Most of them questioning everything I knew about Fillmore's murder.

One-handed, I clawed my way back from the precipice until I was able to scramble to my feet. Then I waded through mud, away from the death-drop, slumped against the trunk of a tree and massaged my throbbing shoulder. There was blood on my hand, leaking from my mashed wrist. Skin red-raw. The whole of my side wrenched and twisted. Everything askew.

But I was alive.

My left shoulder was dislocated, arm hanging limply. I pressed the elbow into my side, lifted the weight with my right hand, then rotated my arm back and to, pressed. The ball joint popped back in place and I bit down against the pain.

I couldn't drag my eyes away from the drop.

Jefferson had known he was done. He could have taken me down with him. He hadn't. Instead, he'd brought down Trenton Fillmore.

Distantly, I could hear the rhythmic *thwack-thwack* of an approaching helicopter. A bright light appeared from behind the trees farther along the curve of the quarry. A spotlight played over mounds of rubble and stretches of slushy water. A cone of light illuminating a steady shawl of sleet.

Woods had called for backup. Cops scrabbling toward me through the woods. I thought I heard dogs.

I wiped mud from my face.

My cell phone began to chime.

I wasn't the only thing to survive the mudslide. At first I didn't realize what it was. I listened to it warbling away. Then I dug it out and wiped droplets from the screen.

Rae's name glowed brightly in the night.

Heart burning, I jammed it to my ear. "Rae?"

"Gabe."

Something like giddy milkshake frothed in my gut.

She sounded terrified: "They're making me do this."

"Who, Rae? Are you okay? Where are you?"

"I don't know; I'm blindfolded. They took me to – "

I heard a dull slap, immediately followed by Rae yelping with pain. Someone had hit her.

"Rae!"

Her next words came out through a sob and busted lips: "Gabe, they know you're in Missouri. They want you back here, in LA. They want a trade. Me for you. They say if you tell anyone . . . they'll kill me. Listen, Cornsilk's –"

I heard another slap, interrupting Rae's words.

Then the connection died.

With fear wringing my gut, I gaped at the glowing screen as the police helicopter roared by overhead.

52

That was it. I'd had all I could stomach of Springfield. Done.

It was excruciating just to hang around, knowing that Rae's life was in peril, her death an increased likelihood with every wasted minute passing me by.

From the back of a paramedic unit, I provided a quick-fire statement to the local cops, then recounted it again to Woods' colleagues as they showed up and shook their heads. They didn't approve of my clipped answers. I didn't give a damn. My wrist was patched up and I got a shot for the pain. Take it up with Wilshire, I told them. Within the hour I was back onboard the Gulfstream jet, as its only passenger, heading west with the Rolls-Royce engines running flat out.

Even with a strong tailwind, it would take three hours or longer to reach LA airspace. I wasn't sure if I'd have any nerves left by the time I got there.

Didn't matter.

Rae was alive. In danger. But alive.

An exchange. My life for hers. I could buy that.

What bugged me was she'd said *they* several times. I figured on purpose. Not just *Snakeskin*, then. More than one kidnapper. She wanted me to know. But who? I'd already seen the result of someone helping *Snakeskin* – the firework display on Hollywood Boulevard – and knew that snakes weren't social creatures.

Besides, *Snakeskin* had never struck me as the sociable type.

I couldn't imagine him enlisting anyone's help to bring his wrath raining down on me, nor on anyone else he associated with his disfigurement. So who were *they*?

285

One hour down. Two to go.

Only so much pacing a man can do.

I used the hand dryer in the Gulfstream's modest bathroom to blow-dry my sneakers. It took the best part of the next hour. My clothes were on the right side of damp. The sleet had rinsed away most of the mud and filth and body heat had done the rest. God bless Levis. No one would believe just by looking me over that I'd survived a mudslide and a dance with death.

Finally, my thoughts returned to the murder at the Imperial Motor Lodge and to Jefferson's subsequent death.

The unit officer from the Fed Med had confessed to his involvement in murdering O'Dell and staging it as a suicide. A deathbed confession – inadmissible in court, but good enough for me. Frank Bridges was in that mix, too. Not sure exactly how. But he'd been at that motel room, for sure, the day before Christmas Eve – the keycard attested to that. He'd played a part in O'Dell's murder, somehow, at some point, before he'd signed me out of the Fed Med.

Bridges and Jefferson had worked together.

But was that the only murder the pair were involved in?

Trenton Fillmore.

Jefferson's last dying breath had implicated Fillmore in a threat to kill Jefferson's son.

It seemed absurd. Out of character. But Jefferson had no reason to make any of it up.

How did that song go? I wondered.

Blackmailing somebody to commit murder wasn't the Trenton Fillmore I knew. Fillmore was a gentle soul. In touch with his inner peace. I'd seen Fillmore catch spiders in his cell, then release them out in the yard. He'd spend hours studying a blade of grass and philosophizing about it being no less important in the grand scheme of things than him or me. Fillmore had been harmless. He'd relinquished a life of crushing others for one of crunching numbers. No way was he a killer.

But Jefferson had sworn Fillmore had threatened to kill his son unless he did his bidding, and I couldn't ignore his deathbed confession.

Had Jefferson shanked Fillmore to save his boy?

As a parent I could understand part of that thought pattern. Protecting our children is paramount. I'd been all set to kill *The Maestro* in order to save my daughter, Grace, back in Florida. Not sure I had it in me to take an innocent life to save my son's. Not after what he'd done. Then again, who knows how we'll act once we're in that play. Would I kill to bring him back?

The real question was: why had Fillmore made the threat in the first place? To buy an easy life on the inside? The Fed Med wasn't exactly a modern-day Alcatraz. Inmates broke tears, not rocks. Not so much Easy Street, but a quiet corner of federal suburbia nonetheless.

For the life of me I couldn't see a motive.

Unless it was a lie. A cover story to hide the real reason why Jefferson had shanked Fillmore: *to stop him from talking to me.*

Thinking back, that was my first conclusion when talking it through with Stone on his hotel balcony: a mole inside Stone's inner circle had tipped off Fillmore's employers and they had acted to silence the accountant. They'd bought someone on the inside, influenced him to take Fillmore's life. The only good snitch is a dead one, right? That someone turned out to be two: Jefferson and Bridges. But now I was thinking they hadn't been bought at all. Instead, Fillmore's unknown employers had made deadly threats against the prison guards. Threatened to kill Jefferson's son and maybe somebody close to Bridges if they didn't act together to stop Fillmore from speaking to me.

Kill or be killed.

In Jefferson's own words, they'd had no choice – or at least felt they hadn't.

Ask me three days ago if both Jefferson and Bridges would have collaborated in a murder and then both ended up dead three days later and I would have sooner put odds on the Texas Rangers winning the World Series.

That's how far outside the ballpark this thing was.

And what about Doctor O'Dell?

The only thing that came to mind was he'd discovered their sinister plot to shank Fillmore and then to make it look like the work of another inmate – namely, me. Maybe they'd tried convincing him they were doing the right thing. Maybe O'Dell had told them he was going to the warden with his information. Maybe they'd killed him to keep him quiet and get away with murder, twice.

What neither of them had bargained on was Cornsilk killing Bridges and leading me right back to the scene of the faked suicide.

And what none of my supposition even attempted to explain was why *Snakeskin* had targeted Bridges in the first place.

I went back to pacing, twiddling thumbs and spinning scenarios.

Two hours down. One to go.

My cell phone rang. I recognized the number: *Tim*.

He had news about the Tussauds security footage.

"I'm about to send you four images I think you'll find interesting," he told me. "The first shows the human torch. The second reveals his accomplice. The third shows the human torch before he rigs his disguise. And the fourth is of their driver."

"A third party?" I was conscious of Rae's use of the word *they*. "How'd you know it's the driver?"

"He's with their vehicle. What I'm sending you are stills from the video. The tape shows them arriving in a van and leaving in it after the human torch bows out."

I heard my phone beep as the first image came in on a text message. "Thanks, Tim."

"No problem, Gabe. Listen, before you hang up on me, there's been a last minute change of plans. Lucky old me has a date tonight. So if you arrive back before I do, don't deadbolt me out."

I hung up and dropped into one of the cream-leather chairs. Ten seconds later, all four images were in. I opened up the first, full screen.

It was a color image looking toward Hollywood Boulevard from about ten feet off the ground, taken from a camera attached to the wall outside Madame Tussauds. The street was busy with people. Tourists ogling the world-famous sights. Vehicles freeze-framed on the road. Bright winter sunshine, and Christmas street decorations scattered strategically throughout.

I peered closer.

In the middle of the shot, standing on the street corner, was a guy in a blood-red Santa suit. There was a large flat parcel covered in Christmas wrapping paper leaning against his leg. He had one hand raised in the air, frozen in the action of a wave.

The camera angle meant I was looking down from behind. Impossible to see his face.

I switched my focus to the top of the shot – to the area across the street, to where the guy in the Santa suit was waving at. I could see the big glass windows of a coffee shop on the corner of North Orange Drive. People milling about on the sidewalk. And somebody seemingly standing stock still, directly facing the guy in the Santa suit.

The detail was too small and too blurry to confirm an ID.

But I had a suspicion who it was.

I opened up the second photo.

It was a zoomed-in shot of the guy standing across the street. The accomplice. I rotated the phone so that the figure grew to four inches tall. He was wearing a black fedora and a gunmetal-gray Tennessee State University sweatshirt over black jeans. Scaly skin visible around a pair of designer sunglasses.

Unmistakably *Snakeskin*.

There was a sneer on his half eaten pizza face.

I felt my own lip buckle.

I stared at his ghoulish image for long seconds, thinking about all the devilish things I'd like to do to him. Cornsilk hadn't just overstepped the mark, he'd rubbed it out as if it had never existed. He'd killed my son and gone on to kidnap Rae. No leniency from me when I caught up with him. I wanted to rub him out of existence, too.

I swept his picture aside and tapped on the third photo.

This was a close-up of the guy in the Santa suit, caught as he'd crossed the street toward the camera, moments before donning the Santa Claus disguise.

He was a blond-haired kid with a golden Californian tan. Lean and wiry. One of those Colgate kids you see surfing up and down the beaches, even in the wintertime.

I perked up with a jolt.

I'd seen this face before and I felt my brow knot.

"The surfer dude from Huntington Beach? What the hell?"

His real name was Richard Schaeffer, but I thought of him by the moniker I'd given him back in January when I'd first laid eyes on him at a crime scene in Bel-Air. Schaeffer was the one-time live-in butler of Marlene van den Berg, a wealthy widow murdered for her charitable deeds by *The Undertaker*.

I couldn't believe it. I had to force the air into my lungs.

What was this kid doing with *Snakeskin*?

I'd last seen Schaeffer being carted away by paramedics following his shooting during a foot chase at Cedars-Sinai. Another failed capture, another story and another fiasco. He'd been charged for interfering with an ongoing police investigation and banged up for the night. But come morning, his bigwig daddy lawyer had gotten him off on a technicality and I hadn't heard a peep from him since.

Richard Schaeffer had been burned alive on Hollywood Boulevard, his gruesome death watched by millions on YouTube.

I couldn't believe it. I didn't want to feel sorry for the stupid kid, but I did.

How had he gone from meddling to being murdered?

I didn't get the connection between him and Cornsilk, not directly. *Snakeskin* had sworn vengeance on all those he felt had contributed to his downfall. Not sure how far down the food chain Schaeffer was. Equally, not sure why Cornsilk had chosen him, out of everyone, to kill publically.

More than that, how had *Snakeskin* convinced Schaeffer to walk down that street wearing a Santa suit and a sandwich board that would later engulf him in flame?

For the life of me I couldn't imagine Cornsilk and Schaeffer moving in the same circles. They were worlds apart. So what did they have in common?

Then it struck me. From nowhere. Out of the blue.

As always, I was the common denominator.

And they had a common motive: they both hated my guts.

Schaeffer hadn't held back from making that known. He'd resented me for giving him a hard time during our interview in the aftermath of his mistress's murder. Spoilt brat syndrome with a narcissistic personality disorder, out to get revenge for being duped out of his inheritance. He'd gone on to blame me for his getting shot and nearly falling to his death from the hospital rooftop. In his eyes, I'd humiliated him. And his sociopathic cross-wired logic couldn't let that go. Schaeffer had held a grudge. All this time.

How did Cornsilk factor into it?

Somehow, *Snakeskin* had learned about Schaeffer – probably when he was delving deeper into The Undertaker Case, looking for innocent people to burn – and spied an opportunity.

Cornsilk was ex-FBI. Friends still in the Bureau. People owing him favors. Maybe he'd used one of them to give him copies of the case files. Schaeffer's name featured prominently in the first days of the investigation. The kid was a soft target.

Thinking it over, I could see how the meeting had gone down. Cornsilk expressing his loathe for yours truly. Playing Mr. Empathy, so that Schaeffer would feel he'd found an ally. Together they could tell the world what an obscenity the Celebrity Cop really was. *Snakeskin* using his snaky charm to coerce Schaeffer into doing his bidding. Embarrass the Celebrity Cop in a very public place. Somewhere close to home, but where the message would reach around the world, in minutes.

THIS IS ALL YOUR FAULT

There, written as if in blood. For my benefit.

Prior to the pyrotechnics, the sandwich board had been covered with Christmassy wrapping paper. Schaeffer had removed the giftwrap mere seconds before the sparks had flown. It was a safe bet he hadn't seen what was on those boards. A sure thing *Snakeskin* had told him it was something other than what it was – possibly a picture of me, together with my name and a bunch of very strong words.

In reality, Schaeffer had been a puppet. A message bearer. Delivering a personal damnation from Gary Cornsilk.

Schaeffer's fiery death is all your fault, Quinn.

And, if I were brutally honest, it probably was.

$*$ $*$ $*$

I didn't advance to the fourth and final photograph. Not straight away. I was too busy thumping the padded chair with my good hand and cursing the day *Snakeskin* was born.

Cornsilk had killed an innocent kid.

Not because he wanted a martyr for his crazy cause, but because he wanted me to suffer.

Did he have the same design in mind for Rae?

I took an evidence bag from my pocket. Inside was the nickel I'd confiscated from the motel crime scene. I smoothed the plastic down over the face of Thomas Jefferson.

There was a single word standing proud alongside the president's likeness: *Liberty*.

I thought about Rae – my friend, my partner, my lover – and wondered, miserably, where she was right now and in what conditions she was being held captive.

Try as I might, I couldn't reconcile with Bishop's claim that she and Stone were an item. So why was it bugging me? Why couldn't I dismiss it as Bishop's attempt to undermine my confidence in Rae and move on from it? Maybe because I knew, if I dug deep enough, I'd find they had worked together over the past twenty years, perhaps multiple times, and that there is rarely smoke without fire. Then again, why would Rae hide it from me if it were true?

Wasn't it more important to focus on what was happening in the present rather than in the past?

Bishop had gotten under my skin, I realized. Wormed his way into my subconscious and planted seeds of doubt.

Rae had no reason to deceive me.

But what about the place in Pacific Palisades? Rae had said it was an inheritance, a fixer-upper. All the same, the upkeep on a property like that would sponge up all her salary. Plus, she didn't permanently reside in LA. So what was with that? She'd never mentioned any relatives out in California.

The sums didn't add up.

Maybe I didn't know Rae as well as I thought I did. Scratch that. There was no way I could know the new Rae as well as I had the old Rae. Time and experience changes us all. I wasn't wholly the same person today as I was two decades ago. I couldn't expect Rae to be unchanged. I couldn't expect her not to have updated views and opinions. Other than twenty-year-old memories, what did I really know?

Aside from Bishop's accusation, I knew nothing whatsoever about her recent personal life. Nothing. Zip. When I'd asked her about previous partners she'd gently steered me in another direction. I didn't even know if she'd gotten married, or had kids. Selfishly, I'd been too caught up in the moment to ask.

As for her career, I knew Rae specialized in breaking down human trafficking rings for the Bureau – hence her coming onboard with *Operation Freebird*. Two decades ago, after I'd fled with my family to California, Rae had worked her way to the rank of Police Detective in Memphis, mirroring my own progression in another State. Where I had specialized in Robbery-Homicide, she'd worked in the Missing Persons Unit for a number of years before moving into Sex Crimes, where she'd spearheaded successful operations against child prostitution rings fed by human trafficking. Five years in, her achievements had piqued the FBI's interest and they'd poached her for their own. That was ten years ago. She'd been an integral part of the Bureau's Human Trafficking Program ever since, more recently based at the Human Smuggling and Trafficking Center in Washington, DC.

A lot could happen in twenty years, I knew. Rae had firsthand experience out on the streets, mixing with trouble. Over the years she would have come into contact with all manner of criminal organizations. Bad guys with clout. Lowlifes with leverage. Was this what Bishop had been hinting at? Had one gotten to her, turned her?

Had she worked with Gary Cornsilk when he was still FBI, in Memphis?

An uncomfortable thought pushed suddenly to the forefront of my thinking:

Was Rae the mole and she'd played me all along?

If so, was I walking straight into a trap?

53

With a flick of her wrist, she signed the last check, tore it out and handed it over.

That was it; she had all the information she needed.

The retired cop turned private investigator thanked her for her kind business and left her with his glossy business card and a gaping hole in her bank balance.

She waited until he'd got in his car and drove down the street before letting out a satisfied breath.

Some things were worth their weight in gold.

She didn't care about the money.

She didn't care about the family business falling by the wayside and its suppliers threatening lawsuits.

She didn't care her marriage was wrecked and on the rocks and sinking fast, and that her husband had suggested a trial separation.

She didn't care she was stick-thin and sickly, and refusing to get checked out.

She didn't care her shunned friends thought her mad and possessed.

She didn't care the bank was foreclosing on their house and that everything she had ever worked for was about to be lost.

The only debt she cared for was a personal one, about to be expunged.

With cold eyes, she looked at the name on the piece of paper, at the names associated with it, at the location the private detective had come up with after weeks of searching.

She had thought she'd feel blind rage, revulsion, pure unadulterated hatred, but instead an unexpected calmness had settled over her.

For the first time in almost a year she saw something that gave her hope.

And its name was retribution.

54

Forty minutes to my destination, I gave Stone a courtesy call. I told him the bad news about Springfield. Told him there was nothing left for me to do in Missouri and that I was returning to LA to help find Rae. He wasn't happy, but Stone's happiness wasn't my concern.

I didn't tell him about the trade, or even that I'd spoken with Rae at all.

"Did you at least get to the bottom of the Cornsilk and Bridges connection?" he asked over the satellite link-up.

It sounded like a bluegrass duo. Either way, I hadn't. I'd racked my brains trying to figure it out, with no success.

"Bloody typical," he sighed. "Okay, the good news at this end is we believe we have a lead on the vehicle Cornsilk was using. One of Burnett's neighbors remembered seeing a white van driving down the street shortly before the first nine-one-one came through. We showed her some photos and we narrowed it down to a Ford E-Series Wagon. Possibly with smoked windows. As we speak, we're rechecking the traffic camera tapes."

"And that's our only lead in twelve hours, a white Ford van?"

I didn't hide my incredulity.

The entire resources of the Federal Bureau of Investigation focused on the safe retrieval of an abducted federal agent and all they'd come up with was a white van.

"It's better than finding a bloody body," he countered.

I remembered the fourth and final photograph sent from Tim. He'd mentioned it showing *Snakeskin's* getaway vehicle. Maybe it was the same van. Maybe the image resolution was good enough to reveal a license plate.

I hurried Stone off the phone and opened up the image.

It was another zoomed-in shot, looking across the street from Tussauds, but on a slightly different angle. This view was of the doglegged junction where North Orange Drive intersected Hollywood Boulevard, with the Spanish-style Roosevelt Hotel in the background. Parked about twenty yards down the side of the hotel, in deep shadow, was a white van with smoked glass windows.

It looked like a Ford all right – just one of hundreds of clones in that popular touristy part of town, used to ferry hotel guests.

I looked closer.

There was a guy sitting on the rear bumper, enjoying a cigarette in the shade. A guy with a crop of dark unruly hair and the makings of an evening shadow, even at midday. The third man, his legs in the way of the license plate. According to Tim: *Snakeskin's* driver.

I pinch-zoomed the image to get a better look.

And that's when the impossible reached out and slapped me across the face, hard enough to jar nerves.

*   *   *

In my vocabulary, the C-word is *coincidence*. And I didn't believe in them.

The guy enjoying a relaxing smoke break behind Cornsilk's van was unmistakably George, my son.

I felt the blood in my heart turn to lava.

It was one of those jaw-dropping moments where the Universe reminds us that we're not as smart as it is.

I'd recognize my own flesh and blood from a mile away.

He was facing Hollywood Boulevard, eyes looking to where *Snakeskin* was standing on the street corner, opposite Richard Schaeffer in his blood-red Santa suit.

The breath solidified in my throat.

This was the first time I'd seen my son since our fateful face-off in the Stratosphere Tower in Las Vegas almost a year ago. That cold winter's night, he'd vocalized his hatred for me. Told me in not so many words exactly how he blamed me for his momma's death. Told me it was his mission to make me suffer.

That world-changing night, George had been shot with two bullets from Sonny Maxwell's gun – one to the shoulder and another to his thigh – before BASE jumping to freedom.

He'd been badly injured, but he'd survived. I didn't know how he'd got patched up. Sonny had checked with all the emergency rooms and clinics in Nevada, and none had reported anyone harboring a pair of gunshot wounds. I didn't know where he'd gone, or how. Ashamed, I'd given Sonny a fake description; she'd only seen him from behind, as it was. George had used an alias, or several. I'd misled her through sheer embarrassment and denial. George had taken flight and disappeared in the wind.

Last I'd seen of him.

Later, I'd heard his voice over the phone. He hadn't finished with me yet. He wanted me to suffer more for his loss. I'd tried explaining how I'd lost everything, too. That in some ways I had lost much more than he had. He wasn't interested. Compared to his, my inner turmoil was negligible.

Sooner or later there would be blood.

Probably mine.

I'd spent months trying to track him down, even hiring a private investigator to do the legwork. Then Cornsilk had caught up with the PI and removed him from the equation.

And then *Snakeskin* had finally found my son and killed him, too. Burned him to a cinder on that bleak Alaskan beach. Killing any plans George had had for mortal revenge against me.

Yet here he was: a week ago, with his killer in Los Angeles.

Nothing made sense.

How had he come to be in Cornsilk's company?

Had he fooled Cornsilk, the same way he'd fooled me?

I was still chewing the fat as the Gulfstream jet landed at LAX. I stuffed the phone in my pocket and crossed the apron to a black Suburban with its headlights on. I was totally preoccupied, juggling all the possibilities and afraid to drop any.

I pulled open the door and fell into the passenger seat.

There was a big guy shoehorned in behind the steering wheel. And I mean *big*. Seven-foot-tall, three hundred pounds, big. Only just fitting in the cab. He had a bald head and a face folded up like a wet beach towel. Didn't look like your typical federal suit.

He was holding a stun gun at his hip, aimed at my chest.

"You've got to be kidding me," I said, a split second before lightning struck twice.

55

Word must have gotten around: the Celebrity Cop reacts negatively to electrocution.

I had no idea how long I was unconscious. Long enough to stiffen neck muscles and form a crust of dried dribble in the crack of my lips. I landed with a thud that jolted open my eyes and mouth, both at the same time.

I was lying on my side on the backseat of a vehicle. The Suburban. Knees pulled up. Wrists and ankles bound with plastic zip ties. The vehicle was moving through night-washed city streets, at a steady rate. Alternating bands of light and dark flowing through the cabin. Elvis Presley was singing from the car stereo, lamenting about bruised love at Christmastime. I could see the back and part of one side of the big brute's head, see his rack-of-ribs hands tapping along to *Blue Christmas* on the upper curve of the steering wheel.

He had the interior mirror angled so that he could see me, I realized. Sink-hole eyes filled with shadow.

I coughed up a knot of phlegm and spat it out. "I take it you're working with Cornsilk. So what's the plan, partner? Where we headed?"

I saw a hand leave the wheel and reappear in the gap between the two front seats, armed with the stun gun, saw the twin prongs snake out and hit me on the chest. White fire slammed into my eyelids. Skeletal muscles barbequing on bone. The world flipped over, then crashed in flames, fizzled and went away again.

Only so many knockouts a man can take before his heart throws in the towel.

56

I don't recall sleeping, but I must have. A dreamless length of nothingness, uninterrupted and as dull as dishwater.

No doubt, I needed it.

When I surfaced a second time it was daylight. Midday, judging from the lack of shadows. I was still on the backseat of the Suburban, aching from head to toe. The SUV was stationary. No signs of Brutus squeezed in behind the steering wheel.

My wrists and ankles were still bound with zip ties. A seatbelt was wound around my legs and plugged in, preventing me from achieving a seated position. All the same, I managed to push myself up on one elbow, at least enough to see out of the window.

The Suburban was parked in woodland. It looked tended. Possibly a picnic area. Tall pines glistening with raindrops. More residual moisture on the windows. I pushed higher and glimpsed a steely blue lake through the long limbs, with rolling hills behind. Cold and damp. Not Los Angeles. More like northern California. Maybe even Oregon.

There was a white van parked alongside. Black windows pebbled with rain.

Cornsilk's van.

I could hear muffled voices. All male. Two, or possibly three. It sounded like I was missing out on a heated discussion.

I twisted against the belt and managed to shimmy along the seat a little. At a push, I could see over the center console and into the front of the cab. There was a bunch of loose change and parking receipts in a cup holder. A discarded Happy Meal box in the passenger foot space.

Keith Houghton

Keys dangling from the ignition. And what looked like my FBI-issued cell phone wedged in a slot in the dash.

Could I be so lucky?

I moistened my lips and whispered: "Find a fed."

The phone remained unresponsive.

Maybe I was hoping beyond hope. Maybe the phone was off or the battery was dead.

I sucked a deep breath and repeated it more loudly.

Suddenly, the phone lit up.

"Thank you for using Find-A-Fed," the synthetic voice shrilled. "Please speak the name of the agent you wish to contact."

"Mason Stone."

A pause, then: "Please repeat the name of the agent you wish to contact."

"Mason Stone," I growled, this time louder, with a silent expletive in the middle.

"Thank you. Dialing Special Agent in Charge Mason Stone."

The phone began to bleep through the numbers.

I began to feel wildly optimistic.

Then the door behind me swung open and someone grabbed me by the hair and yanked me hard enough to pop follicles. I heard someone holler *give him the shot* in the same moment something stung at my neck.

The last thing I saw before darkness enveloped was a big hand reaching for the phone and disconnecting the call.

57

After that, reality returned in brief bursts. Over and over. Like time-lapse photography. Glimpses of darkness or daylight. Snapshots of myself in the third person. Skittering along like a puppet on wires. Impressions of movement or stillness. Sometimes a thundering silence. Sometimes a whispering din. Dislocated sensations of eating, drinking, toileting. Never more than a few seconds of blurred awareness between the blackouts. No way to keep track of time or to hold a single coherent thought before the darkness rushed in and swept it into oblivion.

I woke sometime much later, curled in a fetal position, with the worst hangover in recent memory. At first, no idea where I was, when it was, or even who I was.

Everything was blurry. I blinked until the world hardened.

I was on a bunk bed. Bottom one of two. The wooden unit was built into a nook in a short passageway. White fiberglass walls trimmed with varnished pine. I had a sensation of slight movement. A camper van? No sound of vehicular traffic. Not a road vehicle, then. A boat? Too clean for a fishing vessel. A pleasure cruiser.

I stretched stiff muscles and winced as the zip ties chaffed skin already made raw by the handcuffs and Jefferson's weight. I was still bound like a hog, still stuffed in my jacket, jeans and sneakers. Yesterday's clothes smelling musty. Skin in need of showering.

I was cold. I could see my breath, I realized.

Footfalls coming down the passageway.

I braced myself – not much of anything else I could do – as a man in a long wax coat came into view. He was a big guy pushing eighty, with a thick garland of white beard fringing his ruddy cheeks.

"Paul?"

There was a big serrated blade in his hand. Black steel. Possibly military, and about as friendly as a rabid Doberman.

"Your turn," he said, without acknowledging my surprise.

For a moment I thought Engel was going to gut me like a fish, here in his motor yacht. Spoil the bed linens and spatter me all over the wipe-down walls. But he stooped and sliced the ties fastening my ankles together instead.

Then he nudged me with his hand. "Come on, get to your feet. And no funny business, you hear? Or I'll dice you into little pieces and feed you to the halibut."

I was stunned, bruised brain trying to decipher what my eyes were seeing. "Paul? I don't understand. What the hell's going on?" I was having a hard time connecting Cornsilk with Engel, other than the obvious.

The knife flashed past my face and came away with blood on it. A surgical strike. Hot liquid running down my cheek.

"That's for trespassing in my home," he growled. "Now no more talking. Get to your feet and do as I say, or the next swipe will take your nose off."

I did as I was told. No choice. Engel held all the aces.

He pushed me ahead of him, roughly. I moved on stiff legs, head dizzy.

The passageway ended in wooden steps leading up through an open hatchway. Through it I could see a block of inky black sky dusted with stars. Nighttime when Brutus had picked me up from LAX. Midday when I'd been needled with the tranquilizer at the picnic park. Now it was night again. At least a whole day traveling with me out of it. Possibly two.

"Move it." Engel's impatient fist knuckled against a kidney.

I climbed the steps, awkwardly, out into the freezing night air. Breath condensed from my lips.

Immediately, I recognized where we were, and a shiver ran down my spine as I gazed out across the dark expanse of Deadman Bay.

For some reason, Cornsilk had hooked up with Engel and together they'd brought me back to Alaska. But why?

"I said keep moving."

I stepped up onto the deck and made my way to the side of the boat. Engel's flashy motor yacht was moored against the long jetty outside his mansion house on the snowy Alaskan shoreline. There were crates and boxes piled up on the pier – several already stacked on the open boat deck. Somebody was in the process of moving out.

The mansion house was in complete darkness. No garish lights blazing from all the windows. No thunderous music booming out across the bay. The only sound was the gentle swells lapping against the jetty's supports.

I stepped down onto ice-slicked timbers.

"All the way to the house," Engel said, emphasizing it with a fisted push. "We don't want to keep them waiting."

Dead man walking. That's what it felt like. Bound wrists in front of me. Feet heavy. I wanted to ask all kinds of questions. Why had I been brought back to Alaska? Why was Engel working with Cornsilk? What were their intentions? Where was Rae?

Someone was standing on the snowy beach, down the side of the jetty. It was a man, wearing a padded jacket and a fur ushanka.

Officer Locklear.

Hot hope flashed through my chest.

I'd asked the Kodiak cop to keep an eye on Engel's place, to let me know the moment the old doc returned.

Locklear must have been lying in wait, then come out to investigate the second he saw Engel's boat glide up to the jetty. This time, he hadn't let me down.

Engel was close behind me. Not sure if Engel had seen Locklear. Not sure if Locklear could see the combat knife pointed at the small of my back. But he could see that my hands were tied and was probably at a loss to explain what was going on.

"He has a knife!" I hollered and fell into a sprint.

Engel was slow to react. I heard the blade slice fresh air, but I was already bounded along the boards, out of his reach. Locklear was fumbling out his police-issue sidearm. I cleared the water line and dropped onto the beach. Sneakers slipping on the snowy shingle.

"Arrest him!" I shouted in Locklear's face.

But he just looked at me down the barrel of his gun.

"He's with me, you buffoon," a gruff voice called from behind.

I twisted round to see Engel standing on the jetty, sniggering through his bushy beard. Freezing breath forming a halo around his head.

I twisted back to face the Kodiak cop. "You're in cahoots with Engel? But he knocked you down during his escape."

"It was staged," Locklear said. "I told the doc to fake it. Make it look good. It worked, didn't it? Fooled you."

My dizziness was yet to clear, but the turn of events was compounding it. "You wanted him to escape?"

"More than that. We wanted you to keep your nose out of our business."

Now, things were becoming clearer. "You didn't check the house for the body, did you? You lied to me, Locklear. What do the two of you have going on out here?"

"Something that doesn't concern you. And besides, you're not going to live long enough to find out anyway." Locklear motioned with his firearm: *get walking to the house and let's finish what we started*. His arm was straight, at a right-angle to his body. The heavy gun held in one hand, unsupported by his other.

It was a foolhardy stance. He should have known better. I did.

I acted automatically. Years of police training triggering preprogrammed responses. Last thing Locklear expected.

I clamped both hands around his gun wrist and stepped into him, swiveling on my heels as I did so. Within a heartbeat I had my back up against his chest, his elbow locked, with the gun pointing away from me and out of harm's way. Locklear wasn't about to let me get away with it. His free hand came up to claw out my eyes. I head-butted him, backwards, and heard nose cartilage crack. His hand stopped midway to my face, but it didn't stop Locklear's finger from squeezing the trigger and holding it there.

Bullets began to fly, impacting snow and ricocheting off shingle. Thunder crashed around the bay. The Kodiak cop tried to wrench his arm loose. I clung on and head-butted him again for his efforts. Bullets peppered the crisscrossing beams under the pier.

Up on the jetty itself Engel was pulling back his arm, about to throw the knife directly at my face. No way could I avoid it in time. Engel's arm swept forward in an arc. I ducked – all I could do – as cold steel whistled past my ear.

I twisted Locklear's arm and his line of fire swept across Engel. The old doc twitched, once, twice, and he dropped to his knees, gaped, then went down, face-first onto the decking. I grappled the gun out of Locklear's grasp, then swiveled out of his embrace. Stepped back and aimed.

Locklear was unmoving, staring at me with one eye, the rubberized grip of Engel's blade jutting out of the other. A thick splash of blood running down his cheek and chin. His jaw dropped as a ghastly groan leaked from his lips. His eye rolled up in the socket and he crumpled into the snow like a toppled statue.

Engel had killed Locklear.

My heart was racing, banging, hurting.

I checked the gun's magazine: empty.

Dammit!

One last bullet still in the chamber. It would have to do.

Holding the firearm between shackled hands, I scrambled up the beach, heading for the house and whoever else was waiting for me up there.

58

The endgame was fast approaching. Glorious, like sunlight breaking through after a thunderstorm.

Everything he'd put in place over the past few months was about to pay off. Big style.

Players converging toward an inescapable checkmate.

From his vantage point high on the third floor of the house on Deadman Bay, he watched the Celebrity Cop work his way up the snowy shingle.

After months of planning, his archenemy was exactly where he wanted him.

Here to save the day. Rushing in where angels feared to tread. Pity he couldn't even save himself.

59

Two thoughts were battling it out for dominance in my brain: there were others in Engel's place and my son's body was probably in there, too.

As for what Locklear and Engel were up to, I couldn't even hazard a guess. It probably wasn't any of my business. But in trying to kill me – for whatever the reason – they'd made it mine.

The house was in darkness.

The steel front door was locked and dead bolted.

I worked my way down the side, slipping and sliding around the large snow drift reaching a third of the way to the roof. The edges of my perceptions were still blurry in the wake of the drugs used to keep me sleepy. I placed the gun on the ground, scooped up a double handful of snow and scrubbed it over my face, gasped at the chill, then shook off the excess.

Better.

No more compliance from this end.

I picked up the gun and came round back, scanned the deserted yard. Without the deafening music that had scrambled brain cells the last time round, I could hear the throaty hum of the generator in the big shed in the corner, and the murmur of restless dogs in the long caged lean-to.

The outbuildings were in darkness.

There was a pair of bright white rectangles projected on the frozen mud in the middle of the yard. I looked up at the back of the house, to see two illuminated windows on the third floor: my destination.

At ground level, the steel roller shutter leading to the carpenter's workshop was two-thirds of the way up.

No lights on inside. I started toward it, then froze to the spot.

A big guy in a three-quarter leather jacket had emerged from the workshop and had bounded out into the middle of the yard.

Brutus.

He was a white-skinned Grizzly with a shaven head. He'd swapped the stun gun for a snubnosed revolver – a thirty-eight special – which was sweeping across the shadowy backyard in time with his gaze.

He must have heard the gunshots and come out to investigate. What were they up to here?

No time to ponder. Right now, I was a sitting duck. Nowhere to hide. Nowhere to run. One bullet and no fair fight.

Suddenly his sink-hole gaze found me and he barked something in a foreign tongue. Sounded Russian. I wasn't intimate with the language, but I got its meaning.

He raised his weapon.

Mine was already pointing at his big gut. No time to take better aim. I squeezed off the remaining bullet in Locklear's gun. The resounding crack spooked the dogs in their caged run and they went mad, barking and howling and gnashing at the wire.

But the big Russian bear looked unharmed. Bewildered, but still on his feet. I saw him feel around his waistline with a big hand, as if wondering what had happened to the bullet.

I didn't wait for him to regroup.

I charged him down.

The golden rule in close quarter combat is to use your opponent's weaknesses to your advantage. Like most hired muscle, this brute was top-heavy. An inverted triangle. One of those bench-pressing nightclub bouncers bloated on anabolic steroids. I pulled my head in and went for his waist.

He wasn't prepared.

My shoulder made the tackle. It was like running headlong into a tree trunk. I knuckled down into his thighs and heaved, using momentum to sweep his legs from under him. He tried to counteract, bring the revolver crashing down on my back, but gravity had other plans. His legs came up as I bulldozed through to the other side, floundered on my knees as he toppled to the ground behind me. The bigger they are the harder they fall, right? I heard the air slam from his lungs and the revolver clatter across the frozen yard.

Suddenly I had the advantage.

I spun round and hooked bound wrists over his head, pulled hard until I had the plastic ties garroting his throat. Him or me. His head came up and he let loose a mean howl, started thrashing against the frozen dirt. I hung on, with the zip ties biting into my flesh and his. Then the goliath was pushing himself up, onto his knees, and for a moment I was a daredevil rodeo rider on the back of an incensed bull. He didn't stop. He staggered to his feet with me dangling down his back. No way could I get loose. I swung and kneed him weakly in his side. He didn't even flinch. His big paws reached over his shoulders and grabbed my forearms. Fingers like steel talons. Seemingly effortlessly, he hoisted me up and over his head. Then I was sailing through the air. I twisted and hit the side of the wire cage containing Engel's hell hounds. A half dozen sets of snapping teeth chomped at the wire next to my face. Saliva flying. Claws scratching the mesh. Maddened mutts trying to break out and tear me to shreds.

The Russian bear was coming at me.

I was pinned down. Breathing hard. Senses spiraling from the collision with the cage. No escape.

Was this it? Was I destined to die in another backyard brawl, here in the freezing snow of Deadman Bay?

Thick fingers reached down to snap my neck.

I reacted without thinking. Survival instinct kicking in.

I flung my foot skyward. Right between his legs. Aiming the toe of my sneaker into the soft nerve bundle behind his testicles. It was a last desperate effort. A puny attempt to hit his Achilles heel and bring him down, or at least buy me enough time to find the revolver and even the odds.

Brutus straightened and released a reverberating howl. The dogs joined in the chorus. Going crazy against the mesh.

I spied my chance. I rolled aside and scrambled to my feet, scanning for the gun. Couldn't see it; too many deep shadows and ruts in the mud.

The big brute was clutching his crotch and firing off Russian expletives. Face screwed into a ball. Only a matter of seconds before he recovered and came after me to finish the job.

I needed a weapon. Anything.

The Russian bear snarled and started his advance.

I grabbed up the nearest thing to hand – a weighty propane cylinder – and slung it hopelessly at his head.

He caught it in his big paws.

I was doomed.

But the impetus was enough to knock him off balance. He staggered backward with the cylinder held above his head. I didn't give him the chance to recover. I rushed at him, pushing with all my remaining strength in the direction of the dog cage. No way I was about to let him crush my skull. His heels hit the lean-to and his feet lifted off the ground. I kept pushing. His legs came up and his hips seesawed on the edge of the caged run. Then he went down like a falling wall. The combined weight of the gas cylinder and his spinning top physique proved too much for the wire roof. His bald head and broad shoulders broke through, and the furious hounds were on him in a flash.

I backed away as his blood-curdling screams rang out across the backyard. I saw him thrash at the mesh, trying futilely to disengage himself from the wire trap.

By the time I'd reached the workshop, all I could hear was the mushy sound of hungry dogs feasting.

*   *   *

Inside the unlit workshop, I paused a moment to gather my wits and my breath. But only a moment.

It was my thinking that Brutus wasn't here for the guided tour. Hired muscle usually came ahead of their hirers. I needed to arm myself, and fast.

In the dark, I fumbled around the workbenches and machinery until my hands closed on the circular saw. I rubbed the plastic ties against the teeth until I was free. I massaged screaming wrists, then picked up an ax on my way to the steps leading into the house.

I wanted my son's body back.

And nobody was going to stop me.

*   *   *

The short hallway reeked of gasoline. An invisible fog of noxious fumes capable of shredding lungs.

I stifled a cough and kept my breathing shallow.

Same toxic vapors in the crisscrossing corridor.

Someone had splashed gasoline all over the walls and the floor. Carcinogenic chemicals irritating the airways.

I moved cautiously in the dark, heading for the foot of the staircase. Even so, I bumped into something blocking the way. It was weighty, stout, metallic. A propane gas cylinder – like the one I'd thrown at Brutus. Deathly cold to the touch. I pushed past it, came to the head of the main hallway and glanced toward the big front door. Even in the dark I could make out several more propane cylinders, positioned against the wooden columns supporting the upper floors.

Someone intended to raise hell here. One spark and the whole place would go up like a rocket on New Year's Eve.

I didn't want to be around when that happened.

I continued to the staircase, bumping around another gas canister, and leapt up the stairs two at a time.

I didn't know what I was expecting to find, or who.

More henchmen, maybe. Their big bad boss, hopefully.

My captors had brought me here for a reason – not just to reclaim my son's corpse. I needed answers.

More darkness on the second floor. All the previously locked doors were now wide open. The caustic odor was less concentrated up here; I breathed a little easier. I ran to the stairs at the far end and kept going up. Same on the third floor – except for a pool of light spilling out into the hallway about halfway down.

Two of the rooms were occupied and lit up.

I could hear muffled voices. All male. One with a distinct Russian accent.

I hefted the ax and strode toward the light. I must have looked like a deranged madman prowling down that hallway. Sodden with snow. Skin reddened with the cold and a fight to the death. Blood on my cheek. One of those rare moments where I could have misquoted Jack Nicholson from *The Shining* and gotten away with it.

I glanced in shadowy rooms as I passed them by. No Overlook Hotel, this. More like the hostel from hell. Impressions of bare mattresses on bare timber floors. Coiled chains and slop buckets. Stout iron bars on windows, and the words *abandon hope all ye who enter here* hanging in the air.

I came to the pool of light and stopped on the threshold of the first doorway, peeped cautiously inside.

The illumination came from a long florescent strip bulb protected by a wire grille. Its bleaching glow revealed several single mattresses heaped on their sides against a wall. No linens. No bedroom furniture. No breakfast trays with leftovers and tips for good housekeeping.

Three people.

Two were men. They were looking through the barred window, with their backs to me. The third was a women. She was sitting cross-legged in the middle of the floor, her head tilted toward her lap, so that her fiery hair cascaded in thick swags over her shoulders.

Rae!

Fire surged through my system.

There was a manacle on her left wrist, attached to a chain running through a metal loop bolted to the floor.

I'd been too busy dealing with Engel, Locklear and their dancing Russian bear to even consider the possibility of her being here, too.

But here she was.

Alive!

But why was she here, in Engel's home?

Snakeskin had burned my boy's body on the beach at Akhiok. Engel had taken charge of the recovered corpse. Then he'd absconded with it after I'd returned to Kodiak. Later, *Snakeskin* had abducted Rae from her home by the sea. Engel had then used his motor yacht to ferry us all here from the mainland.

My dead son connected them both.

None of it answered *why*.

Rae must have sensed me gawping, because her face lifted enough to allow her teary eyes to meet mine. She had scarlet bruising on one side of her face and around her eye, a strip of silver duct tape across her mouth. More dried blood in her scalp.

My fingers tightened around the ax handle.

Someone was about to pay for hurting her.

Then cold steel pressed against the side of my neck.

"Don't." A single word, breathed against my ear.

Engel.

He'd somehow survived his shooting and pulled the dagger out of Locklear's eye socket, brains and all. Now he had that same knife pressed hard against my throat, drawing blood. If I moved so much as a fraction of an inch the blade would slice straight through my jugular.

Déjà vu.

Engel reached around and relieved me of the ax, tossed it into the corner of the room.

The sudden clatter caused the two men at the window to turn our way.

And that's when the situation went from bad to absurd.

60

I didn't recognize the shorter of the two. I was hoping it would turn out to be Cornsilk. It wasn't. He was a wiry punk with beady eyes and bad teeth. He looked Russian – if there was such a look. No idea what part he played in this charade, other than the fact he had a snubnosed pistol pointing at me. But I knew the taller one. He had the mincemeat face and gangly physique of a middle-aged bare-knuckles fighter. Two hundred pounds of gristly muscle and gnarly knuckles.

"Fillmore?"

It was all I could do not to gape like an idiot.

"Brother," Fillmore acknowledged with a nod. "This is one for the books, isn't it? I should have known it was you causing all that commotion down there."

His face. His voice. Definitely Trenton Fillmore. But he had no right being here – not after being shanked to death in Springfield. No right being anywhere other than in a morgue or a box.

He nodded at Engel. "You're wounded, brother. What happened?"

"Quinn killed Locklear and fed Sergei to my dogs. Tried killing me, too. Guess I took a through-and-through in the shoulder."

Fillmore's gaze returned to me. "Gabe? Really? Such violence is beneath you. Shame on you, brother."

"You're supposed to be dead," I growled.

It was a stupid statement – borne from stupidity – and everyone in the room knew it.

"I'm supposed to be many things: an accountant, a fighter, a lover. Dead isn't one of them."

"Maybe not yet."

That won me a half-smile. "Somehow, I don't think you're in any position to make threats."

"So what's the deal, Fillmore? Why are you in Alaska? I'm assuming Moscow here is your big boss?"

"Dmitri is middle-management, and I'm disappointed you haven't figured it out yet."

"Let's just say I'm still groggy from your henchman's sleeping pills. Enlighten me. But first, let Rae go."

"Then what? We all live happily ever after, give each other hugs and kisses and depart as friends?" He shook his head. "Let's be honest here, brother, I'm never going to be on your Christmas card list. You and me, we're from different worlds. No amount of brotherly love is ever going to change that. Me, I'm a realist. You, you're a romanticist. And that marriage ain't never gonna work out."

I was thinking furiously, keen to keep him talking, to buy time while I figured out exactly what was going on and how to extricate myself and Rae from this mess I'd got us in.

"So why bring us here, Fillmore? If you wanted us both dead it would have been quicker letting Cornsilk finish what he started. What's the score with you two, anyway?"

Fillmore dismissed my comment with the flap of his hand. "Gary Cornsilk is incidental. An annoyance, at best. Let's not waste what little time we have left talking about that fly in the ointment. Let's talk about us, this. You're the great Celebrity Cop, brother; I'm sure you can conjure up a better line of questioning than why I brought you to Alaska. Which, by the way, is to kill you. Both of you. You left me with no choice where that's concerned."

"We all have choices, Fillmore. Our choices define us. They make us who we are."

He snickered. "Listen to you: textbook Springfield. How nice. If that's true, all I can say is you've made a great deal of bad ones in your time, brother." He nodded at Engel.

Engel twisted the knife, forcing me to my knees.

"You don't have to do this," I said.

"What's the alternative? We all go to prison for a very long time, some of us to death row, while you two love birds fly off into the sunset? This is the end of the road, brother. There's no way out of this for you. See what I mean, about your grip on reality being tenuous at best?"

Fillmore's Russian comrade came over and slapped a manacle around my wrist, effectively anchoring me to the iron loop in the floor. I was staked to the boards, like Rae, with Rae.

Immediately, I reached out and grabbed her hand. "Stupid question: you okay, Rae?"

She nodded, sharply, and I could see she wasn't. There was dried blood in her nostrils and on one edge of the duct tape. More signs of bruising near her hairline. I squeezed her hand. She squeezed back, but I could feel the weakness in her grip, feel her shake deep inside in the way people do when they fear the worst. Either Fillmore or *Snakeskin* had slapped her around. Worked her over. I made a vow to do the same to them, and worse.

"I'll get us out of this, Rae. I promise."

She didn't look like she believed me. Not sure I did either.

I glanced at Fillmore. "The Bureau knows where I am. They keep track of all our cell phones. They'll be here any minute. You won't get away with this."

It was a pathetic attempt to sound fierce. It failed.

Fillmore still had the snicker Scotch-taped to his lips. "But I already have gotten away with it, brother. As far as the authorities are concerned, I died in the Fed Med on Christmas Eve. Apparently, I'm due for a warm send-off in the New Year – or at least some unfortunate soul is. Cremation destroys all the DNA, you know? No one any the wiser." He smiled. My friend from the Fed Med, alive and well, smiling through his false teeth. "I knew all about your hidden agenda from day one. Who would have thought we'd end up here? We've come a long way, haven't we? No doubt you're dying to find out how I came back from the dead."

I'd already figured most of it out.

Fillmore – or his Russian employers – hadn't bought the services of Jefferson and Bridges to kill Fillmore. They'd pressured them to fake Fillmore's shanking, forced the prison guards to turn the other cheek while Fillmore had set the scene. O'Dell was a part of it. They'd made the prison doctor falsify the paperwork afterward. Maybe had him smuggle in a bag of blood beforehand, to make the scene look convincing. O'Dell had shipped out Fillmore's body, but switched it with another on the way to the Greene County Medical Examiner. Probably a down-and-out lookalike with a fresh and fatal knife wound to the stomach. Jefferson had rented out the motel room in advance, as a planned halfway house. Somewhere Fillmore could ditch his prison-issue khakis and take stock. Then, to cover everything up, Fillmore had blackmailed Jefferson and Bridges to kill O'Dell – maybe because he'd gotten jumpy and was having an attack of good conscience. O'Dell had to be silenced, permanently. Only a matter of time before Jefferson and Bridges followed suit, which they had.

"I know the how," I said through grinding teeth. "It's the why I don't get."

Fillmore spread his hands. "Take a look around you, brother. This is the why. This place and the business we ran through it, until you ruined all that. Thanks to your friends at the Justice Department, it's been on hold since my detention. Meanwhile, we've lost millions of dollars, including some very lucrative contracts."

"The human trafficking ring," I nodded. "This is your base of operations. And you're the brains behind it."

It was one of those dawning moments when the smoke clears to reveal the wasteland and the loss suffered. Fillmore had hid in plain sight. Fooling not just me but the rest of Stone's team. The Bureau had been peeking in the wrong Dumpster from the start.

Trenton Fillmore was a fake.

Trenton Fillmore was the ringleader.

"I can't take all the credit," he said. "There has been a recent breakup and a subsequent change in management – for the better. The old boss was getting a little too sentimental for our liking." He tapped his chest. "With this new captain now at the helm, our ship will soon be back on course."

Ferrying sexual slaves into the country.

I felt sick.

Everything was unfolding in my mind. Pieces of the puzzle interlocking to form an uncomfortable picture: Russians shipping abducted teenage girls over the Bering Sea. Maybe meeting up with Engel's motor yacht in international waters. Girls and dollars changing hands. Fillmore and his cronies using Engel's remote motel-sized mansion house to imprison the girls, while Engel used his medical experience to keep them in good health for prospective buyers. Locklear keeping the peace and the rest of the Kodiak PD out of their hair. A simple setup running like a high-end sports car. Everyone paid handsomely for their troubles and everybody happy. Everyone except for the kidnapped girls, that is.

Then the mass grave had been discovered by chance out in the Santa Ana Mountains, with dead girls found in varying stages of decomposition. The FBI had been brought in, begun an investigation. Stone's department taking the lead. *Operation Freebird* had poked its nose into Fillmore's business. He'd reached out to a disaffected federal employee – the spy inside Stone's camp; someone like Lee Bishop, I was thinking – and made whatever deal he had to use him as an information channel.

With the mole's help, Fillmore had kept the operation one step ahead of the Feds. Then the FBI had caught a break: they'd somehow linked Fillmore's accountancy practice to major funds being laundered through the sale of the Russian girls to rich white guys in and around the LA area. They'd picked him up on a technicality and interrogated him about his employers. Fillmore had kept his lips sealed. Stone had come up with the plan to install me at the Fed Med – to kill two birds with one stone – then detain Fillmore there for evaluation, give me the task of jimmying the information out of him. But the mole had forewarned Fillmore about me and he'd played me from the start, even setting me up to take the fall for his faked murder.

I shook my head. "They always say it's the accountants who run the companies. It must have come as a big blow when they picked you up for tax evasion."

"Let's just say, it was more than a minor inconvenience."

"You thought you were untouchable, didn't you?" I said, keeping him talking. "Then your FBI insider got wind of the Akhiok homicide and Stone's plan for me to investigate it. It must have messed up your own plans: my imminent departure to the very place from where you were conducting your illegal enterprise, knowing I'd eventually make the connection. You knew you had to come up with a scheme to get you out and to keep me in. I have to hand it to you, Fillmore, it might have worked, too, if it hadn't been for Cornsilk killing Bridges and leading me right back to Springfield. I guess you have him to thank for putting you under the microscope. That's the one thing I don't understand: you and Cornsilk. Sounds like a marriage made in hell. Speaking of the devil, where is he? Where is that milky-eyed bastard?"

Fillmore nodded to his Slavic sidekick. The Russian went over to the mattresses stacked on their sides against the wall. He pulled the first one down to the floor to reveal a burned body seated in the lotus position. It was the same crisped corpse I'd seen on the examination table in Engel's clinic – *my son!* Engel had brought George's remains out here and stuffed them unceremoniously in the corner of the room.

I felt my stomach draw into a knot and adrenalized rage surge through my veins.

"I know what he did, Fillmore. Stop playing games with me. Tell Cornsilk to get in here. Now!"

"That is Cornsilk."

I baulked, saw Fillmore's indifferent expression, and knew from it that he was deadly serious.

Didn't make any sense.

I stared at the blackened body, at the cracked flesh and red-marbled skin, at the milky white eyes staring blankly from lidless sockets on a melted face. One noticeably whiter than the other.

"It can't be." Breath like diesel fumes.

Still not making any sense.

"Cornsilk came snooping around up here. He saw a little too much and his prying got him killed."

I leveled my disbelieving stare on Fillmore. "You're not making any sense. If that's Cornsilk, who the hell killed Bridges and torched Rae's home? And where's my son?"

Fillmore straightened to his full height. "The answer to both questions is standing right behind you."

I twisted round, expecting to see yet another incarnation of one of Fillmore's lies. What I didn't expect was to see George, my homicidal son, standing in the doorway, smiling lopsidedly.

"Hey," he said. "Been a long time, Dad. Glad you could make the party. Miss me?"

61

The impact came with a delay. The sea level shying from the shore in the quiet moments before the killer wave strikes. In that tranquil interim I was suspended in a limbo of uncertainty, unable to process. I stared at the smiling image of my son, the father in me elated that he still lived, while the lawman in me deflated that he did. Then the emotional tsunami swamped, bringing with it a deluge of questions and throwing me into a mental tumult.

"George?"

There was a Zippo lighter in his hand, a blunt thumb flicking the cap open and shut. Gasoline vapors out in the hall. A manic sparkle in his brooding eyes.

Fillmore patted my son on the shoulder. I sensed George tense, inside – I knew my son – but no one else saw it.

"George has been a great help to us, brother. An asset. That ex-FBI piece of shit Cornsilk was about to expose us. George happened to be in the neighborhood at the right time. He dealt with the problem quite efficiently, don't you think?"

I couldn't take my bulging eyes off my son. "You torched Cornsilk?"

"Sure thing, Dad. It's what you wanted, wasn't it: him off your case? I did you a favor. Besides, I didn't appreciate him gatecrashing my party and all. He who lives by the sword and all that baloney."

I was speechless. Utterly thunderstruck.

All this time I'd believed Cornsilk had caught up with my son and killed him, when in fact the complete opposite was true.

Fillmore squeezed my son's shoulder. "Remember, brother, we're on a tight schedule. We need to close this chapter and move on. Post haste." He turned to me. "I'd like to say it's been fun, brother, but it hasn't." He gave Engel a nod. "Slice her up first, then him."

Engel went straight for Rae.

He grabbed a handful of her hair and yanked her head back, viciously, so suddenly that her eyes sprang wide. Her whole body turned rigid. He had the combat knife against her throat in the same moment I hollered *No!*

*   *   *

A line of blood surfaced on her neck.

"Wait," George intervened.

And Engel paused.

My pounding pulse didn't.

Rae was breathing hard through bloodied nostrils. A trickle of blood pooling in the dip where her clavicles met.

"May I remind you we have a deal," George said to Fillmore. "I disposed of Cornsilk and this here is my reward. This is my endgame, remember? That's why I brought them here. Y'all give us a little privacy now."

"You sure, brother?"

"Positively. Just a little last minute father and son business I'd like to take care of. For old time's sake. You boys carry on now. I won't keep y'all more than a minute or two." He flipped the Zippo open and closed. "Then I'll burn this place down."

Fillmore checked his watch. "Okay. But make your goodbyes quick; I want to be on the water in ten minutes, tops."

"Like I said: a minute or two is ample enough."

Fillmore nodded at Engel, who uncoupled his fingers from Rae's hair. Then the three of them left the room. George waited until they were out of earshot before squatting down next to us.

His feral gaze prowled across my face. "How've you been holding up, Dad? I heard they had you locked up in the nuthouse for a while. How'd that work out for you? Learned what a bad dad you've been? I expect you've got a truck load of questions buzzing round in that head of yours. I wish I could say I wanted to stay and answer them all, but I don't. The time for niceties is long past. We both knew we'd end up here someday." He put a hand to the small of his back and produced a handgun. It looked like Rae's, taken during her abduction, taken when George had burned Bridges.

He waved it menacingly in my face. "See this, Dad? Consider it your one-way ticket to Redemptionville. Your last chance to make good on all those promises you failed to deliver. All those times you built up my hopes and then dropped them in the trash. That's right, Dad. The time has come for you to make amends." He dropped the magazine out of the grip. "See, no bullets. Just one lonesome in the chamber. And it has your name on it." He slapped the clip back home. "I'm going to make you a deal, Dad. Best deal of the day. Best deal of your entire life, probably." He waggled the gun. "Your life in exchange for Libby Rae's."

"You're insane." It got to my lips first, ahead of a string of obscenities which crashed into the back of my gritted teeth.

He sniggered, "Isn't that a little like the pot calling the kettle black – considering I wasn't the one in Springfield? Anyways, that's the deal, Dad. Your life for your floozy's. Take it or leave it."

Rae shook her head, vehemently. Blood and snot flying.

"Now don't go getting all hysterical on us, Libby Rae, or I'll shoot you myself, here and now."

My fingers curled to form fists. Instinctively, I wanted to grab hold of my son and hug him, squeeze the demon out of him, but I also wanted to knock some sense into him with my knuckles.

"So what's it going to be, Dad? Are you with me? Are we both on the same page here? It's a good deal. The best there is. You shoot yourself dead – dead as a doorknob – and I promise on Momma's sweet southern soul I'll let your floozy here have a fighting chance."

Again, Rae shook her head. Fear-stricken eyes pleading with me to ignore my son's crazy offer.

My knuckles were white. Lips peeled back.

We both knew he's never see good on his promise.

"Of course, I can't guarantee she'll survive. That all depends on her, and you. I take it you've seen the setup downstairs. Fillmore's fixing to jump ship. Raze this place to the ground. Burn the two of you with it. I'm saying I'll cut her loose, but only if you give your life for hers." He waved the gun in my face again, threateningly, then raised an eyebrow. "What do you say, Dad? You going to man-up and do the honorable thing for once in your miserable life?"

I snarled: "It'd be madness trusting you."

He cuffed me on the cheek with the butt of the gun. Pain spiked through my skull.

"Show some respect! I just swore on Momma's soul, goddamit." He shook his head. "Honestly. A guy tries his best. He tries to be all civil and all. And what thanks does he get? I just saved Libby Rae from Engel's knife, didn't I? Show a little gratitude."

He tapped the muzzle against my cheekbone, on the cut from Engel's blade. For a moment, I contemplated grabbing the gun from his hand, using the single bullet to put him out of my misery. But that would leave both Rae and I manacled and trapped, while Fillmore set the house on fire.

"Any way you look at this," George continued, "you don't really have much in the way of a choice, and that's the truth. Me, I can walk away right this second. Let y'all fry for all I care. Makes no difference to me; you're already dead in my eyes, Daddy dear. At least this way, I'm offering one of you a stab at life."

I looked at Rae. There were big tears pooling in her eyes. A look of sheer terror that screamed silently *don't listen to him!*

George shoved the Glock into my hand, forced my finger over the trigger. Then, in a surprise move, he pressed the muzzle against his forehead.

"It's what you're thinking, isn't it?" He grated the muzzle against his brow. "Blowing my brains out. Kill your pain."

I resisted his grip.

He pressed the gun harder against his skin. Eyes savage. "Go ahead, Dad. If you're lucky, maybe killing me will exorcise your own demons."

I was sorely tempted. God help me, I was. One shot and my psychopathic son would be no more. Zero chance of him ever hurting anyone ever again. But he was my son. My own flesh and blood. I'd raised him wrong. His condition was no excuse, but neither was my neglect. Either way, my unconscious mind had cut off the signals traveling down the nerves to my trigger finger. I could no sooner kill him than I could save him.

"All right," I growled.

Tears were rolling down Rae's cheeks. Chest heaving as fear-induced tremors coursed through her.

"You have a deal."

We were in a dire situation for sure, our prospects less than grim. I knew my son well enough to know he wouldn't let Rae live, at least not long after I'd taken my own life. It was all a game to him. His way of heightening our suffering. I had to let him believe I'd go through with it, give Rae a fighting chance to escape.

George released my hand. The Glock came away, leaving a red pressure ring in the center of his forehead.

"Let me say my goodbyes, George, in private?"

"Sure thing, Dad." He got back to his feet. "I wouldn't want to come between you and your misguided romanticism." He backed up toward the door. "Just no lollygagging, you hear? If I don't hear your brains being blown out in less than a minute, I'm going to let Engel carve your floozy here a new face, and then I'll shoot you myself."

He disappeared into the hallway. I heard him go to the room next door, heard muffled voices as he explained his plan to Fillmore and his henchmen.

The first thing I did was carefully peel the duct tape from covering Rae's mouth. She flinched as it came free, blotted with blood. She spat out red glue and sniffed back a bubble of snot.

"Gabe." A single, shaky word, drenched in fear. "Don't do this. Please. Not for me. I'm begging you. There must be some other way."

I wrapped an arm around her. She leaned into the embrace, warm and tender, trembling. Her hand cupped the back of my head and held me close, tight, so that my lips caressed the soft hollow beneath her ear.

"Rae, I'm sorry for getting you into this." I emphasized it with a squeeze. "I never meant any of this to happen. This is all my fault."

"No," she whispered back.

She pulled away a little, just enough to look me directly in the eyes. Her pupils were as big as black holes, sucking me in. My heart quaked.

"Don't say that," she said, sniffing. "I chose this life. It was my choice to make a career out of chasing down bad guys. Sooner or later one was going to bite back. If it ends here and now, with you by my side, so be it. I know I've made a difference and I can live with that. So long as we're together."

I felt a quiver run through her. She was scared. So was I.

"Rae, listen to me. It's going to be alright. This isn't how it ends for us. Not here. Not today. Not if I have my say."

She sniffed through tears. "Gabe, you need to know there's no way he's going to let me live. George blames me for causing the rift between y'all. I'm the other woman, remember? I took away his daddy. And the truth is, Gabe, he's right. If we're assigning blame here, then right now I'll hold my hands up and be accountable. I took his precious daddy away from him when he needed him most, and it's unforgivable."

Rae had listened to all the terrible tales I'd told about my son. About his hatred of me. About his warped desire to make me pay for the death of his beloved momma. About his premeditated killings, going right back to Jeanette Bennett, his first psychiatrist from Philadelphia. Rae had every right to be scared out of her wits; I wasn't far behind her.

"Being with you back then, Rae, that was my choice. That's on my shoulders. You don't deserve to die because of my mistakes."

Rae stared at me through welling tears.

"Dammit. I didn't mean for it to come out like that. Men say clumsy things." I brushed damp hair from her face. "What we had was real, *is* real. No regrets. None. And never a mistake. If I could go back in time, right now, I wouldn't change a damn thing."

She smiled weakly. "I hate saying this: but your boy's elevator doesn't go all the way to the top."

I went to kiss her, but was stopped by a fist banging against the wall.

George's voice came though: "Hello? Anyone blown their head off yet? I'm waiting impatiently for the sound of gunfire."

Rae pulled back, dread darkening her eyes. "Don't do it," she whispered fiercely. "Don't kill yourself for me. I mean it."

"It's going to be okay," I breathed. "Trust me, Rae, I know what I'm doing."

Famous last words.

I dug a hand in my jacket pocket, feeling for the small hole in the seam. I located it with a fingertip and pulled at it until the lining ripped, wide enough to get my hand in. Then I rummaged deeper, into the corner of the jacket until my fingers found the wayward bullet that had been out of reach since chasing Jefferson through the rain-soaked woods in Missouri.

I fingered it out.

Rae looked at the solitary bullet in my open palm. I could see her adding things up and coming up with the same answer as me: even counting the bullet already in the chamber, we were short by two.

I dropped the magazine and fed the bullet inside, clipped it back into the handle. Then I pulled against the chain fastening my wrist to the floor, pressed the muzzle against a link.

Jefferson had given me the idea.

But I knew the moment I fired the gun, George and the others would come rushing in to savor my suicide. I'd have barely seconds to reach the ax over in the far corner before Fillmore and his henchmen intervened. I could use the second bullet to take down the Russian with his snubnosed pistol. Then it would be Engel's blade against my ax. Three against one. Not great odds. But better than sitting here burning to death.

I looked at Rae, saw my own desperate hope mirrored in her big pupils.

She reached out and touched my hand. "Gabe, you can do this. We can do this. I believe in you."

I shuffled my feet underneath my buttocks, so that I was folded like a frog – poised to hop to it the moment the link broke – then put my full weight against the chain.

"Do it," Rae breathed.

Gritting teeth, I squeezed the trigger.

Like stapling Christmas tinsel to a wall, right?

*   *   *

Wrong. To every action there is an equal and opposite reaction.

Up close, bullets hit harder than jackhammers. No way to fully anticipate which way they're going to jump.

The force of the impact sent vibrations zinging up the bones of both arms. Jolting teeth. The Glock vaulted vertically out of my hand by about a foot, sailed through the air and clanked onto the floorboards behind Rae. It felt like it had wrenched my thumb from the socket on the way out. I straightened my legs and heaved – only to realize with horror that the link was still intact and unbroken.

Adrenaline flashed through my system.

Instinctively, I threw myself sideways to grab at the gun. In the same moment, George rushed into the room, closely followed by Engel and the others. I hit the floor and the chain went taut with a *twang*, tugging me back. Fingertips less than an inch from the weapon. I saw Rae snap to and go for the gun. I saw a boot crush her hand against the boards before it got there. I heard her release an agonized scream. I twisted to see Engel grabbing Rae by the hair once more and yanking her head back. The vicious combat knife was against her throat in a heartbeat.

"Don't!" he bellowed at me.

I froze.

Rae's eyelids were peeled back with fright. Neck sinews tight as wires. Veins throbbing. Chest palpitating as she resisted Engel's hold on her hair. One slip and it would be game over.

"Yet another disappointing result on your behalf," George mocked. "How on earth do you ever hope to save the day when you can't even kill yourself properly?"

Fillmore's impatient voice sounded from the doorway: "Let's be done with this, brother; we have a deadline to meet."

Engel's wrist flicked as the blade came clear of Rae's neck.

Just like that.

Not a sweeping slash as I'd feared, but something just as deadly.

A surgical incision.

A half-inch red line appeared on her skin where the knife had nicked her jugular. A red gash blossoming as pressurized blood began to spurt from the slit.

*　　*　　*

Then everything happened in slow-motion.

Engel stepped away. Rae began to slump to the floor, her eyes fixed on me with fear. I reached out, screaming my own blood-chilling scream, as her hot blood fountained in my face.

"This is all your fault," I heard George say on his way out. "Her death is on your hands, Dad. Have a very Merry Christmas!"

I was too busy gathering Rae into my arms and aiming to stop her blood loss to think about George's twisted sense of parity. I clamped a hand over the pumping cut. Blood squirted between my fingers. I applied pressure, trying desperately to seal the wound. I knew that I had to pad it with something, anything to keep the vein closed and Rae's precious blood from leaking out.

I heard the door slam shut and a bolt being slid across.

We were alone. Imprisoned in the house on the shore of Deadman Bay. Minutes away from being burned alive.

And Rae was dying in my arms.

I swapped hands, quickly. Hot blood jetted into the air. I applied more pressure, felt her pulse thudding against my fingers. Her whole neck had become sticky and slippery, her breathing erratic. I reached into my inside jacket pocket and pulled out the evidence bag with the nickel inside.

Rae was staring up at me with big unblinking eyes. "Gabe."

"Rae, don't speak. Save your energy. It'll be okay. I promise. Just hold still. I can stop this bleed."

I'd done it before: stem the blood loss with wadding and keep the pressure applied with a tourniquet. Keep the victim alive until the emergency services could get on scene and take over. The only stumbling block here was getting the tourniquet to work effectively without strangling her in the process.

A whole other ball game had Engel sliced the carotid artery feeding blood to her brain.

I shucked the sports jacket over my head so that it hung down the front, inside-out. Tore a strip of the silk lining away and bunched it up to make a thick gauze pad.

Speed was critical, I knew. The more I messed around with the pressure, the more she bled out.

"Hold still."

"I'm not going anywhere."

I lifted my hand just long enough to slap the plastic bag over the wound, followed by the silk wadding, pressed the makeshift dressing onto the gash. Then I ripped more lengths of the jacket lining and wrapped it around her neck like a scarf, pulled it as tight as I could without cutting off the blood supply to her brain. I knotted it over the wound, then, experimentally, I eased off on the pressure and watched for signs of blood seeping out into the silky bandage.

"Looks like it's holding," I said. For now.

Rae's eyes were shut.

A pang of fear sliced through my chest.

Quickly, I checked her pulse. It was weak, but steady. Breathing shallow. I examined the bandage again: no signs of blood other than that already soaked up.

I dragged a deep breath and let it rattle out.

My nerves were jangling, sweat pouring down my sides, senses flayed and crying out for comfort.

I flipped the ruined jacket back over my head and wiped gooey blood from my face.

Rae was unconscious, but alive. Even so, I was all too aware that without the proper medical attention she could easily continue to bleed out internally. The makeshift dressing would only last so long. No saying when it would rupture. I had to get her out of here, summon help, somehow.

But we were stuck.

Something shifted in the corner of my vision: a ghostly whisper of smoke, curling up through a crack in the floorboards. It was followed with a smell of burning timber.

The house was on fire!

I had to get Rae out of here.

I knew it was only a matter of time before the propane cylinders would explode, blasting through the wooden beams supporting the upper floors. When that happened, the building would come crashing down like a house of cards, with us in it.

We had to be out of here before that happened.

I strained against the chain. No give. No chance. The bullet had taken a sizeable nick out of the link, but it was still too sturdy to snap with brute strength alone.

Longingly, I gazed at the ax over in the corner of the room. No way to reach it, and nothing else nearby to use as a crowbar against the chain.

I stretched for the Glock and came up woefully short. I changed my approach and kicked out a leg instead, managed to hook the toe of a sneaker over it and scoot it to within reach.

Not all was lost.

I checked on Rae: still breathing shallowly. Chest rising and falling. Her brain had gone into hibernation mode, conserving valuable energy.

Hand shaking, I held the gun in my bloodied fist and weighed up my options.

One bullet left.

One shot at freedom.

One chance to break the chain and escape before the fire consumed the entire building, and us with it.

I sensed a sinister warmth pervading the floorboards, smell the acrid wood smoke as varnish bubbled and paint peeled.

Only one chance.

I looked at Rae. Sleeping beauty. Critical, but stable.

Her life solely dependent on me and my choices.

I sucked in a breath and held it. I flattened the chain against the floorboards, this time hovering the muzzle of the Glock about an inch above the weakened link.

This was it.

Do or die.

The demon in my chest was pummeling my ribs.

I blew a droplet of sweat from the tip of my nose, aimed and squeezed the trigger.

*   *   *

Incredibly, the bullet seemed to pass completely through the chain and take a splintered chunk out of the floorboard, leaving the link intact. For a heart-stopping moment, crazy fear plumed inside of me. I'd doomed us to die a horrible death, here in the house on Deadman Bay.

Then, as I lifted my wrist, the chain fell away from the manacle and I realized I was free.

Fear almost gave way to frivolity.

No time for celebration.

I picked myself up and rushed for the ax. I came back and flattened Rae's chain out on the boards, raised the ax high for a long swing, then struck it cleanly and shattered a link.

I couldn't believe my luck.

I levered the ax out of the boards, giving vent to more smoky phantoms rising from the depths.

I tried the door: locked. I hefted the ax and kept swiping at the wood until I'd smashed a panel away. Jack Nicholson eat your heart out. I groped a hand between the splinters, found the big bolt and slid it back.

There was white smoke in the hallway, boiling along the floor and ceiling. Denser to the right where the stairwell acted as a chimney stack. Lights flickering. I went to the head of the stairs and peered over the handrail. Smoke as thick as Atlantic fog. Swarming with burnt paint flakes. I wafted at it, coughed. Through smarting eyes I caught a glimpse of fiery demons skittering around in the bowels below. Timbers cracking and splitting. The constant crackle of fiery teeth as they gnawed through wood.

The first floor was completely ablaze, with fire spreading rapidly through the second. The building's sheet metal exterior was acting like the wall of an oven, keeping in the heat. Gas cylinders nearing ignition point.

No way down. Not here. No signs of any fire extinguishers or a hose reel. No other option but to go up, away from the raging inferno.

I ran back down the hallway, leaving swirls and eddies in the gathering vapor. The attic hatch was closed-up. I pushed at it with the ax and it yawned open. A block of cold air slid out and spooked the smoky specters. I reached up and extended the folded ladder down to the deck.

Long flames were visible in the stairwell as I headed back for Rae. The air was getting uncomfortably hot, itchy. Hard to breathe. It's not the smoke that kills, it's the invisible fumes that eat up all the oxygen. I coughed and blinked away tears. Rae was lying on her back where I'd left her, surrounded by a shallow sea of moving mist. Carefully, I rolled her over my shoulder, firefighter-style, and prayed that her bandage would hold.

I grabbed one last look at *Snakeskin's* cremated corpse sitting cross-legged in the corner, then made my way to the aluminum steps and up into the cold attic space.

*   *   *

'You must have killed a priest in another life,' my former partner, Harry Kelso, had said on several occasions, and I'd never had any cause to dispute it.

I lay Rae on her side and then threw open the skylight, paused a moment to clear my lungs in the freezing night air.

Down below, Engel's swanky yacht was still moored against the jetty, its long windows reflecting flames. I could see Engel and the weasel-faced Russian moving crates onto the boat's aft deck. Clearing out. Relocating their sexual slavery operation to an undisclosed location. Closer to home, geysers of smoke were rising past the edge of the roof, gushing out of the first floor windows.

A dull *thwump* sounded from inside the house. The attic floor wobbled beneath my feet.

Gently, I rolled Rae into my arms and eased her out through the skylight, head first, halfway onto the thick layer of crisp snow covering the roof. She was limp, heavy in the way limp bodies tend to be. One wrong nudge and she'd go sliding down the gradient and fall thirty foot to the ground below. I needed to tether us together. I unbuckled my belt, pulled it out and looped it through Rae's at the small of her back. Then I fed it back through the buckle and wrapped the leather around my fist. Not the best safety line, but better than none. I pushed her all the way through, sending disturbed snow skittering off the roof. Then I hoisted myself out and crawled to the apex, slowly, dragging Rae with me.

I reached the crown of the roof and kept crawling, hands and knees slipping on the icy peak. Rae was folded at the waist, arms and legs trailing behind her. I passed a long gouge in the snow where Engel had slid downslope on Christmas Day. I heard another muffled *thwump* from far below, then another. Only a matter of time before the whole house collapsed in on itself. And I was losing strength. Muscles shaking. Hands and face numb from the cold. I gritted teeth and plowed on. I came to the end of the apex and peered over its icicled edge.

Heat had shattered the downstairs windows and flames were flapping through. Shadows dancing across the nearby tundra. The snowdrift piled high against the side of the house was visible in the orange glow, ten feet deep, easy, but melting. I rolled onto my stomach and heaved Rae to the brink. Impossible to say if her necktie was doing its job, but I had to hope that it was. No time to stop and worry. I braced thighs against the apex and slid her off the roof.

Instantly, her weight tried to pull me over with her. I held on as the leather belt snapped taut and the bones in my hand crunched together. I bit down against the pain as Rae dangled in mid-air, fifteen foot above the snowdrift, turning slowly.

Then I let go.

I had no choice; my wrist was a mess thanks to Jefferson.

She fell, face-first, and crashed into the snow bank. Blood-red hair making a splash against the white. She seemed to sink into the drift by a couple of feet before coming to a stop.

Another *thwump* sounded behind me, followed by two more, and this time the entire roof wobbled like a drunk doing a sobriety test.

Without a second thought, I slung my legs over the edge and pushed out into the air.

I landed on my back about three feet in. Snow crumbling into my eyes and mouth. From above, it must have looked like the impression Wile E Coyote makes in the canyon floor. I flapped and kicked my way over to Rae, hooked hands under her arms and slid us down to the ground.

Unbelievably, we'd escape incineration.

But there was a red streak on the slope behind us.

I rolled Rae onto her back and fearfully checked her bandage. Blood everywhere. Frantically, I redressed the wound and tightened everything up. I felt for her pulse and found it, barely.

"Don't die on me, Rae."

At this rate she'd hemorrhage fatally before I'd even summoned help.

I had to get her to safety. I had to stop moving her around.

Above us, the house started moaning. Demons lamenting. I could hear wooden beams rupturing. Glass shattering. Metal whining, sizzling. Shovelfuls of snow skating off the roof and crashing into the yard. I looked up to see intense flame raging from all the windows. Thick smoke billowing from under the eaves.

The whole place was about to cave in.

I carried Rae over to one of the outbuildings, out of immediate danger. There was a smaller snow drift down the side. I kicked a wedge out of it and laid her down, so that her head and shoulders were surrounded by snow. Then I shoveled it in around her with my hands, compacting it down to form a snug blanket.

I'd heard of trauma victims surviving longer by reducing body temperature. I was hoping the cold would shrink the cut and keep the blood from leaking out. Maybe slow everything down, at least enough until rescue arrived.

An almighty roar rumbled across the yard. Something like a plane crash in slow motion. I turned to see the roof of the main house collapse inward and fifty-foot-high flames reach for the sky. Thick smoke churning. The aluminum sidings began to buckle, screeching and tearing as they leaned inward into the inferno.

I needed a phone.

I needed to get to Engel's motor yacht.

I needed a weapon.

62

I retreated into the backyard and scanned the compacted gravel for Brutus' snubnosed revolver. Heat scratched at my skin. I had a rough idea where it had landed after Brutus had let it fly. But it wasn't where I'd expected it to be. I found it yards away, hiding in an icy rut, grabbed it up and ran back down the side of the burning house. I splashed my way through snow-melt and slurry streaming from the shrinking snowdrift.

Then . . . disaster.

Engel's boat was already moving away from the pier.

I'd missed it by seconds!

I fell into a sprint. Legs pumping. Arms slicing air.

I had to stop it, somehow. I had to get to a phone.

Rae's life depended on it.

I leapt onto the jetty and banged across the boards.

The motor yacht was picking up speed; already fifty yards out and widening the gap.

I raised the thirty-eight special and squeezed off two rounds.

I didn't know what I'd expect to achieve. Maybe get their attention. Maybe force my way onboard and to a phone.

The bullets either fell short or missed their target completely.

I came to a juddering halt, breathing hard, and steadied my aim.

I could do this. I had to do this.

I squeezed off another couple of rounds.

The yacht was a fifty yards out and accelerating.

Then . . . catastrophe.

A bubble of blinding light blossomed from the spot where Engel's boat had been a moment earlier. I shielded my eyes against the silent fireball expanding and rising, lighting up the surrounding water like a miniature atom bomb blast. It mushroomed into a glowing cloud of hot gas as the boom of an explosion barreled across the bay and thumped me in the face.

I stared, numb from the feet up, as the cruiser blazed brightly. Suddenly going nowhere. Everyone on board dead or burning. The boat about to sink, taking my heart with it.

One of the bullets must have hit the fuel tank – that's all I could think. A delayed reaction as fuel had leaked out, then spontaneous combustion as it had come into contact with the electrical system.

Then . . . *boom!*

I'd killed Fillmore and his cohorts.

Moreover, I'd killed my boy.

The boat was gone.

And with it any hope I had of saving Rae.

63

"Hot diggity dog! Now that's what I call a firework display!"

I swiveled on my heels. I wasn't alone on the pier, I realized.

There was a man, sitting on the end of the jetty, swinging his legs over the edge like a kid with no cares in the world.

George!

There was something in his hand: a cell phone.

He waggled it at me. "Remote detonation. Worked like a charm, didn't it?"

My son was alive!

I reacted on autopilot.

In that moment all I could see was red. Rae's blood on my hands, red. Rage red. Descending like a satanic mist.

I grabbed George by his collar and hauled him flat against the slicked boards.

He just laughed, deep and loud. Didn't even try and do anything about it. He laughed like a son goofing around with his dad – which he had been, all this time, with me: the fool.

"You're under arrest," I snarled.

"For what? For opening your eyes?"

"For being a disappointment, dammit."

His eyes were wild, reflecting stars – only they weren't stars, they were motes: images of the people he'd murdered in cold blood, including Harry, Jamie and little Jennifer McNamara. All the souls he'd reaped on a whim.

How had we come to be here?

How had my son grown from a boy into a monster?

Nature of nurture?

George's maniacal laughter rang out through the night.

I clipped him between his eyes with the butt of the revolver, hard enough to slam his eyelids closed. He sagged unconsciously to the cold boards and lay there, purring like a baby.

I scooped up the phone from his hand, then pushed away from him. All at once I didn't want to be anywhere near my son. Not even in the same State of the Union. Maybe anywhere at all.

I dialed nine-one-one as the remains of Engel's boat hissed and sank.

64

There was a greasy handprint on the one-way glass, left behind where somebody had leaned close, probably disbelieving their ears. It looked like my hand shape. Same dislocated thumb mark.

Beyond the smudged fingerprints I could see someone wearing my son's face. He had the same dark hair and pale skin. Same brooding eyes and bruised circles. But he was an imposter. He'd taken my son hostage a long time ago. Killed him. Now he was wearing my son's skin like a suit.

He was seated at a brushed steel table, both wrists handcuffed to loops welded to its spotless surface. He was wearing a cheery orange jumpsuit over a plain white undershirt. A conceited look tugging at his thick eyebrows.

At a glance, the resemblance to my son was remarkable. But this wasn't my boy. My son had died when he was five years old. Cracked his head after falling from a carousel at the zoo. All my fault. A demon had seized him that day. Taken over his mind and forced George into a dark corner, permanently. This wasn't my son. This was a cold-blooded serial killer. A monster responsible for the deaths of more than a dozen innocent people. A madman who believed in blood prophesies and dispatched people dispassionately because of them.

I knew him as *The Undertaker.*

But everyone in the room knew him as George Quinn.

Captivity had oiled his jaw and he was talking openly, freely answering the endless barrage of questions posed by the three FBI agents grilling him in the interview room. Like an actor auditioning for a role, he was playing to the camera recording his confession. More than that – he was enthusing, eager to share, to boast. Gushing about his supernatural visions – apparently a side effect of his *condition* – and his consequent missions to right future wrongs.

It was all bullshit.

The killer believed every word escaping his lips. Hard to imagine him being anything other than in total control over his life and his destiny. Possessed with passion and dynamism. Deriving immense pride and pleasure from imparting his dark secrets.

Cuckoo.

He was facing serious charges: several counts of premeditated murder; conspiracy to commit murder; obstruction of justice; kidnap; impersonating a police officer; identity theft; fraud; arson; planting bombs; killing a federal agent; killing two police officers; malice aforethought; being a bad son. He knew the charges and it hadn't dented his hide one bit.

Psycho.

The killer had already come clean over everything and washed his bloodied hands. *The Undertaker's* hour-long confessional had covered every base. He'd confessed about how he'd seen a vision of our calamitous coming together in Kodiak, about how that revelation had revealed the faces behind the human trafficking ring. And about how he'd visualized a way to prolong my suffering while exposing the evil behind the sex slavery being run through Akhiok.

Another good deed – like killing everyone associated with Harland Labs back in January.

He'd confessed about how he'd discovered Gary Cornsilk hunting him down and how he'd decided to do something about it. He'd spoken about how he'd orchestrated a chance encounter, using a false identity to garner Cornsilk's trust, and about how he'd sympathized with Cornsilk's plight to do me harm. He'd told of how he'd introduced the disaffected ex-Fed to Richard

Schaeffer – the surfer dude from Huntington Beach – who was also keen to blight my name in public.

He'd confessed about how he'd convinced Cornsilk to travel to Kodiak with him. About how he'd masterminded the plan to deliver me right into his hands. And about how he'd deliberately used the Westbrook ID to pique the Bureau's interest, gambling on the fact I would be sprung from Springfield and sent to investigate.

The fulfillment of a prophesy.

He'd confessed to killing Cornsilk, to cement confidence with those running the human trafficking ring, admitted to burning Cornsilk to a cinder on that cold Alaskan beach, then using his credit card to spin me back to California. Never knowing that I would misidentify the body, then spend the whole of Christmastime believing my son had been brutally murdered.

A fool and his logic soon come unstuck.

He'd confessed to manipulating those behind the human trafficking operation – especially Paul Engel, who he had first met during our father-and-son expedition to Kodiak years earlier. Confessed to exposing their operation and then to killing them for their heinous crimes.

The irony was tearful.

I'd already worked out that Engel had been the one to patch him up following his fall from the Stratosphere Tower in Las Vegas. The killer had been shot with two bullets from Sonny's gun. He'd timed everything to perfection. Engel had been in town that night, visiting his folks. The killer had forced him to fix him up, then convinced Engel to allow him inside his inner circle out at Deadman Bay.

He killed, cheated and lied.

No way was he ever coming out.

Already, a date for his trial had been set.

The press would want their pound of flesh, and I had no illusions about how it was all likely to pan out.

The Undertaker was a readymade media sensation.

Soon to be a household name. Like his dad.

In the coming weeks and months, the whole world was going to learn everything there was to know about the killer: about how his condition caused him to kill, about how his hatred for me was his driving force. For a brief moment in time he'd become famous, infamous. His name, face and atrocities splashed across all the papers and Internet feeds. News programs running feature-length reports. Crime analysts giving their honest verdict. Supporters of the death penalty citing his inhuman crimes as justification to uphold Old Testament mentalities.

The Celebrity Cop dad with the Celebrity Killer son.

A perfect recipe for a media feeding frenzy.

I felt sorry. But not for me. And certainly not for the killer.

I felt sorry for the families and the friends of all his victims, whose lives had been irreversibly traumatized by his condition. The media attention would force them to relive their pain under a global spotlight.

In court, on nationwide TV, *The Undertaker* would live it up. Charm the cameras. Turn his condition into a godsend. He'd run through his confessional again, as many times as they liked. Not to glorify his actions, but to justify them. To show the world how he saved a million lives by taking one. He'd use his trial as a forum from which to point the crooked finger of blame at the one person he held ultimately accountable for creating the monster:

Me.

Back inside the interrogation room, his evil eyes looked my way and the coolness inside of me turned to a chill.

No words can describe the indescribable.

Only feelings.

And mine were frozen in time, twenty-five years in the past.

The killer looked directly at me.

352

Of course, there was no way he could see me through the mirrored finish. No way could he see the dread and disappointment drawing down my jowls. Rather, he could sense my presence – just as I could feel the gravity of loss pulling us together.

He mouthed a silent sentence.

I placed my palm against the glass, leaning in to hear his whispered words:

This is all your fault.

Then, abruptly, his wild eyes returned to his inquisitors, and the words bubbling from his mouth were no longer aimed at me.

My son had died that day at the zoo and he was never coming back.

65

The sky was the color of a Memphis Tigers jersey. A lackluster sun had shown up out of obligation. And a fruitless breeze was trying to encourage leaves to take the plunge.

Last day of the year.

I followed my feet across the neatly-trimmed lawns, carrying a bunch of flowers like the Olympic torch. Heavy as lead. Watery eyes fixed on my destination. There were other visitors scattered across the cemetery. Ravens flocked around dead relatives.

I arrived at a headstone and leaned the bouquet against the polished granite. I placed both hands against the cool marble, closed my eyes and prayed for forgiveness.

Condemned.

A lifer, with no hope for parole.

No court in the land able to judge favorably on my failings.

Life is cruel. Sometimes we make it that way,

Even mass murderers are entitled to due process.

*   *   *

I stayed there until demonic shadows were reaching out across the grass to pull me into an early grave. Then I returned to the black sedan parked on the narrow roadway and fell inside.

"You okay?"

"Sure," I lied. "Reckon I'm about as happy as a father whose son is headed for death row."

"Maybe it was a bad idea my coming along; it's not exactly my place to be here."

I turned to face Rae Burnett.

She was seated behind the steering wheel, her wavy red hair spilling in thick swags over the shoulders of her long woolen coat. She had a green scarf looped around her neck, partly to hide the needlework stitching her jugular together, but mostly because it brought out the verve in her eyes.

"The last thing I want to do is intrude."

I reached out. She grabbed my hand in hers, squeezed.

"Trust me, Rae. Hope would approve. You're just about the best thing to happen to me in ages. You make me happy. And that's what's important right now. My very own ray of hope."

She pulled me into her embrace. I didn't fight back; I knew what battles I could win. We clung onto each other for long moments while the rest of the world revolved around us in a blur.

Then, hot breath swirling in my ear: "I'm here for the long haul, Gabe. You saved my life and right now that makes you responsible for me."

I eased back and looked into her eyes. "Rae, that's sweet. But it's also a cheap Hollywood trope."

"I know, but it got you smiling, didn't it?" She smiled, levering one from my own lips. "See. Now listen to me, Gabe. I'm serious. It's New Year's Eve. I know you're in no mood for celebration and all – God knows it's way down on my priority list, too – but hear me out. Stone's given us a week's leave, with instructions for rest and recuperation. Maybe I'm being disrespectful and inappropriate, but right now I'm fixing on making good on the debt I owe you. Gabe, you saved my life, and I want to show you exactly how grateful I am."

"You're right," I said, "it is inappropriate and disrespectful." I leaned over and kissed her, gently. It felt good. Scratch that – it felt *right*. "Let's go somewhere. You and me. Far from here. And I don't mean the nearest hotel room either."

"You don't?"

"Rae, I am sorely tempted. Trust me, I am. But no. Let's do this right. Let's find a room in another country. For the New Year, at least. Preferably someplace sunny. God knows we could use a little sunshine after all that snow. Let's be impulsive. We can be packed and on a plane by tonight."

Rae was looking at me like I was talking gibberish, and maybe I was. I didn't care. Upset had kept me suffocated too long. I needed to breathe, to taste fresher air, and to do so as far away as possible from my homicidal son.

It was Rae's turn to lean over and kiss me, hard. "All at once I can see why they had you locked up in the Fed Med; you're certifiably crazy, Gabriel Quinn."

I smiled, this time of my own volition. "Rae, that's what happens when you get too close to crazy people: some of it rubs off."

66

The plain cement walls were an institution gray. A shade lighter than the sheets covering the bedroll, which was no thicker than a tombstone and just as forgiving.

No pillow to nest bedbugs or rest a bugged head.

He had his shoulders pressed against the cool wall, legs crossed in the recognized lotus position, meditating.

Late afternoon sunlight was slicing through a single row of glass bricks high up, painting a burnished gold stripe across the opposite cell wall. Dust motes dancing, revealing events yet to be played out, forming and dissolving within the light.

There was a dog-eared book on the bedroll. One of the classics. Something by Hemmingway. It had been left there to keep an insane inmate from going stir crazy. Fat chance. A giant marlin and a small boat on the worn jacket.

He picked it up and turned to the first page.

A former internee had scrawled the words *'You're in deep shit now, brother'* in what looked and smelled like old feces.

Loser.

He tossed the book into a corner.

Out in the hallway, several sets of footfalls grew louder as they approached. It sounded like four men, suited up, agitated. A lock mechanism rotated. The door squeaked open. A curved riot shield appeared in the doorway first, closely followed by a shuffling guard and his buddy, holding a Taser, spooning him from behind. Tight on their heels was another pair of burly unit officers in body armor, taking up the back line, armed with nightsticks and determined faces.

Springfield overkill.

"On your stomach!" The guard with the Taser commanded.

He did as he was told; he knew disobedience was met with unnecessary brute force. He flattened his cheek against the poured cement floor. He saw boots scuffle, felt hands grab his wrists and slap manacles over them, tight enough to cut off circulation. Same restraints around his ankles. Both sets of handcuffs joined with a chain.

Prison bling.

Rough hands hoisted him to his feet.

Then two of the guards fed their batons through his arms and marched him out of the cell, at a speedy shuffle. The guard with the Taser brought up the rear. No one spoke. Testosterone soup. Not exactly a Sunday stroll.

Who did they think he was – Hannibal Lecter? Or something much worse – if there could be a monster worse than a serial killer with a proclivity for eating his victims. Dr. Lecter with a predisposition toward premonitions, then. Real life much scarier than the fictional.

Fear is weakness.

The guard with the Taser was itching to unleash electric discipline; he could smell his unease.

He wouldn't give him the satisfaction.

With his arms behind his back, he was walked down one underground passageway after another, the pace sustained. Inmates mopping floors moving aside, eyes averted. He might have been the President of the United States, being escorted by the Secret Service, had it not been for his prison-issue khakis and his shackles.

They ascended concrete steps, passed through doors, eventually arriving at a processing station. His name was checked against a roster. Words were exchanged. The green light was given and he was shepherded into a large room with plastic-covered tables and chairs bolted to the floor.

There was a woman seated at one of the visitor tables: a small redhead with a boyish figure and a sallow complexion. Hair scooped up and held in place with a long clip. Bony hands placed palms-down on the tabletop. Everything still and orderly. She looked thinner than the last time he'd seen her. Gaunt. No more than a skeleton with shrink-wrapped skin.

She didn't get up to acknowledge his arrival as he was forced between empty tables, then forced again to sit in the chair facing her. His chains were fed through a clasp on the back of the chair, keeping his hands safely secured at the small of his spine.

Then his entourage hovered behind him in silence, like servitors attending a king.

"Hello, Anne," he said through a slanted smile. "I like what you've done with your hair. I have to say I didn't care much for the pageboy cut. The scoop-up suits you much better. You might say, it redefines your head shape, making it look less like a rutabaga." He leaned forward, just enough to take up the slack. "How's Seattle? Moreover, how's Peter, that big bumbling hubby of yours? Has he got himself another German Shepherd yet? How's the health food business working out for you? You're not exactly a poster child."

All the while – from the moment her eyes had first fixed on his entrance – the woman hadn't breathed.

Until now.

"You took my daughter from me." Six cutting words, each as cold as an icicle dagger. Emotionless despite the crippling content.

She was the cool epitome of self-restraint.

Good for her.

"Your child was destined to kill a million other children," he corrected. "She was going to be a brilliant scientist. Create a super-vaccine. Only she was fated to factoring in a flaw. And that mistake would cost the lives of millions of babies. I did the world a favor, Anne. One less mass murderer for the history books. You should thank me for putting it down."

Her hand moved quickly, in a practiced blur, faster than the eye could track. Small fingers pulling the long alligator clip from her hair. Red locks unfurling as her arm swung round, fist gripping the prong like a knife.

The movement caught everyone by surprise.

But not him.

He'd seen it coming – a long time ago. And he was ready.

"Her name is Jennifer," she snarled as she staked the metal clip into the side of his neck, pushing it in deep with all her strength, twisting it, forcing it in. "And she didn't deserve to die."

A heartbeat later, the guards reacted: two rushing in to restrain her, one barking orders to his buddy to get the medic in here ASAP.

They dragged Anne McNamara away from the table, her cool eyes unmoving from his.

He knew it had cost her her life savings finding him.

He knew it had cost her her family business and her home.

He knew it had cost her her marriage and maybe her sanity.

And now he knew it would cost her her freedom.

He stared at her, smiling lopsidedly, as luminous blood arced from the puncture wound in his neck and painted a pretty pattern across the plastic-covered furniture.

EPILOGUE

A tropical breeze lifted the hairs on my arms, stirring me from a sweaty midday slumber.

At first I was at a loss to understand where I was.

Blistering sunshine and a distant sigh of surf.

I was on my side, cuddled-up on a sun lounger like a toddler having an afternoon nap, a cheek damp with drool. I could see sun-kissed people packed together on a golden beach. Tans deepening. Stringy men playing soccer in the sand, watched by smiling girls in skimpy swimwear. Behind them, a bleached cliff of towering hotels stretched along the promenade as far as the eye could see.

Copacabana Beach.

We'd made it, Rae and me, all the way to Rio. Lovebirds migrating south in search of winter sun. We'd nested in a cozy condo with breathtaking views over the city and all the way to Sugarloaf Mountain. Lost ourselves in finding each other.

Pure madness.

Doctor's orders.

Emotionally, I was full and empty, both at the same time.

Unquestionably, Rae illuminated the darkness within, pushing the sadness for my son to the outer limits. Like a galaxy of warmth and light, kept in check by the dark energy surrounding it. But the hurt was a constant echo of my past, as inescapable as my skin.

I rolled onto my back and stretched muscles weakened by long days lazing.

Almost a week had passed since our arrival in Brazil.

Officially, I hadn't heard anything about *The Undertaker*, other than he'd been flown to Springfield for psychiatric evaluation and to await trial, bail denied. Unofficially, I'd heard there was a big name Hollywood producer trying to get an interview with him over movie rights.

If it weren't so sad it would be laughable.

As for me, I'd done my part: I'd caught *The Undertaker*. My secret was out. In many ways it was a relief. In many ways it wasn't. Now it was down to a jury of his peers to decide his fate. Not mine.

Truth was, I'd washed my hands of him and walked away. I didn't want anything to do with him. Not yet.

But never say never.

The sea breeze ruffled the frill on the parasol, bringing with it a scent of coconut and caipirinha.

So far, Brazil had been good for Rae and me. Bodies and minds on the mend. But I knew our escapism had to come to an end sometime. Once reality bites, it rarely lets go – and even if it does, scars are left behind.

Tentatively, I'd thought about my future under Stone's hooded watch. I wasn't sure if I wanted to continue my role with the Bureau; I missed my old gang at Central Division. Maybe I wouldn't be given a choice, either way. Maybe for the better. One thing I did know was that without something to stimulate my brain I'd go mad.

And I'd already been there. Got the bumper sticker.

I scooted into a seated position, screwed my eyes against the midday glare.

There was another sun lounger huddled up in the shade. A jazzy beach towel and a pair of women's sunglasses on the top. A dog-eared paperback with a vampire on the cover.

I put on my Wayfarers and pulled a swig of tepid water from a plastic bottle.

I could see Rae farther down the beach, where the flatter sand slipped under the water's edge. She was playing beach volleyball with three women half her age, and keeping up. Fiery hair flying. Freckles frying. Hour-glass figure and orange two-piece checking all the boxes.

The skin-tone Band-Aid on her neck was virtually invisible.

Rae had cheated death. Engel and Fillmore hadn't.

Days ago, the Coast Guard had recovered their burned corpses from the black waters of Deadman Bay, together with their Slavic sidekick. Laptops and accounting books salvaged from the boat's wreckage. Techies at the Bureau were retrieving data from hard-drives and piecing things together. Already, arrests had been made – mostly rich white guys with abused Russian girls chained up in their basements. Stone had got a congratulatory pat on his back for a job well done, and people were speaking highly of Rae on Pennsylvania Avenue.

No one knew how to deal with me: the killer's dad.

I didn't mind being left alone, for once.

I was making the most of the calm before the media storm.

I saw Rae launch herself into a long dive, scooping up the Day-Glo ball an inch before it was about to hit the sand. Nice move. Everything synchronized. Everything perfect.

Just laying eyes on Rae made me smile, I realized. I was happy to sit here all day and stare like an idiot.

I had no idea where we were headed. I hadn't broached the subject of her and Stone. Possibly through cowardice. Rae had obligations back in Washington, DC. I didn't. With Stone's nest of vipers crushed, she had no reason to stay in California – aside from me, that is. We hadn't discussed specifics. The subject hadn't come up. But I had a feeling she'd suggest I return with her, to Washington, if we were to return at all. There was nothing keeping me way out west. A base on the East Coast made sense; not only would I be nearer to Grace, I'd also be closer to Kate and my grandson. And, in the coming months, they'd need me – or I'd need them.

Rae's cell phone jangled in her beach bag.

I leaned over and rummaged it out. Ordinarily, I would have let it go to voicemail. For some reason, I didn't. Unsure why.

The number on the screen was a long jumble of digits. Probably international.

I glanced at Rae. She was in the full throes of the game, laughing and ribbing her opponents. Brushing off sand. No point dragging her away from her fun and an impending win.

I put the phone to my ear and hollered *hello?*

"Fillmore? I was expecting Burnett." It was an accented voice, Eastern European.

I straightened up with a jolt, thinking I'd misheard. "Who is this?"

"Fillmore, it's me: Alexander. I have been waiting patiently for your communication. Burnett made it clear never to contact her directly, but your combined silence has left me with no other option. The merchandise is backing up, my friend. The pipeline must be reconnected. I trust your issue has been successfully dealt with and we are now back on schedule? . . . Fillmore?"

I didn't answer. Not simply because my throat was suddenly strangled, but because the cell had become as heavy as a brick and gravity had pulled it away from my ear.

A Russian. Calling on Rae's FBI-issued phone. Thinking I was Fillmore.

The universe can change in a heartbeat.

Fillmore had spoken about a change in management and, under interrogation, Bishop had proven not to be the mole in Stone's department. Could it be that Rae had run the ring all along? Was she the mole? Had

Fillmore decided to kill the competition, kill Rae, because he wanted to be the boss and take her place?

No such thing as coincidence, right?

I dropped the cell on the lounger, as if it were contaminated, my thoughts suddenly in disarray. Blood running cold. I could still hear the Russian mistakenly calling out Fillmore's name. It sounded like an obscenity.

From down near the rolling surf, Rae saw me gaping and threw me a big grin, followed it up with a playful wave.

Nothing is ever what it seems.

Beyond her I could see thunderclouds on the horizon.

An omen of trouble ahead.

Beautifully deadly.

Words from the Author

Thank you for reading my novel!

also available
Gabe Quinn Thrillers #1 and #2

Killing Hope and Crossing Lines

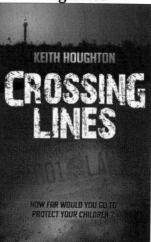

Out Now!

Book and Author updates available by adding your email
to **keithhoughton.com**

**If you enjoyed my book, please consider writing a
quick review on Amazon for me. Great reviews help
other readers decide on my books and hopefully
enjoy them as much as you have!**
Also, I really appreciate feedback and love hearing from
my readers. Please stay in touch by leaving your email on
my website or by dropping me a line to
contact@keithhoughton.com

Thanks for all Your support!!

Book and Author updates available by adding your
email to my spam-free mailing list at:
www.keithhoughton.com

Twitter
https://twitter.com/KeithHoughton
Facebook:
http://www.facebook.com/KeithHoughtonAuthor
Gabe Quinn Fan Group
https://www.facebook.com/groups/gabequinn

Thanks once again!

Keith

=)

Special Mentions to my Facebook Friends
& Gabe Fans worldwide

You Rock!

Jackie Offen, Kerry Clifford, Gaye Croft, MeLissa B. Mattaliano Davidson, Steve Reninger, Patti Hammond Blask, Jen Rowedder, Charlotte Roys, Karen Smith, Lorna Donna Robinson, Brenda Rochefort, Sue Garner, Matty Matuk, Laurie Tucker, John Bent, Carol Lynn Chilton, Bev White-Billyard, Alfie Robins, Ann Shiel, Julie Hudic Yost, Kelli Woods Jameson, Sarah Kuesel, Jan Jessup, Kim Cooper Couling, Elaine Elliott, Henry C. Cocker, Jeri Carlino, Paul Dawson, Janice Mckenzie Houghton, Tracey McPhail, Mary Endersbe, Maryruth Barksdale, Candi Warner, Glenn Hillyard, Donna Galanti, Tasha Laro, Dee Tregaskis, Mag Minor, Richard Nuttall, Jim Rooney, Bec Weir-Stoddard, Kiana Griffin, Sandy Walden, Amber Colleen, Jennifer Ward Wright, Traci Cappiello, John Michalak, Denilee Dedek, Carol Covato, Alice Weissman, Andy Snelle, Bonnie Phillips, Cara Gilligan, Bill Tharp, Cathy Ball, Christina Hall, Darrel Smith, David Pownall, Debbie Sams, David Ingram, Diane Martin, Elsa Maroon, George Mackrill, Gloria Stein, Herbert Asherman, Ali Bambridge, Mary Connelly, J. Scott Sharp, Jack Everett, Jack Rearden, Jaime Tennille, James Columbo, Jim Dunn, Joanne Patterson, John Gregory, Julie D. Richards, Kathy Mason, Katie Janes, Kim Hennessy, Kristie Haigwood, Laina Tiller, Larry Teply, Laura Pulsifer, Len Bernstein, Leslie Skidmore, Lise Voigt, Lucille Young, Lyn Askew, Marilyn Chapman, Marilyn Petrie, Marilyn Royle, Melissa Etheridge, Michele Wesselman, Michelle Miller, Mike Gibbons, Mildred

Drake, Naomi Buckley, Norma Pryor, Pamela Dalton, Paul Higginbottom, Penny Bolla, Pete Houghton, Phil Calkins, Phyllis Manning, Raymond McCullough, Robert Garr, Robyn Brown, Rosie Connolly, Russell Waters, Sarah Conway, Shannon Johnson, Sharon Pollock, Shiela Fabiano, Shiela Puckett, Sheri Bush, Stacey Gunkel, Steven Hardesty, Steven W. Dalton, Sue Bath, Sue Geibl, Theresa Gonzales, Tracey Baxter, Trish Arrowsmith, Vicky McCaffrey, Karen Charlton, Nick Quantrill, George Polley, Kathleen Hewtson, Jeanette France, John Holt, Christine Robitaille, Babs Morton, Missie Mauldin, Liz Hoban, William Stephen Taylor, Harry Dunn, Sara L. Wielenberg, Fabyan Kio BetRan, Neil Thom, Keith Nixon, Patricia Johnson Laster, Diane Chan, Markie Robinson, Iain Purdie, Cheryl Richmond, Michael Turashoff, Tmonique Stephens, Martin Cooper, Tammie Buel, Pilar Guillory, Valle Fregeolle, Diane Boyd, Kathleen Patel, Megan Thakkar, Ann Bailey, Dianne Hill, Angel Eicher, Holly Kobe, Emma Alston, Joni Harrison, Nancy Thomas, Frederick Falchook, Roger Scott, Kelly Thormodson, Emmy Swain, Billy McCoy, Shara Mcdonald, Jason Jones, Hadiyah Lysko, Alejandra Rivas, Beckey Delaney, Lisa Freeman, Jodi Eubanks, Eri Nelson, Marilou George, Julie Goldsmith, April Hanson, Walt Denman, Linda Moore, Megan Mason, Ashley Blake, Roxanne Smolen, Renee Blakely, Christy Kidd, Neha Sarode, Kathryn Davis, Roger Lansing, Tracy Manley Moore, Dianne Smith, Janet Whitney, KD Rush, Andy Knott, Mandy Rudd, Tamara Pomponio, Susan Lyons, Dana Gary, Joanne Salapatas, Peg Crippen, Lynette Barfield, John Paul Davis, Heather Carter, Joyce Kirschner, Vanessa Faurot, Diane Schultz, Robbie Revell. Teresa Lowe, Michelle Starns, Roy Jeffries, Melissa Vannoy, Ryan Cable, Darren Burton, Diane Mcdevitt, Jordanna East, Joyce Counter, Dana

Keith Houghton

Cosgrove, Chris Kelly, Amy Metz, Adam Teague, Jennifer Combs, Abby Pudlewski, Kendra Peterson, Aly Attwood, Bette Kincaid, Carol and Gary Curtis, Lorna Major, Joyce Ann Nelson, Emma Glynn, Debbie Knight, Victoria L. Hauck, Sybil Anne Richardson Hadfield, Judy Graves Hayes, Rebecca Tibbs, Julia Barrand, Teri Williams, Adrienne McIntosh, Ethel White-Ransted, Debbie Fowler, Beverly Hand, Tracey Mitchell, Nancy Grow Matteson, Abby Hand, Angel Gainey Eicher, Kathrynn Bell, Nancy Siegel Nasto, Helen Carroll, Ralphe Leboeuf, Char Markey, Becky Fitzgibbon, Kathy Ford, Sharon Murphy, Ian Bichara, Cheryl Cardwell-Brown, Helen Mullins ...

and to everyone who has supported my work by purchasing my books, but are too many to mention –

THANK YOU!

Keith Houghton, Oct 2013

Keith Houghton